HAMMAJANG LUCK

HAMMAJANG *Luck*

A NOVEL

MAKANA YAMAMOTO

This is a work of fiction. Names, characters, places, and incidents are products of the author's imagination or are used fictitiously and are not to be construed as real. Any resemblance to actual events, locales, organizations, or persons, living or dead, is entirely coincidental.

HarperCollins books may be purchased for educational, business, or sales promotional use. For information, please email the Special Markets Department at SPsales@harpercollins.com.

FIRST US EDITION PUBLISHED 2025.

First published in the United Kingdom by Hachette UK Limited 2024.

Designed by Patrick Barry

Library of Congress Cataloging-in-Publication Data has been applied for.

ISBN 978-0-06-343082-2

24 25 26 27 28 LBC 5 4 3 2 1

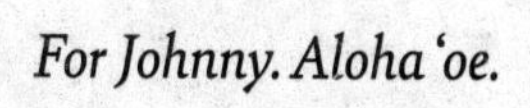
For Johnny. Aloha ʻoe.

HAMMAJANG LUCK

"I live proudly in a body of my own design. I defend my right to be complex."

—LESLIE FEINBERG,
Trans Liberation: Beyond Pink or Blue

Chapter 1

"I'M NOT ELIGIBLE FOR PAROLE FOR SIX MONTHS."

That didn't seem to matter to the surly-looking guard peering into my cell. I couldn't see his face between the light pouring in from the hallway and the flashlight beam in my eyes, but I assumed he looked surly. Every guard here had that perpetual look—a cross between "some jackass spat in my soy synth" and "Mother just grounded me for war crimes." It was better than the other one they wore—a cross between "it's both Christmas and my birthday" and "Mother just ungrounded me for war crimes." That look didn't precede anything good.

The guard grunted. "Must be your lucky day."

Nobody was lucky in this prison, least of all me.

But I bit back the words. There was no way in hell I was really up for parole, nor did I ever have the chance. The warden said as much the last time I was dragged to his office. Though I figured it was still worth investigating, if only to break up the monotony of prison life. What else did I have to do at 0100 hours other than stare at the moldering HVAC unit?

I swung my legs off the top bunk and hopped down, still light on my feet. I didn't have a cellmate, but I liked being off the ground. I've always enjoyed heights. Maybe I was meant to live in the Upper Wards. It was always *her* dream. But—again—nobody here was lucky, least of all me.

The guard kept his flashlight trained on me as I pulled on my boots. I offered my wrists to him at the door, and he cuffed them to my ankles. The long chains rattled as I walked. I was apparently on parole, but within the prison walls, I was meant to be shackled.

It wasn't a long march along the crisscrossing catwalks to the receiving area, but it seemed to stretch on forever. The other prisoners were either asleep in their bunks or uninterested in where I was going. Not that there were many people who would miss my presence in the prison yard—after hustling more than a few of them out of their weekly commissary funds, I didn't have the best reputation.

Another even surlier guard met me at the receiving area.

"Warden's not here to meet me?" I asked.

Guard the Surlier spoke in a thick colony drawl. "It's the middle of the night, why would he?"

"Thought he'd like to see me off, we've become such good pals."

Guard the Former scowled at me.

I still had no idea how or why I'd been granted parole. It felt like an unlocked cell door—a trap. Like the warden was just waiting for me to leave and break some law I'd never even heard of.

I recoiled at the thought. After *she* fucked me over, Joyce Atlas threw the book at me during my sentencing. It made sense he'd try to make me even more miserable now.

I glanced between the two of them, then directed my next question at Guard the Surlier. "You don't happen to know who released me, do you?"

He scowled at me too. "Not lookin' a gift horse in the mouth, are you, Morikawa?"

Other people may have jumped at the chance, but I knew too well that there were no gifts or grace on Kepler. Everything had a price. I just didn't know how much this would cost me—yet.

But even so, as Guard the Surlier undid my shackles, the freedom of movement eased the constant anxiety I'd been living in for the past eight years.

I didn't have much in the way of personal effects. My junk phone, a binder that no longer fit me, clothes that were no longer in fashion, and a deck of novelty cards I'd bought *her* as a joke. I had half a mind to throw the deck back in the attendant's face. But I didn't. I just muttered my thanks and took the bag offered to me.

I dressed in what I had—minus the binder, despite my temptation. The jeans didn't reach my shoes and the shirt stretched across my chest, the sleeves tight around my arms. I grimaced in the mirror. With my too-short jeans and my too-small shirt, I looked like a tattooed sausage splitting out of its casing.

After I dressed, I returned to the receiving area. Guard the Former had what appeared to be a staple gun in hand.

Didn't like the look of that.

He gestured for my hand. Warily, I proffered my right one. He yanked it forward, then, with a *snick*, the gun pierced into the flesh between my thumb and forefinger.

I winced.

He let go. "Behave. Someone's always watching you now."

I hated the sound of that.

Guard the Surlier led me to the prison entrance. "Best of luck, Morikawa," he sneered.

I looked back at him. "How the hell am I supposed to get home?"

"Not my problem," he said, then gave me an unceremonious shove on my back.

And suddenly, I was on the outside.

It was always cold on the trashy rock that Kepler orbited. Good for nothing but a few strip mines and a prison. There were haphazard banks of dirty snow strewn across the pock-marked landing pad, frozen solid from a dozen freezes, thaws, and refreezes over the course of the Rock's near-constant winter. Remarkably, a few leaves still clung to the branches of the native trees. The night sky was overcast with fast-moving clouds, and a frigid breeze nipped at my bare arms.

It didn't feel real until that moment.

I'd been bracing myself for impact, waiting for the warden to leap out like a jump scare and laugh in my face as the guards threw me back in my cell. But despite my initial wariness, I felt a weight lift off my shoulders. Maybe it was my need for more, my need to fill the negative spaces in my life, blinding me to the consequences. But for now, I savored my freedom.

I breathed in deeply. The guards used to make me crawl through the airducts, repairing the ancient HVAC units. I used to choke on the chemical smell of harsh detergents as I scrubbed the prison walls and floors. Here, on the Rock, the chilly air was unrecycled, and I could faintly smell the scent of oily smoke and gasoline.

After eight long fucking years, I was on the outside.

And I knew exactly who I wanted to call first.

I pulled my phone from my pocket. My last call with my sister was in my allotted comm time two weeks ago, and I knew the landlord was breathing down her neck. If anyone needed good news, it was her. That lightness in my body only grew as I thought about it: I could lend a hand around the house. I could take the kids to school. I could get a job—a real, legitimate job—and help pay our mounting bills. I never considered the prospect of parole. Now that I had it, the possibilities for me and my family were endless.

But when I tried to power up my phone, it stayed dead. And all those light feelings sank to the pit of my stomach.

Now what?

I was still staring at my phone, willing it to come back to life, when I heard a sharp whistle from across the landing pad.

I lifted my head.

And I saw her.

She was taller. Or maybe it was her high heels, tucked beneath a pair of slim black chinos. She wore a white blouse under her open wool coat, and her jewelry was all classy sterling silver. Her hair was now a brilliant shade of platinum blond, cut into a chic bob with razor-sharp edges. Her eyes were shadowed in the dark, but I remembered the color of them: the deepest, darkest brown I had ever seen, just verging on absolute black.

"Edie," she said. "It's been a long time."

It took everything in me to not walk backward back into the prison.

She must have known, because before I could make a graceless escape she said, "They won't take you back. I made sure of that." She stepped forward, and in the fluorescent lights of the landing pad I could see the depths of her brown eyes. "If you're interested in ruining your life again, you'll have to do it the old-fashioned way."

"Not gonna do it yourself?" I said through gritted teeth.

"I think you've proven yourself capable of doing it all on your own," she said coolly.

I tried to shake loose the anger locking up my mind. "What do you want, Angel?"

"I want to give you a ride." She nodded at the dead phone clenched in my fist. "I think you'll find your options are a bit limited without me."

I swept my eyes across the landing pad. There was one sleek black flyer parked a few paces behind Angel, and a decrepit old shuttle that transported the guards to and from the Rock and its prison. The staff rotated on a weekly basis, the flight to Kepler Space Station too much of an undertaking for a commute. It would be another week before I could *maybe* bum a ride, depending on the lenience and goodwill of the guards. Both of which were in short supply, especially with this lot.

I was considering the possibility of carving out a shelter from one of the snowbanks and stowing away on the shuttle when Angel interrupted my thoughts.

"Whatever you're planning, I can guarantee it's stupid."

"All of my plans are at least a little stupid."

"You say that as if I've forgotten."

I looked at my phone again. Still dead.

Angel sighed. "It's one hour in the flyer. If after that hour you never want to see me again—"

"Bold of you to assume I want to see you now."

"—I'll leave you alone. I swear."

"Your oaths leave a lot to be desired."

Angel's gaze was sharp. "I swear on my father's grave."

That startled me out of my anger. Last I heard, Angel's father was still alive. Miserable, but alive. I wasn't sure when in those eight years he would have died, at the rate his mind had been deteriorating.

I shifted from foot to foot. "I'm sorry," I said. Despite everything that happened between me and Angel, it felt like the right thing to say.

"Don't be," Angel replied, her voice cold.

A frigid wind blew through the landing pad, rattling the leaves on the trees and stirring Angel's hair. It fell back into its perfect angle. I shivered.

Angel gestured at the flyer behind her. "Just one ride, Edie."

I gave my phone one last look, willing with all my might for it to spark to life. It didn't.

There was a time in my life when I would have accepted

Angel's offer without hesitation. I thought of all the times we'd ridden somewhere together: in the crush of the monorail on our way to school, crowded in the back of a friend's flyer for a job, or drunkenly swaying in a speeding cab from a party. Back then, we were inseparable. Back then, we went everywhere together.

But that was long before Kepler System Penitentiary. That was long before we fell apart.

I didn't know what all this meant now.

I looked up at Angel, who was watching me expectantly. Impatiently.

"One ride," I agreed.

Angel gave me a brilliant smile, one that lit up her entire face. It was a smile that made my heart race in my chest, my palms sweat in my tight fists. It was a smile that could persuade someone to do anything for her. Move mountains for her. Slay dragons for her. Fall on their sword for her.

"Perfect," she said. "Because I have something to ask you."

"You're out of your fucking mind," I said.

Angel didn't react to that, placidly sipping from her teacup.

"Joyce Atlas is the richest man in this quadrant, in the running for richest in the galaxy." Despite the empty pilot's seat, I lowered my voice to a hiss. "And you mean to *steal from him*?"

"I'm glad you were able to grasp the basic concept."

"You're out of your fucking mind."

"So you've said."

"That man has more security than any senator. Guards, cameras, codes, keys. Even his lunch box is biometrically sealed."

"You would secure yours too, if you spent so much on real fruit."

"And what makes you think you can crack his lunch box, let alone his proprietary vault?"

Angel met my gaze evenly. "Because I'm his chief of security."

I gaped at her. She sipped from her tea again. Her lips left a smudge of vermilion on the edge of the teacup.

I shook myself out of my daze. "How'd you manage that?"

"Eight years is a long time, Edie. Enough time to straighten out, get credentialed, build a reputation." Angel smiled, her lipstick still perfectly smooth. "I'm respectable now."

"You won't be, after this job."

"Who needs respectability when you're rich?"

I gestured to the cabin of the flyer, with its paneled interior and leather seats. "This isn't rich?"

"Joyce Atlas is a multitrillionaire." Angel put aside the teacup. She folded her hands in her lap and crossed her legs. "This is nothing compared to what that kind of money can buy." She smiled again. "Ever wanted to own a moon, Edie?"

"What the hell am I supposed to do with a *moon*, Angel?"

"I hear it's a nice place to raise a family."

I scoffed. "When have you known me to be domestic?"

"Doesn't have to be for you."

The Morikawas had lived in the same apartment in the Lower Wards for generations now. A sprawling family tree of aunts, uncles, cousins, and their children were ever-present in my life. And even as the neighborhood changed around us, my family never left. It was the closest thing we had to roots, long after we were driven from the rising waters of our homeworld. If nothing else, the Morikawas had each other, had the memories of our culture.

"We're not looking to move," I said flatly.

Angel reached into her bag and removed a bright green apple. From her sleeve she drew a butterfly knife—she'd gotten faster with it since I'd last seen her. She flicked it open and began to peel.

"The plan is already in motion," Angel said, the apple's skin curling in an unbroken ribbon around her fingers. "It's just a matter of whether you want to be involved."

I leaned forward in my seat. "Need I remind you what happened the last time we tried to rob Atlas?"

The knife slipped and the ribbon of apple fell to the floor. For a moment I saw naked anger on Angel's face, anger that I didn't quite understand.

She wasn't the one who'd spent eight years of her life behind bars.

But before I could say anything, Angel's expression smoothed back into icy calm. "If anyone needs reminding, it's you, Edie. Now you know a little of what I'm capable of. Betray me, and I'll ruin your life."

"You've done it once, already," I said through my teeth.

"And I won't hesitate to do it again."

Angel could have carved her initials out of the tension in the air. I didn't know what she was thinking, offering me a moon in one hand and threatening to stab me in the back with the other. I didn't know why she would come to me, of all people. Not after everything had gone so wrong between us.

"Why me?" I asked.

"Why you?" Angel repeated. "Because you know the catacombs better than anyone else. Because you're the best runner I've ever known. Because you and I—" She paused. Rethinking. Recalculating. After a moment, she met my eyes again. Her gaze was hard with cold resolve. "Because I know you, Edie. Better than anyone else."

"Eight years is a long time," I said. "You don't know me anymore, Angel."

Another tense silence filled the cabin as Angel held my gaze. I noticed then that there was a ring of cold, glowing blue that cut through her irises. A mod. Smart implants like those were just becoming fashionable among Kepler's rich and powerful when I was imprisoned. They still gave me the creeps—they felt inhuman, unnatural, machinelike. The mods were an outward representation of the world of difference between people like me, and them.

After a few moments of silence, Angel settled back into her seat, carving the apple into slices in her hand. "I'll give you three days," she said finally. "If I don't hear from you by the fourth day, the deal is off."

"And then what?"

"Then you enjoy your freedom. Think of it as a gift, for old times' sake." I scoffed. "Just be sure to stay on the straight and narrow, or you may end up back where you started."

"Is that a threat?" I growled.

"You don't need any interference from me to send you back to the Rock." The knife cut smoothly through the flesh of the apple. "Understand this, Edie. I can have any runner I want. I can succeed with any runner worth their salt. But I want the best. I want you."

That was one thing eight years hadn't changed in her. Always seeking perfection.

She lifted her gaze, and I met it defiantly. "Three days from now, you'll want me too."

"You really think I'll change my mind?"

"I do, actually."

I scowled. "Why is that?"

I went rigid as Angel ran her tongue along her forefinger, licking the apple's juices off her skin. Then she smiled a wicked smile, her lips still perfectly lined. "You've changed, Edie. But not that much."

Angel dumped me at Kepler's rail station. Her goodwill only seemed to extend to the docks, and not much farther. But it suited me just fine. The tense silence in the flyer was suffocating, and I was eager to be out of this new Angel's presence.

"Think about it, Edie," she said from the flyer. "I'll be waiting for your call."

I grunted in response, turning away from her and moving toward the rail station. Another sharp whistle made me stop midstep. I turned back slowly. Angel had my phone in her hand. "Dropped this."

I approached her warily, then reached out to take the phone. Angel pulled it close to her chest and met my eyes. "Remember, Edie," she said, her dark eyes searching mine. "Remember that I can do this without you. Can you survive on the outside without me?"

Angel proffered the phone and I had to resist the urge to snatch it out of her manicured hand.

I shoved it in my pocket, then turned on my heel and started toward the station again. I half expected her to call out to me, but she said nothing. As I slipped into the crowds—the rail station was always crowded, even in the dead of night—falling in step and changing my posture, I hazarded a glance over my shoulder.

Angel was gone.

I sighed. Lost in the crowds, out from under her scrutinizing gaze, I felt more at ease. That feeling of weightlessness continued, Kepler's gravity lighter than the constant downward pull of the Rock. The faces may have been unfamiliar, but the feeling of being in a crowd wasn't. The low light of Kepler's simulated night was familiar. The brushed steel walls—once polished to a shine, now grimy with generations of handprints—were familiar. I approached the turnstiles leading to the tracks and smiled. The roar of the monorail was familiar, and so was the ride to Ward 2.

But when I slipped my rail card from my wallet clip and

touched it to the sensor, a grating *beep* stopped me in my tracks. I tried again, and the *beep* was more insistent. I glanced at the screen. *Insufficient funds.*

I braced myself on the turnstile, preparing to vault it, and froze. I glanced down at the chip in my hand. The flesh was raw and red.

I thought of what the guard said. Someone was always watching you on Kepler, and I wasn't willing to risk my freedom on petty crime. Who knew what obscene punishment there was for fare evasion under Joyce Atlas's watch.

I turned away from the turnstiles with a frustrated sigh. It was nearly an hour's walk from the docks and through the Lower Wards. If Kepler was such an impressive feat of human engineering, why were the lifts never in service, and why did it have so many goddamn *stairs*?

I exited the rail station onto the quiet streets. It was always dark in the Lower Wards, where the towers loomed and the skybridges blotted out Kepler's simulated night sky. Screens on the towers' faces cast flashing neon light across the streets, advertising vids and products and mods I'd never heard of. A waifish model appeared on a screen beside me as I passed, dancing and striking poses that showed off the sleek mod on her belly as it changed colors from electric blue to neon green to hot pink. The friendly rounded lettering of the Atlas Industries logo appeared above her head with a tagline for the mod: *Performance. Precision. Perfection. BioTelos.* The model smiled at me, tracking my movement. I scowled back at her and picked up my pace.

I turned back toward the street, where a lonely figure far off in the distance was drunkenly staggering down the sidewalk. Their footsteps faded as they turned the corner. A lone flyer passed overhead in a pounding of bass and whining of engines before it shot off toward its destination. In the silence that followed, it was quiet enough to hear the low, constant thrum of Kepler's monolithic engines, the hushed breath of its life-support systems. At this hour, when all its people were asleep, it felt like it was just me and it.

"Miss me?" I asked softly.

Angel was right: I knew Kepler better than anyone else. I spent my childhood racing through its narrow streets, exploring its labyrinthine catacombs, and climbing its soaring towers. In combination with an apprenticeship learning the ins and outs of the station and all its systems, I was more knowledgeable than any mechanic, any lab coat. Any cop too. Whenever a lift went sideways or a job went south, I could disappear into Kepler. I knew it would keep me.

Maybe it owed me and Dad that.

I picked up my pace as I moved down the street, from a leisurely walk to a jog to a run. Before long, I was sprinting across open streets, vaulting over walls, and sliding down railings. My mind coursed a path on instinct, and though my body had changed and its movements were unfamiliar at first, after a few blocks, it began to respond just the way I wanted it to. An exhilarated grin rose on my face, and I let out a *whoop* that echoed through the silent night.

Maybe in eight years I had changed, but Kepler hadn't. Beneath the fresh coats of paint, the trendy advertisements, and the new pavement, Kepler was the same as it always was. I always had Kepler to keep me. And if I returned the favor, it would keep my family too.

That was all I needed. I didn't need money. I didn't need notoriety.

I didn't need Angel.

All I needed was myself, my family, and my home.

That was enough.

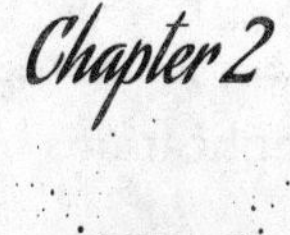

Chapter 2

IT WAS THE DARKEST PART OF KEPLER'S NIGHT CYCLE WHEN I FINALLY made it home. The shop's lights were off, its windows were shuttered, and the blinds were drawn in the apartment window above. I realized with a start that they probably had no idea I was coming. *I* had no idea I was coming until two hours ago, when Angel apparently paid my way out.

I pushed the implications out of my mind. I'd always worked with a singular purpose, one step at a time. Didn't make sense to worry about it now.

With a silent prayer I drew my keycard from my wallet clip. I tapped it to the sensor, then blew out a breath when it gave an affirmative beep and the lock slid open with a *clunk*. I pulled open the door, bypassing the lift to take the stairs. The automatic lights came on in the stairwell, illuminating the handprints on the dirty walls and stains on the concrete steps. I climbed to the second floor quietly, then paused outside the apartment door.

I wasn't sure whether to knock. In my younger days, when I was more rascal than felon, it wasn't uncommon for my family to find me passed out on the couch after a late night on the streets. They hated it when I was just a rascal and would probably hate it more now as a felon. I was six months out from the possibility of parole; they'd probably think it was a jailbreak. Which it sort of was, I guess—but instead of chipping away at the wall of my cell, Angel had negotiated my freedom behind closed doors.

Again, I pushed the implications out of my mind. One step at a time. I knocked.

I stepped back from the door and shoved my hands in my pockets, shifting awkwardly from foot to foot. Everyone always seemed happy to see me on visit days, but that was through a grainy video feed. There's so much more to communication than words. To be in someone's physical space, really be *there* with them, was something no vidfeed could capture. It was easier to bullshit when all you can hear is someone's voice, all you can see is their smiling face. The real grift is in the way you occupy that space. Be *there* with the mark.

Angel taught me that.

The door opened to an expectant Andie, and all thoughts of Angel fled my mind.

"Edie," Andie said, her face lighting up with a smile. "You're home."

"Surprise," I said with a sheepish grin.

Andie opened the door wider, revealing a floor carpeted in balloons and a banner across the far wall, lettered in a child's scrawl in rainbow colors: *Welcome Home!!!*

"Surprise," Andie said in a hushed voice, matching my grin.

My eyes widened and my mouth dropped open. "How did you . . . ?"

"The warden called," Andie explained. "Something about new policies regarding good behavior?" She slugged my shoulder. "I knew you could pull it together if you really tried."

"Yeah, sure," I said absently. How many strings did Angel have in her hand, exactly?

"Well? Aren't you gonna hug your big sister?"

I pushed thoughts of Angel out of my mind and fixed Andie with another grin. I pulled her into a hug and she wrapped her arms around my back, holding me tight. Her heavy belly pressed against me—she looked way more pregnant in person than over a vidfeed. As I held her, the knot of apprehension that had settled in my stomach slowly began to ease. I gave her a tentative squeeze and she laughed.

"You're crushing us."

"Sorry," I said. "It's just easy to crush you when you're so small and weak and I'm so big and strong."

Andie laughed again. "Shut up."

She drew away from me, and I took her in. She was shorter than I remembered, but I was always tall, like our dad. Her dark hair was piled on top her head in a tita bun—long Hawaiian hair, like in the pictures from Old Earth. I cut mine off with a pair of safety scissors in middle school and refused to grow it back. I don't think Mom ever forgave me for it.

"Come on in," Andie said, waving me into the apartment. "Just be quiet, the kids are sleeping."

My stomach dropped. "You weren't waiting up for me, were you?"

"Yeah, but no worries. Warden said he wasn't sure when you'd be back, and believe me, I've gotten used to waiting up for your miscreant ass."

"Miscreant no longer," I said as I followed Andie into the apartment and took off my shoes. "I'm out on good behavior, remember?"

Andie settled herself on the apartment's faded couch, the upholstery worn smooth from years of use. "And you intend to stay out?"

I sat down beside her. "Das da plan."

Andie leaned on the couch and rested her head in her hand. She smiled at me fondly. "Good. Because the kids missed you. You made a big impression on them at the funeral."

I shrugged. "Kids can be bought, Andie."

"Not Paige. She sees through everyone's bullshit. Always have to warn the doctors not to baby her, because she's not afraid to call them out."

"How is Paige?" I asked, carefully.

"Pretty good!" Andie answered brightly, and a little too loudly. "Hasn't metastasized at all, which is great. Doctors are optimistic about finding a donor, we all are."

I watched her warily. I was never as good at reading people as Angel, but then again, Andie had never been a very good liar.

"I think I told you about the Caduceus Cancer Fund," Andie continued, unprompted. "They've been paying for a good chunk of the treatment, which has helped a lot."

"Not enough for gene therapy, though."

"No, but who's got the cash for that?"

I frowned at her. She shifted uncomfortably on the couch. But before I could press, Andie moved on.

"Tyler's been watching the kids while I'm at the shop, but I'm sure they'll be excited to spend time with their aunty."

I'd hated Tyler from the moment I met him. A contractor with one of the housing developers on Kepler, he spent a lot of time at the shop. In no small part to hit on my sister. Even years later I resented him for pulling Andie away from me. He pulled Andie away from everyone, kept her away from everything she loved. When Andie filed for divorce a few months ago, I could've danced for joy.

At least, I thought she did.

I tried to hide my annoyance. "Are you and Tyler back together?"

"No, no. We're still separated. He's just been helping watch the kids while we figure out custody," she said quickly. "But it'll be good to have an extra set of hands."

My annoyance faded. "Am I being volunteered to babysit?"

"Unless you'd rather snake drains and fix pipes."

"I'll get back to you on that."

Andie laughed. "Or you could stock shelves with Mr. Fong."

"You know that old fut wouldn't let me anywhere near those shelves."

"For good reason, after you broke half a case of lightbulbs."

"It was *one time*!"

"And once was enough!"

Andie laughed again, and I did too. She smiled, then laid a hand on my arm. "I missed you, E."

"I missed you too."

She gave my arm a gentle squeeze. Then her eyes widened with surprise, and she squeezed again.

"Jesus Christ, Edie."

"What?"

"You've grown so much!"

"Eight years'll do that to a person."

"No, I mean"—she prodded my shoulder—"where'd my scrawny lil' Edie go?"

"They got bored and started hitting the gym." I grinned. "Mr. Fong can't slap my head now."

Andie laughed. Midway through, it shifted to a yawn.

"You should sleep, you look tired," I said.

"I *am* tired—been up since 0400." Andie gave me a weary smile. "But I wanted to see you."

I met her smile. "Thanks. Appreciate it."

I rose from the couch and offered my hand. Andie accepted it and stood on unsteady legs.

"I made up your room," she said. "Go get some rest."

"Thanks, Andie. Really."

"You're welcome." Andie pulled me into another hug. "I'm just glad to have you back."

She hummed contentedly as I held her close, now more mindful of the baby. I could smell her perfumed shampoo as

I held her—she had changed it, in the years since I'd last seen her. No longer indistinctly floral and sweet, she smelled like cool aloe now. I wondered if it was weird to ask her about it. But before I did, she stepped out of my grasp and waved me toward the bedroom.

"Go to bed so I can go to bed. I'll be here in the morning before the shop opens."

"I'll see you in the morning, then."

"See you in the morning."

Andie and I went to opposite ends of the living room—her to what used to be our parents' bedroom, me to what used to be mine.

The furniture was still the same: my creaking bed and scuffed desk, though the chair in the corner had been cleared of unfolded laundry. A dozen half-finished models and tech kits crowded the bookshelf, my textbooks and technical manuals stacked in haphazard piles around it. The closet could hardly close around the rails hung with clothing and the overstuffed boxes labeled with Mom's scrawl. I navigated through the mess and flung myself on the bed, mussing up the neatly made blankets.

As I sank into the stiff mattress, my body felt heavy with exhaustion. Yet my mind kept returning to Andie. Much as I despised her dirtbag ex, he'd at least been there to support her through Mom's sickness, managing the shop, raising the kids, and taking care of Paige. Now Andie was on her own, and I'd left her to it. All I could think about was how I could possibly make up for my eight-year absence.

I'd figure something out. It seemed like the least I could do for her.

I woke up early the next morning. Which in itself was unusual, not accounting for the late hour I got home. Maybe it was a holdover from prison life—they used to wake us before the Rock's shitty little sun had even risen over the prison walls.

At first, I wasn't sure where or even *when* I was. Waking up in my old room in my old clothes, I felt like a kid again. Twenty-one years old and reckless with ambition; chasing the high of success, the rush of adrenaline. At the time I felt invincible, like nothing could stop me. One day I would be somebody, not just some lowlife from the Lower Wards. All I needed was one big score, that last big job—

But every high has its low.

I sat up in bed and rubbed at my bleary eyes. I wasn't twenty-one anymore. I wasn't that person anymore. I was a felon on parole, waking up in clothes that were eight years out of fashion and a size too small. A felon who overdid it on their run last night. A felon in desperate need of a shower.

So I dragged my tired, achy, old ass out of bed and trudged to the closet.

It was packed. I guessed that Mom had repurposed my room for storage over the years, based on the towers of boxes with labels like *Kids' Toys, Dad's Books,* and *Family Photos*. I unstacked some of them, but as I rifled through the clothes hanging on the rail, my stomach dropped.

I pulled a shirt from the closet and held it. One of Dad's aloha shirts: a nice one, patterned with outrigger canoes with billowing sails. It wasn't made of real silk—we'd never had the credits for that—but it was the nicest synthetic shit we could find. I found more in the press of clothes: aloha shirts in shades of muted blue and pale red, ties in subdued patterns, a suit in tasteful gray.

Grief made my stomach heavy in my gut, my heart ache in my chest. Twenty-one-year-old me might have felt stinging tears in their eyes, might have tried to still their trembling hands.

But twenty-nine-year-old me—felon me—put the shirt back with a sigh.

I found my things shoved to the back of the closet. Luckily, I used to buy my clothes oversized, baggy enough to conceal my chest when squeezed into a sports bra. I pulled a gray henley, a pair of dark-wash jeans, and a black canvas coat from the closet with some underwear and a binder then closed the door behind me.

When I entered the living room, it didn't look like the kids were up yet. I heard Andie rummaging through cabinets in the galley kitchen but opted to say good morning after I showered. So I picked my way through the balloons strewn across the floor to the bathroom.

The bathroom itself was clean but untidy. Andie had apparently washed everything in a whirlwind between shifts at her jobs and me coming home. The counter was crowded with toiletries, and the medicine cabinet was so full the door was ajar.

I took a little longer in the shower than maybe I should have. The water was warm on my skin, and the pressure felt good on my shoulders—I hadn't had a real shower since I was last out for Mom's funeral, two years ago. It felt like I was rinsing away the last eight years of my life.

Satisfied, I washed my hair and scrubbed the last of Kepler System Penitentiary off my body. I toweled off, struggled into my binder, and dressed.

As I looked myself over in the mirror, I felt like a different person. Now that I was clean, bound, and wearing clothes that fit, I might have been someone else. I didn't think it was twenty-one-year-old me, but I didn't think it was quite felon me either. I didn't know who that someone else was, but maybe it was worth finding out.

I opened the door and was immediately greeted with the *BANG* of a balloon popping.

I jumped at the sound. It drew my gaze to the little boy sitting on the floor outside the bathroom door, a limp balloon in one hand and light-brown eyes fixed on me.

"Hey, Casey," I greeted him.

The boy beamed at me and waved with his free hand.

"Don't you want to say hi to Aunty Edie?" Andie called from the kitchen.

Casey shook his head vigorously.

My heart sank. I wasn't sure how I'd fucked up so badly to draw the ire of my six-year-old nephew.

Andie appeared from around the corner. Her dark hair was twisted into a loose braid and she wore a threadbare robe that just barely accommodated her hāpai belly. "C'mon, at least give them a hug."

Casey dropped the balloon in his hand and rushed forward, throwing his arms around my waist. A little stunned, I hugged him back.

Relief washed over me as the little boy settled into my arms. Casey was born during my stint at the penitentiary, and I'd only seen him in person for a few hours at the funeral two years ago. I always thought that he liked me—if not for me specifically, then for the sleight of hand tricks I showed him—but it was still nice to know that he was happy to see me. He gave me a squeeze, and I held him a little tighter.

"There you go," Andie said cheerily. "Now go get dressed, you have to leave for school in half an hour."

I gave Casey's brown hair a tousle. "Bettah brush yo' hair too."

He gave me a fearsome scowl, shaking his head to settle his hair back into place.

I lowered my voice to a stage whisper. "And if you brush yo' teet good, I'll pull some candy outch yo' ear."

"Edie—" Andie protested.

But Casey was already gone, shutting the bathroom door behind him with a snap.

I laughed. Andie smiled. "You're such a bad influence."

"For the candy or the crime?"

"First one, then the other."

I nodded in the direction of the bathroom. "What's with the silent treatment?"

Andie moved to stand beside me. "He took a vow of silence."

"What—" I laughed. "What kind of vow does a six-year-old make?"

"I wouldn't know, he took the vow before telling any of us."

"Maybe I'll take him on my next job." I grinned. "He'd make a good witness."

Andie's smile fell. "What next job?"

My stomach dropped at her expression. "It was just a joke."

"Don't joke like that, Edie."

"Why not?"

"Mom?" a voice called from the bedroom.

We both turned. Standing in the doorway was an adolescent girl, newly thirteen. She was dressed in the uniform of one of the nearby private schools—a white blouse and plaid skirt with stockings and black dress shoes. Her brown hair was braided into two neat tails, without a hair out of place. But her immaculate appearance was betrayed by the dark circles under her eyes and the pallor of her light skin. It took me a moment to recognize her.

"Hey, Paige."

She smiled, and immediately I could see Andie in her face. She crossed the living room and I knelt to give her a hug, holding her loosely, as if she might shatter.

"How you doing, kid?" I asked.

"Good," she answered noncommittally. "We get a pizza party today for meeting our class reading goal. How was prison?"

"Paige!" Andie said sharply.

"Good," I said, equally noncommittal. "But we nevah get one pizza party, even though I read a whole book."

"A whole book?"

I shrugged. "Life's busy in prison."

I was rewarded with a snort of laughter, which made me grin.

Andie laid her hand on Paige's head. "Let's try and eat something before school, yeah? E hele kākou." She urged the girl toward the kitchen. Then she gave me a rare frown. "We'll talk about it, okay?"

I shifted uncomfortably. "Yeah, sure. Anything you say."

Andie lumbered away, leaving me in the living room with the balloons. I sighed and followed.

As I walked into the kitchen, I deeply breathed in the scent of fried canned meat, rehydrated eggs, and fresh rice, overlaid by sharp coffee and sweet guava. I was always trash at cooking, but Andie had taken to it easily. By the time we were teens she was cooking for the whole family, in between school and work. At first it was because she wanted to—after Dad died, it became more of a necessity. Andie was always good at stretching twenty credits.

I made my way down the counter, spooning heaping scoops of rice and fluffy eggs onto my plate. I piled some slices of canned meat on my plate and poured myself a cup of coffee. It was a feast compared to the prison rations I'd been living on for the past eight years. My mouth was watering by the time I sat down at our scuffed kitchen table.

Paige brushed past me to sit at the table as Casey dashed into the kitchen, tugging on a vest with one hand and holding a cowboy hat to his head with the other. Andie turned away from the food and sighed. "I already said you can't wear that to school," she chastised. Casey scowled.

"Why not?" I asked, adjusting the little boy's vest.

Andie shot me a look. "Because they're taking class pictures today and have to wear their dress uniforms." She redirected her gaze to Casey. "You can wear it on funny hat day."

"This classy thing? On *funny hat day*?" I straightened his hat and affected one of the Western drawls I saw on TV. "I think Tex here is lookin' mighty fine."

"What's a Tex?" Paige asked.

"It's short for Texas," I answered sagely.

"What's a Texas?"

"It's—" What the fuck *was* a Texas? "It's, uh—"

"It was a place on Old Earth," Andie answered tersely. "Why are you being such a pest?"

"He's taken a vow of silence," I said, solemn. I put an arm around Casey and pulled him close. "Someone must defend him."

Andie threw up her hands. "Fine. But you can't wear it in the pictures. And if it gets taken away, it's not my problem."

I tipped Casey's hat. "Thank you kindly."

Andie sat down heavily at the table. "Now everyone sit down and eat, please."

We did as we were told, gathering around the table in a clatter of cutlery. I put my hands together and grinned at Andie over my fingertips. "Itadakimasu."

"Yeah, yeah," she grumbled. "Eat your food and shut your mouth before I put you back in prison."

Andie ushered the kids out the door not long after breakfast. I insisted on clearing the dishes, which Andie grudgingly conceded that I could wash if she dried. For a while we cleaned in silence, stacking the dirty dishes in the sink. Then she said, "About your next job . . ."

"There's no next job."

"Are you sure?"

I stacked the skillet on the untidy pile in the sink and pushed up my sleeves. "Of course I'm sure."

"Because you said something different."

I ran the skillet under the tap. "I was just joking, Andie."

"You can't joke like that, Edie."

I didn't say anything for a moment, focusing my attention

on one stubborn spot on the skillet. After a while I asked, "Why not?"

"What if someone overhears you? What if they misunderstand you and think you're going to try something? The courts are watching, E. Watching both of us."

"I'm not gonna try anything." I handed the skillet to her. "I'm out on good behavior, remember?"

Andie dried it. "But if you don't keep up that good behavior you'll be right back in again."

"I won't, though." I contemplated the plate in my hands. "People need me now. Paige is sick, Casey's just a kid . . . and you're on your own." I glanced her way. "I think you need me too."

Andie took the plate from me and set it aside. "You don't need to worry about me. I just want you to stick around." She smiled. "We all missed you."

"I missed you guys too."

"So, stay out of trouble," she scolded. "I've gotten pretty good at this mom thing, and I'm not afraid to turn it on you."

I laughed. "You know I'd hate that."

"Then keep your hands clean, E."

"Yes, ma'am."

I turned back to the dishes in the sink. We cleaned in comfortable silence for a while, leaving me to my thoughts. Andie never liked the crime; she always thought it was too dangerous. She thought that no matter how bad things got, I shouldn't let myself get pulled down into that world. But despite that, she never snitched—even covered for me when she could. I could always count on her to have my back, even through the worst of Mom's tirades. I think she knew I was trying to help the only way I knew how. And much as she hated it, she knew she couldn't stop me when I put my mind to something. So she tried her best.

She always tried her best.

After the dishes, Andie went to open the shop. I was left sprawled on the couch, idly shuffling my old deck of cards and staring into the field of balloons on the floor.

I was going legit. I needed to go legit. I promised Andie. It was unthinkable to me that any of my bad behavior might reflect poorly on her in court. But what did people even do to make legit money? Would the tea shop down the street hire a felon fresh on parole? Probably not. The docks might be more likely. Though Kepler was becoming more of a tech hub, product always needed to be moved and there was always work at the docks. I heard Cy had cleaned up his act and taken a job there—maybe I could win someone over and start from the bottom up.

I pulled out my phone from my pocket and tapped out a quick message:

I'm back bitch

Before I could even resettle my phone in my pocket, he responded:

Good.

I grinned. Charismatic as ever.

I need a favor. can we talk?
I am working Dock 2A-4. I get one break in an hour.
I'll be there

I turned over onto my back and stared at the ceiling. Cy would have my back. And more than that, Andie believed in me. I could do this. I *had* to do this.

Angel said I couldn't survive on the outside without her, but I was determined to prove her wrong.

Chapter 3

I TOOK THE MONORAIL UP THE NEAREST SPOKE TO THE CENTER OF Kepler's ring, where a spire extended outward into space. All the docks were housed there, and they were always busy these days. Originally a refueling station for ships on their way to a handful of outer colonies, there was a time when the traffic through the system ebbed and flowed with the needs of the inner worlds. But as humanity expanded farther and farther into the edges of deep space, Kepler grew from backwater station to interstellar hub, each new generation building on the work of the last. My family came here generations ago to man the docks on the government's dime, the first of the spacefaring Morikawas.

It was also the point of origin for Atlas Industries, the tech empire of the big man himself, Joyce Atlas.

The docks were packed with ships branded with the company's logo. From my vantage point at the entrance to Dock 2A, I could see the columns of ships above and below me, up to dizzying heights and down to terrifying depths. Each was anchored to the scaffolding with mag locks the size of a small flyer. The dockworkers scurrying up and down the ships looked like swarms of ants, climbing hand over hand in the zero-g. Just beyond was the honeycomb wall of individual airlocks, and behind that was the frigid darkness of space.

Dock 2A-4 was three rows above the entrance. I secured a tether to the harness I'd grabbed and climbed up the scaffolding. Outside the spin of Kepler's ring, there was no gravity at the docks. But even in the cold and zero-g, I was sweating by the time I reached 2A-4.

The dock was occupied by a smaller freighter, probably one that made the short trips between Kepler and the many colony worlds within jumping distance. A stylized bird at rest was painted at the ship's midsection, bisected by its open cargo hold. A tall figure moved with purpose among the crates, the efficiency and certainty of his movements familiar.

I felt a twinge of apprehension watching the figure. Had Cy changed, in the years I was gone? He went straight since I last saw him. He was happy enough to talk story on visit days, but if he left his old life behind, would he welcome me into his new one?

I kicked off from the dock and let momentum carry me to the ship.

"Cy!" The figure looked up from the crates to watch me approach. I caught myself on the scaffolding just outside, swaying as my momentum came to a stop. "That you?"

The figure moved out of the shadow of the ship and into the fluorescent lights that bathed the whole dock in harsh white light. He was just as tall, but everything else had changed. Not only had the T filled out his frame, but the bulk of his cybernetics made his clothing bulge. His head was shaved, and the light glared off the brown skin of his bald scalp, the matte black of his cybernetic hand absorbing the light. His eyes were sharp beneath his heavy brows, one a deep brown and the other a disconcerting black and red. But the slightest quirk of his moustache at my call made me grin.

"Edie," Cy greeted me, his voice a low rumble. "You out!"

"Hell yeah, I am!" I shifted my tether onto another rail and moved toward the ship to meet Cy halfway. I offered my hand, and he grasped my arm and pulled me into a loose hug. He gave me a pat on the back with enough force to make me cough. "Good to see you too," I wheezed.

Cy gestured for me to follow, and we both drifted into the cargo hold of the ship.

"How long you been out?" Cy asked me.

"Jus' yestahday," I answered. I anchored myself to one of the secured crates as Cy went back to checking the contents of the hold against the roster on his datapad. "Out on good behavior."

"Huh." He sounded incredulous.

"What so hahd to believe?"

"You nevah seem like da good behavior type. Even from hanabata days."

"What? You no believe I can change?"

"Nope."

I laughed. "Faka."

It felt good to be back, talking to an old friend, talking in my own language. The prisoners in the system penitentiary didn't speak much Pidgin, and after Dad died we didn't speak much of it at home. It was a language I only spoke with his side of the family, or with my friends at school.

Cy drifted to another crate. "You going stay out dis time?"

"Das da plan. Why I come talk to you."

Cy paused, scrolling through his datapad. Satisfied, he hooked it to his belt before fixing me with his intense gaze. "What you like talk about?"

"Brah, I need one job. Tought I'd ask how you get dis one."

He shrugged. "My cousin's da foreman. Owed my tūtū one favor."

"Your tūtū likes me, yeah?"

He scoffed. "Not enough for one job."

I frowned at his back as he left the cargo bay. A moment later he returned leading the arm of a crane. He started untying one of the crates.

"What I suppose to do, den?" I asked.

"You talk to Angel?"

I stiffened. "No," I lied.

I wasn't sure whether Cy didn't pick up on my tension or if he simply didn't care. "You like one job? Talk to Angel."

"Fo' why? She talk to you?"

Cy fixed the crane's arm to one of the magnetic pads on the side of the crate. "Yeah."

"You going take it?"

The hydraulics of the crane hissed as it withdrew the crate from the cargo bay. "Yeah."

"*Why?*" The question came out sharper than I intended. What was Cy thinking, getting pulled back into Angel's web? He seemed to have it good here. He seemed to have his shit together. I couldn't imagine throwing all that away on Angel's word.

Unconcerned, Cy turned away from the crates to face me. "Iz a good plan, E. Maybe da bes' we evah had. I know you guys get pilikia, but she like have you on dis job."

"No can, Cy," I said. "I'm out. Fo' good."

He shrugged. "If can? Can. If no can? No can. But at least tink about it."

I won't, I thought.

"I go talk to my cousin about da job fo' you," Cy continued. "No guarantee but."

"Tanks, cuz. Appreciate it."

"I come by when I pau hana. We can talk story later."

"Shoots. Sounds good."

I pushed off from where I was floating to meet Cy at the cargo bay's entrance. I held out my hand, and again he pulled me close. His mismatched eyes met mine, and his gaze was intense. "We need you, E. And I tink you need us too. Try tink about it."

"Shoots," I said.

"Shoots," he replied.

He let me go, though I could feel his gaze on me as a I left. I climbed back to the scaffolding, pausing until Cy returned to his work. Instead of kicking off downward to the entrance to the docks, I hooked my tether to the rail that ran up and down the scaffolding and let it pull me up to the very top.

As usual, the docks up this high were fairly empty. Nobody paid attention to me as I reached the ceiling, nor did anybody stop me as I opened a service hatch, untethered myself, and climbed inside.

Eight years had passed since I'd last been up here, and I half expected the way to be blocked. But I followed the winding shafts, avoiding every dead end, dodging the sparse camera coverage, every hatch opening to my command. I unlocked the final one and pulled myself through..

If you climb to the highest point of Kepler's docks, you can find where the traffic controllers coordinate the movements of the docks and nearby shipping lanes. The newer ones were all cameras, vidfeeds, and displays. But if you knew the path, you could find the old command center with a plex window, with a real view of the space around the station. I smiled to myself as I closed the hatch behind me, drifting toward the window crowded with chairs and consoles.

From here you could watch the flow of supplies to the colonies, or manpower to the mines, or raw material to the inner worlds. Up here, you could look out into the depths of space and try to count the stars, each of them orbited by countless planets. From up here, you could see every possibility.

Dad showed it to me just before he died. I showed it to Angel just before we fell apart.

As I settled into one of the chairs at a decrepit console, I wondered how my life could have changed in these past eight years, if only things hadn't gone so wrong between me and her. Maybe I would have straightened out, found a real job, like Cy. Maybe I would have gotten caught up with another person, started a family, like Andie. Maybe I would have conned my way to the top, made a fuckton of money, like Angel.

Maybe I'd just be dead.

One of the airlocks below me cracked open, and a massive freighter lumbered into view. I didn't recognize the crest painted on its hull—some new conglomerate, probably born in the time I was gone. It was a hulking thing, but in zero-g it was almost graceful. It floated just beyond the reaches of the station, almost out of sight, before its engines flared and it blinked out of existence—to reappear somewhere else, far away.

Angel and I used to talk about where we'd go, where we'd jump, if we were on one of those ships. She wanted to go to an inner world, make a name for herself where all humankind could know it. I always wanted to go home, see the ocean, touch the real earth my family always talked about. Feel that connection—the one my dad maintained we all still had. Even after all the change and ruin, there was still a piece of me there.

But here I was.

I stayed in the control room for a while longer, until the cold made me shiver despite my coat. I slipped out of the hatch and locked it behind me.

I spent the next two days looking for work, wandering through the Ward and walking into every shop with a Help Wanted sign. As I suspected, the fancy tea shop down the road wouldn't take me. One glance at my record ended that opportunity. Neither would the new supermarket, or the pretty little boutique, or the greasy spoon in need of a dishwasher. I even searched for station mechanic jobs, but without a trade school degree I was shit out of luck. Everything else required a high school diploma if not a college education, both of which I was sorely lacking.

Just another testament to me being the family fuckup.

Mom always said as much.

Cy came by late in the evening of the third day, after the shop closed. Andie was in the kitchen after shooing me out when I tried to help. She said I burned everything, which was only partially true. The kids were settled in front of the television—to my great surprise, they were watching a cartoon that had been running since before my prison stint. Paige had carefully explained the plot to me, though I couldn't completely follow. There were talking dragons and invisible cats. I think there were flying horses too, but I wasn't entirely sure.

One of Atlas's programs was struggling to personalize an ad for me—eight years of missing data messed with the algorithms—when there was a knock at the door. I leapt to my feet, opened the door, and was greeted by Cy, an offering of malasadas in one hand and a six-pack of beer in the other.

We left the kids to demolish the malasadas and sat on the stoop outside. Cy offered me a pack of cigarettes, which I eagerly accepted. He cracked open one of the beers and for a moment we sat in silence, savoring our respective vices.

After a while, I asked, "So, how tings?"

"Good," Cy answered. "Been working a lot. Helping my tūtū when I can."

"How's yo' tūtū?"

"She no can see too good, so my cousins do a lot of da sewing now. But she like boss 'em around, so it's not too bad."

I grinned. "You still running around da Wards looking for real-kine wool?"

"You tink I can get away wit going to da Upper Wards looking li'dis?" Cy asked, gesturing at himself. In his short sleeves the nanofiber muscles and hydraulics of his cybernetic arm were exposed. Pretty far from the slick smart mods of the Upper Wards. "Dummeh."

I laughed. "What kine help you get, den?"

"I wen move da sewing machines, brah. I get choke, now."

"Ho, so you one operation now."

"Da numbah one," he said proudly.

"And how's yo' papa?"

Cy shook his head. "Make. He wen die six months ago."

I looked down at the ground. "Sorry, cuz."

"No need. You been gone a long time."

"Yeah."

Cy took a long pull from his beer. I took a long drag from my cigarette.

I pointed at my eye. "Wen dis happen?"

"Tree o' fo' months ago."

"Dat quick?"

"Buggah stay healing up pretty good, yeah?"

I shuddered and tried not to think too hard about what getting that cybernetic eye must have entailed. "How many moa you going get?"

"Not too much moa. I almost happy wit what I get."

It was hard to imagine Cy being happy with what he had. All our lives he'd been chasing perfection, chasing his perfect body. I knew a little bit about that. Puberty was hell for both of us, bitching and moaning about our new breasts and hellish periods. Grasping for words for what we were—not women, but not men either. Dad called us Māhū—in the middle. We would've been special, back on the homeworld, a long time ago. Now though, we were scraping together anything we could just to *be*. Whatever leftovers Cy had from the score, he put it toward transition—hormones, surgeries, and mods.

"Mus' be expensive," I said.

"I get choke debts to pay, brah. But iz worth it."

"Yeah."

Choke debts to pay. I knew a little about that too. Maybe that was why Angel was pulling him in—trying to pull me in too.

"How's Andie?" Cy asked.

"She good. Busy. Da house, da keiki, da shop . . . doing too much, as always."

"She tough. She going make it."

"Yeah. She no ask for help, but."

"What you like help wit?"

I took another thoughtful drag, considering my words. "Everyting." I sighed out a plume of smoke. "She like me go straight, settle down."

"And you like do dat?"

"Yeah. I like do dat."

There was a beat of silence.

I turned to him. "Speaking of, you heard from yo' cousin about da job?"

He sighed. "Yes and no."

"Waz dat suppose to mean?"

"He no can give you a job."

My heart squeezed in my chest. I took a deep, clear breath, then let it out slowly. "So das da yes. Waz da no?"

"Buggah wen get real cagey wen I ask why. Said you get some kine mark on your record."

"Well, yeah, I one fucking felon," I said, annoyed.

"But we get plenny felons. I said dat no make sense."

"And what he said?"

Cy put a heavy hand on my shoulder. "I sorry, E. You blacklisted."

My heart squeezed again. I had no idea how I could have gotten blacklisted in the years I'd been away. Maybe I'd underestimated Atlas's reach.

"So what I going do, den?"

"I tink you know, cuz."

I glared at him. "Ahready tol' you I no can, Cy. I going straight, settling down."

He shrugged. "I not going tell you what to do. Jus' telling you da facts."

I was about to reply when the door swung open behind us. I twisted around and saw Andie standing in the doorway with her hands on her wide hips.

"Dinner is ready," she said, scowling down at us. "Not that the kids will eat it, now that they're full of sugar."

Cy looked unremorseful.

"Thanks, Andie. We'll be up in a sec," I said.

Andie left us on the stoop. Cy climbed to his feet, then crushed the beer can in his metal fist. He looked down at me, his red eye sharp in the fading light. "Like I said, E. If can, can. If no can, no can. We going do dis wit or witout you. Tink about it." Then he disappeared inside.

I ground out my cigarette on the concrete with more force than necessary. If I was really blacklisted, there was no hope of finding work here. Atlas had his fingers in every industry, every business on the station. But I had to think of something. I had to survive on the outside.

I had to.

With a sigh, I followed Andie and Cy back into the apartment.

Two hours later, Cy left with a plastic container of chili and rice. Despite the scant contents of our fridge and shelves, Andie couldn't abide sending him home without leftovers.

Andie only had a few hours between shifts, so I helped herd the kids into bed after Cy left—with more bribery than persuasion. I made some promises I couldn't keep. I had no clue what kind of lizards lived in Texas, let alone how to find one—but it placated them enough to brush their teeth and go to sleep.

When I came back to the kitchen, Andie was still sitting at the table with her chin in her hand, half-asleep.

"Hey, tita," I said gently, laying a hand on her shoulder. She stirred beneath my hand. "Go sleep, I got this."

"Tita?" she mumbled, turning her bleary gaze up at me.

"Yeah, you. What other tita in this kitchen would I be talking to?"

"No, I just," she laughed, "I'm trying to remember the last time you called me 'tita.'"

"Eight years ago?" I offered.

"No, longer." She smiled up at me, but her dark eyes were sad. "I don't think you have since Dad died."

"Oh. Yeah." I rubbed the back of my neck. "I guess so."

She gestured for me to sit down. I took a seat beside her.

"It's weird," she said, "I keep looking at you expecting to see my kid sibling, but you're so different now."

"It's the gains," I joked.

"No." Her eyes were sad again. "It's the time."

My heart sank. "Andie . . ."

"I keep having to remind myself that you're all grown up." She shook her head. "It's just weird."

"I'm not a kid anymore, Andie. I haven't been for a long time."

She laughed. "And you would never let me forget it."

"No, I won't, because you don't need to take care of me anymore. I want to help you."

She laughed again, softly. "You've been gone a long time, E."

"But I'm here *now*." I reached out and took her hands. "I'm here now and I want to help."

She went quiet, staring at our folded hands.

I gave her a squeeze. "Just talk to me."

I wasn't sure if she would. She was staring so intently at my hands. Finally she said, "The neighborhood is changing, E. They've raised the rent on us three times in the last four years. It wasn't so bad when Tyler was here, but we were sinking half his paycheck into the shop. Now that he's gone—" She inhaled sharply, as if the words pained her.

"Let me take some shifts from you. Or send me out on some repair jobs, I can manage that."

"It's not just the shop," she said. "Every cent is going toward Paige's medical bills. Even with the cancer fund, we're barely making our minimum payments." She sighed. "The doctors are so kind to us, but there's only so much they can do."

"I can help with that," I said. "Maybe Cy's lead didn't pan out, but there are other places."

"Places like where, Edie? If the docks won't take you, where else could you possibly go?"

I tensed.

Andie looked pained. "I'm sorry. I didn't mean that. I'm just tired." Then she dropped her head into her hands and drew in a long, shuddering breath. She let it out in what was dangerously close to a sob. "I'm just so tired. I'm so tired, all the time."

"Hey." I stood, moving around the table so I could pull Andie into my arms. She buried her face in my shoulder. "Hey, it's okay."

"I'm trying so hard," she said into my collar.

"I know."

"I'm trying so hard, but I'm just so tired," she said, voice quavering.

"I know, Andie."

"It's just been so hard, Edie."

"You don't need to carry this all on your own," I soothed. "I'm here."

She took in another shuddering breath. "I know," she said. "I know." Then she drew away from me, sniffling into her sleeve. "I just don't know what to do."

"We'll think of something. We always do."

Andie gave me a thin smile. "Yeah. We do."

I lifted my chin in the direction of our parents' room. "Go sleep. I'll clean up."

"Okay."

I helped her to her feet. She started toward the bedroom but paused at the doorway. I looked up from clearing the dishes, and she was wearing a brighter smile. "Thank you, Edie. I don't think you realize how much you do for us, how much you mean to us. Things are better with you home."

"Yeah," I said. "I hope so."

"They are. I know so."

"Goodnight, Andie."

"Goodnight, Edie. I love you."

"I love you too."

Andie slowly made her way to the bedroom as I cleared the last of the dishes. As I washed, I kept turning her words over in my mind. Much as I hated to admit it, she was right. If the docks wouldn't take me, who would? No one would cross Atlas by hiring someone off his blacklist. If I wanted work, it would have to be off the station. Maybe even out of the system. Toiling away in the rare-earth mines, or processing helium-3, or cracking an asteroid.

No matter what though, it would be far away from Kepler. Far away from the Ward. Far away from Andie and her kids. And without Mom, or Dad, or even Tyler, she would be completely alone. I couldn't do that to her. Not again.

And there was no guarantee the money would even be enough—we needed something else. Something more.

I put away the dishes before crossing the apartment, snatching up my coat on the way. I shut the apartment door softly, then stepped lightly down the stairs. The lights flickered on in the stairwell, but I knew it wouldn't be visible inside. I pushed open the front door and stepped onto the street, pausing to tap a cigarette out of the pack.

Sneaking out to smoke—it made me feel like a kid all over again.

I wandered aimlessly down the street. The buildings crowded

around like nosy onlookers, and my footsteps echoed between them. I paused outside an unfinished storefront, separated from the sidewalk by a chain-link fence. A banner was draped across it: *Centennial Tower, a new shopping experience!* I looked farther up the tower, where the windows had been removed and the insides torn out. I remembered it used to be an apartment building—a lot of my friends from school lived here. Andie told me most of them were already priced out. As my eyes went from empty window to empty window, I could feel the pain of their absence.

I glanced up and down the street. Nobody was around, and I was feeling nostalgic. I climbed the fence, dropping lightly to the other side.

The area around the tower was littered with construction equipment and raw building materials. I picked my way through the detritus, then swung my leg through the open window of the storefront and stepped inside.

The lower floors of the apartment tower were in the middle of being transformed into a massive galleria, the upper floors torn out in a complete waste of space. The stairs leading farther up the tower were blocked off by a locked gate, and the lift was out of service. But the ceiling was open to the floor above, and the scaffolding still sprawled over the walls.

I tilted my head back to look up through the empty ceiling. I was feeling nostalgic, and a little daring.

I started to climb.

My climbing drove Mom crazy when I was a kid. Dad too, but like he always did, he turned it into something worth doing. Told me that if I became a station mechanic, I could climb through the catacombs all I wanted. He figured I was climbing shit anyway, might as well make it a vocation.

I scaled to the very top of the galleria, up the metal scaffolding and ladders and across windows and ledges. I didn't stop until there was nothing left to climb. With nowhere else to go,

I settled myself on a windowsill and lit another cigarette, looking out over the Ward.

Distantly, I could hear the sound of music playing from an open window higher up the tower, conversation on a stoop a few buildings down, and the sound of a flyer alarm a few streets over. From my vantage point, I could see the whole of my neighborhood, dark in the way all the Lower Wards were, with only the light of glowing neon, flashing billboards, and digital graffiti cutting through the gloom.

Most of the shops and restaurants on the street were familiar—neighborhood establishments that had existed through my childhood: the little bodega that never carded, the twenty-four-hour diner where we'd go for lunch when we skipped class, the bus stop that I'd take to school, whenever I actually went. But a lot of them were new, probably built within the last eight years: trendy boutiques with frothy dresses in the windows, bougie coffee shops, a whole block cleared for a chain supermarket. All of them staffed by faceless virtual-intelligence shopkeeps and stocked with overpriced goods courtesy of Atlas Industries and our harvested data.

Andie was right: the neighborhood was changing. And with so many outsiders moving into the Ward, it was easy to see why the rent would rise. I felt a pain in my chest as I took in every empty window and darkened sign. Uncle Liu's Asian market, Aunty Clara's bookstore, my cousin Leilani's flower shop. How many of my friends and family had been pushed out, the same way Andie and I were being pushed out? Where did they go? Where *could* they go? So many of us had lived here for generations upon generations—there was no homeworld to go back to.

Anger burned in my chest. I knew then that I couldn't leave. I couldn't leave my family, who always supported me. I couldn't leave the Ward, the last connection I had left to the homeworld. I couldn't leave now, not with what was happening to the neighborhood. Not after three short days with them. Not with no return in sight.

I smoked my cigarette to the filter. A few streets over, I saw our own shop: Morikawa Hardware and Repair. Once upon a time it was my father's pride and joy, a side hustle that had grown into a real livelihood. Between watching his kids and feeding his family, he fixed televisions. After days spent maintaining the life-support systems that kept us all alive, he repaired vacuum cleaners. And in any time he had left, he taught me everything he knew. But that was how Dad was: always hustling. Hustling because it was the only way he knew to support us. The only way he knew how to build a better life for us.

I took after him in more ways than one.

Things are better with you home.

I pulled out my phone, then navigated to my contacts list. I scrolled through, though I knew I wouldn't find what I needed. Or so I thought.

I scowled at the screen when I saw the last contact listed:

XOXO Angel

I dialed the number. It rang a respectable two times before she picked up.

"*Edie,*" she said pleasantly.

"Don't sound so smug," I growled.

"Are you calling just to hear my voice?"

I scoffed. "As if."

"Then what is it you want?"

My eyes went to the sign above our store. Just above, I saw the light in the window wink out. My hand tightened into a fist at my side, mustering all my resolve.

I know so.

"I'm calling to tell you that I'm in."

Chapter 4

ANGEL CAME BY THE NEXT DAY, IN THE AFTERNOON WHEN THE KIDS were at school and Andie was minding the shop. Dressed in a sharp suit in Etrian style, the richest of the inner worlds, tailored to fit her long legs and slender frame. She looked so out of place sitting at the kitchen table in our shabby apartment, with its dated decor and scuffed, threadbare furniture.

She declined my offer of coffee, instead drinking from a thermos of tea.

"So, what's the play?" I asked, setting down my mug and pulling up a chair.

"Atlas keeps all of his intellectual property in a proprietary vault," she said. "Research, designs, prototypes—it's all there. I know for certain there are a handful of projects underway being kept in that vault, some that he claims could change the face of human-machine interface as we know it." She sipped her tea. "We're going to steal them."

"And do what with them? I'm no lab coat, Angel."

"We ransom them. He'll do anything to keep them out of the hands of his competitors—it's why his security is so tight in the first place. I know Atlas's enemies. But I know Atlas better."

"If you know Atlas so well, what do you need me for? I

would've thought as his chief of security, it'd be an easy job."

"For one, Atlas is intelligent but paranoid. Everything is dual custody—his own codes, his own biometrics, his own keys, in addition to mine. I need help acquiring those. For another, I'm the only other person with access to the vault. If I did it myself using my own credentials, I'd be implicated."

"So you're implicating me."

"I have a plan," she said, lifting her teacup to her lips. "We'll all walk away from this with our hands clean, I can assure you."

"If his security is so tight, what makes you so confident?"

"I have an exceptional crew."

"Oh yeah?"

Angel set aside her teacup. "Take a look."

She flicked her wrist, and half a dozen haptic screens flew from the silver band of her comm and hovered in the air over the game of go fish I'd started with the kids on the kitchen table. Carefully, she arranged them into a semicircle. Then, with an expansive gesture, she swiveled them all to face me. My eight years out of date junk phone couldn't do that.

I leaned forward on the table. She settled back in her seat, cup of tea in her hands.

The first one I recognized. I pulled it closer, and Cy's face glared at me. Beneath his picture was the name *Cy Yoshino.* I scanned the dossier, and it was like reading through the greatest hits of our delinquent childhood. "You're missing some," I noted. "The hotel job isn't here."

"I figured your memory would suffice."

I brushed Cy's dossier back into the semicircle and pulled up another. It showed a smiling woman about my age with an immaculate blond braid, light skin, and lively green eyes. There were medals of silver and gold around her neck, and she was posed in front of a balance beam. The name beneath her picture read *Sara Morris.*

"Our acrobat," Angel said helpfully.

I pulled up another. A young woman with dark curling hair cut into a shaggy bob, light-brown skin, and big brown eyes grinned back at me. She had a crescent-shaped mod fitted to her ear and was dangling coins from her fingertips. The name read *Tatiana Valdez*.

"Our thief," Angel said.

"We need another thief?" I said, scrutinizing the picture.

"For our purposes, yes."

"What's with the mods?"

"An auditory amplifier in her ear, an RFID chip reader in her hand, and subdermal magnets in her fingertips," Angel answered. At my questioning look, she continued. "It changes the sensation of metal on the skin. Newer thieves say it makes safecracking easier. They're very fashionable."

I frowned at her. I pushed the dossier aside and pulled up another. In the picture were two women. One had brown skin and wavy, dark hair pulled into a low ponytail under her hat. She was dressed in a button-down and jeans. The other had light skin and sleek black hair worn loose around her face, dressed in a low-cut blouse and a short skirt that showed off her full bosom, wide hips, and rounded belly. They were both clinging to each other and laughing. Under the butch one, the name read *Kapua Duke*. Under the femme one, the name read *Chloe Nakano*.

"Our grifters." Angel sipped from her tea. "They come as a pair."

I drew another one. *The Obake*. "This one doesn't have a picture."

"Our hacker."

I scrolled through the ten lines of dossier. "Pretty sparse too."

"The Obake chooses all of their own clients. There's no way to contact them directly. They've claimed dozens of security breaches, but we don't know much about them beyond their skills. They're very good."

"So how are we supposed to meet this guy?"

"I've made a connection."

"How?"

"You'll see," she said cryptically. I knew I wouldn't get anything else out of her.

"Where did you find all of these jokers?" I asked.

"When you're in the business of security, you meet people, make connections."

I scoffed. "Networking?"

"You could call it that."

I looked over the edge of the dossier. "You're not blackmailing these people, are you?"

Angel looked offended. "Do I look like a blackmailer to you?"

"Well."

A flicker of annoyance passed over her face. "Blackmail never gets you what you want. Not in the long run." She poured herself another cup of tea. "No, they'll join of their own accord. They'll be just as invested as you or me."

I raised a brow. "What investment do you have?"

"Other than being disgustingly wealthy?"

"Yeah."

"I want to take Atlas down," she said simply.

"Why?"

"Why not?"

"Because he's more powerful than half the senators put together, that's why fucking not."

Angel's eyes gleamed, the blue of her mods standing out against the darkness of her irises. "And isn't it exciting?"

I stared at her. "You really are out of your mind."

She just smiled.

I flicked the dossier into the pile and sat back in my chair. "Okay. So, what now?"

With a gesture, the dossiers flew back into the cuff on Angel's wrist. She unfurled her fingers and another set of documents, lists, and maps appeared.

"The vault is a physical location—much as Atlas loves his tech, he's not willing to put all his trust in a firewall."

"What are we dealing with?"

"The vault is behind a three-ton steel door locked with manual keys, a dual-custody keypad, and sealed with a five-ton mag lock. We'll need to pick the manual locks, steal the codes, and cut the power to disengage the mag."

"Pretty straightforward."

"I'm not done. The security system is rigged with pressure-sensitive floors, motion and IR sensors, and a biometric scanner."

"Nothing we haven't done before."

"All of this is behind a wall of cybersecurity. Encryption, firewalls, passwords, fail-safes, logs—it's a suite to rival any warship."

"Okay," I said slowly. "Anything else?"

"Once we break through the main firewall and crack the vault, the proprietary information is inside. The most valuable tech is stored within a Liberty 1890 manual safe."

I raised my brows. "Hard to find someone who can crack something so low-tech."

"It's why we needed another thief."

I pulled up one of the documents. "And what's the human security like?"

"Atlas maintains a private security force. Mostly ex-military or ex-police, mostly dishonorably discharged or forced to resign."

"I see your taste in men hasn't changed."

Angel's lip curled. "It was Atlas's idea. Something about loyalty and brutality, I don't know." She paused. "And any interest in men I thought I had is long gone."

Duly noted.

Angel waved her hand dismissively. "Our hitter should be able to take care of them, anyway."

"Cy," I said in understanding.

"Exactly."

I wasn't sure how to feel about Cy taking on Atlas's security forces. If Cy was anything, he was competent. But this was beyond anything we'd done—though I couldn't be sure what he'd been up to while I was in prison. He was always scrappy as a kid, and the mods certainly helped.

I pushed aside the document and reached for the map of Kepler's catacombs. "So where is this vault, then?"

"Leeway, beneath Ward 1."

I looked up at her, surprised. "That way is impassable."

"Which is why I have you," Angel said, leaning forward in her seat. "You're going to grant us physical access. I know my security system, but you know Kepler. We need you to find a way in and out."

I paused, considering her plan. Individually, these were all obstacles Angel and I had seen before. Combined, it made for one hell of a heist. Angel said the job would be worth my while—with all the failure points and ways it could go wrong, it better be.

"What's my cut?" I asked, lifting my mug to my lips.

"What's one trillion split eight ways?"

I nearly choked on my coffee. "Did you say one *trillion*?"

Angel looked amused. "I did."

"What makes you so sure that Atlas would pay out *one trillion credits* for some fucking tech?"

"Losing this proprietary information could destroy Atlas Industries. That's billions of credits flowing out of Joyce Atlas's pockets and into his competitors' every year. A galactic monopoly, gone."

"You don't think he'd just give it up? You don't think he'd just retire with what he's got?"

"It's not about the money, Edie." She smiled. It looked out of place now. "It's about mastery over the galaxy."

I was about to reply when I heard the trill of the door unlocking. I swatted the screens away from me, and with a sweep of her arm Angel extinguished them all.

"Edie?" Andie stepped through the door, her arms laden with groceries. "Could you help me carry—oh!" She blinked. "Is that you, Angel?"

I glanced at Angel, sitting across from me at the table. She had a smile on her face, one that actually looked genuine. "Andie," she said, "it's so good to see you."

"It's been a long time," Andie replied, carefully setting down her groceries. "What are you doing here?"

"She's helping me find a job," I answered. "Might have something for me at Atlas Industries."

"You're still in the Upper Wards?" Andie asked.

"I am," Angel replied. "I'm sorry I haven't been by to visit. Work keeps me busy."

Andie tried to hide her grimace. "I'm sure."

It was weird, seeing Andie react to Angel like that. The three of us grew up together. Went everywhere together. For the longest time we were like siblings, totally inseparable.

But Angel's betrayal had blown all of us apart.

I glanced Angel's way. To her credit, she looked unperturbed.

"Will you stay for dinner?" Andie asked politely.

"I can't tonight. I have an engagement I can't miss."

"Maybe some other time."

"I'll be by again, I'm sure."

I stood from the table. "I'll walk you out."

Angel followed me out the door. We didn't speak until we

reached the street, where Angel paused in front of a sleek black flyer at the curb. She turned to me. "I've arranged a meeting with the Obake. Tonight, at Cherry in Ward 4."

"The club?" I asked, surprised.

"Yes. Meet me there at 0100."

"Since when was Cherry haunted?" I joked.

Angel didn't acknowledge me. "Can you manage that?"

"Yeah, yeah, I'll be there."

Angel nodded. She moved to her flyer, and I turned back toward the apartment building. I had my hand on the door when Angel called to me again. "Edie."

I turned back toward her. "What?"

She held up a hand, one of my playing cards between her fingers. She must have lifted it from the table on the way out. The back was printed with a painted landscape, and the face card was a cartoon lion dressed as the king of hearts. "This was a gift, if I remember correctly."

"I would have returned it, but the prison didn't care about takebacks," I said flatly.

Angel didn't reply. She flicked the card in my direction, and I caught it out of the air. "And one more thing," she said.

"What?"

"Keep Andie out of this," she said.

I scowled at her. "Of course I'm gonna keep Andie out of this, I've always kept her out."

"Not just the job. Whatever's going on between you and me? Keep her out of it."

"Why?"

Angel met my gaze evenly. "Because I care about her, just as much as you."

"You have a funny way of showing it," I said, coldly.

Angel didn't answer, but instead climbed into her flyer and shut the door. She rolled down the window and peered at me through it. "Cherry at 0100. Don't be late."

I gave her a mock salute. She rolled up the window, then started the engine.

I waited as she lifted from the curb, joining the traffic overhead. We were so far away from where we were as kids. She was my family, hānai'd in with her dad's blessing. Uncle Daniel was like my dad in that he was always hustling, but more in the vein of get-rich-quick schemes and shady dealings. I couldn't tell you how many bad situations the man got himself into, only to have my dad bail him out. We were all tight like that.

Maybe that's why she followed me into this life, all those years ago.

There once was a time when I would've considered Angel family. There once was a time when she was a daughter to our father. There once was a time when she was a sister to Andie.

I didn't know what she was to me.

It didn't matter now.

I went back into the apartment.

Andie was putting away groceries when I walked through the door. She was struggling to put a bag of rice above the refrigerator when I tapped her shoulder. "Let me."

Andie passed me the rice and stepped back. "I just couldn't reach."

"You shouldn't be carrying this anyway," I chided.

"Thanks, Dad," she said sarcastically. She paused. "I haven't seen Angel in so long."

"Has she been by at all?"

"She hasn't visited since you were in prison. And I haven't seen her in the Ward at all since her dad passed, four years ago."

Funny way of showing that she cared.

"What was she doing here?" Andie asked.

"Heard I was looking for work," I grunted, heaving the rice into the cabinet. "Said she'd see about offering me a job."

"Really? That's surprising."

"You're telling me."

"I wouldn't have expected her to help, given what happened." She paused again. "You know, you never told me the full story."

"It's . . . complicated," I said.

Andie led me to the kitchen table. "I'm pretty akamai." She sat down, then pulled out a seat beside her. "Try me."

"You always hated hearing about our jobs," I said as I sat down.

"Yeah, but I hate not knowing what happened between my kid sibling and my hānai sister more."

I raked my fingers through my hair. I wasn't sure how to go about this.

She touched my hand. "Just talk to me, E."

After a long moment, I sighed. "You know what our last job was?"

"A little. Just what they went over in court."

"It was a bounty," I explained. It felt weird to say it out loud. I'd spent so long denying and pleading innocence, it was strange to admit the truth. Especially to Andie.

"Atlas Industries was moving some new tech out of the station," I continued, "and some big Earth conglomerate wanted it . . . and were willing to pay a fortune to have it. The brief was light on details, but the money was too good to pass up. The job was time-limited, and we needed to move fast. Angel almost said no—said it was too sloppy, said we needed more time—but I convinced her to take the job."

I convinced her to take a lot of jobs, back in the day. The first, the last, and countless in between.

"What was the job?" Andie asked.

"The tech was being held in a warehouse near the docks, but nobody knew which one. Angel was supposed to gain access to the records and find the location and codes. I would break into the warehouse and steal the tech later that night." My gaze fell to the pool of cards on the table. "It should've been easy."

"What happened?" Andie asked softly.

"Angel sold me out. The codes she gave me were no good, and before I could run I was surrounded by station security. The cops told me everything: they picked up Angel earlier that day, and she took a plea deal in exchange for her cooperation. Instead of having my back, she let me take the fall."

I raised my eyes. "It should've been easy, Andie. I should've been set for life. But instead I lost eight years to Kepler System Penitentiary. Because of Angel."

Andie was quiet for a moment, considering my words. "I just don't understand. The Angel I know would never do that to you. There must have been something else."

"You didn't know her like I did," I said quietly.

It was always Andie, Angel, and I. But even within the three of us there were little alliances. The blood siblings. The sisters. And then there was me and Angel.

Dad used to joke we were like the ʻōhiʻa lehua. The stories said that a spurned Pele turned ʻŌhiʻa into a tree. Taking pity on his lover, Lehua, the other gods turned her into a flower. They said that when you separated the flower from the tree, it would rain down the lovers' tears. And we cried like hell the first time Angel and I were in separate classrooms in the first grade.

But we were never together. Not like ʻŌhiʻa and Lehua, much as our friends and family teased us. Much as we danced around it, never fully in or fully out. Much as I feared what could go wrong if we ever took the chance.

Given what happened, I was glad we never did.

I used to know her so well. Better than anyone else. But the Angel I knew was so far from the Angel I met outside the prison. She was always cool, always confident, but never cold.

Not like this. I thought of the blue rings in her eyes and wondered what changed her.

Andie went quiet again, collecting her thoughts. Finally, she said, "And you're sure working with her is the right call?"

"What other choice do I have?"

Andie opened her mouth to object, but all that came out was a sigh. "I don't know. I just worry about you." She gave my hand a squeeze. "I always worry about you."

I felt a twinge of guilt in my gut. "You don't have to worry about me."

"But I will anyway," she said with a small smile.

It hurt to know that she worried about me. It hurt even more to know that she had reason to worry about me. Worry about herself, even. If this went wrong, it wasn't just me who would go down. The courts were watching, and Andie needed every scrap of evidence that she was the right choice for custody of the kids. If I got caught again, it would be over for all of us.

I had to believe that taking Angel's job, risking it for the payout, would be worth it in the end.

Andie gave my hand another squeeze. "Just remember you can always talk to me."

"I know." I absently flipped over a card. "I will."

Andie fixed me with a brighter smile. "Everything's gonna work out. You'll see."

I glanced down at the card: seven clawed paw prints. The seven of diamonds.

Lucky.

"Yeah. I think it will."

Chapter 5

I TOLD ANDIE I WAS GOING OUT. I WAS PRETTY CERTAIN THAT I COULD'VE snuck out without her or the kids noticing, but I figured that there were more and bigger lies coming—didn't make sense to lie about the harmless things.

Maybe going to a shady club to recruit an infamous hacker for a dangerous heist wasn't exactly "harmless," but it was on the lower end of the type of bullshit I'd be doing over the next few weeks.

I dressed in clothes that wouldn't stand out in a crowded club: dark-wash jeans, a T-shirt, and a black leather jacket. I slid my lock-picking kit into a hidden pocket and secured my reprogrammable keycard into another. Though I was never the hitter in a crew, I always carried a switchblade in my pocket. Hopefully I wouldn't have to use it.

It was a Friday night, and the monorail was crowded. I kept to myself at the rear of the car, back to the wall and watching the passengers warily. As we left the Lower Wards, most of the riders were night shift workers on their commute. As we passed through to the Upper Wards, the commuters left, and the revelers got on.

The atmosphere in the car was giddy, with more than a few

of the occupants already drunk. Watching them sway and bump into each other as the monorail rumbled through the Wards, it would have been easy to disappear in the crush of the crowd. It would have been easy to slip my hands into coats, pockets, purses. On a night like this, I could have walked away with enough credit chits, phones, IDs, and other valuables to cover half a month's rent for the apartment.

But that was a long time ago.

So I kept my hands to myself.

Ward 4 was the transition between the Lower Wards and the Upper Wards. It used to be Koreatown, full of bustling restaurants and tiny markets, populated by scrappy yobo kids and little old aunties pushing their shopping wagons. But as Atlas Industries expanded and Kepler grew into hotspot for tech research, it drew more and more lab coats and execs to the station. So many that they spilled over from the Upper Wards, working their way down the towers and skybridges to the Wards below, pushing out everything else. In the eight years I'd been gone, it had completely transformed. Even on the short walk from the monorail station to Cherry, I passed two trendy O_2 bars, three VR hubs, and half a dozen biofeedback boutiques.

There was a line down the street when I arrived at 0100. I could hear the bass pounding from the other end of the block, just under the excited chatter of the people waiting. There were two bouncers checking IDs and swiping chips at the door, though they were only letting people in whenever someone stumbled out. It must've been packed in there.

Unsure of where to go, I loitered at the end of the block, trying to ignore the overly familiar Atlas VI trying to sell itself to me.

Cherry was one of the last holdouts from the old Ward 4. Among the transplants, it had a reputation for being edgy and dangerous. Everything in the Lower Wards was li'dat with them, but in the case of Cherry it was at least somewhat based in truth. The club was one of the few places the locals still liked to hang out, and it was also where a lot of shady business deals were negotiated. Cherry was the interface between the Wards, where the commands of the Upper Wards were transmitted to the workings of the Lower Wards. Software to hardware, brains to brawn.

"Edie," a voice called.

I looked up from my phone and saw Angel striding toward me, her high heels clicking on the pavement. She was dressed in a black pencil skirt and a snowy-white blouse, her vermilion lipstick, and her blond hair sleek and shining in the streetlights.

I frowned at her. "You're not going in dressed like that, are you?"

Angel looked at her outfit. "What's wrong with the way I'm dressed?"

"You look like a fed, that's what's wrong."

She looked offended. "I do *not* look like a fed."

I smirked. "You've been corporate for too long, A. Forgot what it's like to get down and dirty with the locals."

"Then what do you suggest?" she snapped.

"Here." I shrugged out of my leather jacket. "Put this on."

She took it from me warily. Satisfied I hadn't booby trapped it, she slid her arms through the sleeves.

"Don't lose it, I've got my shit in there," I warned. "Now hike up your skirt."

"What?"

"You wanna get us thrown out of Cherry for looking like a narc?" I demanded. She pursed her lips but said nothing. "Then hike up your skirt. And undo a button, for God's sake."

Through the crack in her ice, I could see she was pissed—the same look she wore when she knew I was right but hated to admit it. I met her dark eyes without flinching. We stood at an impasse for a moment before she reached down and grabbed fistfuls of her skirt. She held my gaze as she hiked it up, and it took conscious effort on my part to keep my eyes on her face. My heart pounded in my chest when I caught a glimpse of the garters holding up her stockings.

She reached for her collar, and despite my best efforts, my eyes fell to her hands. She unbuttoned her blouse, down far enough that I could see the band of her bra. Black satin.

"Satisfied?" she asked, her voice icy.

I met her gaze again. "Yeah. Satisfied."

She brushed past me toward the club, and I could feel the chill in the air. She strode down the block, straight by the line hugging the side of the building. I followed her closely, trying to ignore the muttering of the crowd. I never liked drawing any kind of attention.

The bouncers looked like they were about to say something when Angel came to a halt in front of them. "I'm meeting someone," she said, authoritative. "But I don't know their face."

The bouncers exchanged a glance. Then one of them gestured for me and Angel to pass through. I gave them both a nod. Angel walked right in.

Stepping into the club, I was immediately overcome by the pounding bass, the smell of liquor, and the humid heat of bodies packed together. The house lights were dim, the room lit with neon shades of pink and red. Angel slipped into the crowd, and I followed. She moved easily between the writhing mass of people on the dance floor and the crush of patrons at the bar. Angel always had a way with people, always knew how to move within their space. She could command a room with a gesture or disappear without a word. The crowds seemed to part at her touch, and I followed in her wake.

We made our way to the far end of the club, where a spiral staircase led upstairs. Cherry was divided into three floors, each with a different theme. We passed through the pink-and-red room to the neon floor, then to the black-and-white ballroom. The pulsing lights brought back years of memories, dancing and drinking and money changing hands. Angel led me to a door marked Private Parties, guarded by two more bouncers. I couldn't hear what she said over the roar of the music, but the bouncers nodded and let her pass through.

The next room was quieter. It was set up as a lounge, with plush sofas, armchairs, and tables arranged around a central stage. There didn't seem to be any other exits. Angel sat in a chair at the front of the stage and facing the door, looking imperious. I paced the perimeter of the room.

We waited in silence for a few minutes, with only the sound of the muffled music playing in the other room.

"Where did you find this guy?" I asked after a while.

"They hacked the Cassius system in four minutes," she answered.

"I've been in prison for eight years, Angel, I have no fucking clue what that means."

Angel sighed. "They were able to break through the previous iteration of Atlas's security measures in an impressive amount of time. And they got very close to breaking through the current one."

"And you think we can trust them?"

"I think they'll be just as invested as we are."

I frowned at her from across the room. But before I could speak, the lights in the lounge dimmed. I jumped, my hand flying to the switchblade in my pocket. A spotlight flared and a figure appeared on stage, dressed in loose black pants, a baggy black hoodie with the hood pulled up, and a mirrored mask that glinted in the harsh light. The holographic image flickered as a deep voice with a velvety timbre said, "*Angel Huang. It's a pleasure to finally meet you.*"

"The pleasure is mine, Obake," Angel said smoothly, utterly unfazed. "Though I would have liked to meet face-to-face."

"*You can never be too careful, in these troubled times,*" the voice rumbled.

"I hope to earn your trust, then."

"*That remains to be seen.*"

I looked around the room, puzzled. The voice sounded familiar.

"*I understand you're looking for someone with my skill set for a job,*" the image said as they paced across the stage. "*Why did you not seek me out?*"

I glanced Angel's way, confused. I thought she'd already contacted the Obake.

"You're very hard to find," Angel said simply.

The image paused its pacing. "*But you sought out others.*"

"That I did."

"*I see everything that happens within the Net,*" the voice continued, slightly aggrieved. "*I saw you seek out others. Others that are far inferior to me—mere fools with clumsy hands bumbling their way through the Net. So I ask again—why did you not seek me out?*"

Angel smiled. "I did seek you out, Obake. You're here now, aren't you?"

She drew out the Obake by playing off their pride. Of course she did.

There was a long, heavy pause, the music thumping through the walls. Then the voice chuckled, a low thrum not unlike the bass outside. "*Clever.*"

I frowned at the speaker in the corner. I could almost place the voice.

The figure crossed its arms behind its back. "*You have my attention, then. What would you ask of me, Angel Huang?*"

"I'm in need of someone with your skill set. Someone who can crack Cassius II."

"*And what could you offer me in exchange?*"

"Exactly what you wanted when you contacted me, Obake. I can offer you galactic notoriety—the only hacker to break

Cassius II. The best in the business, the best in the galaxy. Your name would be synonymous with greatness."

"*Greatness...*" The voice sounded pensive.

"Wait a minute," I interrupted. "You're a dragon."

Angel whipped around in her chair to glare at me. A lesser human may have withered under that look, but I'd seen it enough times in my twenty-one years of knowing her to ignore it. "Your voice changer. It's a dragon from that one fantasy show. What's that about?"

The voice chuckled again. "*An appreciator of fine arts, I see.*"

"I mean, if you're into kid's shows."

"*It's not just a kid's show.*" The voice sounded offended. "*There are a lot of mature themes at play. The dragons, for instance—*"

"*Anyway,*" Angel cut in. "I don't mean to take up too much of your time, Obake." She settled into her icy calm, back to business. "Cassius II has never been breached—not even you could crack it. But I am someone intimately familiar with the system. I'm offering you the opportunity to try again. Should you succeed"—she smiled—"you would be the very first, and perhaps the very last, to bring Atlas Industries to its knees."

The voice went quiet, considering. Then, the lights went out again. I moved to stand at Angel's side, my eyes on the door. She was tense beside me. After several long moments of silence, the door opened, casting white light into the darkened lounge.

The same figure stood in the doorway. As the door swung shut behind them, we were once again left in darkness. The figure strode forward and climbed onto the stage, and the spotlight flared to illuminate them.

They pushed back their hood and pulled off their mask.

A girl stood before us, with brown skin, long locs pulled into a ponytail, and dark monolid eyes that seemed to gleam in the low light. She grinned at us, and in a high, soft voice said, "All right. I'm in."

"Hold on," I objected. "How old are you?"

The girl stiffened. "Old enough."

I whirled on Angel. "She's too young."

"Hey!"

Angel met my gaze. "Is she?"

"She's what, sixteen? Seventeen? I'm not pulling a literal child into this, Angel."

"I am *not* a child!" the girl protested.

"How old were you when we pulled the credit chit scheme?" Angel asked evenly.

I scowled. "That's different."

"How so?"

"Because there was nobody there that knew better."

"And you know better?"

"*Yes*, I do."

"You have no idea who I am!" the girl cut in. "You have no idea what I'm capable of!"

I gestured at her wildly. "She watches *cartoons*."

"What's wrong with watching cartoons?" the girl demanded.

"I'm not dragging some kid into this life, Angel."

"She's already in this life, Edie."

"But—"

"The Obake is our best shot at the vault, E," Angel said impatiently. "If you're worried about things getting dangerous, she'll be behind a screen. She'll be off-site." She paused. "And if we don't take her, who knows what she'll do."

"Yeah," the girl agreed. "Who knows what I'll do."

I looked between them, the girl with her defiant stare and Angel with her expectant gaze. I gave a frustrated sigh. "I can't win this, can I?"

"Nope," the girl said.

I dragged my hand down my face. ". . . Fine. But if things get hot, I'm sending you straight back to junior high."

"I'm in high school," the girl said irritably.

I threw up my hands.

Angel ignored me. "Can we set up another meeting to go over the details, Obake?"

The girl grinned. "As cool as it sounds to hear you say it, you don't need to call me Obake. I'm Malia."

"Malia. It's good to meet you." Angel gestured at me. "This is Edie."

Malia met my scowl with disinterest. "Edie. That short for anything?"

"Nope," I answered.

Malia shrugged. Then she hopped down from the stage and approached us. "If you want to meet again, I can send you a secure message tomorrow." She gestured at my wrist. "Let me see your comm."

I took out my phone from my pocket and held it out for her. She stared at it in disbelief. "What the hell is that?"

"What?"

She took it from me, turning it over in her hands. "This thing is ancient!" She looked up at me. "Can it even connect to the Net?"

"What, like the intranet?"

Malia shot Angel a pleading look. "I can't work like this."

"She means the GhostNet," Angel explained, as if I were a child. "Atlas has been developing it over the last ten years, but it only went live three years ago, while you were gone."

"Okay," I said slowly, "what is it?"

"A new form of human-machine interface," Angel continued. "A network that interfaces directly with the human brain."

"Brain mods?"

"Exactly."

"The mods are mostly used for multi-threading in the prefrontal cortex and semantic retrieval through the hippocampus," Malia said. I looked at her blankly. She sighed. "Think of it as overclocking your brain or using a search engine. But instead of using multiple cores or hits on a website, you're tapping into the processing power and semantic memories of thousands of other people." She grinned. "Cool, yeah?"

Not at all. "You mean to say the GhostNet connects to other people?"

"Yup!"

"Who the fuck puts a computer in their brain?"

Malia tapped at her temple. "It's pretty handy!"

I recoiled in horror. "But why?"

"Think about it! The processing power to rival Atlas Industries' most advanced supercomputer, encyclopedic knowledge, and, if that's not enough, access to any electronic system on this station with just a thought?" Her grin turned sinister. "I'm the Obake, E. I was made for the GhostNet."

"You're okay with people poking around in your brain?"

"Nah, brah, my connection is one-way. I closed up the backdoor, and I get firewalls for days. Nobody's messing with my head."

Even with Malia's security measures, I felt sick to my stomach. It reminded me of the flyers and advertisements that would appear in the Ward, when Joyce Atlas was building his empire. They promised huge payouts—cash payouts—for participation in the human trials for his new tech. Patches and subdermals, chips and implants. There were even reports of extra vials of blood going missing, extra samples of healthy tissue disappearing. The rumors were that Atlas was stealing them himself in some bid for eternal youth. I didn't know what to believe.

But no matter how dire things got at home, I never took the bait. I heard so many horror stories of the tech going wrong and people getting hurt—I couldn't imagine giving someone access to my body like that. I couldn't imagine it then, couldn't imagine it now.

I looked uneasily at the phone in Malia's hand. "You're not going to stick another chip in me, are you?"

"What? Of course not!" She looked offended. "I'm just patching you into my private network."

"Here." Angel tossed a comm to her, one that was worn on the wrist. Malia tapped out a few commands, then held it out for me to take. Angel gave me a cool look. "You can keep that."

"Thanks, I guess," I said, slipping the comm around my wrist.

Malia gestured for my hand. "You said you had another chip. Show it to me."

I extended my hand cautiously. She pulled it closer, examining the wound. She reached into the pocket of her hoodie and withdrew a chip reader, then swiped it across my hand. It beeped in confirmation.

"What'd you just do?" I asked, a little alarmed.

"Copied your RFID. Now we can spoof the signal, make it look like you're having a chill day at home. Don't want the feds following you around." Satisfied, she let go of my hand and stepped back from both of us. "Now we can talk."

Angel nodded. I gave my hand another uneasy glance.

"All right, well, you seem mostly cool," Malia said. She pulled up her hood and put on her mask. "I'll message you about meeting again." She gave us both one last appraising look as she turned to leave. She addressed Angel: "Nice outfit, by the way."

Angel stiffened beside me, and I did my best not to look too smug.

Malia threw a shaka at us as she left. "Shoots!"

We both waited until she was gone before I turned on Angel. "Did you know she was that young?"

"I had my suspicions," she said.

"You should've told me."

"Why?" She brushed past me toward the door. "So you could lose this argument sooner?"

"Fuck you, Angel," I growled. But I followed her out anyway.

There was still a line down the street when we pushed the doors open at the front of the club. We walked together for a while before Angel paused in front of her flyer.

"I'll discuss next steps with Malia," she said. "We need her to track down our next contacts, Kapua Duke and Chloe Nakano."

"The grifters."

"That's right. I don't know what their current play is, but I believe Malia can find out."

"Just tell me where to be."

"I will."

I moved past her toward the rail station. She called out to me again. "Edie."

I looked at her over my shoulder. "What?"

"Don't get squeamish," she said.

"I'm not squeamish," I said, annoyed.

"Keep it that way. Because if I think you're going to compromise this plan because of your own discomfort"—she met my gaze evenly—"I'll cut you out."

"Noted," I said flatly.

I turned to leave. Angel unlocked her flyer and climbed inside. "Goodnight, Edie."

I waved at her over my shoulder.

The music faded as I walked to the monorail, until I was alone with just the sounds of Kepler itself: humming machinery, sighing air vents, dripping water. Ward 4 was quieter than the other Lower Wards—the transplants preferred the quiet, I guess. I reached for my cigarettes, only to realize that Angel still had my jacket. My curse echoed between the buildings.

I gave a frustrated sigh and walked the rest of the way to the monorail with my hands in my pockets.

As I walked, my thoughts kept returning to Cherry, and my memories of the place. It used to be where Angel and I went to party with our friends. Until we started taking jobs there, and it became our place of work. It started off with a few harmless lifts. Then it moved on to breaking and entering. Before long we were on full-blown heists and cons, making names for ourselves in Cherry's back rooms.

It was all my idea, of course. What was the harm in doing a little more, reaching a little higher? We were so close to buying our way out of this life, pulling ourselves and everyone we loved out from under that crushing weight. My parents could retire. Andie could come back home. Angel's dad could go straight, leave all his debts behind. More than that, with the bounty of our last job we could've lived like royalty. We could've had it all, could've had everything we ever needed. We could've never wanted for anything again. All we needed was one more job, one last score—

But the higher they climb, the harder they fall.

And Angel let me take one hell of a fall.

I convinced Andie to give me weekend shifts at the shop. It gave her time to rest and be with the kids on their days off from school before her shifts at the market down the street. It also kept Tyler out of the house, which was a bonus.

When I put up the shutters and unlocked the door, I was overcome with nostalgia. I remembered all the weekend mornings, the after-school shifts, the holiday hours. As I stepped over the threshold, I smelled the familiar scent of paint and cleaning solution. I remembered sweeping floors and mopping spills, popping open Atlas tech when it hit its planned obsolescence, picking locks and cracking safes when their owners had lost their keys or forgotten their combinations. Even before that, I remembered playing Marco Polo with Andie in the aisles, poking at the cash register before I could count change, listening to Dad talk with customers about things I didn't understand, but desperately wanted to.

The grief hit me all at once. I couldn't help but feel like this was all so unlucky, so unfair, so undeserved. I lost my dad to a station accident at fifteen, Andie to Tyler at sixteen, Mom to cancer at twenty-seven, and I was staring down the possibility of losing Paige at twenty-nine. What did I ever do to deserve this? Whatever I did, what could I ever do to make up for it? Because I was tired, I was so goddamn tired.

I knew then that I would do anything to keep Andie, Paige, and Casey.

Anything and everything.

The door chimed behind me, and I crushed all those feelings deep down where I couldn't feel them anymore.

I turned toward the sound to see Old Mr. Fong standing in the doorway. His head was bald; he must have shaved off the scraggly hair that used to grow there. His beard was no longer gray, but snowy white, and he peered at me through glasses perched at the end of his long nose. He smiled. "Edie, it's so good to see you."

I smiled at him too. "It's good to see you too, Mr. Fong."

I held out my hand and he gave it a firm shake, stronger than I expected, then pulled me into a tight hug. "It's good to see you out," he said. "It's good to see you going straight."

He released me. I smiled again, but all I could do was nod. He shuffled past me into the shop, moving with slow but steady purpose toward the back room. "You plan to stay out?"

"Yes, sir."

"Good," he said, fishing for the manual keys in his pocket. Even Dad didn't like to keep electronic ones. "The whole neighborhood missed you."

I leaned against the counter. "I missed them too."

Mr. Fong pushed open the door and the lights flickered on. He started rifling through the open boxes. "I been helping your sister, but she doesn't listen to me." He clicked his tongue in disapproval. "So akamai, but you cannot replace age with anything."

I laughed. "At least not without a lot of time."

"Exactly!" He stooped down, out of my sight, then grunted with exertion.

"You okay in there, Mr. Fong?"

"Aiyah! I cannot." He poked his head out. "You look strong. Try carry this."

I grinned to myself.

I pushed off the counter and joined Mr. Fong in the back room. He gestured at what he was trying to lift—a case of fluorescent lightbulbs.

My heart sank. "You never used to let me carry these."

"Well, you going have to soon. You and Andie going take over here. Your dad is long passed, and I won't be here forever."

"That's not true." It was a lie, but I wanted to believe it.

Mr. Fong tutted. "Time stops for no one, Edie."

I didn't know what to say to that.

He pointed at the case of lightbulbs. "Go on. I supervise."

I turned my eyes down toward the floor, then picked up the case of lightbulbs and carried them to the front.

Chapter 6

IT WAS EARLY MONDAY MORNING WHEN I GOT A TEXT FROM ANGEL:

> Meet me at the Common in Ward 7 at 1000.

And a follow-up:

> Dress presentably.

I wasn't sure what that meant, with the way she'd shown up to Cherry. But given this was the highest of the Upper Wards, I figured I'd be conservative. I opted for dark slacks and a slate-gray button-down, the sleeves buttoned to hide my tattoos, and only slightly out-of-fashion gloves to cover the still angry chip wound on my hand. I hazarded a guess that prison tats weren't presentable in Angel's mind—they were pretty far behind the bougie smart-tats the transplants had.

After showering and dressing, I went to the kitchen and poured myself a cup of coffee. The kids were already there, engrossed in their bowls of cereal. Andie did a double take when I entered the kitchen.

She grinned. "Look at you, all dressed up!"

"Job interview," I lied.

"Did Angel set it up?"

"Yeah. I'm meeting her in a few hours to get ready."

A flash of concern passed across Andie's face. But before I could press, she moved on. "What would you be doing?"

I sat down beside her. "Customer service. Just answering phones and fielding complaints, you know."

Angel and I had rehearsed this lie. While lying was a necessity in what I did, I never took to it naturally like she did. I made a passable grifter, but Angel . . . Angel made lying into an art form.

"That's tough though, dealing with angry customers," Andie said.

"Not as tough as prison. A customer can't shank you." I sipped my coffee. "Legally."

"What's a shank?" Paige asked.

Andie shot me a warning look across the table.

"A shank," I said carefully, "is something people in prison use to hurt each other very badly."

"Did you ever get shanked?"

I wasn't sure how to answer that.

Andie saved me. "That's a very rude question to ask, Paige."

"Sorry." She poked at her cereal. "I was just curious if it was like the time you hit Aunty Edie with their skateboard and they got a concussion."

Andie whirled on me. "You told them about that?"

I put my hands up. "They asked if we fought! I wouldn't lie to a kid."

"It was an *accident*!"

"Allegedly."

Casey mimed swinging a skateboard at Paige and she rolled her eyes.

"Don't hit your sister, Casey," Andie scolded.

The little boy scowled and folded his arms.

Andie turned back to me. "What else have you been telling them?"

"Whoa, it's so late, already," I said, looking at my wrist. "Better go meet Angel."

"Edie!" Andie said sharply.

I downed my coffee. "Love you, tita!"

I made a quick retreat from the kitchen, acutely aware of Andie's stink eye on my back. I rushed to gather my wallet clip and the switchblade, though my lockpicks and keycard were still in my jacket. They went into my pocket along with a multitool and a nicer wallet, then I hustled out of the apartment.

It was a nice day out. There wasn't much variation in Kepler's climate, but if you knew it well enough, you could sense when things were running smoothly. The temperature was cooler, the air smelled cleaner, and the light was bright, even in the Lower Wards. I decided to take it as a sign.

I was almost an hour early for my meeting with Angel, so I made my way leisurely to Ward 7. From their roots in the Lower Wards, Kepler's towers reached for the simulated sky that stretched across the inner hull of its ring. The Wards had always been stratified, but the difference between Wards 7 and 2 was literally day and night. With no towers, skybridges, and flight traffic to obscure it, Kepler's simulated sun shone brilliantly down on its highest Ward, unlike the perpetual twilight of the Lower Wards. Here it was always light and warm and dry, which Ward 2 wasn't, even on its best days.

I wandered aimlessly for a while, watching the people of the Upper Wards on their commute to work. They seemed to walk with a spring in their step, one you didn't see much in the Lower Wards. The spin of the station made the pull of the artificial g weaker. Feeling the lightness in my limbs, I wondered what it might be like to live in this weightless luxury. What it would be like to exist outside the downward pull of the Lower Wards.

I made it to the Common a few minutes early. I didn't come here often. Seven Common was one of two green spaces on

Kepler. A wide skybridge, it arced over the monorail tracks, casting a deep shadow over the Lower Wards. The skybridge itself was carpeted with neatly trimmed grass and well-kept ornamental trees, tall, leafy, and green—utterly unlike the scraggly gardens people attempted to keep in the low light below.

I walked casually down the street and scanned the thinning crowds for Angel. Then my comm buzzed on my wrist with a message from her:

Van at your 3.

I looked to my right, and next to the sidewalk hovered a comm utility van. I made my way toward it, and the side opened to allow me inside.

The interior of the van was crowded with gear for every crime—hacking, climbing, burgling, even simple disguises. Angel was sitting in the front seat. Malia was seated at a console set against the wall of the van, fussing with a metal puzzle while the screen beside her populated itself with lines of code. I assumed interfacing directly with the mod allowed for multitasking. I shuddered and climbed inside.

"Howzit, E," Malia greeted me, without looking up from her puzzle.

"Howzit," I said in answer, averting my eyes. I sat down on one of the supply crates. "Did you track down Duke and Nakano?"

"I did," she answered. Finishing a line of code, she looked up from her puzzle. "Angel tell you the details?"

I glanced at Angel, who met my eyes impassively. "No."

"They were pretty tough to find, actually," Malia said. "They tend to hit marks that are new to the station or just passing through, ones that don't have the connections or resources to track down the people who scammed them." She paused. "Or ones that would be implicated slash humiliated if they came forward."

"What are they doing now?"

Angel answered, "Their mark is a collector of Old Earth art, antiquities, and exotic animals. They—"

I held up a hand. "Wait a minute. Did you say exotic animals?"

"Peacocks," Angel replied.

"Peacocks as in . . . ?" I made a rude hand gesture.

Malia snickered. Angel's lip curled. "You're disgusting."

"Then what the hell is a peacock?"

Malia leaned forward to show me her tablet. She pointed. "That's a peacock."

I stared at the screen. "That's fucked up, is what that is."

"*Anyway,*" Angel interrupted. "Duke and Nakano are posing as fellow collectors. They're selling pedigree peacock eggs to the mark."

"And they're not really pedigree peacock eggs," I said in understanding.

"No, they're not."

I'd be impressed if they were. Real animals were hard to come by this far away from the homeworld. Genemodding a real animal to survive so long in space was an extravagant expense. Most people just kept electronic knockoffs.

"What's the play?" I asked.

"You're an interested buyer, late to the game," Angel answered.

"Wait, me?" I asked, startled. "Why me?"

"I'm a high-profile security consultant," Angel explained, "they almost certainly know my face. You, on the other hand, are an unknown quantity."

Eight years off the station would do that, I guess.

"Unless you can't handle it," Angel said coolly.

That got me. "Of course I can handle it," I said with a scowl.

"Good." She reached into the front seat of the van to pull out a dark blazer and tossed it at me. "Wear this."

I caught it in the air. I ran my hands across the fabric and checked the pockets. There was a card with Angel's tidy handwriting in the right one. Then I peered closely at the buttons. "Button cam?"

"You got it!" said Malia. She brought her chair closer to me, then held out a hand. In her palm was a small earbud, clear and flexible. "You can send and receive through this."

I took it from her and fit it into my ear.

"What about the mark?" I asked.

"Her name is Trinity Chau," Angel said. "She made her fortune smuggling drugs into the colonies, but has recently expanded into art, artifacts, and exotic animals. She has a fondness for pretty things. The more expensive and useless, the better."

"Hence the peacocks," I said.

"Hey, peacocks have a use," Malia objected. "They eat snakes."

"Malia. If I ever saw a snake on a space station, I would have far bigger problems," I replied.

Angel ignored us. "The deal is happening at one of Chau's art galleries. Duke and Nakano are supposed to arrive at noon, which gives you time to pique her interest. Make her think you're a serious buyer but need a demonstration of her connections before you'll commit to a relationship."

"Got it," I said, adjusting the earbud.

"But remember that Duke and Nakano are the real objectives, and they'll be harder to hook than Chau. If you can't hook them, at least don't spook them."

"I can do that," I said, tightening my cuff.

"Malia and I will be here to support you. I suggest listening to what we have to say."

"Yeah, yeah," I said, shrugging into the blazer. "You always liked bossing me around."

"And mind your tells. You always touch your face when you're nervous."

"Noted," I said flatly. "Anything else?"

Malia gave me a thumbs-up. "You got this, brah."

"Thanks." Then I climbed out of the van into the warm midmorning light.

The art gallery was a few blocks down and around the corner. I walked purposefully, as if I belonged here. Never in my life had I felt like I truly belonged in Ward 7, and after eight years in prison, I felt even more out of place. But if I'd learned anything in my twenty-one years on the station, it was how to pretend I belonged.

The gallery was on an upper floor of a shared office space. To my left, there was a set of glass double doors with the name of the gallery, Chau Collections, printed across them. I pulled them open and stepped inside.

The space was huge, with open floors and a floor-to-ceiling window that let in Kepler's light. White walls hung with paintings partitioned the space, while matching pedestals set with sculptures dotted the floor. Most of the paintings were of nature: landscapes, animals, natural phenomena, with a few nudes scattered here and there. The sculptures were primarily abstract, organic shapes, except for a collection of tiny birds nesting in a bronze tree. The whole place was minimalistic in the way that rich people liked—purposeful in what they bought, because they had the money and power to be choosy.

I swept the room with my eyes. Not seeing anyone, I moved toward the closest painting. It was a landscape, almost large enough to take up the whole wall. It depicted an ocean sunrise in elegant brushstrokes, with a sandy shore and foamy waves, the pale blue water stretching out until it met the pink hues of the sky. It was pretty. Who could say if it was accurate—the only real sunrise I'd seen was over the prison walls of the Rock. But I liked it all the same.

Light footsteps on the floor made my ears prick. I inhaled

deeply and exhaled slowly. As the footsteps rounded the corner, I let my mind settle into a practiced calm.

"Lovely, isn't it?" a soft, seasoned voice asked.

"It really is," I answered.

Angel spoke into my ear: *"What you're looking at is a Sierra Vann, known for painting cityscapes. She painted this piece around 2150. It's probably worth upward of seventy-five thousand credits, so don't undersell it."*

"I've always had a soft spot for Vann," I said. The woman moved to stand beside me, just on the periphery of my vision. "I haven't seen many natural landscapes of hers."

"She only painted a handful of them," she said. "Her heart was in the city."

Remembering the contents of the gallery, I said, "Though I suspect yours is back on Earth."

"Oh?" The woman sounded surprised.

I looked at her. She was older than me, maybe mid- to late forties. Her black hair was swept into an elegant chignon, one graying strand framing her face. She wore a long dress of iridescent silky fabric with a high neck and long sleeves, with tasteful cutouts that showed off the shimmering lines tattooed on her skin. Her dark irises were encircled by a violet ring, similar to Angel's. Her expression was curious.

"This gallery," I explained. "All of the art is of the plants and animals of Old Earth. This whole collection is a testament to the beauty of our homeworld. Everything you could ever love about where we came from, it's here."

The woman looked bashful. "You must think it's silly."

I smiled at her. "Not at all. I think it's romantic."

Angel once told me my smile was lopsided. I tried to fix it, but she told me to keep it. She said she liked it. Made me feel more real.

The tattoos on the woman's skin shifted to a delicate pink. "You're too kind."

I extended a hand. "I'm Jay. Jay Kuroda."

She took my hand. "Trinity Chau."

I gave her hand a gentle squeeze, letting my touch linger for just a moment.

"A pleasure," I said.

"Likewise."

I released her, then moved away from the Vann painting. "You have quite a collection, Ms. Chau."

"Please, call me Trinity. And thank you."

I gave each of the paintings an appraising look as I moved through the gallery. My gaze fell on one of the nudes of the collection at the same time Angel spoke in my ear.

"At your eleven. That's an Eirin Yu. They're making a name for themselves painting mythological scenes. It's a newer piece, painted in 2167, but it's already worth twenty thousand credits. Express your interest, but don't lay it on too thick."

I approached the Yu painting. It depicted a nude woman reclining in a forest glade, a fruit in one hand and a snake grasped in the other. The juices of the fruit ran down her arm in rivulets, and the snake's grip left imprints on her wrist.

"*The Fall of Eve*," I read from the placard. "Funny how a story as old as that one stays fresh in our memory."

"It's certainly one that persists across time."

I put on a pensive expression. "Makes me wonder what stories of ours will be painted."

"Isn't it striking?"

I met her eyes. "It's beautiful."

Trinity's tattoos darkened to a rosy red.

"*I said not to lay it on too thick*," Angel said, annoyed. "*Now look at the sculpture at your three.*" I glanced that way and saw the bronze tree filled with little polished birds. "*That's a Kemp, he specializes in extinct fauna of Old Earth. Use that as a lead-in to the deal with Duke and Nakano.*"

I ambled to the tree, peering through the pounded bronze

leaves at the birds. "What birds are these?" I asked, genuinely curious.

"They're lovebirds," Trinity said. Her skirts swished around her ankles as she moved to stand beside me. "They used to mate for life, and deeply mourned the loss of their partners."

"Amazing." I circled the statue, still peering into the branches. "I wish I could have seen a real one."

"Have you seen a bird before, Mx. Kuroda?"

"Jay," I corrected gently. "And yes, I have. I keep an owl at home. He's very cute."

"Oh?" Trinity said, her interest piqued. "Where did you get him?"

"A collector friend on Etria." I met her gaze. "Do you keep birds, Trinity?"

"A few parakeets. A macaw." She laughed. "It's quite a trial keeping them away from the cat, though!"

"A cat!" I smiled brightly. "What pretty animals."

"And so full of personality!"

"What's your cat's name?"

"Boots."

"Clever! I see what you did there."

She beamed. "And your owl?"

"His name is"—I searched through my thoughts and came up blank—"Frank."

Angel blew out a sigh in my ear.

Trinity blinked. "Frank?"

"Like the virtue," I tried. "My niece named him." I put on a sheepish smile. "It's a little childish, but I think it suits an owl well."

Despite the fuckup, Trinity smiled. "You let your niece name him? How sweet."

"*The deal with Duke and Nakano, please,*" Angel said tersely.

"I thought I'd get her one for her birthday," I said to Trinity.

"Through your friend on Etria?"

I allowed a little unease to cross my face. "They're not much for trading anymore, unfortunately."

"Oh. Well, that's a shame."

"You don't happen to know any collectors looking to trade, do you?"

I could almost see the wheels turning in Trinity's head, weighing the rapport I'd built with her against the experience of a seasoned smuggler. I schooled my expression into one of innocent curiosity—the face of a naïve rich person who was only just dipping their toes into the criminal underworld, instead of a felon who cut their teeth on marks just like them.

"I . . . might know somebody," Trinity said slowly.

I perked up immediately. "Really? That would be amazing! Maybe you could—"

The bell on the door chimed, and two sets of footsteps followed.

I looked past Trinity toward the door, where two familiar women stood waiting. One was dressed in pressed slacks and a tailored sport coat, her wavy dark hair pulled into a tight bun. She was carrying a hard-sided suitcase. The other was wearing a skirt that accentuated her curves and a blouse in muted blue. Unremarkable. Unmemorable. They could have easily blended into the crowds of Ward 7, into any police lineup. If not for Angel's dossiers, I may not have remembered them either.

"Ms. Chau," the femme one—Nakano—said in greeting. "Do you have a moment?"

"I do." Trinity put a hand on my shoulder, guiding me toward the two. "And this is someone you might want to meet."

"*Remember*," Angel said in my ear, "*if you can't hook them, just don't spook them*."

I extended a hand to Nakano. "Jay Kuroda."

She took my hand. I noticed there was the faintest scar between her thumb and forefinger. Her grip was gentle. "Hana Sato."

I turned my attention to the butch one, Duke. I extended my hand, and she took it. She had the same scar, in the same place. Her grip was strong, certain. "Lani Cooke."

"Jay is a collector of animals," Trinity explained. "They're in the market for an owl, and I thought you might have connections."

The two regarded me curiously. I put on another sheepish smile. "I have my own. This one is for my niece."

"We might have a connection," Nakano said smoothly. "How do you know Mx. Kuroda, Ms. Chau?"

"Oh, I"—Trinity stammered—"truthfully we just met, but they seem like a good connection to make."

"*They're testing your cover,*" Angel said. "*Rely on that rapport and keep it simple.*"

"Trinity was showing me around the gallery," I said. "We got to talking about Earth and her beauty"—Trinity's tattoos flushed again—"and she mentioned she was a collector. I'm a bit of an amateur, I admit, but I would appreciate any connections you're willing to make."

"You said this is for your niece?" Duke asked.

"For her birthday," I answered. "She's been taken with owls lately, something about witches and familiars." I grinned. "Probably too much of that fantasy show."

Duke matched my grin, and Nakano had the decency to laugh politely.

I knew one thing about the world I'd returned to, and I was going to milk it for all it was worth.

"How long have you been collecting, Mx. Kuroda?" Nakano asked.

"Jay," I corrected. "Not long, maybe three or four years."

"Who are you working with?" she asked innocently.

I resisted the urge to touch my face.

"No one right now," I answered carefully. "I had a contact on Etria, but he's no longer trading."

"There's a high turnover in this business, I'm afraid."

"So I've gathered."

"You said you were looking for an owl?" Duke asked.

"Yes, that's right."

"They're hard to keep, owls," Duke said, a charming smile on her face. "I'm impressed you kept a predator for so long—most people can only handle prey."

"You're blown," Angel said. *"Don't spook them—back off and we'll regroup."*

"I should let you get to it," I said. "I'll leave my contact information for you both."

"No, please stay!" Duke said. "If Trinity vouches for you, we believe her. We'd be glad to make a connection."

"I—"

"Don't spook them. Just go with it, Edie."

I rubbed my jaw. Then I forced a smile. "That sounds excellent."

Duke passed Nakano the suitcase. Nakano gave me a nod, then followed Trinity deeper into the gallery. Duke unbuttoned her sport coat and sat on a plush ottoman opposite the Yu painting. She watched me closely, still smiling that confident smile.

"How did you hear of us?" she asked.

"Like I said, I mentioned to Trinity that I collect, and she put me in contact with you."

"And you just met her?"

"I did."

"On the day that we were going to make a deal?" She laughed. "That's lucky!"

"I've always had that kind of luck," I said warily.

"Well, hopefully you don't run out," she said, maintaining that winning smile.

We sat in silence for a few minutes more, until Trinity and Nakano returned. We stood, Nakano joining Duke and Trinity pausing beside me.

"I'll forward you my information," Trinity said to me. With a blink of her eyes, my comm beeped affirmatively as it received her information. She smiled. "Do call me, sometime."

I smiled back. "I will."

"Please, come with us," Nakano said to me. "We'd love to make your acquaintance, maybe discuss that owl."

"*Do it, Edie,*" Angel said.

"Of course," I replied. I smiled at her too. "I'd hate to disappoint a thirteen-year-old girl."

Duke led me out of the gallery, Nakano following close behind. When we reached the street, I glanced in either direction for an escape route. Nakano must have sensed my intentions, because I felt something hard and cylindrical press into my back. I stiffened. I'd had enough guns pointed at me to know to stand still.

"Please don't make me use this," Nakano said softly.

Duke and Nakano led me down the street to the Common. We followed the winding path under the boughs of the green trees until we reached the midway point of the bridge, where we veered off into a shady grove.

Nakano urged me forward with the gun. Duke whirled on me. She looked pissed. "We've been working that job for a month," she snapped, "and you could've blown the whole thing. Who the hell are you?"

"I already told you," I said slowly. "My name is Jay Kuroda, and—"

Duke cut me off by lunging forward. I tried to react, but Nakano was insistent with the gun. Duke grabbed my arm and yanked it forward. Before I could protest, she ripped off my glove, revealing the wound where the prison had chipped me. "What animal collector has an ownership chip?" she demanded.

The grove was tense and silent for a moment. I met Duke's gaze defiantly. "My name is Edie," I finally answered, "and I have a message for you."

"How did you find us?" Nakano asked.

"It wasn't easy, you cover your tracks well. But I work with some well-connected people."

"Are you here to blackmail us?"

"What? No. I'm here to offer you a job."

Duke and Nakano shared a look over my shoulder.

"What's the job?" Duke asked cautiously.

"We're stealing proprietary information for ransom."

"Who's the mark?"

"Joyce Atlas."

"*Joyce Atlas?*" the two said in unison.

Duke gave me a disbelieving look. "You can't be serious."

"Wish I wasn't, but it's true."

Duke looked like she was getting ready to tell me off, but I felt Nakano lower the gun. I sighed in relief. "Why us?" she asked.

"Because you're the best. And we need the best to pull this off."

Duke scowled. "We don't work with amateurs."

"They may be an amateur," a voice said, "but I'm not."

All of us turned toward the entrance to the grove, where Angel stood with a hand on her hip.

"Angel Huang," Nakano said, breathy with shock.

Duke moved between Nakano and Angel. "Is this a setup?"

"No setup," Angel answered. "And no hard feelings, if you pass on this job." She took a step into the grove. "But I have a feeling you'll join us."

"Why is that?" Nakano asked.

Angel smiled. "Because I've heard you have a cause."

"A cause?"

"Your MO. Your last four jobs have targeted drug smugglers

and weapons dealers in the colonies, all for almost everything they're worth. But the money always seems to disappear before it can be found. Could it be connected to the absurdly large and suspiciously timely donations funneled through shell corporations to organizations on the ground in the outer worlds? An easy way to make the money disappear, but I think there's something else at play."

I remembered the scars on their hands. Some corporations chipped their colonists, same as Kepler System Penitentiary chipped their prisoners. Duke called them "ownership chips"—seemed like someone once owned all of us.

"You're thieves with a conscience," I said in understanding.

Nakano smiled. "You could say that."

"What does our MO have to do with your job?" Duke demanded.

"Imagine," Angel said, "all the good you could do with 125 billion of Joyce Atlas's credits."

Duke barked out an incredulous laugh. "You mean to tell me you're stealing from your own boss?"

"I'm in an excellent position to do so."

"Why Atlas?" Nakano asked.

"Atlas has blood on his hands," Angel replied. "He hides his dealings behind a screen of philanthropy, but you and I know the truth. He has contracts with every police force in the inner worlds and half the defense contractors in the galaxy. His technology has killed millions, and imprisoned millions more. That's the type of man I'm stealing from."

Duke and Nakano exchanged another long look, both considering. Duke looked like she was about to say no. But then Nakano gently touched her hand, and Duke sighed.

"Okay. We'll hear you out."

Angel smiled. "Good."

I circled the two of them warily, searching Nakano for the

gun. Noticing me, she smiled. She lifted her hand, and in it I saw a tube of lipstick. I gaped at her.

Fucking grifters.

"Have my number," Angel said, gesturing at me. I passed Duke the card in my pocket. "Call me and we can set a time to discuss the details."

"We will," Nakano said.

"It was a pleasure meeting you both." Then she turned and started out of the grove. I gave Duke and Nakano a nod, then followed her.

"Amateur?" I said, falling in step beside her.

"Duke and Nakano are professionals," Angel said. "You were never going to hook them, I just needed you to make the connection. With any luck you won't have to do that again."

"You're welcome. Glad I could help," I said, sarcastic.

"*I think you did pretty good, E,*" Malia said. "*Do that again, bumbai you'll get a hot MILF girlfriend.*"

"Malia. Never speak to me about MILFs again," I grumbled.

Angel ignored us. I followed her out of the Common.

I couldn't say that I was surprised by the way things went down with Duke and Nakano—my strength was as a thief. I never took to grifting, not like Angel. She always had a way with people, even when we were kids. She knew exactly what to say to get what we wanted, or get us out of trouble. I couldn't count how many double scoops of ice cream, or extra time on the playground, or skipped time in detention she had negotiated for me.

And her grifting only improved as we grew older. As we graduated to bigger jobs, worked with better crews, she never faltered. She was making a name for herself. Where she would be if things hadn't gone so wrong, I couldn't be sure.

Though did things really go wrong for her, given where she was now?

When we reached the main path, she turned to me. "Now that we've contacted Duke and Nakano, we can move forward with the rest of the plan. Sara Morris is our next recruit. I'll forward you more information about her whereabouts closer to our meeting."

"Sure," I said.

She gave me a brisk nod. "I'll be in touch."

"Shoots."

I watched Angel stride away, dappled in Kepler's sunlight. She looked so in her element. Like she belonged here, high in the Upper Wards. She seemed so far away from the person I used to know.

My mind turned back to the look Duke and Nakano shared. It was a look that conveyed everything they wanted to say, without speaking it aloud. It was a look that could only come from years of communication, of knowing another person so intimately you could almost read their thoughts. It was a look with years of history behind it.

I remembered a time when I could read Angel just like that.

A crowd of people passed me on their way to lunch, and I disappeared into the press.

Chapter 7

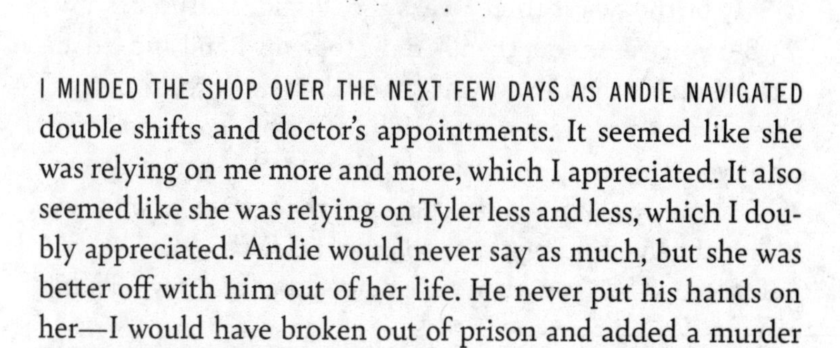

I MINDED THE SHOP OVER THE NEXT FEW DAYS AS ANDIE NAVIGATED double shifts and doctor's appointments. It seemed like she was relying on me more and more, which I appreciated. It also seemed like she was relying on Tyler less and less, which I doubly appreciated. Andie would never say as much, but she was better off with him out of her life. He never put his hands on her—I would have broken out of prison and added a murder charge to my sentence if he had—but that wasn't the only way one person could hurt another.

So I was happy to watch Casey and smile at customers if it meant Andie got a break.

It was late afternoon on Thursday when my comm pinged with a message from Angel:

> We're meeting Morris tonight. I'll pick you up at 2300.

I did wish she would give me more of a heads-up, but what else did I have to do on a Thursday night?

After I closed the shop that evening, I climbed the stairs to the apartment and tapped my keycard to the sensor. I opened the door and nearly toppled down the stairs when I was met with a scream of "*Surprise!*"

"*Motherfucker!*" I shouted involuntarily.

I put a hand to my chest, trying to slow my racing heart. I peered through the door and saw Andie, Casey, Paige, Cy, and about two dozen relatives crowded in the living room, looking a little scandalized by my language.

"What's going on?" I asked, stepping cautiously into the apartment. The floor was carpeted with balloons. The kitchen table was laden with trays of steaming food, coolers of drinks stacked around it. A handmade banner, hung over the kitchen table, read *Hauʻoli Lā Hānau*.

Andie smiled at me. "Happy birthday, Edie."

"My birthday was three weeks ago," I said, confused.

"But you weren't out then!" Andie took my hand and led me into the apartment. "Now you can celebrate with your ʻohana." She looked a little remorseful. "I didn't always get to celebrate while you were away, so I wanted to do something special now."

"Did you do all this?" I said, taking in the apartment with awe.

"I had help minding the shop," she said with a grin.

I matched her grin, then pulled her close for a hug. "Thank you, tita."

I spent the evening surrounded by relatives: aunties who brought their best food, uncles who told their same stories, and cousins and their children who had grown so much in the years since I last saw them. Most of them I hadn't seen in two years, since Mom's funeral. Some of them I hadn't seen in eight, since I went to prison.

There was Uncle Reggie, who always told me and Andie embarrassing stories about our dad. He sent me pictures while I was away, so I could keep family close. And there was Aunty Maria who made the best chili chicken, and always sent me the good-kine snacks. Even Cousin Kacen, who I maintain stole one of my hologames as a kid but never admitted to it. But even they crowded into the family calls every month.

It was surreal to see how much had changed and how much

had stayed the same. But we picked up right where we left off, as if no time had passed at all. All night we talked and laughed, joked and teased, and ate and drank.

Midway through the night, Cy pulled me aside, into the kitchen.

"So," he said, "you in?"

I finished off my beer and put it on the counter. "Yeah."

"Yessah! You doing da right ting, E. No worry, everyting going be okay, watch 'em."

"Why you go so hahd on dis plan, though?"

"Cuz you no moa any options. What I going do if you get kicked off the station? I knew you from babytimes. Who else going have my back in a scrap?"

I laughed.

He slugged my shoulder. "You doing da right ting. Iz a good plan."

"Bettah be," I replied, "if we working wit Angel."

He sighed. "We doing dis again?"

I leaned against the counter and crossed my arms. "Waz dat suppose to mean?"

"Dis fight? I no tink iz different den any oddah time. You scrap, you make up. You scrap, you make up. You guys always been li'dat, since hanabata days."

"Dis time different, cuz. You no undastand."

"I undastand plenny." He pulled another beer out of the cooler and handed it to me. "We going do dis job, we going get choke kālā, den bumbai we going be braddahs and sistahs again. You watch."

Unlikely. Even with 125 billion credits, how could Angel ever make it up to me? But I didn't ask the question out loud.

I pointed the beer in Cy's direction. "Dis goes wrong, I going bus' you up."

"Ho! You tink a few reps in da gym make you one moke now?"

I grinned. "You like scrap and find out?"

He laughed, a low rumble that reverberated in the room.

"You bettah not scrap in my kitchen," Andie said from the doorway, an empty tray in her hands.

"Jus' jokes, tita," I reassured her.

"Tanks for the grindz, cuz," Cy said to her. "Broke da mout."

"We get plenny more," Andie said, brushing past us to exchange the empty pan for a full one. "No shame, grin' somemoa."

"Shoots," Cy said. He gave me a last look, then followed Andie out of the kitchen.

I sighed and followed.

Three hours later, I was helping clear dishes while my relatives portioned out leftovers for themselves when Angel messaged me:

Outside.

I frowned at the message. "Sorry, Andie, but I need to head out."

Andie looked surprised. "So late?"

"I'm going out for drinks with Angel."

"Oh." Her expression fell. "Is she here?"

"Downstairs."

"She like come up for dinner?"

I almost wanted to tell her she didn't have to offer, but I knew Andie would always offer, anyway.

"I don't think we'll have time," I said instead.

She sighed. "Try wait while I fix her a plate."

"You don't have to—"

But Andie was already hurrying into the kitchen. She found a recyclable plate, then bustled around the table loading it up with food—kalua pork and cabbage, a ladle of katsu curry, a fat laulau, a scoop of mac salad, a precious helping of poke, and a mound of steaming rice. She heaped the plate with food and covered it tightly with tinfoil, then foisted the heavy plate into my hands. I made the rounds saying goodbye to the family, hugging and kissing and making promises to see each other again soon.

I already had a terse nudge on my comm by the time I made it downstairs, and through the window of her flyer I saw Angel drafting another. I rapped on the window, then climbed into the passenger side. Angel dismissed the message with an irritated flick of her eye.

"Sorry," I said. "Family was over."

Angel frowned at the plate in my hands. "Don't eat in my flyer."

"It's for you," I said irritably. I handed it to her. "Andie wouldn't let me leave without it."

Angel actually looked surprised at that, and a glimmer of affection passed through her dark eyes. She took the plate from me, then carefully placed it in the back seat. "I'll eat it at home."

"Sure."

She pressed the start button. "What's everyone doing here?"

"It's my birthday," I explained.

Angel met my gaze impassively. "Is it?"

"Well, no, it was three weeks ago. But Andie wanted to celebrate."

"I see." Angel reached into the back seat, then pulled out the leather jacket I'd lent her at Cherry. She tossed it in my direction. "Happy birthday."

I caught it, then checked the pockets. My lockpicks, cigarettes, and keycard were still there. "Thanks for not losing my shit, I guess."

"You're welcome."

I sat back in the seat. "So where are we going, anyway?"

"Venus, here in Ward 2."

"Never heard of it."

"It opened a few years ago." She lifted away from the curb. "You'll see."

* * *

It was about a twenty-minute flight to Venus, on the far side of the Ward. Angel parked at a curb a few blocks away from the club, killing the engine and stowing her keys in a small clutch. Another detail I was surprised hadn't changed. She always insisted on manual locks and keys wherever she could—you can't hack those. And you couldn't pay her any amount of money to willingly hand over her biometrics.

I pushed open the door and stepped out, shrugging into my jacket. Angel waited for me on the sidewalk, clutch in one hand and the other on her hip. In the streetlight I saw that she was dressed more appropriately for a club: a slinky black dress that accentuated her slight curves, black heels, and bare legs. Classy and timeless.

Noticing my lingering gaze, she said in an icy tone, "Do I look like a narc to you?"

I met her dark eyes. "Not tonight."

Something flickered through her expression—too subtle for me to read.

"Let's go," she said, turning on her heel and walking away. I followed.

She led me down the shadowed streets at a brisk pace, past crowded liquor stores and cramped bodegas, their neon lights casting flickering reflections in the puddles on the street. Angel stepped over the scattered ʻōpala on the sidewalk, the politicians in city hall having cut the funding to clean the Lower Wards' streets. As we walked, the sound of music grew louder, the pulsing and pounding of songs unfamiliar to me. I followed Angel around a corner and saw the lighted sign of Venus ahead of me. And beneath it a sign that said Adult Entertainment.

I stopped in my tracks. "Are you fucking joking?"

Angel turned to face me. "Do I look like I'm joking?"

"I'm not going in there."

"Why not?"

"It's a strip club!"

Angel looked at me impatiently. "Don't be such a prude, Edie."

"You know I'm not a prude, Angel."

"Then compose yourself. Morris is inside."

"We couldn't meet Morris anywhere else?"

"She's working," Angel said simply.

"She's—what? Here?"

"If you won't come in, you could always walk home."

I scowled at her. "I'm not walking home."

"You can't sit in my flyer," she said coldly. Then, inexplicably, she smiled. "I don't want you eating my dinner."

I stared at her. "Was that a joke?"

Angel didn't answer. She turned away and started back toward the club. "Do whatever you want, Edie."

I stared for a while longer, still working through my options. Then I gave a frustrated sigh and followed her into the club.

It was dark inside, with only the dim house lights to supplement the stage lighting. It smelled like sweat and stale beer, and it was hot near the stage lights. There were three circular stages, each one with a woman dancing and patrons crowded around it. Angel paused at what turned out to be a currency exchange, plugging her credit chit into the machine and taking a fifty-credit bill emblazoned with a naked woman in return. It reminded me of the old arcades I used to frequent with her, but way sleazier.

Angel led me to a shadowed booth at the far end of the room, where a scantily dressed waitress came to take our order. She took water, I needed a beer.

"So, what's our acrobat doing at a strip club?" I asked.

"You'll see," Angel said cryptically.

I was about to object when the crowd erupted into whoops and whistles. I turned toward the main stage, where the dancers were trading places. The one entering the stage had light skin and long blond hair falling in waves around her face. She was dressed in sheer white lingerie and walked in towering platform heels. Her face was familiar.

I turned to Angel. "*That's* Sara Morris?"

"You'll see," Angel repeated.

Sara started her routine with a series of slow, languid spins, circling the pole. She braced herself with her arms on the pole, spinning and arcing her shapely legs. Gradually the spins became faster, lifting off the ground higher, arching her back and letting momentum carry her. She climbed higher and higher, almost up to the ceiling of the club. She twisted on the pole, holding herself up with just her arms and core to extend her legs, sensually rolling her body as if she were swimming in the air. My abs hurt just watching her. She wrapped her legs around the pole again and did another spin, then the crowd gasped when she let go of the pole and fell, only to catch herself midway down.

Her routine went on for another few minutes, the crowd totally enraptured. She was good. *Really* good. As she writhed and spun on the pole, I had to notice her grace and poise.

I watched in awe.

"Stop salivating," Angel said irritably, drawing my attention back to the booth.

"Okay, I see it. Now how do we talk to her?" I lifted my beer bottle to my lips.

Angel carefully folded her card into the fifty-credit bill. She held it out to me. "Go put this in her thong strap."

I choked on my beer. "I'm *sorry*?"

"I need her to have my information—go give it to her."

"I will do no such fucking thing."

"She's working, it's a tip. What's the problem?"

"Because I don't want to fondle the woman I'm robbing a man with, that's the problem," I hissed.

Angel looked annoyed. "Just give her my card, Edie."

"No!"

"You're being childish."

"You're just giving me heat!"

"I'm not." She leaned forward on the table and lowered her voice. "I can't be seen because I know some of these girls."

I stared at her. "You—you do?"

Angel's annoyance was growing. "Just give my information to Morris. Please."

My head was full of questions. How could Angel know these girls? When would she have met them? I opened my mouth to ask them, but Angel's expression left no room for protests.

I gave a frustrated sigh. "Fine. Give me the card."

Angel handed it to me. I made my way to the stage, weaving through the crowd and trying to be as unobtrusive as possible. I stood right at the stage and raised the bill, trying to draw Sara's attention.

She made her way through the crowd accepting tips, tucking the bills into her bra and the elastic of her panties. I affected nonchalance as she paused in front of me. Her green eyes brightened at the sight of the fifty credits in my hand. I held it out for her to take, and she slid it into the band of her bra. She winked at me. "Thanks, handsome."

"Find me later," I replied. "I've got more to offer."

She smiled at me blankly—probably the same smile she gave to every patron that propositioned her. I just hoped Angel was right and the card would interest her enough to speak to us.

I left the stage and made my way back to Angel.

"What now?" I asked.

Angel sipped her water. "We wait."

Sara performed four more times over the next two hours, just as energized as the first. Angel kept to herself in the shadows for the most part, leaving me to watch the stage. Every so often I thought I felt her gaze on me, but when I looked at her, she was engrossed in her comm.

After a while there was a shift change as new dancers took the stage.

"So what's Morris's deal?" I asked, turning my attention back to Angel.

"She's a former gymnast," Angel answered. She extinguished her comm with a blink and turned her attention to me. "A very good one. Ten years ago, she could have competed on a galactic stage."

"Hence the acrobatics."

"Exactly."

"Why didn't she compete?"

"Gymnastics is a sport rife with abuse. Sara blew the whistle," Angel continued. "Being put on the blacklist meant she couldn't afford her training anymore, at least not at that level. Sponsorships fell through, endorsements were canceled, and Morris was left with the bill."

"And now she's here."

"Now she's here."

"What makes you think she'll take our job?"

"Given her history? A payout like this one would be highly motivating."

I was about to reply when a woman approached our table.

She was wearing a white dress beneath a long coat in muted gray, dressed unremarkably except for her shocking pink lipstick. Her blond hair was in a loose braid at her shoulder, and her green eyes were alight with curiosity.

"Sara Morris," Angel greeted her. "It's a pleasure to see you again."

See her again? I looked between the two of them, confused.

Angel gestured at a seat in the booth. "Please, sit."

Sara accepted the invitation, and I shifted to the middle of the booth to make room.

Her face broke into a smile. "I saw the card and thought it might be you! Didn't think you'd ever come back once you found your way to the Upper Wards."

"It's for business," Angel explained.

Sara shifted her gaze to me. "And who's this?"

"This is Edie," Angel answered for me. "My business partner."

Business partner, eh?

"Edie. Is that short for something?"

"It's not," I answered.

"Well." She winked at me. "Thanks for the tip."

I rubbed the back of my neck. "You're welcome."

"I remember you promised you had more to offer," she said. She put her elbows on the table and rested her chin in her hands, looking between me and Angel with amusement. "Tell me more."

"We're here to offer you a job," Angel explained.

"What kind of job?"

"A crime-kine job," I said.

Sara's eyes widened. "Crime?"

Angel shot me a glare. "They mean," she said, "a discreet job with under-the-table pay."

"Is that what you were doing while you were here?" Sara asked. "Is that why you always acted so weird?"

"I didn't act—" Angel began. Then she paused, composing herself. "Yes. I committed crime while I was here. And I need your help."

"What's the job?"

"You know Joyce Atlas?" I asked. Sara nodded slowly. "We're robbing him."

"Ransoming his intellectual property," Angel corrected.

I shrugged. "Yeah, sure."

"But what would you want with me?" Sara asked.

"We need someone with your skill set," Angel answered. "You're our way into the vault where the technology is housed."

Sara took us in with her big green eyes. "I've never done anything illegal."

"We'll be sure to make it worth your while," Angel said. She leaned a little closer. "How does 125 billion of Joyce Atlas's credits sound to you?"

Sara's shocking pink lips parted, just a little, at the number. Angel met her eyes, nearly black to heather green, and held Sara's gaze for a long moment. The music stopped, and the crowd cheered and hooted as the dancers collected their tips. A waitress strolled by, and Sara reached out to grab the hem of her sheer plastic skirt.

She met the waitress's puzzled look and said, "Could you tell Joey I quit?"

Both the waitress and I stared at Sara. The waitress recovered faster than me, nodding slowly before walking away. In my peripherals, Angel looked pleased but unsurprised.

"That's quite a vote of confidence in a plan you haven't even heard," I said to Sara.

She grinned at me. "Angel's smart, and her plans always worked out. I trust her. And if there's one thing I've learned, if you want to succeed at something, you've got to give it more than your all. I'm in—one hundred and ten percent."

Trusting Angel. That sounded like a mistake. Given who she was, what she did—what she did to *me*—it seemed like a huge mistake.

Then again, wasn't that exactly what I was doing?

"Perfect," Angel said. She rose from the booth. "I'll be in touch about talking through the details."

"I'm excited!" Sara clasped her hands together. "I've never done anything illegal!"

"You'll get used to it," I said, following Angel out of the booth.

Sara waved at both of us. "I'll see you soon!"

I waved at her as we left, Angel striding back to the entrance of the club.

"Well, that was surprisingly easy," I said as we exited Venus and started toward her flyer.

"Like I said, a payout like this one is highly motivating," she replied.

"You can say that again."

Angel walked briskly down the sidewalk. Despite her concerns earlier about being seen, outside the club she walked with familiar confidence. I wondered what Angel had been doing here that she would know Sara and the other girls.

Angel unlocked the flyer, and we shut the doors behind us. As she settled into her seat, I couldn't bite back my questions any longer. "How did you know her?" I asked, only half expecting an answer.

"I used to work there," Angel answered.

"When?"

"Through college. My employment at Atlas Industries was contingent on having a degree. But Dad couldn't exactly afford tuition."

Uncle Daniel could barely stock shelves at the market last I saw him. I had no idea what state he was in during the time she was in college.

"Why there?" I asked.

"It was the only place that would take me," she answered. "Not many options for a thief trying to go straight."

I turned my eyes down toward the center console. "Oh."

It made sense, I guess. Butches like me and Cy, we ended up in warehouses and docks. Femmes like Angel and Sara, they ended up in clip joints and street corners. All of us trying to survive, in our own ways.

But isn't that how it always was? I felt a sudden twinge of guilt, of all things. She was out here in this Ward 2 club on her own, without me there at her side.

Her voice took on a wistful tone. "I always liked to dance. Just didn't expect to be dancing on a stage in Venus." She reached for the start button. "I've had enough of men leering at me to last two lifetimes."

I shook my head. "You don't need to be ashamed—"

"I'm not," Angel interrupted. I raised my eyes, and she met my gaze evenly. "I worked hard to get to where I am, Edie. Waiting tables, hustling customers, studying between shifts... I busted my ass to get here. I'm not ashamed of that."

I rubbed the back of my neck. "I just didn't want you to think I was judging you."

"I don't think about your judgments," she said coldly. She pressed the button and started the engine. "I don't think about you at all."

"Then I won't feel bad for telling you to go fuck yourself," I said, just as cold.

Angel flew me home in silence. I kept my eyes on the window, watching the Ward go by. Venus had opened not long after I went to prison, and like Venus, the rest of this part of Ward 2 was a mix of new and old. It was the same cheap restaurants and bars, but overhead were the apartment towers, skeletal where their guts had been torn out for renovation. They loomed above us, as if waiting to descend on the Ward.

But here, at street level, it felt like I had never left Ward 2. Had I not gone to Kepler System Penitentiary, I may have never left at all.

Angel, though.

I glanced at her reflection in the window as she wove through the streets of what once was her home, expression impassive. While I may have never left, Angel had clawed her way up and out. From dancing on tables in clubs to sitting behind a desk in an executive office. Once she had her degree, once her father was dead, once I was out of the picture, there was nothing to hold her down. And once she was free, she never looked back.

It made me wonder—if it were me, would I do the same?

Angel dropped me off at the curb outside my apartment. She addressed me through the open door before she left: "Tatiana Valdez is our next recruit. I've arranged to meet her in three days."

"Sounds good," I replied.

I made to close the door, but she stopped me. "Wait." She met my eyes, and her gaze was intense. "Tell Andie thank you, for me."

"Sure," I said, a little surprised.

Angel gave me a nod. I closed the door, and she pulled away from the curb. As I watched her leave, I reached into my pocket for my cigarettes. I tapped the pack, but only a slip of paper fluttered out.

These will kill you. And on the other side, *You'll thank me later.*

I looked up, just in time to see Angel's flyer lift into the nighttime traffic. I scowled after her.

"Bitch."

Chapter 8

IT WAS ALMOST 0100 WHEN I GOT HOME FROM MEETING SARA MORRIS. I creeped back into the apartment without waking Andie or the kids, brushed my teeth and undressed, then threw myself into bed.

I wasn't sure how long I was asleep when my comm began to chime.

I stirred, lifting my head off my pillow to open the line.

"Angel?" I croaked. "Why are you calling me?"

"*You weren't answering my texts,*" she replied.

I glanced at my comm. "Because it's four fucking thirty in the morning."

She ignored me. "*There's been a change of plans. We're meeting Valdez in thirty minutes.*"

"Why?"

She ignored me again. "*Be ready in ten.*"

"Angel—" I said sharply.

But the line was already dead.

I dropped my face back down into my pillow and groaned. Angel never liked change, and while she was good at improvisation, she always hated any deviation from the plan. If she was pivoting so hard to acquire Tatiana, there must have been a huge fuckup somewhere along the line. That fact curbed my resentment about being woken up at godforsaken o'clock in the morning. A little.

I dragged my ass out of bed and dressed in whatever clothes I could find scattered across the floor. I didn't have time to shower, and the noise may have woken Andie anyway. I felt a twinge of guilt as I crossed the apartment, glancing toward our parents' bedroom. Eight years later and I was still sneaking out, leaving Andie to worry. It seemed like I had kept all my worst habits.

Surprisingly, Angel wasn't at the curb when I stepped out onto the street. It was still dark out, well before Kepler's simulated sky cycled into dawn. I stood beneath a streetlamp, wishing for a cigarette.

I didn't know what to expect of Angel's thief. From the dossier I knew she was still young, a year or two younger than me when I went to prison. She had a record with a couple of misdemeanors—shit you could expect from a miscreant teen. Nothing major. But according to Angel, she was the key to cracking the safe after we broke into the vault. What she could do that any of us couldn't already, I wasn't sure.

Angel's flyer descending to the curb interrupted my thoughts. She came to a stop, and I opened the passenger side door and climbed inside.

"Good morning," she greeted me.

"Does 0430 really count as morning?" I grumbled.

"There's been a change of plans," she explained.

"So you said."

Angel lifted from the curb and started down the street, flying upward through the sparse traffic toward an upper Ward. "Valdez has been made. She's being held at Solstice Corp's headquarters right now."

"Made? She was on a job?" I asked, surprised.

"I was hoping to catch her before it started. It seems the timeline was moved up."

"What now?"

"I know the chief of security at Solstice. I called in a favor, and they're detaining her without calling the police. But just for an hour, and we need to get in and out on our own."

"What's the play?"

Angel reached into her bag and withdrew a police badge on a chain. She tossed it to me. "Officer Sato."

I caught it, then turned the badge over in my hands. It still had its shine. "You kept this?"

"It's still useful, isn't it?"

I glanced over at her, but she didn't meet my gaze. I didn't think Angel was one for sentimentality. But then again, a solid alias is a solid alias, and it was always worth holding on to.

I put on the badge.

We flew the rest of the way in silence. I wasn't familiar with Solstice; it must have been a new corporation formed during the years I was in prison. Over the past few weeks at home, I'd noticed there were a lot of those. It seemed that not only was Kepler changing, but the whole scope of the galaxy was changing. Corporations were born and died, merged and consumed each other. Most apparent of all was Atlas Industries, which was already a behemoth when I was locked up. In the years since, it had swallowed whole corporations, small and large, to become a tech monopoly the likes of which the galaxy had never seen.

I was surprised by Tatiana's alas to go after Solstice. What did it mean for Angel to go up against Atlas Industries?

Angel merged into upper traffic, following a skybridge to an adjoining tower. We flew a few blocks deeper into the Ward before she parked alongside an empty curb. Angel got out of the flyer and waited for me on the sidewalk. Even at 0500 she looked as put together as ever, though today she had forgone her skirt and stilettos for chinos and heeled boots. With a leather coat and her badge, she appeared more like a detective and less like an exec. I thought she might have forgotten how to blend in, but it seemed like it was coming back to her.

"Still look like a narc," I joked.

Irritation passed over Angel's face, but she didn't deign to reply. She started down the sidewalk. "Come on. We don't have much time."

Angel led me a little farther down the block, up to the darkened face of a corporate tower. She rapped on the glass door.

It wasn't long before a weary-looking security guard in a tan uniform approached. "We're closed," he mouthed.

Angel and I held up our badges, and the security guard's eyes widened. He hastily unlocked the door and beckoned us inside. "What can I do for you, officers?"

"We're responding to a break-in," Angel answered smoothly. "I'm Detective Li." She nodded in my direction, "This is Detective Sato." She brushed past the guard into the lobby, and I followed. We swept our gaze across the building's lobby. The floors were polished gray tile, and the furniture was all abstract, organic shapes. The walls were dominated by huge windows that in the daytime would have let in Kepler's light. In the center of the room was a large water feature—a false stone pinnacle with water running down its sides. It was all pretentious as fuck.

"Right," the guard said. "We picked up one of 'em, but we think she wasn't working alone."

"I would expect not." Angel returned her gaze to the security guard. "Where is she being held?"

The guard jerked his thumb over his shoulder. "In the back."

"Would you take us to her?"

"I can, but I'm afraid we can't release her yet."

"Why not?" I asked.

"Need to question her. Can't let her leave until our head of security gets here. He's running a little late, though."

"Then we'll do some of our questioning before he gets here," Angel said. "If you could take us to her, please."

The guard nodded, then gestured for us to follow. He led us across the pretentious lobby to what appeared to be an ordinary door, which he opened with a badge pinned to his shirt. We walked down the hallways and took the second left, then the third right, then paused in front of the first door on the right, marked Security Holding. Another guard was stationed at the door, and opened the holding cell with a ring of manual keys connected to his belt by a retractable cord.

I made note of all of this, since I was sure it would become relevant shortly.

The first guard led us into the room while the second stayed at the door. The holding cell was harshly lit by fluorescent lights, though the gray walls absorbed much of it. I didn't see any cameras. A brushed metal table was set up in the center of the room, with two chairs on opposite sides. A young woman was cuffed to the table in the far chair, maybe eighteen or nineteen. Her curly brown hair was crushed under a black beanie, and she was dressed in dark jeans and a black hoodie. She had light-brown skin and big brown eyes.

"This is her," the guard said to us. "Caught with her hands in the safe."

"What was in the safe?" I asked.

"Just some documents. Not sure why she'd want 'em, but"—the guard laughed—"maybe that's why I'm not a thief."

"Mm," Angel said. "We'd still like to question her."

"Well, I'll just go check in with the boss and see when he'll get here." He turned to leave, then paused at the door. "What did you say your names were?"

"Officers Sato and Li," I answered.

"Badge numbers 4789 and 2702," Angel added.

"Right. I'll be back." Then he left us alone.

I looked at Angel. "Are those credentials still good?"

"Malia updated them yesterday," she answered. Then she turned her attention to the thief cuffed to the table. "Tatiana Valdez. I'm impressed you made it so far on your own."

"I'm not talking without my lawyer," Tatiana responded.

"Do you even have a lawyer?" I asked, incredulous.

"I'm not talking without *a* lawyer," Tatiana corrected.

"It'll be a hard defense," Angel said, moving to stand at the other end of the table. "The best you could hope for is a reduced sentence, with your hands in the safe like that."

Tatiana said nothing, staring down Angel defiantly.

"You could sell out your crew for a plea deal," Angel said, "but the most they could get is conspiracy. And I don't think that's your style."

My eyes flicked to Angel's face. She was watching Tatiana with an even expression, without a hint of guilt or shame. Either she was totally lacking self-awareness, or totally without remorse.

Fucking bitch.

"What if I could offer you another way out of this?" Angel continued. "Leave here with us, and you'll walk away from a lengthy trial and guaranteed prison time." Tatiana's defiant expression slipped, just for a moment. But it was long enough for Angel to notice. "Think of all that lost time. Time away from your friends, your family, your life. Time you can't afford to lose."

My hands curled into tight fists at my side. She was threatening Tatiana with the same thing she did to me, and it seemed like she knew full well the consequences of her actions. I realized then that part of me always believed she didn't understand what she was doing, didn't understand what the cost would be.

Turns out that part of me was wrong.

Tatiana narrowed her eyes. "What do you want from me?"

"Your expertise. You broke into this building, bypassed the security system, and cracked the safe all on your own."

I gave Angel a look. "She did get caught, though."

Angel ignored me. "I need a thief like you for the job I'm planning."

Tatiana's lip twisted into a scowl. "This is entrapment."

"We're not cops," I said.

"No, we're not," Angel agreed. "We're similarly excellent thieves."

"Probably better, since, notably, she got caught," I said.

Tatiana glared at me. "My crew chickened out, I had to do it on my own."

"So you're stubborn and stupid too," I said irritably.

Tatiana started to snap back, but Angel interrupted. She turned to me, her expression stern. "We need her, E. She's the only one who can crack the safe."

"I can crack a safe," I argued. "And I don't need mods to do it."

"You have a problem with mods?" Tatiana demanded. "I don't need them either, it just makes me better than everyone else."

"Not me," I growled.

Tatiana opened her mouth to argue, but Angel interrupted again. "Have you cracked a Liberty 1890?" she asked me.

Tatiana's eyes widened. "A Liberty 1890?"

I ignored her. "You keep forgetting I've been in prison for eight fucking years. Didn't have tons of time to practice."

"Which is why we need her." Angel gestured at Tatiana.

I met Angel's gaze. "I can do it, A."

"Are you willing to bet 125 billion credits on it?"

Angel held my gaze for a long moment. I was weighing my pride against my altruism, whatever idiotic sense of thieves self-esteem I'd developed against my dedication to the job. Deep down, I knew I could do it—even without fancy tech in my body. I could do it.

But 125 billion credits was a lot of money.

And I had a lot of debts to pay.

Finally, I sighed. "No. I'm not."

"Excuse me," Tatiana interrupted. "Did you say 125 billion credits?"

Angel turned her attention back to Tatiana. "Yes. We can offer you that, and more."

"And all I have to do is take this guy's place?" Tatiana asked, nodding at me.

"Who says you're taking my place, you little—" I began.

"Yes," Angel said, cutting me off. "That's all you have to do."

Tatiana went silent again. I wondered what she was thinking. Was it the same thing I thought when I was offered that bounty? Throwing caution to the wind for the chance of a payout big enough to be set for life?

I could only hope that this job wouldn't go the way of the first.

Finally, Tatiana looked at each of us in turn, a grin spreading across her face. "I'll do it."

Angel smiled. "Perfect."

"Great, she's in," I said sarcastically. "Now what?"

"I need you to lift a badge and the keys," Angel said to me. "And get rid of the guard."

I scowled at her. "That's your plan? Make me do all the shit?"

She met my gaze impassively. "I'm working on it."

I grunted in response. I slid my multitool out of my pocket and opened the knife.

"What're they gonna do?" Tatiana asked, alarmed. "Are they gonna stab that guy?"

"I would hope not," Angel replied.

I ignored them both. I moved to the door, watching the hallway through the small window. The guard was still stationed outside, but an employee was hurrying down the hallway, his arms laden with a tray of coffee and a box of doughnuts.

I counted down his steps, then as he was about to pass by, I threw open the door. It hit him in the face with an unpleasant *thud*, spilling coffee and sending doughnuts rolling across the floor.

"Oh, I'm sorry!" I exclaimed, stepping into the hallway. "Shit, I'm so sorry!"

The guard fell to his knees beside the dazed employee, looking between him and the pastries on the floor, back and forth, unsure of where to help. Eventually he chose the pastries. As he gathered up the doughnuts into the box, I crouched beside him. I cut through the nylon cord holding his keys to his belt, dropped them into my hand, and pocketed them.

"Oh man, you're bleeding—fuck! Here, let me help you up." I grabbed the bloody-nosed employee and hauled him to his feet. He slung his arm over my shoulder, and I wrapped my arm around his middle, supporting his weight. I unclipped the badge on his coat pocket and slid it into my sleeve.

"Hey!" I addressed the guard, who looked up at me from the mess on the floor. "You guys got a first aid kit?" The guard bobbed his head. "Can you take him to it? I have no idea where I'm going."

The guard clumsily took the employee from me and together they started hobbling down the hall. "And find your safety officer!" I called after them.

I was surprised at how good it felt, the presence of the keycard in my sleeve and the weight of the keys in my pocket. It felt good to engage in some petty crime—the thrill of almost getting caught, the comfort of the muscle memory, the satisfaction of outwitting a mark. It felt good to know I still had it. I captured a little of that thrill hustling cards in the prison yard, but this was different. Way different.

I realized that I missed it.

When the guard and the employee turned the corner, out of sight, I went back into the holding cell.

I tossed Angel the keys and held up the keycard between my fingers, my expression smug. "Guard's gone too."

Angel gave me an approving nod, which I guess was the best I could hope for.

Angel uncuffed Tatiana from the table. Tatiana stood, shaking out her hands. "Cool," she said. "Now what?" Without warning, Angel grabbed Tatiana by the arms and pulled her hands behind her back. She cuffed her wrists together. "*Hey!*"

She addressed Tatiana. "You're under arrest, make it convincing."

Angel led Tatiana out of the room, the thief sputtering in protest. I followed.

The hallway was still clear when we left the holding cell. Angel set a brisk pace, pulling Tatiana along with her. I used the keycard I lifted from the employee to open the door, then stepped into the lobby. The early risers were just beginning to filter into the building, and they watched in shock as we hauled a protesting Tatiana to the main doors. Someone was kind enough to hold it open for Angel. I lagged behind, timing it such that I bumped into another employee entering the building.

"Sorry," I said, dropping the keys and keycard into her pocket.

Angel loaded Tatiana into the back seat of her flyer, still cuffed. I climbed into the passenger seat, Angel into the pilot's seat. She started the flyer and lifted from the curb, leaving Solstice behind.

"Am I entrapped?" Tatiana asked, leaning forward between our seats.

"I said we weren't cops," I replied.

"Then who *are* you?"

"My name is Angel. This is Edie," Angel introduced us.

At Tatiana's questioning expression, I said, "It's not short for anything."

"Okay," Tatiana said slowly. "Then what's this job about?"

"Let me fill you in," Angel said.

We rounded a corner into the growing traffic, just as Kepler's sky began to cycle into dawn.

We dropped off an uncuffed Tatiana on the far side of Ward 2. Angel flew me home, pausing at the curb outside the apartment.

"With all of the crew secured, we can move forward with the plan," Angel said to me. "I'll be in touch about a meeting with all of us."

"Just tell me where to be," I replied.

"I will." She paused, looking through the passenger side window at the storefront. "Do you need an excuse for getting back so late?"

"I was thinking I'd take the long way up. I'm good."

Angel nodded. I pushed open the door and stepped onto the street, still empty at this hour. Kepler's simulated sun hadn't risen yet, and the streetlights were still on. I approached the store front, then took a left to round the corner into the narrow alley between the two towers. There was a fire escape clinging to the side of the tower that went all the way up from our street to the next Ward, but I only needed to climb up to my bedroom window.

The ladder was retracted, up out of reach. Mom always kept it that way—a feeble attempt to keep me from getting out at night. I climbed onto the dumpster that serviced the shop and nearby apartments, then jumped up to catch the bottom rung. I pulled myself up hand over hand until my feet touched the rungs. From there it was a short trip to my bedroom window on the second floor, which I jimmied open with the help of a lockpick.

I climbed through the window and closed it behind me. I toed off my shoes, then threw myself on my bed with a sigh.

Even as exhausted as I was, my thoughts kept returning to my stubbornness at Solstice, my almost-refusal to go with the plan. I used to be one of the best in the business, a triple threat of a pickpocket, runner, and safecracker. It was a stupid thing to get hung up on, I knew that, but what did it mean if I lost my reputation to Kepler System Penitentiary, along with eight years of my life? What did it mean if I was so easily replaced?

And what about Tatiana, the infant thief? I tried to think back to when I first entered this life, when I took my first step toward Kepler System Penitentiary. But there were so many steps, so many branching paths, it was hard to pin down a point of origin. Maybe it was when I stole Jake Vierra's bike, after he went to the hospital with a broken arm. Maybe it was when I walked out of a store with a toy soldier in my pocket, and didn't ask my dad to return it. Maybe it was when I noticed a cashier put a carton of eggs in my mom's shopping bag without scanning it, and didn't say anything. I thought of the look on her face when Angel threatened her, and I wondered what had driven Tatiana into this life.

I was just drifting off when there was a knock on my door.

"Edie?" Andie called. "Edie, are you awake?"

I groaned. I briefly considered ignoring her, but if Andie was waking me up, she must've needed something. ". . . Yeah, one sec."

I trudged to the bedroom door and opened it. Andie looked at me in surprise. With my tousled hair and rumpled clothes, I must've looked all hammajang.

"Jesus, Edie. You look like shit."

"Thanks, I feel like shit."

"Are you hungover?"

Great excuse. "Hellishly."

"Then go back to sleep, I'll see you later." Andie turned to leave.

"Wait," I called after her. "You need something—what is it?"

"It's no worries, Tyler can handle it."

A jolt of anger ran through me, and suddenly I was alert. Tyler in the house was the last thing we needed.

"Just tell me what it is, first," I said.

Andie paused, midway across the living room. She turned to face me, twisting her braid around her finger. "I've been trying to get in to see my obstetrician, and they finally have an appointment open I can make it to. But someone needs to watch the kids . . ."

". . . And you wanted me to watch them for you."

"But it's okay, Tyler can take them. He hasn't seen them in a while."

I frowned. "Hell no. You go to the doctor, I'll watch the kids." I passed a hand through my messy hair. "Just give me a minute to get ready."

Andie smiled. "Thanks, E. You're the best."

"And don't forget it."

She laughed. "I won't."

Andie lumbered away toward the kids' bedroom. I heard her open the door, then gently wake them. Better than Angel calling at 0430 in the morning.

I sighed and went back into my room to change.

Chapter 9

IT WAS SATURDAY, AND ANDIE HAD A RARE DAY OFF. SHE AND I WERE sitting with the kids at the kitchen table, all of us drawing on the thin reusable plastic sheets the kids used for their homework. Andie was sketching a bird with a pen. Casey was scribbling a lion with a marker. I was designing a new tattoo—one of the great manta rays I saw on Casey's nature shows. I couldn't afford it now, but I was sure I'd be able to soon.

I glanced over at Paige's drawing. "Who's that?"

"That's me," she answered without looking up.

"Why do you have wings?"

"I'm a fallen angel," she said, as if the answer was obvious.

I pointed at the figure next to her. "Who's that over there?"

Paige gave an exasperated sigh. "That's Ilethor, Knight of the Nine Kingdoms. We've been over this, Aunty."

"All haole guys look the same to me, Paige." I tilted my head to get a better view. "Are you holding hands?"

She flushed, yanking the sheet away from my reaching hand. "No."

I laughed. "Then why can't I see it?"

"Because it's none of your business!"

"I'm your elder," I said sternly. "It's my business to know your business."

"Mom!" Paige protested.

"Edie—" Andie began, but before she could chastise me, her phone began to ring. She checked the number, then stood abruptly. "It's your dad," she said to the kids. "Behave." She looked at me. "*All* of you."

Andie left for the kitchen.

"You don't want to talk to him?" I asked Paige.

"Not really," she said, going back to her drawing. "He's still mad at me for getting a C on my math test. Mom lets me read here, but Dad took all my books away." She paused. "Sorry, Aunty, he said not to talk to you about it."

"That's okay, I get it," I lied. I wasn't a snitch, but the bastard toed the line.

"What about you, Casey?" I asked.

Casey shrugged.

"I guess you wouldn't have much to say either, would you?"

He shook his head gravely.

Even before I went to prison, Tyler was a shit human. He was more invested in his powerful friends, flashy mods, and luxury clothes than he ever was in Andie or the kids. He always wanted to be one of the rich fuckers living in the Upper Wards. Anything that didn't fit that vision of himself, he discarded or destroyed. Or tried to shape in his own perfect image, just the way he did with my sister and her kids. At least the kids actually enjoyed being around me.

I was about to test that by giving Paige more grief when my comm chimed. I checked my messages. It was from Angel.

Meet me today at 1200. 201 8th St., Ward 1. 47401.

I frowned at the message. She couldn't wait for another time, when I wasn't with my family? I sighed. "I need to go in to work, kids."

Casey looked disappointed. Paige looked more than a little relieved.

I stood. "I'll tell your mom." I rounded the table and headed toward the kitchen, but not before leaning in over Paige's shoulder to steal a glance at her drawing. She hunched over the sheet protectively while her ears burned bright red.

I laughed again, then moved off.

I stepped into the galley kitchen, looking toward the far end. Andie stood with her back to me, and she was speaking in hushed tones.

"I know," she said. "I know, but the doctor said I can't work so late in the pregnancy." She paused, wiping at her eyes. "It's not permanent, just until the baby comes. I'll be back—I already told you, Atlas won't take me for any trials. No, I won't come back for—please, don't bring this up in—one second." Sensing my presence, Andie swiped at her eyes one more time and turned to me. "What is it, Edie?"

"Are you okay?" I asked, concerned.

Andie waved dismissively. "I'm fine. What do you need?"

"I just wanted to tell you I need to head out. Angel wants to go over some work stuff."

"Work stuff?" Andie rested the phone on her shoulder. "What work stuff?"

"Well, I told you about that interview," I said. "Angel thinks I have a real shot, wants to prep me for the next one."

Andie beamed. "That's amazing, E!"

It broke my heart, a little, lying to Andie like that. She looked so happy, thinking I was going straight. I think in some ways, it was what she always wanted—to live our lives free from the pressure of debt, away from the edge of losing everything. A life where she didn't have to worry about me.

But that would have to wait, at least for a little while longer.

"Go on and head out," Andie said. "I'll stay here with the kids."

"Are you sure you're okay?" I insisted.

"I'm sure. Get that job and I'll be more than okay." I heard Tyler speaking indistinctly on the line. Andie waved me out the door. "I need to finish talking to Tyler. Go on, I'll be here." She put the phone back to her ear.

I nodded, turning to leave. I gathered my things from where I'd scattered them across the living room, then said goodbye to the kids.

It reminded me of what Andie said, the night I called Angel to accept her job. She said they were barely making their minimum payments, barely staying afloat. There was the cancer fund, but that could only cover so much. Paige had her treatment now, but what would happen if the money ran out? And without Andie working, and Tyler being the controlling, manipulative, heartless dirtbag he was, the money would run out.

I squeezed my hands into fists at my side. Whatever Angel had to say, I had to hope to God it was going to be worth it. I had to hope to God that all of this would be worth it.

The lowest of the Wards, Ward 1 lived in the shadow of the others. Eighth street was a residential neighborhood, where the apartment towers loomed on either side. Even in Kepler's daylight the windows were lit from within, the vague shapes of their occupants shifting back and forth. Neon lights flickered in the darkness, and the walkways were lined with ailing plants in artificial planters. Though it was always a little dark, a little damp, a little crowded, Ward 1 was beloved same as all the other Lower Wards. At least by the locals.

The building Angel directed me to was at the bottom of a recently renovated tower. A huge banner hung down the side of the tower: "luxury condos and rentals, coming soon!"

Apprehensive, I approached the door to the building. When I peered inside, I couldn't see much beyond the sheets of plastic that partitioned the rooms. I tried the door, but it was locked. My eyes fell on a keypad and intercom beside the door. I keyed in the number Angel sent to me: 47401.

The keypad beeped and flashed green, and the door unlocked.

My footsteps echoed on the tile floor as I stepped into the building, sweeping my gaze across the room. Farther into the building I could hear women's voices. I followed the sound, brushing plastic curtains aside, and found myself in what looked like a community space: big, expansive floors, wooden coffee tables, leather chairs and sofas, and a huge screen at the far wall. Some of the chairs and sofas had been crowded around the screen, almost all of them occupied by people familiar to me.

Duke was slouching in one of the armchairs, Nakano balanced on the arm. Malia was sprawled, upside down, across an ottoman. Sara was sitting cross-legged on the couch, Cy on the opposite end. Tatiana was draped across an armchair, legs over the arm. Angel stood at the front of the room, next to the screen.

I made my way to the others. "Am I late?"

"No, you're right on time," Angel answered. She nodded at the couch. "Sit, and we'll get started."

I did as I was told, sitting between Cy and Sara.

Angel addressed us. "I suppose you're all wondering why I gathered you here today."

Here we fucking go.

"You're here because you're the best at what you do," Angel said, looking at each of us in turn. "And I need the best for the job we're about to do."

"And what's the job?" Duke asked, her expression wary.

"Atlas Industries maintains a proprietary vault that houses all their research, prototypes, and designs, the most important of which are kept within a manual safe. The technology within could change the galaxy for better or, most likely, for worse. It is top secret, well protected, and extremely valuable." Angel smiled. "We're going to steal it."

"Who's gonna fence tech like that?" Malia asked, incredulous.

"No fence. We'll destroy the electronic copies, and eventually the physical prototypes will be returned—but only after they pay a hefty ransom."

"What's the ransom?" Sara asked.

"One trillion credits," Angel answered. "If you do the math, that's 125 billion for each of you."

"*Each?*" Tatiana exclaimed, nearly toppling out of her precarious position on the chair.

Angel looked amused. "That's right."

"How the hell are we going to walk away with 125 billion credits?" Duke demanded.

"It's not going to be paid out all at once," Angel explained. "The money will be laundered and invested, to be paid out over time. And if you play your cards right, the money will only grow."

Cy nudged my shoulder. "So no spend it all in one place, dummeh."

Angel paused. "It's incredible what you can do with that kind of money," she continued. One by one, she met our eyes. "Pay off debts. Do some good. Build a reputation. Live like a queen for the rest of your days."

We all fell silent, considering Angel's words. It was a lot of money. We were all here for different reasons, but any way you looked at it, it was a lot of fucking money.

Finally, Duke spoke. "All right, I'll bite. What's the play?"

"I'm so glad you asked," Angel said with a smile. She flicked her wrist, and the screen beside her flared to life. On the screen was a picture of a man—midfifties, light skin, dark salt-and-pepper hair, and a striking face with laugh lines at his mouth and shockingly blue eyes crinkled with mirth.

I recognized him immediately.

"The mark is Joyce Atlas," Angel began, turning toward the screen. "A tech mogul and trillionaire philanthropist. He made his fortune designing communication devices but has since expanded into smart technology and human-machine interface. His greatest breakthrough was AXON and the Master Network, colloquially known as the GhostNet. His fortune has only grown since. He's the very image of a self-made man giving back to his community . . . or so the vidfeeds say." She turned to us again. "I think all of us know that he's not as he seems."

Tatiana raised a hand. Without waiting for an acknowledgment she blurted out, "Is he a vampire?" She shifted in the uncomfortable pause. "Y'know. Are the rumors true?"

Angel met her gaze, deadpan. "I'm not going to dignify that with an answer."

I wasn't sure if that was confirmation or denial.

Tatiana looked put out, but Angel moved on. She gestured and the screen changed to a grainy video of what appeared to be surveillance footage from a police raid on an apartment. Police fully kitted in exosuits and Gauss rifles were knocking down the door and fanning out into the apartment. "Atlas also heavily invested in surveillance technology," she continued. "At first, he just used the data for his own research. Then he sold it to advertisers. Then he sold it to governments and police forces across the galaxy." The screen flicked to another view of the same apartment, where the police were dragging people from their beds and hauling them out the door. "You see, every one of his devices have backdoor accessibility—and Atlas is always listening."

"Hold on," I interjected. "You're not telling me those mods have backdoor access to your thoughts, are you?"

"That's the simple way of putting it," Malia chimed in. "It's not sophisticated enough to translate individual thoughts—

just whatever the algorithm is trained on. Mostly commands, feelings, urges. But if you're constantly thinking, 'damn, wish there was a gym to put more wrinkles in my smooth brain'"—I scowled at her, and Tatiana snickered—"it'll pick up on that."

"And there are new algorithms being put in place every day," Angel said. "Algorithms that can anticipate your needs, discern your beliefs, predict your actions."

"They're using it to find dissenters," Nakano said softly, still watching the police on the screen.

"They can't use the content of your mod data to convict you," Angel said. "At least not yet."

"But what about the new tech? The stuff in R&D?" Malia asked.

Angel gestured again, and a schematic of the AXON mods filled the screen. It was shaped like a wishbone, with spindles of wires branching from the body of the mod. It made me sick to look at. "The current generation of AXON mods only has access to semantic memory—information learned over the course of one's lifetime. Episodic memory—recollections of life events—is more elusive. Every memory is encoded differently in each person, and until now it's been impossible to reverse engineer a memory from a neural pattern."

"Until now?" Tatiana repeated.

"With the newest generation of AXON mods, Atlas has done what was seemingly impossible: Using the data from the millions of people fitted with his mods, he's been able to develop an algorithm to translate the patterns into a coherent whole." Angel paused. "It's now possible to access another person's memories."

"*Ho shit!*" Malia crowed, flipping right side up. "That's fucking *mental*!" She was met with shocked silence from the group. "What?" she asked, indignant. "Atlas just invented a hacker's *dream*, cuz!" Not getting the response she had hoped for, she turned back to Angel. "What kine access these mods get?"

"Like I said, all of Atlas's technology has backdoor accessibility. With the right tools, you could access the memories of anyone with a mod."

Malia gave a sinister grin. "The GhostNet's not ready for me."

Ignoring her, Nakano spoke. "What's Atlas doing with this?"

With a sweep of her hand, Angel shifted the image to another grainy video: a first-person view of someone playing a simple matching game with a deck of cards. "Right now, the algorithm can only read the content of a person's memories. Atlas wants to change that." The person in the video flipped over a card: a single diamond. "Utilizing the inputs of the mod, it's not only possible to read the contents of a memory"—the person flipped over the same card again: this time, a single heart—"it's possible to manipulate them."

"You're not fucking telling me these mods can edit your *memories*, are you?" I asked, horrified.

"The technology is still in its early stages, but the theory is sound," Angel answered.

"And with Atlas's defense contracts—" Nakano began.

"It's possible to retrieve and edit a detainee's memories, yes."

A silence fell over the group. It wasn't just that Atlas was swindling my people in the Lower Wards to test drive his tech, he was turning that same tech against them. Watching them, trapping them, then throwing them into prisons contracted by him to make more tech. And if we got fed up and started making noise, he used that tech to destroy our minds. Chewing us up and spitting us out, over and over and over again. It made me sick with rage.

Sara was the next to speak. "So, he's a bad guy, and we're stealing from him. How?"

Angel made another gesture and a map of Kepler and its catacombs appeared on the screen. I leaned forward in my seat.

"The vault is kept in Leeway, beneath Ward 1," Angel said. The screen zoomed in on a highlighted area of Kepler, near the hull and close to the docks. "As it is now, Leeway is impassable. We need to find a way in." She nodded at me. "Edie is our runner. They'll scout out a way to gain physical access to the vault, as well as an escape route."

"And how do we get *in* the vault?" Duke asked.

"The vault is behind a three-ton steel door and sealed with a five-ton mag lock. We'll need an EMP to cut the power." The screen zoomed in further, to a schematic of the vault. "Beyond that is a security system rigged with pressure-sensitive floors, IR motion sensors, and a temperature-sensing laser grid. Atlas must cross the floor first to drop the grid. It's tuned to his body temperature, which runs lower than your average human due to his mods."

"Vampire," Tatiana muttered.

"Sara will bypass the security system and open a path," Angel finished, ignoring her.

"Oh," Sara said, her eyes wide.

"The door to the vault opens via a dual-custody keypad—I have one code, Atlas has the other. We'll also need Atlas's retinal scan and fingerprint for the biometric scanner. The other is keyed to me."

"What about the safe?" Tatiana asked, twisting to sit upright in her chair.

"It's a Liberty 1890 manual safe," Angel answered. "A Group 1 safe that's heat resistant, shock absorbent, and has a glass relocker." She paused. "Can you handle that?"

I glanced Tatiana's way. She gave me a smug look, which I met with a scowl. Then she nodded.

"It's not enough to just have physical access," Nakano said. "We need someone to keep Atlas occupied."

"That's where you two come in," Angel replied.

"How?"

"Nakano is our poisoned bait. The Financial Crimes Division of the System Security Administration has already opened an investigation into Atlas's illicit business practices. You two will assume fake identities and . . . accelerate the process."

Duke put a hand on Nakano's thigh. "If this goes south . . ." she warned.

Nakano laid her hand over Duke's. "I'll be fine," she said gently.

"Can't she just shut all the security down at once?" Duke asked, gesturing at Malia.

"No can, cuz," Malia answered. "Each element of the system is on its own discreet network—I can break into 'em, but we need to do 'em one at a time."

"Then what are you here for?" I grumbled.

Malia whipped around in her seat to give me stink eye. "You no can even *get* to the vault without me, brah! I'm peeling back the layers of this security system like one fucking onion. You like access to Leeway? You come talk to me. You like crack the codes? You talk to me. You like bypass the firewalls? Talk to *me*."

I opened my mouth to shoot back, but Angel interrupted me. "The last piece is Atlas's security forces." She made a gesture, and a collection of dossiers appeared on the screen. We all leaned forward to squint at the writing. "These are some of Atlas's most recent recruits, just to give you an idea."

Dishonorably discharged. Resigned. Charged. Acquitted.

"They sound awful," Sara said, sitting back in the sofa. "How are we going to get past them?"

"We'll have someone on the inside," Angel said.

I turned in my seat to look at Cy, who until now had said nothing. He quirked a brow at my stare. "What?"

"No offense, cuz, but you nevah seem like da grifter type."

"He doesn't need to be, he's going in as himself. Mostly."

Angel paused. "Connections to me and you scrubbed from his record, of course."

Malia flashed a shaka.

"Edie will find us a way in, and Cy will make sure the path to the vault is clear from there," Angel finished.

Another silence fell over the group, each of us considering. Angel watched us all expectantly. "What do you think?" she asked.

Sara chewed her lip. "It's a lot."

"It is," Angel agreed.

"There's a lot that can go wrong," Duke added.

"I can assure you that I've thought this through," Angel said firmly. "But I understand if I'm asking too much."

"You do?" I asked, surprised.

Angel looked annoyed. "I would never strong-arm any of you into my plan. There's no hard feelings if you decide to walk." She paused. "I only ask you don't bring this to the authorities, as that would be a hassle for everyone."

The group murmured in assent.

"So." Angel swept her dark eyes across the seven of us, meeting our gazes. "Are you in?"

Malia's hand was the first to shoot up in the air. "Hell yeah I am!"

"You know I'm in, cuz," Cy said second.

"I'm in," Tatiana said with a grin.

Sara beamed. "I'm in, and I'm excited!"

Duke and Nakano shared a look—one that only trusting partners could share. Then Nakano said, "We're in."

Angel's eyes fell on me, last. I held her gaze. For an instant, I thought about refusing. What if we failed? I was a felon on parole. If we failed, I'd be in prison for a lot longer than eight years. I thought of all the time I'd lost already, and to lose any more felt unbearable. To miss Casey growing up, to potentially lose Paige, to leave Andie alone . . . It was too much to think about.

And what if Angel let me take the fall again? I didn't forgive her, and I definitely didn't trust her to save me if things went wrong. But what other options did I have? Blacklisted and swimming in debt . . . There was nothing else I could do.

I thought of Andie wiping away her tears in our apartment's tiny kitchen and knew what I had to do.

"Yeah," I said. "I'm in."

It was Dad's birthday on Sunday.

Andie always treated it like a holiday, and this year she got me and the kids to play along. Paige helped Andie weave ribbon lei in Dad's favorite colors, and Casey picked out balloons he thought his papa would like. I had the less glamorous job of picking up Dad's bodega snacks of choice—with a pack of cigarettes snuck in for me. Andie hurried us out of the apartment. We were apparently late to whatever birthday party she planned every year. With our spoils tucked into her tote—which I took despite her objections—we all piled onto the Number 54 bus to the graveyard.

I teased Casey by pretending to lose the balloons, letting them fly out of my hand and reaching up to pull them out of the air before they hit the ceiling. Casey screwed up his face in aggravation, trying desperately not to break his vow of silence with a kindergarten curse. Paige read her book, casting judgmental glances my way over the top of the pages, and Andie dozed with her temple against the bus window.

The graveyard wasn't much of a graveyard—there wasn't much real estate for graves on a space station, nor would it have survived the gentrification of Kepler. It was more like a monument, with rows of false stone walls engraved with the names of the dead. Richard Morikawa was C-34, Margaret Morikawa was C-33.

The four of us claimed a bench opposite the wall, and Andie

began unpacking her bag. Paige carefully arranged the false flowers in Dad's vase, and I laid out the snacks on the shelf below his name. I lifted Casey to help him tie the balloons to the peg on the wall, and Andie draped the lei over all of it.

We stepped back to admire our handiwork. With all the clashing colors and shapes of Casey's balloons, Paige's flowers, and Andie's lei, the grave was festive, lively, and tacky as hell. Dad would've loved it.

Andie set the kids up on the bench with their lunches, and the two of us stood at the foot of Dad's grave.

It was hard to believe we lost him almost fifteen years ago. At turns it felt like it was in another lifetime, at others like it was just yesterday. It was hard to believe how quickly the years go by. Even harder to believe that I'd spent half of those years in prison. I wondered where I would be if Dad were still alive. Would I be working as a runner? Or would I have followed my original path and become a station mechanic like him?

Would he be proud of me, where I am now?

The question hit me like a bolt of lightning. He and I talked a lot about the future. Where I would be, what I would do, who would I be. That was how Dad was—always thinking ahead, always working for something better, always reaching for more. He said he would be proud—but he envisioned a different path for me, a different life. What would he say, if he knew who I was now?

After a while, Andie put her head on my shoulder. "Thanks, E."

I glanced her way. "For what?"

"For everything," she said. "You've been such a help at the shop, around the house, with the kids—I couldn't do this without you."

A pang of guilt went through my heart. I couldn't imagine how she'd managed all these months on her own after she and Tyler split. And I'd been absent for all of it.

"You don't need to do this alone anymore," I said. "I'm here, tita."

"I know. And I'm so happy you are."

I smiled, then pulled Andie into my arms and held her close, her hāpai belly bumping against me. I kissed the top of her head and she let out a contented hum, one that was interrupted by a sharp gasp.

"Is that Angel?" she asked.

I whipped my head around to follow her gaze. And infuriatingly enough, there was Angel. She stood at the corner of the C-row, a bouquet of expensive-looking flowers in her arms.

I felt my face flush with anger. How dare she. How dare she show her face here, after what she did to me. To Andie. To all of us.

I started to say something, but Andie spoke first. "Angel," she said, voice strained. "What are you doing here?"

Angel approached warily. "Andie," she said. "I didn't expect to see you here so late."

"It's Dad's birthday party," she replied. Her eyes fell to the bouquet. "Did you bring those for him?"

"I did. I can leave them with you, though, I don't want to intrude."

"You're not intruding," Andie said politely. I wanted to be much less polite, but I bit my tongue.

She gestured at the kids, halfway through their musubis. "Would you like to sit?"

"I'm between appointments," Angel said. "I just wanted to drop this off."

"I'll take them, then." Andie took the bouquet from her, shifting the flowers in her arms.

Angel stepped back toward the entrance to the graveyard. "I'll let you get back to your party."

"Thank you. I'm sure I'll see you around."

"Goodbye, Andie."

"Bye, Angel."

I muttered an excuse to Andie and followed Angel. I picked up my pace, then grabbed her arm. She whirled around, glaring daggers at me.

"What are you doing here?" I demanded.

"Don't touch me," she said, wrenching her arm free.

"If you needed me, you could've messaged me. You didn't need to come here."

"I'm not here for you," she replied. "I'm here for Uncle Rich."

Hearing his name in her voice made my pulse pound in my ears.

"Why?" I asked, hotly.

"Because I care about him," she said, almost defiantly. "I care about him, and Andie too."

"Do you really?"

"Of course I do."

"You have a real fucking funny way of showing it, then."

"I'm here now, aren't I?"

"You have no right to be here."

"Why not?"

"Because you're not part of this family, Angel," I snapped. "Not anymore."

Angel's eyes widened and her nostrils flared, a crack in her facade.

"You have some fucking balls," I continued, goaded on by her anger. "You have some fucking balls coming here after everything you put us through."

"I didn't do anything, Edie," she said, eyes flashing. "Everything you got, you brought upon yourself."

I wanted to scream. Was ready to scream. But I paused when Paige called my name.

"Aunty Edie!" she called. Then, in an exasperated voice only an adolescent could manage, she said, "Mom wants us to sing."

I took a deep breath. Let it out slowly. "I'll be right there," I answered.

I looked forward again, and Angel's face had settled back into her mask of frigid calm. "Are we going to have a problem, when we meet with the crew next?"

I needed to remember what I was doing this for. Paige. Casey. Andie.

My hands, tightened into fists, loosened at my side. "No."

"Good," she said, cold. "I need an exit strategy. Find me an escape route by the end of next week."

All I could manage was a nod.

Angel gave me one last look before turning on her heel and striding out of the graveyard. "Call me when it's done."

I watched her leave, disappearing around the bend. Then I dragged my hands down my face and made a low noise of frustration.

Fuck her.

I turned and walked back to my father's grave.

Chapter 10

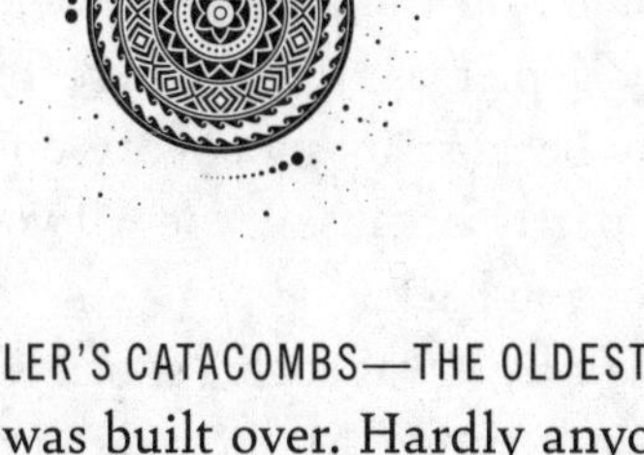

LEEWAY WAS ONE OF KEPLER'S CATACOMBS—THE OLDEST PARTS OF THE station that the city was built over. Hardly anyone accessed them other than the station mechanics, and runners like me. The mechanics ventured into the catacombs to maintain Kepler's aging systems, with hands-on knowledge that the lab coats lacked. They knew the ins and outs of all the systems, their temperaments, their idiosyncrasies. They passed down their knowledge from generation to generation, something no technical manual could replace.

Where the mechanics were elders, the runners were criminals. Their knowledge was ill-begotten, built from years of trespassing and breaking and entering. Runners knew how to navigate Kepler beneath the streets, where the cops couldn't follow. They were highly sought after for that—every crew needed a runner, at the very least to scout a path. Without one, you were doomed to get caught, lost, or worse. And God forbid you piss off your runner.

As an apprentice beneath the best mechanic of his generation, and a delinquent with a penchant for adventure, I made an excellent runner.

Which is why Angel picked me.

I climbed down a ladder into a service tunnel beneath the street, dropping to the floor and flicking on my flashlight. I took everything in. The sweep of my flashlight illuminated the branching pipes and bundled wires behind plex panels that covered the metal walls. The light was low, the air was stale, and the catacombs always ran a little hot, being so close to Kepler's systems. Far down the tunnel I heard the clanging of a system coming to life, echoing through the walls.

Some people said the catacombs were haunted, that every soul killed by Kepler was trapped here forever. I never believed them. Mostly because in my twenty-one years I'd never seen a ghost, and partly because I knew if you respected Kepler, it would respect you back.

Which was why it was such a shock when Kepler took Dad.

"*Eh, E, where you stay?*" Malia said in my ear, drawing me out of my thoughts.

"I'm in the catacombs," I responded. I shifted my bag on my shoulder and started down the service tunnel, my footsteps echoing. "Headed for Leeway."

"Rajah dat."

I followed the branching pathways, my mind coursing a path on instinct. I was surprised to see that so many of the landmarks were still there: a cracked plex window, a bundle of brightly colored wires, a dented pipe. Easy to miss, but clear as symbols on a map for any runner worth their salt. And, if you peered close enough, you could read the scribbles and sketches on the walls. Messages, directions, warnings . . . and the occasional boast about a particularly successful job. All written in code by runners that came before me. A thieves' cant that persisted across ages.

Malia interrupted my thoughts again. "*You ever wonder why it's called 'Leeway'?*"

"It's called Leeway because it houses the redundant systems

on the station," I answered. "Apprentices start their training here." I paused at a service door, pulling out my reprogrammable keycard. "More leeway to make mistakes."

"Oh, so the mechanics were punny too."

"Seemed like a requirement," I said. I held the keycard to the sensor, and Malia manipulated the electronics within, shifting the magnetic strip to match the code. The sensor beeped and the door slid open.

"With your scintillating personality, you must've gotten far."

I scoffed. "I was good enough at everything else to make up for it."

I was never one for books, and exams were always torture. But I was good with my hands, and all the other shit came naturally to me. Dad knew how to make it work. Mom thought I just needed to try harder.

Maybe if I did, things would have turned out differently.

Who knows.

I took a left at the next broken light, then a right at the following tangle of blue wires, pleased and relieved to find that I still knew the way.

"Okay, tell me with your big mechanic brain why Leeway is blocked," Malia asked.

"An airlock blew," I answered. "Took a good chunk of the catacombs with it. But like I said, Leeway is all redundant systems, and there's always other shit that needs fixing, so it was never a priority. It's been impassable for over a decade."

"Perfect place to hide a high-security vault, then."

"Exactly."

I followed the tunnel for a while longer, counting the meters to myself as I approached Leeway. The thieves' cant on the walls warned of a dead end. After a few minutes, another closed door came into view. My flashlight illuminated the reflective tape that crisscrossed the door: Danger! No Entry!

"Found it," I said to Malia. I approached cautiously. There were welding seams between the door's shutters. "It's sealed. You'd need to blow this open to get through."

"And explosives on a space station are a bad thing."

I swept my flashlight across the walls and ceiling. "This is all reinforced, probably done after Atlas moved in." I frowned at the ceiling. "It'd take us days to drill in, otherwise."

"So . . . they're a good thing?"

"If you know how to use them, where to use them. If you know how much stress the bulkhead can take." I grinned. A plan was formulating in my head. "Angel's gonna hate this."

"I wanna be there when you tell her, I like see her face."

"Yeah, yeah." I turned away from the door and started back toward where I entered. "I'll be back in half an hour, make sure you're there."

"*Shoots.*" There was a brief silence on the comm. I thought she'd left, but after a few seconds Malia's voice came back in my ear. "*Eh, E?*"

"What?"

"If you were such a good mechanic, why'd you become a runner?"

I stopped in the service tunnel. "Why do you want to know?"

"*I became the Obake 'cuz I'm nīele, E.*" She paused. "*Also, it wasn't in your file.*"

I sighed, running a hand through my hair. How could I explain? How could I explain the betrayal I felt when Kepler took my father? How could I explain the hate I felt, the day it turned on us? How could I make her understand that I couldn't bear to care for it, heal it, after what it did to me?

I knew I couldn't explain it. But I couldn't dodge the question forever, so at least I could put it off.

"Running pays better," I said. A simplified version of the truth.

"Das it?"

"Das it."

"*Hm.*" Malia didn't sound convinced. I didn't care. If she was so nīele, she could poke around in my file some more, maybe she'd glean something there.

I started toward the entrance again. "Tell Angel I'll be back soon."

The crew were all at the hideout when I arrived half an hour later. Tatiana was tinkering with an autodialer, music blaring through her earbuds. Sara was attempting to engage Cy in conversation, chattering excitedly. Duke and Nakano were milling around near the screen, looking expectant. Malia was draped over an armchair nearby, populating code on her laptop. I didn't see Angel.

I hadn't spoken to Angel at all in the days following our fight at the graveyard. I didn't reach out to her, and she didn't reach out to me. Whatever plans she had in motion, I had no clue what they were. I figured she would tell me anything relevant. Otherwise, we kept our distance, which suited me just fine.

"Howzit," I said to the room.

"Howzit," Malia, Duke, and Cy answered.

The others answered in a chorus of "hey" and "hello." I sat down on the arm of the couch. "Where's Angel?"

"Caught up at work," Malia answered. "Some security catastrophe."

"Oh good," I said. "Glad to hear that's going well."

"Maybe it's good news for us," Nakano said. "Maybe it's a new security exploit."

"Not really," Malia answered. "System Security got a warrant for the payouts from AXON's clinical trials, and Atlas is pissed about it."

"Why would they want that?"

Malia shrugged. "He probably wen cockroach some fo' himself. You know how it is."

"You think we have anything to worry about?" Duke asked.

Begrudgingly, I had to admit that Angel was a good improviser. If there was some fuckup along the way, she'd figure it out.

"No," I answered. "I think Angel will handle it."

"I appreciate the vote of confidence."

We all turned toward the entrance where Angel was striding into the room, looking composed as ever. She gave us a nod. "Thank you for coming. I'm sorry I'm late."

"No worries, brah," Malia said.

Angel moved to stand beside the screen, looking at each of us expectantly. I nodded at Duke and Nakano. "You go first."

"Good," Angel replied. She addressed the grifters: "As you know, your role in the plan is to bait Atlas into revealing his fraudulent business practices. I'm going to brief you on the con."

She gestured toward the screen, and two dossiers appeared. "Duke, you're Kalei Harden, CEO of Clairvoyant, a growing tech start-up just about to break into the galactic scene. Your company is developing new applications of the AXON mods, focusing on health and wellness. You were born on Elysium and graduated with degrees in psychology and business administration from Reine College. Malia has drafted a few articles about your progress, she just needs sound bites from you.

"Nakano, you're Ella Abe, Duke's partner and head of R&D. You're currently developing algorithms for therapeutic memory retrieval, to be used in Duke's apps. You were born on Caelestis and graduated with a dual degree in computer science and cognitive neuroscience from Caelestis University and a PhD in applied neuroscience from Etria University. Malia has created some awards and honors in your name, as well as constructed profiles for use on the universities' websites."

"What's the play?" Duke asked, leaning against the arm of the sofa.

"Atlas will try and buy out your start-up for the proprietary algorithms. You'll refuse. But I know Atlas, and he would never back down from a challenge to his power."

"That's it?"

"Not at all. Atlas is currently in the midst of a class-action lawsuit alleging that his mods caused irreparable harm and emotional distress, largely due to negligent testing and sloppy construction. He's looking for a way out—specifically an acquisition that he can transfer the blame to. Clairvoyant will appeal as an acquisition not only for its algorithms, but as a scapegoat for the lawsuit."

"How do we do that?" Nakano asked.

She shifted her attention to Nakano. "As I said, you're Duke's business partner. Atlas will notice you're unhappy with the current situation at Clairvoyant and try to convince you to sell behind Duke's back. With the time pressure, he'll use shareholder funds to buy the start-up without their approval. After the deal, it's only a matter of time before both the shareholders and System Security learn what he's done. His career will be destroyed . . . and we'll walk away with a few more credits for our efforts."

"That seems like a lot of trouble for a distraction," I said, surprised.

Angel's dark gaze flicked to me, and the blue ring of her mod looked colder than ever. "Are you questioning my plan?"

"The plan is solid," I admitted. "I'm questioning whether it's necessary."

"Believe me, it's necessary," Angel replied. "Men like Atlas are like weeds—you have to pull them by the root to keep them from returning, over and over and over again."

"How is that our problem?"

"Do you want to get away from this clean?"

"Yeah, but—"

"—Then listen to what I have to say," she said, icy. "I've

planned for this for a long time, Edie. And I won't let your doubts stand in my way."

Her adamancy surprised me. Angel was always careful, logical, measured. On the job, she acted with surgical precision—never doing more than what the situation needed. The fact that she was going so hard on Atlas—it made me wonder what warranted the scorched-earth response. Especially if it meant burning a bridge to a legitimate life, one that she built over the past eight years.

"What's our in?" Nakano asked.

"The Beyond Humanism Conference is being held at the Yamato Hotel, in Ward 7," Angel said. "Atlas will be giving a talk there about his research into episodic memory reconstruction. You'll approach him after the talk, to network. Pique his interest with your research, and he'll invite you to a private conversation. That's where you'll be able to hook him."

"And what will you be doing during all this?" Duke asked.

"I'll be at the conference as well," Angel replied. "I'll test your cover, make Atlas feel more secure in trusting you. I'll also be nearby to run interference, should you need it."

"What if our cover's blown?" Nakano asked.

"I and a few others will be on-site if you need extraction. Mention your daughter's dance class, and we'll pull you out." She paused. "Can you handle that?"

Nakano took Duke's hand. "Yes, we can."

"Good." Angel nodded. "I'll let you get your cover together."

The grifters drifted away, talking quietly among themselves as they settled on the sofa. Angel turned her attention to me. "What is it, Edie?"

"I found you an escape route," I said, hopping off the arm of the couch, "but I don't think you'll like it."

Angel didn't react. "Just tell me what it is."

"Getting in is pretty straightforward," I said. I gestured, and an image of the Atlas Industries tower appeared in the air. "There are service tunnels between the vault and the catacombs that are normally inaccessible through either side." I highlighted a series of tunnels that branched out beneath the vault. I zoomed in on one that intersected a long vertical shaft. "This tunnel connects to the lift in Atlas's tower. If we can access the lift, we can get to the service tunnels through the shaft."

"I can get you access, that's easy enough." Angel replied.

"The real trouble is getting out," I continued. I scrolled across the service tunnels to the catacombs beneath the vault. "Leeway is still blocked. The doors are sealed, and parts of the catacombs are fully depressurized. It's a nightmare to navigate."

"Okay," Angel said slowly.

"Even getting in is difficult. The walls and ceilings around the vault are reinforced, so drilling isn't an option. If we want to get out through the catacombs, we need to get through the floor with other means." I paused, waiting for her to fill in the blanks.

"You want to blow a hole in the floor to a depressurized passage," she said flatly.

A few heads turned at that.

"I want to blow a hole in the floor to one of the few pressurized passages left," I corrected. "*Then* I want to go through *this* depressurized passage," I pointed at another one in the image, "out and into the catacombs."

Angel stared at me with a neutral expression. "You're insane."

Malia snickered behind her laptop.

"Malia checked their status, and while the passage is compromised, it's not completely without atmosphere," I said. "Life support is down, but if we're quick we can get in through the floor and out through the last functioning airlock. We can seal everything else behind us, then any buggahs following will have to go up and around. And by then we'll be long gone."

"No," Angel said. "Find me another route."

"There is no other route," I said irritably. "Not unless you want to double back the way we came and do the security shit all over again, but backwards."

Angel went silent, considering. Duke and Nakano exchanged a glance. Tatiana tried and failed to look engrossed in her autodialer, while Malia watched with naked interest. Even Sara and Cy were listening.

It was a stupid plan. But Angel knew that all my plans were at least a little stupid.

"What will you need?" she asked, finally.

"Thirty feet of thermite wire," I answered, and grinned. "And any luck you can spare."

The Yamato was the swankiest spot on the station. It took up the entirety of a Ward 7 tower, where the elite of the elite vacationed in their pricey hotel suites or lived in their freshly renovated condos. From its penthouse it had an unobstructed view of Seven Common, and you could see all the way down to the very lowest Wards. It was a mile above the Ward I grew up in, almost literally.

I never spent much time in the Yamato. Except for a daylong job I pulled with Angel and Cy nine years ago, where our crew boosted a dozen valeted flyers and fenced them to an off-station dealer.

That was fun.

The Beyond Humanism Conference was being held in the Yamato's ballrooms. They were all clean floral carpets, white paneled walls, and tall windows that showed off the hotel's spectacular view. Over a hundred well-dressed people milled around in the foyer, sipping coffee and nibbling at baked goods. I stood apart from the group, leaning with a shoulder against the wall near an open window. Duke and Nakano were in the thick of it, chatting animatedly with the other attendees. If I didn't know any better, I would have thought they were busting their asses networking.

"*Keep it up,*" Malia said over the comm. "*Getting choke hits on your web pages from people looking you up. Makes you look more legit.*"

I bit into the bright green apple I'd swiped from the buffet table, the juices tart on my tongue. We never had the credits for anything other than rehydrated fruit, so I enjoyed it while I could.

"*Are you eating on the job?*" Malia asked, annoyed.

"It's free fruit," I said from around a mouthful of apple.

"*I can hear you chewing, it's gross.*"

"Mute me, then."

"*You no can—*"

"I've got a visual," I interrupted. I stood up straighter, peering over the heads of the crowd and across the room. An entourage of people walked in with purpose. Half of them were poorly disguised bodyguards, half were giddy-looking lab coats, and two were impeccably dressed execs. One of them with a kindly face and graying hair, the other with a neutral expression and an immaculate blond bob. "Atlas is here."

The entourage moved swiftly into the main ballroom. Over the comm I could hear Angel bossing the bodyguards around, arranging them in the space. I made note of their positions: two behind the stage, one at each exit. After a few minutes, the doors to the ballroom opened and the attendees began to filter in. I lingered at the back, shuffling in behind the group.

"*Keep your eyes on Duke and Nakano,*" Angel said quietly into my ear.

I did as I was told, taking a seat a few rows behind them. They were still chatting with some other attendees that they'd drawn into their orbit, but the room hushed when a woman strode onto the stage.

"Esteemed guests," the woman said, her voice amplified. "It is my pleasure to welcome you to the twenty-fifth annual Beyond Humanism Conference." The crowd applauded. She smiled. "Thank you, thank you so much. Beyond Humanism began as a small gathering of like-minded scientists, and over this past quarter century has grown to include some of the most brilliant minds in contemporary human history. And what better way to celebrate this momentous occasion than by opening our conference with perhaps the greatest pioneer of transhumanism in history. Creator of the Universal Communication Device, inventor of AXON Human Modification, founder and CEO of Atlas Industries, as well as a compassionate soul who has donated billions of his own credits to the advancement of human culture. Please join me in welcoming: Joyce Atlas."

The room broke into applause as Atlas stepped onto the stage, smiling and waving. His image was projected on a larger screen behind him for a better view. I noticed in the video that his eyes were an inhuman blue. A blinking pyramidical mod stood out from his graying hair at the temples, and his skin was traced with seams from artificial grafts. But despite his tailored suit and expensive mods, he gave off an air of humility and familiarity. Like everyone here was his equal. It was enough to inspire hordes of people to trail him everywhere he went, and defend him against every atrocity he committed.

I knew it was all a grift. The damage Atlas Industries was causing to the people of the Lower Wards spoke to that. It was clear to me who they considered human and who they didn't. And I had no doubts that most of the well-dressed people here were in on Atlas's con, the hypocritical fuckers.

I suppressed a grimace and clapped along.

Atlas stood at the center of the stage, waiting until the applause died down.

"Thank you, thank you so much for having me. It is my honor and privilege to be speaking with you all today." Atlas cast his gaze around the room, smiling warmly. "I'm delighted to share with you the newest research from our labs at Atlas Industries, where we've been hard at work iterating and improving upon the AXON mods.

"I have always been fascinated with the human mind, particularly the narratives we tell ourselves in moments of reflection, and those moments we cherish within our memories. It is one of nature's last great frontiers: Humanity has conquered space, now it's time to witness our own minds." The crowd applauded again. Atlas waited for the noise to die down, grinning. "Thank you. But humble as I am, I cannot take credit for all our advancement." Malia scoffed in my ear. "I cannot undersell the hard work and long hours our scientists have put into this new technology. They share my vision of the future, and I hope that after these forty minutes, you will share the same enthusiasm as I do."

The crowd applauded again.

"*Forty minutes?*" I hissed into my comm.

"*And sit still through it*," Angel replied.

That was impossible.

"I'm gonna fucking kill you," I growled. Malia snickered on the comm. Angel didn't deign to reply.

The lights dimmed. Atlas gestured with his right hand, and the seams across his hands and face lit up electric blue. The crowd gasped and murmured at the showmanship.

He gestured again, and the screen shifted as he began his presentation.

* * *

The presentation was agony. I managed to make it through by picking at the band of my comm, trying to be as unobtrusive as possible. I was one of the first to leap out of my chair during the standing ovation, if only to stretch my legs.

"Now I would be happy to take any questions," Atlas said to the audience.

I saw Nakano's hand go up, subtly moving her wrist so the gold band of her comm caught the light.

Atlas noticed. "Yes, you in the middle row."

Nakano stood. "Thank you for sharing your research with us, Mr. Atlas. It's an honor to hear you speak," she said in a timid, breathy voice. She smoothed her blouse. "My question is about the potential for memory rescripting through the new AXON mods." A murmur went through the crowd. Nakano stood a little straighter, then continued. "What are AXON's capabilities for memory implantation?"

"Excellent question," Atlas replied. "As of right now, AXON is in the early stages of development for memory reconstruction. It's a little too early to be thinking about memory creation."

"But the mods already use a form of memory creation," Nakano responded, "just in the form of semantic memory. Is it possible to utilize the same capabilities to create episodic memory?"

"Hypothetically, yes. You could use the same stimulating technology to generate memories similarly to semantic memory implantation."

"It's just a matter of refining the algorithms to distinguish one memory from another?"

"Yes, exactly."

"Which could be used later for rescripting, say, a traumatic memory to a more bearable one."

Atlas chuckled. "You're looking very far ahead into the future."

Nakano smiled, a little demure. "I'm a very future-minded person."

"What did you say your name was?"

"I didn't," Nakano answered. "I'm Dr. Ella Abe."

"Dr. Abe," Atlas repeated. "If you could stay behind after the Q&A, I would be very interested to pick your brain a little more, so to speak." The crowd chuckled. Nakano sat down and Atlas turned his attention back to the audience. "Next question?"

"*Nice work,*" Angel said into her comm. "*Atlas will meet you after the presentation. Sit tight.*"

I was no lab coat, and I had no clue what Nakano and Atlas were talking about. But I could read people, and I saw the way Atlas lit up talking to Nakano. The Q&A went on for another fifteen minutes. Atlas seemed interested and amenable, but not in the same way. If he wasn't on the hook now, he would be soon.

After another round of applause, the crowd filtered out into the foyer. Duke, Nakano, and a few stragglers stayed behind in hopes of an audience with Atlas. I kept to myself at the back of the room, watching and listening to the conversation over my comm.

"*Dr. Abe,*" Atlas said, extending a hand to shake. "*It's a pleasure to meet you. I truly appreciated your questions. It's not often I meet someone as forward thinking as you.*"

"*The pleasure is mine, Mr. Atlas,*" Nakano responded, taking his hand. Duke cleared her throat from behind her. Nakano gestured toward her. "*This is my colleague, Kalei Harden.*"

"*I'm Ella's business partner,*" Duke said with a laugh. She shook Atlas's hand. "*It's great to meet you.*"

"*So, tell me a little about yourselves,*" Atlas said, standing with his hands in his pockets. "*How did you find yourself in this field?*"

"*I founded Clairvoyant two years ago,*" Duke said, before Nakano could speak. "*Been interested in this field since AXON hit the market, to be honest. Saw the potential for a new brand of therapeutic interventions and had to get involved.*" She laughed again. "*Now here I am!*"

"*Wow, what an asshole,*" Malia muttered over the comm.

Had to agree with her there.

"*And you, Dr. Abe?*" Atlas asked.

"*I've always been interested in this problem space,*" Nakano explained. "*My thesis was on memory formation.*"

"*You said something about traumatic memories, didn't you?*"

Nakano opened her mouth to answer, but Duke cut her off. Nakano's mouth snapped closed. "*That's right. We're developing an intervention to rescript traumatic memories. Get in there and change the associations, you know? We used to do it with talk therapy, but with your mods you could zap them right in.*"

"*Preliminary trials are very promising,*" Nakano added.

I was halfway convinced Duke and Nakano had degrees themselves—downloaded them off the Net overnight, maybe. I had to admit, these grifters knew what they were doing.

"*I see,*" Atlas said. "*You're working on these algorithms now?*"

"*Yup!*" Duke answered. "*So far, we're able to find the memories, and we're working on distinguishing them. After that, it's all about creating new associations that are more adaptive.*" She grinned. "*Which is why your tech is so important.*"

"*Fascinating,*" Atlas said. "*I would love to hear more. Are you in town for much longer?*"

"*For two weeks,*" Nakano said. "*I'm visiting family on the station.*"

"*Then can I interest you in dinner, this weekend?*"

"*I would need a day or two to run a background check,*" Angel said, emerging from backstage.

Atlas frowned. "*I hardly think that's necessary. It's just a simple dinner.*"

"*This is highly sensitive information you're discussing,*" she said. "*It doesn't hurt to be cautious.*"

"*I think there's such a thing as over-cautiousness, Angel.*"

"*I must remind you of ongoing*"—Angel gave Duke and Nakano a sidelong glance—"*complications, Mr. Atlas.*"

Atlas looked annoyed. "*Fine. Run a background check if you must.*" Then he smiled. "*In fact, if you're so concerned about security, perhaps you could secure us a place for dinner.*"

"*That's not really in my purview,*" she replied, flatly.

"*Of course it is. You took up the mantle of my second in command, did you not?*"

Angel went silent. To her credit, she remained impassive. "*Very well, sir. I'll find you a suitable place.*"

"*Excellent.*" Atlas gestured toward the door. "*Wait for me outside, I'll be just a moment.*"

"*Of course, sir.*" Angel gave Duke and Nakano an appraising look. Then, cold as ever, she strode out of the room.

"*Please excuse my chief of security,*" Atlas said. "*She's always been a little humorless.*" He paused, then smiled. "*Though one of these days, I'd love to find a crack in that ice.*"

Duke laughed, Nakano smiled, and weirdly enough, I felt a twinge of irritation.

"*Here's my direct line.*" Atlas flexed his hand, linking the mod to the comm on his wrist. After a few keystrokes, Duke and Nakano's comms chimed in answer. "*I'll reach out to schedule a time to meet.*"

Duke smiled. "*I look forward to it.*"

Duke, Nakano, and Atlas exchanged final handshakes. Then the bodyguards ushered Atlas out of the room, leaving me and the stragglers behind.

"*Nice one,*" Malia said over the line. "*With Atlas's direct line I can spoof his number, potentially access his messages.*" She gave a mischievous laugh. "*You like start a scandal?*"

I shook my head but didn't reply. I knew by now that whatever Malia set her mind to, she'd do it anyway.

"*We're headed out,*" Duke said. "*We'll meet you at the rendezvous point, E.*"

"Shoots," I replied.

I stood and walked back into the foyer, where the hotel staff was clearing the breakfast table. I plucked two apples and an orange from the fruit platter and pocketed them. Andie would lose her mind for the real kine.

I watched Duke and Nakano say goodbye to the little entourage they'd formed at the convention. They were far down the foyer, approaching the lobby, when Nakano made the smallest movement to touch Duke's hand.

Even professionals had their soft spots.

I made my way through the Yamato's ballrooms toward the lobby, where the chandeliers caught Kepler's sunlight and cast it across the tiled floors. I crossed the lobby and out to the valet. A woman wearing a fine dress tailored in all the right places brushed past me to where a slick flyer was idling. The valet passed her the key fob and she climbed inside, shutting the door with a snap.

It reminded me of the day I spent here nine years ago, with Angel and Cy. That woman would have been a prime mark. I remembered back then, the lifts were easy—when you're that rich, everyone beneath you is basically invisible. I remembered that Cy had a black eye and had to sit with the crew in case things went sideways. I remembered that Angel wore a red dress—her favorite color.

It made me wonder what it would be like to live in the luxury of the Yamato Hotel, pilot a fast flyer, eat expensive food whenever I wanted. I felt a flash of envy. It could've been me, if only I'd been lucky enough to be born a mile up. It could've been me, if only I'd made that last big score. There were so many "could'ves" and "what-ifs" it could drive a person crazy.

Angel and I used to daydream about what we'd do if we ever scored big, made it to the Upper Wards. All she wanted was to be known. Me? I wanted everything.

But deep down I always knew I would never be one of them. Not with the money we were making.

Maybe with 125 billion credits, I could be.

Chapter 11

ANDIE AND I WERE CLEARING LUNCH DISHES ON SUNDAY WHEN SHE SAID to me, "I was thinking about picking up an extra shift at the market tonight. Do you think you could watch the kids?"

I frowned at her over the stack of plates in my hands. "You worked this morning."

"Sure, but I feel fine enough to go in again."

I placed the stack in the sink and pushed up my sleeves. "Didn't the obstetrician say to stay off your feet?"

"I really can't afford to stop, though." She reached for a plate in the sink and ran it under the tap. "It's just one more shift, E. I applied for more support from the cancer fund, but we need any extra income we can get."

Extra income. I was reminded of the discretionary funds Angel deposited into my account, for any expenses relating to the job.

"What if I had some extra income?" I asked.

Andie turned off the tap and looked at me, surprised. "Did you get the job?"

I put on a sheepish grin. "I wanted to surprise you with a paycheck, but if it keeps you from going in today, I'll tell you now."

Andie's face lit up with a grin, and she pulled me into a soapy embrace. "Edie! That's amazing, I'm so proud of you!"

I hugged her back, swallowing down my guilt. "Thanks, tita."

It hurt to lie to her. I tried to tell myself that this wasn't any different from all the other lies I told, growing up. But back then, Andie had no illusions that I was going straight—now she did. And it seemed like she really believed it. Really wanted to believe it, anyway.

"Will you stay home now?" I asked. "Rest up, spend time with the kids?"

She stepped back from me, her face still glowing with a smile. "Only if you're okay with it."

"Of course I'm okay with it. You're due soon, I don't want you having your baby on the grocery store floor."

She laughed. "All right, all right. At least let me watch the kids while you're at work."

I narrowed my eyes at her. "I'll allow it."

Andie pulled me into another hug, resting her cheek against my shoulder. "You're the best, E."

I held her close, swallowing another wave of guilt. It would all be worth it. The lies, the sneaking around, the crime—it would all be worth it in the end. With 125 billion credits, Andie would never have to work again. I would never have to lie again. We would never want for anything again. We could have everything.

I just hoped Andie would forgive me for it, when it was all over.

I didn't know what I'd do if she didn't.

"Now that the grift is underway, the next part of the plan is gaining access," Angel said.

We were all gathered around Angel in the hideout, sprawled across the couches and chairs. Duke was sitting on a love seat, her arm around Nakano. Sara sat on the edge of an armchair, looking attentive. Cy sat beside me on the couch. Tatiana was sitting cross-legged on an ottoman, making a coin walk across her fingertips. Malia had even closed her laptop. Angel stood at the front of the room, her screen projecting a schematic of Atlas Industries' tower.

"First is accessing Atlas Industries' internal systems," Angel continued. "Everything is on a discrete network, and I can't access all of it with my credentials. I can grant Malia access to our internal security. Then it's a matter of getting into the financial records, R&D systems, and Atlas's personal files.

"Physical access is more difficult." The image zoomed in to the path I identified. "Edie found us a way in, through the lift in the tower. We can get to the vault through the service tunnels between floors. Cy will be waiting for us on the other side, after clearing a path to the vault from within. From there, you'll disable the mag lock on the vault door through a planted EMP."

Sara raised her hand.

"Yes, Sara?"

"How do we get to the service tunnels?" she asked.

"I've identified three marks whose credentials you can steal," Angel answered. She gestured and three dossiers appeared: a shy-looking blond woman in glasses and a lab coat, a young man with impeccably styled brown hair in a suit, and an older man with gray hair dressed in a custodian's uniform. "A developer, defense contractor, and custodian, respectively. We'll clone their keycards and steal their PINs to get past security."

"What happens to them after we get their keycards? Will they get in trouble?"

Angel remained impassive. "Does it matter?"

Sara looked taken aback. "I—I don't know. I just thought—"

"Don't." Angel cut her off. "Don't think about them. They're inconsequential. Insignificant. And if you're having doubts about the minor details of the plan, you'll need to seriously reconsider your place on this team. Do you understand?"

Sara's mouth snapped shut. She nodded.

"Good." Angel swept her cold gaze across us. "And any of you? Any other doubts?"

We traded glances. Slowly, we shook our heads.

In any job, there was always collateral damage. It was the nature of the work. But Angel and I had always made a point of reducing the damage as much as possible. Or at least containing it within the mark and their circle. Three people in Atlas's periphery wasn't enough to stop me, but I didn't take any pleasure in burning them either.

Angel, though.

"Any other questions?" Angel asked.

"What about the mag lock?" I asked. "How do we get the EMP in place?"

"Same way as the day of the job. We'll spoof credentials and smuggle the EMP inside the service tunnels. After that—"

"That won't work," I interrupted.

Ordinarily I would've kept my mouth shut—not my crew, not my plan—but I knew running, and I couldn't let the manini details of Angel's plan ruin us.

"You send us through the service passages early and we'll be made," I continued, "if not then, the next time we're in the building. They'll close it all up and we'll be shit out of luck."

Angel's jaw tensed. "Then what do you suggest?"

"There's a conduit, a small one, that discharges ambient electricity built up on Kepler's hull. It runs through Leeway, just under the vault. We can access the mag lock and plant the EMP through there."

"Why didn't you tell me about this sooner?"

"Because it's not practical," I said, annoyed. "The discharges are a high enough voltage to kill you three times over, and they pulse every twenty minutes. That, and the chamber's only big enough for one person to move through at a time, and getting there is a nightmare."

"Sounds fun," Tatiana said dryly.

"Then why bother with it?" Angel asked, matching my annoyance.

"Because it might be our only shot at taking out the mag lock. At least without blowing the whole operation."

"It's an unnecessary risk."

"Are you really going to give up a trillion credits to break into the same vault twice?" I challenged.

Angel went quiet for a moment, considering. I wasn't much for planning, but I knew running. You never took the same route twice as a runner—selling the same route to multiple crews was a recipe for getting caught or killed, either by the cops or your own crew. And with a job as high stakes as this one, there was no way going over the same route wouldn't end in disaster.

"I'll think about it," she said, finally.

I knew that meant I won, but I tried not to look too smug.

Angel's face settled back into her characteristic icy calm. She gave each of us a cool look. "That's all I have for you. Malia, stay here to work on accessing Atlas's files. Cy, be back tomorrow for Duke and Nakano to brief you on your cover. Duke and Nakano, check in with me before your dinner with Atlas. Everyone else, stay available. I'll meet with you individually in one week for the next phase of the plan."

Angel wanted to keep me around over the next few days. Something about being ready to run interference if I was needed—some flimsy excuse li'dat.

I set up a home base in an unfinished storefront on the first floor. The floors were still concrete, and the walls were open and hung with plastic sheets. But the scaffolding was still up, and something to climb was all I really needed. Just like when I was a kid.

I threw my backpack, jacket, and shirt in a pile on the ground while I worked out. Midway through a set of pull-ups, I heard the click of high heels on the concrete floor. I glanced behind me and saw Angel standing in the doorway, hip cocked and arms crossed.

"What do you want, Angel?" I asked.

"I want to talk about us," she answered.

Well, that was an opener.

I resumed my pull-ups, affecting nonchalance. "What's there to talk about?"

"Our demeanor," she said. "How we talk to each other."

"What about it?"

"We need to keep it professional. Especially in front of the crew."

"Why is that?" I grunted.

I could sense Angel's annoyance through the glare I felt on my back. "They're starting to see you as some kind of second in command," she explained. "They look to you to for leadership, follow your example, especially when I'm not around."

I hadn't really thought about that. I was never in any kind of leadership role in my past crews, I was mostly along for the ride. It felt a little weird to be seen as a mastermind in any kind of capacity.

"That's why we need to put up a united front," she continued. "When you dissent, it makes us seem of two minds. Ultimately it puts the crew in a position where they have to choose between us. That's bad for cohesion."

I finished my last pull-up and dropped to the floor lightly. I crossed the room to my pile of stuff, picking up a towel to wipe the sweat from my brow. "You want me to stop voicing my opinions."

"I want you to stop arguing with me," she corrected. "There's a difference between voicing an opinion and being petulant."

I scowled at her. "I'm not petulant."

"Are you really?"

I dropped the towel back into the pile and picked up my shirt. I turned to look at her. "Maybe if you listened to me, I wouldn't have to drive my point home so hard."

I felt Angel's gaze on me, taking me in. Appraising me like something valuable she'd stolen. I briefly wondered how much I'd changed, in her eyes. Even more briefly I wondered if she liked the changes, but that thought I violently shoved into the back of my mind.

Angel met my eyes again. "Okay. I'm listening."

"Send me in alone," I said. I pulled my shirt on. "I move faster on my own. If I'm not managing two other people I can get in and out of the passage in fifteen minutes, before a discharge. Worst-case scenario, I'm made and I can't access the vault on my own. It's better than all three of us getting our covers blown."

"The worst-case scenario is you're electrocuted in the chamber," Angel said flatly.

"And that would be so inconvenient for you."

Angel didn't say anything, just held my gaze.

"You know I can do it, A," I said. "And you know that I'm right."

Angel searched my face for any sign of hesitation or trepidation. She wouldn't find any. When I set my mind to something, there was nothing that could dissuade me. She knew that well enough.

"Fine," she said. "But keep in constant contact with Malia. She'll assist you in the chamber."

I gave her a mock salute. She turned on her heel and walked away. I went back to my things. Her footsteps paused at the door.

"Edie," she said.

I lifted my gaze. She had her hand on the door frame, and she was looking at me over her shoulder. Her expression was unreadable. "Be careful."

"I will," I said, a little surprised.

"Because I'd hate to replace you," she finished. "I never like to settle." Then she walked out the door, leaving me more than a little bewildered.

Getting to the conduit in Leeway was a twenty-minute walk down the main passageway, a ten-minute crawl through labyrinthine vents and ducts, and a three-minute climb straight up the conduit itself to the inner workings of Leeway and the underside of Atlas's vault. I could only assume the way wasn't blocked because nobody in their right mind would climb through an active conduit. It was insanity.

I wasn't sure what that said about me.

I entered the catacombs through an access hatch in Ward 1, not far from the hideout. I followed the winding passageway, sweeping my flashlight across the walls. The machinery became more dilapidated as I moved toward Leeway, the sounds of banging machinery, dripping water, and my own echoing footsteps. At the intersection of two passages, where the branching wires formed a Celtic knot, I unslung my bag and pulled out my toolkit.

I unscrewed a panel directly below me, swinging it upward on its hinges, and lowered myself into the duct below, letting the panel swing back into place behind me. I started toward the exterior of Kepler's hull on hands and knees.

Down here the noise was even louder, filled with the buzzing of wires and stuttering of machinery. I could barely hear Malia ask me, "*Eh, E, where you stay?*"

"Halfway to the conduit," I replied, pushing through a tangle of wires. "Little busy."

"*Angel told me to stay on the line with you,*" Malia said. "*In case you, y'know, die.*"

I scowled. "I'm not gonna die. I'll be in and out well before a discharge."

"*If you say so.*"

"And what can you even do from the hideout?"

"*I'm the one with the access codes, brah. I hold your life in my hands.*" I could almost see her kolohe grin. "*So try be nice.*"

I shook my head and continued on.

It was another five minutes through the ducts. I took a right at the next cracked plex panel, and at the next junction I consulted the map of the catacombs on my comm. Eventually I came up against a grate leading to another, larger passageway. I undid the screws, popped it open, and straightened to my full height.

I swept my flashlight across the walls and floor. The lights were low, with some of them burned out entirely. Most of the walls were filled with monitors and machinery, all of it well insulated from the electricity that discharged just beyond the far doors. The air was buzzing. I could feel the hair on my arms and nape rise, and when I pulled myself out of the duct I was shocked by static.

Cautiously, I approached the far door. A monitor mounted on the wall beside it showed a red light indicating the building voltage in the chamber, and a timer. I stepped back from the door as the timer turned over to seventeen minutes.

"I'm at the conduit," I said into my comm. "There's a discharge in three minutes. I'll enter the chamber once it's clear."

"Rajah dat. The access codes rotate every thirty minutes, but you should be back before then."

"What happens if the access code rotates?" I asked, knowing I didn't want to hear the answer.

"You'll be stuck, brah. But I get 'em now, and you'll be back no problem. Garans."

I sure hoped so.

The timer turned over to twenty minutes, and the chamber discharged. The resounding crack of electricity filled the air, even through the door.

I took a deep, steadying breath as I fixed my eyes on the door. My heart was racing in my chest, adrenaline coursing through my blood. I was aware of the danger. Kepler could kill you at any moment, and I was putting myself right in its teeth. Kepler always demanded respect, and a little fear. But even beneath the fear, there was always a little thrill.

Once the indicator light turned green, I pressed my keycard to the sensor and the door slid open.

The door opened to another hallway lined with dim white lights that led to the conduit itself. It was long and narrow, only wide enough to accommodate a single person. I jogged down it, my footfalls on the grate below me echoing off the metal walls. I paused at the edge of it.

The conduit was a vertical shaft, leading upward to the underside of Ward 1 and downward to the hull of the station where the electricity was discharged into space. More of those dim lights lined the conduit on either side, illuminating parallel ladders that ran up the walls. I gripped the nearest one and began to climb.

"Where you stay?" Malia asked.

"Climbing. Busy," I replied tersely.

It was cold in the chamber so close to the vacuum of space outside. I could feel the chill of the metal ladder even through my gloves. It was a three-minute climb, and I was shivering by the time I reached the top rung. I looked overhead and saw that the bridge between the ladders was listing dangerously to the side.

I cursed under my breath and scanned the chamber for another route, but saw only the ladder on the opposite side. I shifted my hold and reached for it tentatively, but it was just beyond my grasp.

With another curse, I twisted on the ladder and jumped across. The ladder rattled but held.

"*What was that?*" Malia asked, slightly concerned.

"Almost there," I grunted.

I climbed the last few rungs of the ladder with ease, pulling myself into the access passage. I let out a sigh of relief.

"I'm below the vault," I said to Malia. The passage was small and low, and I had to hunch to move through it. I paused a few meters in, lifting my flashlight to illuminate an access panel above me. I pulled out my toolkit, then unscrewed the panel and peered inside.

Unlike the passage in Leeway, this ceiling wasn't reinforced. I imagined Atlas would have run into resistance trying to mess more directly with the systems. I knew that these were backup systems to the air circulators of Ward 1 and wouldn't cause any kind of blackout in functioning if disabled. But the EMP's effect was temporary, and a system reboot would reset it easily.

It would give us just enough time to enter the vault itself.

I pushed aside tangles of wires and unscrewed a few more panels to uncover the power source for the mag lock. A thrill went through me, looking at it. This was my first step toward 125 billion credits. My first step toward being free of debt. My first step toward being richer than my wildest dreams. I grinned. "I found it."

"*Cherreh. Now attach the EMP to the underside and hele on.*"

I unslung my bag and pulled out the EMP, packaged within

an unassuming black box. With all the care of a trained station mechanic, I duct-taped it to the underside of the power source.

I reached for my screwdriver to re-secure the panels, but as I leaned down, a readout meter caught my eye.

"Hold on," I said.

"Hold on what?"

"This is the power supply for a CO_2 scrubber. It interfaces with air filtration."

"So?"

"*So*, it's bearing the entire load of Ward 1. If we blow this thing, it'll knock out the air filtration system for an hour."

"And?"

"*And* I'm assuming you'd like to keep breathing for an hour."

"What do we do?"

"Fix it," I said, reaching for my toolkit.

I popped open the panel behind the readout meter and started rooting through the wires. "Are you in Kepler's life support systems?"

"Yeah, but—"

"Can you spoof an all-clear signal from this location? I need to take the system offline for about five minutes."

"Five minutes is cutting it real close, brah."

"Just do it."

Malia went silent for a moment. *"It's done."*

I pulled out the plug that connected everything and the meter dropped to zero. I went to work with my tools, rewiring the power supply. As I did, my mind settled into quiet. Everything else seemed to fall away, and all that was left was working through one problem after the next, with singular focus.

"You need to go, cuz, you've got less than ten minutes left," Malia interrupted.

"Working on it," I said through gritted teeth.

Kepler always demanded respect, and a little fear. Its jaws

were closing around me as the minutes ticked by, and that fear grew and grew. I tried to push it aside and focus on my task.

I clicked another wire into place. "I just jerry-rigged the power supply to piggyback off Ward 1's climate control. Now, redirect power from climate control to life support."

Malia muttered to herself under her breath. Then she said, "*There.*"

The meter jumped back to full.

"It's working!"

"Great! Now get the fuck out of there."

Satisfied, I slammed the panel shut and threw my tools into my bag. I left the wires askew and the panels open, hustling down the low hallway toward the ladders. The metal of the ladder shocked my hand as I touched the rung. I slung my bag over my shoulder and started to climb.

"*Brah, where you stay?*" Malia asked again.

"Climbing. Busy," I snapped.

Midway down the ladder I heard a growing electric whine, coming from all around me in the conduit. I braced my hands on either side of the ladder and slid the rest of the way down.

I hit the ground running.

My footfalls echoed through the chamber, metallic and pounding as the electric whine grew louder and louder. The fine hairs on my arms and the back of my neck rose, partially from the electricity in the air and partially from the adrenaline rushing through my blood.

I skidded to a halt in front of the access hatch. I fumbled out my keycard and slapped it to the sensor, only to be met with a grating beep as the indicator light flashed red.

"*Oh, shucks,*" Malia said.

"*Shucks?*" I echoed.

"Access code rotated. Try wait."

"I cannot try wait, Malia!" I shouted over the line.

I yanked open a panel to the left of the hatch and scanned

the tangle of wiring within, picking out a mess of chips and fuses beneath. Forgoing my tools, I popped a chip out with my fingers and plucked out a handful of wires, exchanging their places. I left the panel open as I lunged for the sensor again. The same grating beep sounded.

I made a low noise of frustration. I glanced behind me at the chamber, where the lights were shutting down with loud *clunks* in succession.

"*Malia!*" I shouted again.

She muttered something back at me that I couldn't catch.

I lowered my shoulder and threw my weight at the door. A shock of pain went through my shoulder. I hit the door again. Another one went all the way down my arm. I hit it again. This one went through my whole body.

The last light went out. A Klaxon began to sound. The electric hum in the air pitched up to a scream.

I threw myself at the door one last time.

The doors sprang open. I sailed through them, then landed hard on my stomach. The doors snapped closed behind me.

The chamber discharged with a *CRACK*.

Then it was silent.

I lay on the floor for a long time, my whole body trembling with adrenaline and exertion, my breath coming in ragged pants. The silence rang in my ears.

Malia spoke first. "*. . . Eh, E?*"

I groaned.

"*You stay make?*"

I groaned again, this time in the affirmative.

"*Chee hoo!*" Malia whooped. "*Whatever you did, it left the back door wide open! You lucky, cuz!*"

I didn't respond. I lifted myself on shaking arms, testing my strength before standing upright. I ran a hand through my hair, pushing it off my sweaty forehead. I picked up my bag off the ground and slung it over my shoulder, then touched my pocket. My last few cigarettes were all crushed inside the pack. I dragged a hand down my face, then started down the passage.

"Eh, where you going?"

"I'm going the fuck home," I replied, hoarsely. I kicked open the grate. "Tell Angel I'll see her in the morning."

Chapter 12

"ANGEL ASKED US TO GO OVER YOUR COVER BEFORE YOUR INTERVIEW tomorrow," Duke said. She was standing by the screen, arms crossed, Nakano at her side. Cy sat on the couch, looking attentive. Tatiana was sitting on top of the card table, fiddling with a safe door, an earbud connecting her mod to the front. Sara was sitting cross-legged in one of the armchairs, watching curiously. I was perched on the arm of an armchair, as moral support for Cy. "There's a few things you need to know before we send you in," Duke continued.

"Like what?" Cy asked.

"Malia's cloned your record," Nakano explained. "With a few notable exceptions." She made a gesture, and a dossier appeared on the screen, Cy's scowling face in the picture.

"Your name is Makaio Iwata," Nakano continued. "You were born in Ward 2 to a family of tailors. You attended First District High School, until you dropped out at seventeen. You bounced around the Ward for a while before you got pulled into working as the hitter in a few low-profile jobs."

"Das it?" he asked.

"Not yet," Duke answered. "The stories diverge here, when you joined Station Security at twenty-one." Nakano highlighted a few lines of the dossier. "You did pretty well for yourself, until your superiors realized you were taking kickbacks from civilians."

"Ho, so I one crooked cop," Cy said in understanding. "And dat Atlas buggah like 'em li'dat?"

"He does," Nakano answered. "Malia has a stellar resume for you, it's just a matter of keeping the job."

"And you like teach me?"

"Yes. Things like how to keep up a lie, how to carry yourself."

"Would you like me to speak proper English?" Cy asked, dropping his accent with great effort.

I laughed. "Don't strain yourself, cuz."

"No need fo' dat," Duke said. "You need to be as authentic as possible if this grift is going to work."

"But practice wouldn't hurt," Nakano chimed in.

"How you like practice?" Cy asked.

"A roleplay." Nakano scanned the room. "Would anyone like to volunteer?"

Sara's hand shot up. "I would!" She grinned. "I could probably use some grifting lessons too."

"Great, come up here with Cy."

Cy and Sara moved to the front of the room and faced each other. Duke stood beside Cy, Nakano beside Sara.

"The first and most important thing is to appear confident," Duke said. "You belong here. You're meant to be here. You deserve this job." She modeled how to stand—back straight, shoulders squared, feet apart. Cy shifted on his feet. "No, that's too stiff. Try relax a little, don't think too hard about it." Cy shifted again, shaking out his hands and rolling his neck. "That's better."

"That's perfect, Sara," Nakano said. I glanced her way, and Sara had mimicked Duke's pose, down to the set of her jaw. I raised my brows, admittedly impressed.

"Now, Sara, I'd like for you to pretend to be the interviewer," Nakano continued. "As you grift, think about your motivations. You're looking for someone dependable, someone tough, someone willing to do the dirty work to get something done. And remember that you're not trying to hire, you're trying to exclude. Can you do that?" Sara nodded, schooling her face into a grim frown.

"Your motivation, Cy, is to get this job," Duke said. "You're off the force, and you're pissed about it. Bussing things up is all you know how to do. It's not just that you need this job to keep your family fed, you need this job to keep doing what you love to do: bussing things up. Got it?" Cy nodded, shifting his weight like he was about to enter the ring. "All right, go."

"Thank you for making the time to meet with me today," Sara said to Cy, pitching her voice low and rough. "I'm sure you're a busy person."

"Yeah, but I get time fo' dis," Cy replied. "Dis important, yeah?"

"Very." Sara glanced over Cy's shoulder at the dossier on the screen. "I understand you were with Station Security for almost ten years."

"Das right."

"What was your favorite aspect of your job with Station Security?"

Cy cracked his knuckles. "I like work wit my hands."

"Nice," Duke said as an aside.

"And your least favorite?" Sara asked.

". . . paypawork."

"Okay, Imma stop you right there," Duke interrupted. She stepped up to Cy, tapping his boot with hers. "You shifted your weight, like you were off balance. It reads as nervous, unsure." Duke planted her feet again, demonstrating her stance. "Always stay rooted, like one tree, braddah. Try again."

Cy resettled into a power stance. Sara collected herself. "I see," she continued. "What do you think your greatest strengths are?"

"I dependable, responsible, loyal—"

"—But you were going behind the backs of your superiors. Is that really loyal?"

Cy's eyes widened with shock. I turned my laugh into a cough, but Cy still fixed me with a glare.

"Oooh," Tatiana said, unplugging the earbud from her mod. She grinned at Cy. "She got you, cuz."

"Why you gotta ask me dat?" Cy asked, turning his glare on Sara. She smiled sheepishly.

"She's testing you," Duke said. "You need to be ready for curveballs li'dat."

"I no even undastand what my strengths *are*, cuz," Cy complained.

"Sometimes it's easiest to model yourself off someone else," Nakano suggested. "Think of every crooked cop you've interacted with. What were they like? What did they say? How did they move?"

"Eh," I said, drawing the room's attention. "You remembah dat one guy, who wen help us wit da kine? You know. Mikey always like talk to him befo' one job."

Tatiana perked up. "Mikey the mastermind?"

I raised my brows. "Mastermind now?"

"Yeah." Tatiana twisted in her seat. "I've been on his crews a few times. His cop's name is Officer Ripley."

"Da one who get permanent stink eye and da fucked-up leg?" Cy asked.

"Das da one."

"What were you doing on Mikey's crews?" I asked, incredulous.

Tatiana shrugged. "Same thing you were doing, probably." She went back to her safe, plugging the earbud back into her mod. "Just younger and sexier."

"Not something to be proud of," I replied, annoyed.

"Being young and sexy?" She grinned at me. "I mean, I can see why you'd give up on that, but . . ."

I took a breath, ready to shoot back, but Cy interrupted me.

"So you like me walk around wit one permanent stink eye and a fucked-up leg?"

"Not such a big stretch, is it?" Duke joked.

"Maybe leave out the leg," Nakano corrected. "But think about Officer Ripley when you're on the job and draw inspiration from him. Try again."

Cy drew up to his full height, planted his feet, and crossed his cybernetic arm across his flesh one. To her credit, Sara was staring down a six-foot moke built like a dreadnought and didn't even blink.

"I asked you a question," she said coldly.

"I left Station Security 'cuz they no can handle da truth of tings," Cy said. "We no can operate da way we do. We need someting moa den jus' government kālā. I doing my paht to keep dis city clean." He paused. "Wit skosh taken off da top." He looked down at Sara. "Das why."

"Ho, shit!" Tatiana crowed, tugging the earbud out of her mod again. "It's like I'm seeing Ripley in da flesh! Somebody try call Mikey and tell him we get one zombie on our hands."

"Ripley wen make?" I asked, surprised.

"Ripley is dead and Mikey's in prison," Tatiana said. "Not that you would know, old fut."

"Who you calling an old fut, you little—"

"You two like shut up a minute?" Cy snapped. "I try'n fo' tink."

"No, this is good!" Duke said. "There'll be distractions on the real grift—tune 'em out as best you can."

Cy turned his attention back to Sara. "Dat a good ansah?"

Sara looked impressed. "It is."

"If I'm an old fut, you're a little shit," I hissed at Tatiana.

"At least I still have my youth and senses." She waggled her fingers at me. "You're stuck in the Stone Age."

"What would you say are your biggest weaknesses, then?" Sara asked.

"I get one bad tempah," Cy said. "Hanabata days I use to scrap all da time. Get in trouble wit my boss too. But now I like channel dat aggression, do good tings wit it."

"I'm not even *thirty*!" I snapped at Tatiana.

"And you're already washed up," Tatiana shot back.

"Well, you have the opportunity to do some good here," Sara said. She clasped her hands behind her back and widened her stance. "What drew you to Atlas Industries?"

"I'm not washed up," I growled.

"Then why am I here?" Tatiana retorted. She grinned again. "Angel doesn't trust you to get the job done?"

I didn't have an answer for that.

"Didn't think so," Tatiana said, triumphant. She turned back to her safe. "Everybody else knows. Just admit it to yourself."

I felt my cheeks flush with anger. Who the fuck did this kid think she was? What the fuck did she know about me, about me and Angel?

But I still didn't have an answer for her.

"I like a man wit powah," Cy answered, drawing my attention back to the roleplay. "Da powah to do real good in dis city. I like be paht o' dat."

"Good," Duke said. "Good job, both of you."

Sara dropped her affect and grinned, and I could swear it was like night and day. She threw her arms around Cy and gave him a hug. He reciprocated stiffly.

"That was fun!" she said. She drew away from Cy, looking remorseful. "Sorry for hassling you, though."

"Nah, nah, nah," Duke said. "It was good practice."

Cy put a hand to his forehead. "Ho, dis grifting shit is *hahd*, cuz!"

"It just takes more practice," Duke assured him.

"You make it look so easy!" Cy exclaimed.

Nakano smiled. "We've been doing this a long time."

"How long?" Sara asked, settling herself on the edge of the sofa.

"Ten years?" Duke said. She glanced at Nakano. "When'd you start your transition, babes?"

"Tenth anniversary is in a month," Nakano answered.

"So, eleven years."

"Oh! Congratulations!" Sara said with delighted applause.

"Thank you. I wouldn't be here without Duke, though," she said, taking Duke's hand.

"Nah, it was a team effort," Duke said, smiling warmly at her.

Eleven years was about when I started, at least professionally. I wondered if we had ever crossed paths.

"How'd you start?" I asked, curious.

"We're colony girls," Nakano explained. "Pelias is one of the larger ones, but still a colony. We were both destined for the rare-earth mines. But the corporation wouldn't cover my transition, so . . ."

". . . we took matters into our own hands," Duke finished. "And you know how one thing always leads to another. We started with small cons to make some quick cash. Then we started working with other crews on bigger jobs. Before long we weren't just hassling tourists and salarymen, we were playing investors, CEOs, corrupt politicians. Never staying in one place too long, never working with the same crew twice. It's how we've stayed alive this long." Duke gave Nakano's hand a squeeze. The scars on their hands almost touched. "How we've stayed together this long."

"Awww." Sara put a hand to her chest. "That's so sweet."

"A couple that cons together, stays together," Tatiana said, without looking away from her safe.

"C'mon," Duke said, jerking her head toward the entrance. "Let's take a break, go kau kau. I know a place not far from here."

Duke and Nakano started toward the door, Cy following. Sara stood from the couch and straightened her skirt. Tatiana hopped off the table to join them.

It was hard to imagine working with the same crew, the same person, for eleven years. Angel, Cy, and I were free agents, and we rotated through crews. Sometimes for longer, sometimes for shorter. But while Cy always came and went, Angel was a constant. And even before we went pro, we were working together long before that. Even longer if you counted the petty crimes and confidence tricks of juvenile delinquents.

When I put it all together, I realized with a start that while Duke and Nakano had been a team for eleven years, even separated at twenty-one, Angel and I had been a team for ten.

"You coming, E?" Duke asked, pulling me back to the present.

"... Yeah, sure," I answered, following them out of the building.

Duke and Nakano led the way. Sara and Cy followed, reviewing their exercise together. Tatiana was strolling with her arms crossed behind her head, apparently without a care in the world. I trailed after them. I wondered how long she'd been working, whether she'd ever worked with someone else. Her dossier didn't mention any partners, so I had to believe she was a free agent. With her shitty attitude, I had to think she wouldn't fit in well with a crew, at least not for very long.

Even harder to imagine was working without a crew, without a partner. It must be lonely. I never could have done it. I could never stand to be alone. Especially now, after eight years apart from everyone I'd ever known. Apart from my family, my friends. Apart from Angel.

Ten years together as kids. Ten years together as partners. Eight years apart as enemies. I felt a weight in my chest, heavy with anger, grief, and hurt. In my work I always tried to take it one step at a time, with singular focus. I didn't like distractions. But in this moment, feeling this hurt, it was all I could think of. I had to wonder where we would be if things had turned out differently.

Or where we would be next.

* * *

Later that night, it was time for Duke and Nakano to meet Atlas.

Atlas asked to meet them at the Starlight, a restaurant that took up the entirety of the top floor of one of the Ward 7 towers. Even more impressive, the whole restaurant rotated, giving each seat a panoramic view of Kepler's skyline. It was another one of the swankiest places on Kepler, another one that I'd never been to. Probably never would, outside a job like this one.

Angel and Malia were in the crew's van a safe distance away from the restaurant, listening in. Tatiana and Cy were stationed at the doors, should things go south.

Sara and I were on a "date," there to snoop.

The houselights were low, and the flickering flames of real candles set in little crystal dishes cast dim light across the tables. Everything was dressed in white tablecloths and sparkling place settings. The gold-rimmed china alone would've cost me a week's wages to replace. The whole perimeter of the restaurant was dominated by floor-to-ceiling windows with a dizzying view of the Wards below. Outside, Kepler's sky was cycling to sunset, and the skyline glittered with artificial light.

I tugged at the glove on my right hand, acutely aware of the chip buried in my skin.

Sara reached across the table to lay a hand on mine. She was gorgeous in her off-the-shoulder black dress and plum lipstick. "Don't be nervous."

I laughed. "Aren't I supposed to say that to you?"

She smiled at me. "Everyone gets nervous. Even me, sometimes, when I get up on stage, or step on the balance beam. It's okay to be nervous."

"I'm not nervous," I assured her. "It's just—" I paused. What was it? I wasn't nervous, so much as hellishly aware of how much I didn't belong here. I had more in common with the waitstaff than anyone seated at these tables. I spent time in Ward 7 before, rubbed elbows with its people, and over time I got good at pretending I was one of them. I was content with that, for the longest time—just pretending. But now I felt self-conscious in a way I never had before. It wasn't enough to just pretend, not anymore. I wanted to belong. I wanted to be one of them.

I wasn't sure how to articulate all of that to Sara, but Angel spoke over me. "*We're all in position*," she said over the line. "*Ready when you are.*"

"*Heard*," Duke replied. "*Going in now.*"

The elevator chimed and its doors opened, Duke and Nakano stepping out into the restaurant. The two of them approached the maître d', who seemed to be expecting them. Duke exchanged a few quick words with him before he led them past Sara and I, to one of the tables with Starlight's famous views. Atlas was already seated at the table, and he rose to greet Duke and Nakano as they approached.

"Ms. Harden, Dr. Abe," Atlas said, "it's a pleasure to see you again."

"The pleasure is ours," Duke replied, shaking his hand. "Thank you for meeting with us."

Atlas gestured for the two to sit, and all three took their seats at the table.

"I've been doing some reading," Atlas said. "Your thesis was a fascinating read, Dr. Abe."

"You read my dissertation?" Nakano asked, a little thrill in her voice.

Atlas chuckled. "I did. And the applications of your research seem limitless."

"You could say that again," Duke cut in with a laugh. "Clairvoyant's on the cutting edge of memory research."

"Indeed it is," Atlas agreed. "I've done some reading on you and Clairvoyant as well, Ms. Harden."

"Please, call me Kalei," Duke replied. "And I hope you liked what you read."

"I did! What you've accomplished in so short a time is incredible, Kalei."

I could see Duke's grin from a table over. "Thanks, appreciate it."

A waiter came by to fill the group's water glasses. Angel took the opportunity to say, "*Good work, Malia.*"

"*Was easy, brah,*" Malia replied. "*Once I found a thesis to rip off, we were cherreh.*" She cackled. "*Some doctoral candidate on Caelestis is mad confused though.*"

"Are we going to give it back?" Sara asked. I gave her a look across the table. She flushed in the candlelight. "Oh."

"I understand your current focus is on memory reconstruction," Atlas continued after the waiter left. "Care to share a little bit more?"

Nakano started to answer, but Duke cut her off. "Right now, we're in the process of developing algorithms to distinguish episodic memories from one another. But I'm not really involved in the R&D side of things."

"I am," Nakano said, her patience with Duke's character visibly fraying. "We're using machine learning to discern the subtle differences between neural patterns for different memories, particularly those related to trauma."

"How is that going?"

"Well!" Nakano answered, pleased. "We're able to distinguish different memories at a 97 percent confidence interval."

A waiter approached our table. "How are we this evening? Are you ready to order?" they asked.

"Well, thank you," I said with a smile. I opened the paper menu, then tried to hide the way I startled. The Starlight served real meat and fresh vegetables, imported from the farming colonies of the outer worlds. Not lab grown, not rehydrated. *Real* food.

Sensing my panic, Sara said smoothly, "I think we need a few more minutes."

The waiter nodded and moved off.

"And what is the end goal for distinguishing these traumatic memories?" Atlas asked.

"To identify them for rescripting," Nakano said. "If we're able to specifically target the traumatic memory, it's possible to rescript it without interfering with other related memories."

Duke jumped in. "We don't want to overwrite any other memories that might have been built on the trauma," she explained. "Particularly if those memories are adaptive."

The same waiter approached Duke and Nakano's table to take their order. I used the break in conversation to hiss into my comm: "What the hell should I order?"

"*Something expensive*," Malia said.

"*Something fancy*," Tatiana suggested.

"*Someting ono*," Cy said.

"*Just keep it under budget, please*," Angel added.

"I see," Atlas said as the waiter left with their order. "Tell me about the rescripting aspect of your research."

"Well, distinguishing the memories is only the first step," Duke answered. "The next step is pulling apart the neural pattern to figure out what corresponds to specific details of the memory. Only after we do that is it possible to change those specific parts of the pattern to create new associations."

"What's a veal?" I asked the group.

"*Baby-kine cow*," Malia answered instantly.

"*How'd you know that?*" Tatiana asked.

"*GhostNet, brah! The executive chef get a mod too!*"

"I imagine these are all very minute changes, then," Atlas said.

"Oh, for sure," Duke replied, ignoring our conversation. "Don't want to be held liable for any big changes in personality or processing downstream, you know."

"Should I order something different?" Sara asked.

"*Try ordah someting else, we eat 'em if you no like 'em*," Cy answered.

Sara flipped through the menu, chewing her lip. "I don't know, the veal sounds good."

"Eh, E, you get someting else den."

"Fascinating." Atlas gave a long look at Duke and Nakano in turn. "And how do you intend to change those pieces of the pattern?"

"That's pretty far in the future," Duke said with a laugh, completely unfazed by the breakdown on comms.

"But I've given it some thought," Nakano cut in. Duke twisted in her seat to give her a frown. Nakano turned her eyes down toward her water glass, demure.

"Please, I'd be interested to hear your thoughts," Atlas encouraged, picking up his water glass.

"Yeah, same," Duke added, incredulity in her voice.

"*Just pick something, Edie,*" Angel said, irritated. "*You're taking over comms.*"

I flipped back and forth through the menu. The waiter was approaching, and I felt another flash of panic. I scanned the page for anything remotely familiar.

Nakano ran her finger along the edge of her glass. "Well. Since your presentation, Mr. Atlas, I've thought about the implications of using the new iteration of AXON in my research. With the nuances of the pattern identified, it's possible to use AXON's stimulating capabilities to simulate an altered memory. With enough repetition, eventually it could overwrite the old memory entirely."

"You're not talking about rewriting the memory itself, are you?" Duke asked, shocked.

"Are we ready to order?" the waiter asked me and Sara.

Sara smiled. "I'd like the port-braised veal, please."

"I'll have the swordfish," I said. I saw one once on Casey's nature shows. I didn't even know you could eat them. It felt kind of badass.

I blew out a relieved breath as the waiter left. Hopefully I'd bought us enough time to get through the rest of Duke and Nakano's conversation.

I glanced over at their table. Atlas's grip on his water glass tightened, almost imperceptibly. But if I saw it, there was no doubt the grifters had too.

"It's just a theory," Nakano said hastily. "I'm not sure the technology as it exists right now would be able to accomplish that, anyway."

"How would you go about testing this, Dr. Abe?" Atlas asked, affecting nonchalance.

Nakano looked at Atlas askance, through her lashes. "Well. Like Kalei said, the first trials are to distinguish the memories within individuals. From there, it's comparing the neural patterns of one individual against another, ideally with the same controlled memory. That would allow us to identify the common elements in the memory into objective fact and subjective interpretation." She paused, as if unsure.

"Go on," Atlas urged.

"With the pattern corresponding to the objective facts," she said, slowly, "it would be possible to stimulate another, naïve brain with the identified pattern, thus implanting the new memory."

"But that's not what Clairvoyant's doing," Duke interrupted. "We're in the business of altering associations between memories, not creating new ones wholesale."

"It was just a theory," Nakano said quietly.

"Good, because that would be a liability nightmare," Duke said with a nervous laugh.

"But it's an interesting thought experiment, isn't it?" Atlas said, his kindly blue eyes gleaming in the candlelight. "Given that the technology exists, of course."

A brief silence fell over the party. Atlas drummed out a pattern on the table with his fingers. Even to my eye I could read that he was thinking hard about something.

"He's interested," Angel said quietly. *"But don't let him get what he wants so easily."*

"Well," Atlas said, breaking the uncomfortable silence. He raised his glass. "I'm excited to see what the future holds for all of us."

"I'll drink to that," Duke said enthusiastically. The three clinked their glasses.

"Kalei," Atlas addressed Duke. "What are your goals with Clairvoyant?"

"Other than fame and fortune?" Duke laughed.

Atlas smiled. "That's a given, isn't it?"

"I'm hoping to attain a five percent growth rate through the third quarter, pay out some of our investors," Duke answered.

"Those are quite modest goals," Atlas said.

"Are they?" Duke sounded surprised.

"They are." Atlas leaned forward on his elbows. "I could offer you a lot more than breaking even."

"Offer?" Wariness crept into Duke's voice.

"Let me tell you something, both of you. Your algorithms are valuable. Worth more than whatever you got from your investors. And I'm willing to pay you for them."

"How much, exactly?"

Atlas reached into his breast pocket and withdrew a card and pen. He wrote a number down in a rigid scrawl. He slid it across the table to Duke. "That's my opening offer."

Duke examined the card. I couldn't quite make out the numbers, but I saw a hell of a lot of zeroes. Even that would be enough to buy the entire floor of my apartment building, and then some.

Nakano reached for the card, but before she could read it, Duke slid it back. "That's very kind, Mr. Atlas, but I'm sorry, we can't accept. We're not interested in selling."

Atlas, to his credit, looked unfazed. "I understand the sentimentality," he said. "This is your first venture—your first successful one, anyway. And I'm not going to lie and say that what you have isn't special. But there's only so much you can do with these algorithms, at least without my technology."

"And will getting access to that technology prove to be a problem?"

"I can make no promises about what accessibility will be like in the future," Atlas said evenly.

Nakano drew in a hushed breath. Atlas's eyes flicked to her face, then back to Duke's.

"There are other avenues for our research—" Duke began.

"Are there?" Atlas cut her off. "There's nothing in the galaxy like AXON. There are cheap imitations, ones that are just as likely to transform you into a superhuman as they are to turn you into a vegetable. What happens to your liability then?"

Duke went silent, as if she didn't have an answer.

Atlas crossed out the original number on the card, wrote a new one, then slid it across the table again. "Another offer."

Duke slid it back without looking at it. "We're not interested."

A muscle in Atlas's jaw jumped. "I suggest you take the offer," he said. "You'll find it very hard to get anything out of your research without it."

"Is that a threat?"

"Not at all." Atlas smiled, but his blue eyes were malicious. "It's a warning."

"Kalei—" Nakano began, but she quailed under the look Duke shot her.

Duke stood, jostling the table. "I don't think we have anything else to discuss," she said. "Thank you for inviting us out, Mr. Atlas."

Duke started away from the table. A few paces later, she turned around to see Nakano frozen in her seat. She gestured for her to follow. Nakano slowly folded her napkin on the table and stood, smoothing her dress. She gave Atlas a last look before following Duke out of the restaurant and into the elevator.

After the doors closed, we let out a collective sigh of relief. "*We're clear,*" Duke said. "*Nice job, babe.*"

"*Ho, that Atlas buggah stay hūhū,*" Malia said with a laugh.

"*Fo' real,*" Cy agreed.

"You think he bought it?" I asked, directing my question at Angel.

Just then, I saw Atlas's mods flare to life, electric blue in the candlelight. With a few taps of his fingers, he opened his comm.

"*Quiet,*" Angel commanded. We all shut up. "*Yes, sir?*"

I heard Atlas's overlapping voices: one in the restaurant, the other over the comm. "I need the results of your background check," he said. "Give me everything you've found on Ella Abe."

"*Of course, sir,*" Angel answered. "*Forwarding it to you now.*"

Atlas closed the line, the light of his mods fading in the dim light. A waiter approached with a bottle of wine, and Atlas nodded his approval. He leaned back in his seat as the waiter poured, looking self-satisfied.

"*Everyone, meet at the rendezvous point in thirty minutes,*" Angel said. I could hear the smile in her voice. "*He's hooked.*"

Chapter 13

NOW THAT DUKE AND NAKANO HAD ATLAS ON THE HOOK, THE NEXT phase of Angel's plan was for me, Tatiana, and Malia to gain access to Atlas Industries' internal systems to steal the electronic copies of the prototypes, as well as gain access to the physical building. Over the next three days, it was all about the lifts. I wasn't particularly looking forward to being bullied by the teens, but anything for the job, I guess.

"I have something for you," Malia said, rummaging through the pile of tech, junk, and ʻōpala she'd collected around her armchair in the hideout. "Try wait," she said, "everything's all hammajang."

"Take your time," I said, leaning against the table with my arms crossed. "Not like I have anywhere else to be."

"Would've thought you'd be busy," Tatiana said breezily, dropping herself into Malia's armchair. "I thought you'd be in high demand, once you were out."

"I work one job at a time," I said, annoyed.

"For a payout like this? I do too." She grinned. "Had to turn a few down, already."

"Must be hard," I said.

"I mean, you knew all about that, didn't you?"

"What's that supposed to mean?"

Tatiana sat up in the chair. "You used to be the best runner on the station, one of the best thieves too."

"Right . . ." I said, waiting for the follow-up.

"So, it must suck to know that there's a young, sexy upstart here to take your job."

"You aren't gonna take my job," I growled.

"Aren't you even a little afraid? You've been out of the game so long—mistakes are to be expected. And with Angel's high standards . . ." She trailed off.

"Angel trusts me," I said, with a little less conviction than I wanted.

"For now," Tatiana replied.

"If you're trying to rile me up—" I warned.

"It's working?"

"Aha!" Malia interrupted, straightening up with a cardboard box in her hands. She handed it to Tatiana. "For the job."

Tatiana opened the box, and her brows went up in surprise. She reached inside, then pulled out a button with a slogan printed across it: An Earth for All of Us.

"What the hell is this?" she asked.

"Your cover!" Malia said. "The janitor is our way into the general offices, and he's big into nature conservation and animal rights. You need to lift and clone the RFID in his chip, then get him to wear this button." Malia handed another pin to Tatiana. At first glance, it was the same as the others. "This one's got a camera we can use to capture his PIN."

Malia paused, her eyes brightening with realization. "It's a *button cam*!"

Tatiana groaned.

"Can you handle that?" Malia asked.

"Of course I can," Tatiana said. She took the box from Malia. "I'll get it to you tomorrow." She gave me a meaningful look, which I met with a scowl.

"What about R&D and the defense contracts?" I asked Malia.

"Angel's working out the details for the defense contractor, but we've got you on getting into the R&D area of the building as well as its internal systems. You'll need to lift and clone her keycard, then get me access to the systems."

"All right. What've you got for me?"

"Here," Malia said, foisting another cardboard box into my hands. "I need you to get the mark to plug this into her computer."

I opened the box. "This is a fucking dildo."

Tatiana screeched in delight, nearly spilling her buttons on the floor with the way she doubled over laughing.

"Not just a dildo!" Malia exclaimed over Tatiana's laughter. "It's a dildo loaded with *malware*."

I looked at Malia blankly. "You expect me to convince the mark to plug a malware-loaded dildo into her computer."

"Nah, nah, nah. Just swap the malware-loaded dildo with her perfectly ordinary dildo. She'll plug it in on her own."

"Why?" I asked flatly.

Malia took the box from me and pulled out the dildo. She turned it over in her hands, displaying a port at the flared base. "It's meant to plug in! It syncs with a proprietary app. From there you can create profiles, manage settings, download programs, grant a hacker access to security information . . ." She grinned at me. "Cool, yeah?"

"Malia. Everything I've learned today about dildos I have learned against my will."

"*I* think it's cool," Tatiana said, her laughter subsiding. "I'm all for new tech on new jobs." She gave me another look. "Gotta evolve with the times, y'know."

"See! You get it, cuz!" Malia and Tatiana high-fived.

I scowled. "Anything else?"

Malia passed the box back to me and shrugged. "Just get it on her desk."

I took it from her. "What makes you so sure she'll plug it into her work computer, anyway?"

"You'd be amazed at the kinds of lōlō shit people do on their work computers." Malia cackled. "This one time—"

"No, nope, 'a'ole, I'm good." I tucked the box under my arm and made a hasty retreat. "Shoots!"

The first mark was Yusef Saab, a custodian with access to the general offices of Atlas Industries. Tatiana parked herself on his usual route to work with a stack of flyers and her box of buttons, heckling passersby with her save-the-animals spiel. Malia and I watched from the van, through the video feed of the button cam pinned to her shirt.

"*I'm passing out choke flyers,*" Tatiana said. "*Gonna need more at this rate.*"

"Too bad Angel wouldn't let us take 'donations,'" Malia said ruefully.

"Stay focused," I said. "We have a job to do."

"*Yeah, yeah, yeah,*" Tatiana replied. "*It'll be easy, no worries.*"

"Never go into a job thinking it'll be easy," I said. "That's how you get caught."

"*Maybe if you're still analog,*" Tatiana quipped.

"*Analog?*" I repeated, aggrieved.

"Oooh." Malia twisted in her chair to grin at me. "She got you, cuz."

"Mods just make shit more complicated," I argued. "I'd take 'analog' over 'unnecessary' any day."

"*Wanna bet?*" Tatiana challenged. "*I'll pay you twenty credits if you can do the lift faster than me.*"

I was about to say no. But then I touched the light pack of cigarettes in my pocket and reconsidered. "Deal."

"*Cool. Now watch and lose. Sir!*" Tatiana called out to Yusef, catching his attention. "*Sir, can you spare a minute for the animals of Earth?*"

"*I'm on my way to work,*" he said.

"*It'll only take a minute,*" Tatiana pleaded. She waved a flyer at him, emblazoned with a picture of a whale and her calf. "*You could save her life!*"

Yusef glanced at his phone. Then he approached Tatiana, guard up.

"*Did you know,*" she said, "*that Earth is experiencing an extinction event to rival the end of the Cretaceous period?*"

"What's a Cretaceous?" I asked Malia.

"It's when the dinosaurs died, brah," Malia replied.

"*I did,*" Yusef answered. "*It's been going on for a while.*"

"*I'm glad you're aware,*" Tatiana said. "*It's easy to miss, living thousands of light-years away. But Earth needs us. We're all her children, after all.*"

"You're overselling it," I said, annoyed.

Yusef sighed heavily. "*It's a tragedy. But what can we do, so far away?*"

"*Vote!*" Tatiana exclaimed, whipping a flyer out of her stack. "*Earth for All has compiled a list of Senate candidates who are friendly to conservation efforts,*" she said, handing him the flyer. "*All you need to do is fill out your ballot this coming election cycle.*"

Yusef bobbed his head. "*I would be happy to.*"

"*Awesome!*" Tatiana thrust out her hand to shake. "*We appreciate it, really.*"

He took her hand, smiling. The RFID reader embedded in Tatiana's hand read the chip in Yusef's, and a moment later Malia's laptop beeped in confirmation. "Got it," she said.

"*I almost forgot, I have something to go with it!*" Tatiana said. She undid the pin on her shirt, jostling the video feed as she handed the button cam to Yusef. The video feed righted itself when the man pinned it to his shirt, showing Tatiana's grinning face. "*Wear it with pride! You're saving the animals, after all.*"

The man laughed. "*I will!*" He turned away from her, then started back on his path.

"Nice one, cuz," Malia said. "That'll capture his PIN at the door."

"*Like I said: easy,*" Tatiana replied. "*Heading back now.*"

The second mark was Vera Decker, a developer with access to the R&D floors and the systems containing the prototypes. After tracking her spending habits across the past few months, Malia found that she sent all her mail to her work address—including the dildo that was our way into the vault. Amateur mistake.

A squirrelly-looking Vera was waiting at the door for the mailman when I arrived just outside Atlas Industries' tower.

"*All right, Analog, let's see those skills,*" Tatiana said in my ear.

I grunted in response.

Vera looked relieved when she saw the mailman approaching with a stack of packages. I tightened my grip on the box under my arm and picked up my pace. She was just reaching for the box the mailman was offering her when I brushed by, too close, knocking it and a number of other packages to the floor.

"Shit, I'm sorry," I said. Vera looked like I'd just sabotaged her career, falling to her knees to sift through the boxes on the ground. "Here, let me help."

I crouched down to help Vera and the grumbling mailman. First, I reached for a package near Vera's side. On the way, I lifted the badge clipped to her lab coat pocket. I tapped it to the keycard reader in my pocket.

"*Got it,*" Malia said.

I dropped the keycard to the ground. Then I scanned the

packages on the ground, picking out the one Vera dropped. I exchanged it with the one under my arm.

"Here, I think this one is yours." I offered the switched package to Vera, and she nearly snatched it out of my hand. "And I think you dropped this," I said, pointing to the badge on the ground. She snatched that up too.

I helped the mailman gather up the last of his packages as Vera made a hasty retreat into the building. Then, with one last apology to the mailman, I started back toward the hideout.

"Time," I called.

"*It's close, brah,*" Malia said. "*But Tati edged you out.*"

"*Yes!*" Tatiana cried. "*Machine over man! How you like that, Analog?*"

"Don't call me that," I growled.

"*You like your full name better, Edith Jay Melehau'oliokalani Morikawa?*" Malia cackled.

"*Edith?!*" Tatiana screeched.

"Don't call me that either!" I snapped.

I scowled to myself. It was a clean lift, any thief could tell you that. I could have argued that the jobs were different, there were external factors, but I knew the teens would just think I was being a sore loser. I was almost thirty fucking years old, I didn't need to bitch about being beat by a teenager.

Maybe mod did edge out analog.

I pushed the thought out of my mind.

"I'll wire you when I get back," I grumbled. Then I looked down at the package in my hands. "Now what the hell do I do with this?"

"*Keep it,*" Malia said. "*Consider it a consolation prize from Atlas Industries.*"

"Atlas?" I repeated. "How do I know this shit won't listen in on me?"

"*Run it under a magnet and wipe it,*" she said. Then she and Tatiana snickered. "*Unless you're into that.*"

"Fuck. No." I paused over a trash can, the package hovering over the opening.

At least it was *something.*

I sighed and tucked the package back under my arm, resuming my path to the hideout.

The last mark was Craig Burns, a defense contractor with access to the highly restricted areas of Atlas Industries. Malia spent the last few weeks tracking his movements and came up with a pattern: every Wednesday night he went to happy hour at a pretentious Ward 7 lounge with his buddies. But a few spoofed emails sent them to some nonexistent meetings, leaving Craig alone.

"You can't send in anyone else?" I asked.

The group of us were crowded around the open doors of the van, Angel surveying us from the raised interior. She met my gaze. "Would *you* like to flirt with a man?"

The group muttered a collective no.

"But what about Nakano?" I asked, gesturing at her. "She's flirting with Atlas, she can pull it off."

Duke nudged Nakano with her shoulder. "She really could."

"Nakano is already involved, and he knows my face," Angel said. "Besides, Burns has"—her lip curled—"particular tastes."

"Then come up with another play," I argued. "We can't send Sara in alone."

"But I'm not alone," Sara chimed in. She smiled. "I'll have all of you."

"It's true," Angel agreed. "Malia has a camera on her, and you'll all be inside to run interference if needed."

"She's never been on a job alone before," I said.

"She's hustled before, though. Everyone at Venus has," Angel replied. "As for jobs, we all have to start somewhere. And she's a natural."

Sara beamed.

"Will you be okay?" Nakano asked, touching Sara's arm.

Sara took her hand and patted it reassuringly. "I'll be okay."

"Remember your tells," Duke added.

"Don't bounce my leg and don't chew my lip, I got it," Sara replied.

"Everyone get ready," Angel said. "We'll send her in when you're in position."

I sighed. Wasn't going to win this one. "Fine. Cy and I will go in first."

Cy paused, giving Sara a long look. "Dat buggah give you any heat, I going bus' him up."

Sara smiled. "Thank you."

I clapped Cy on his metal shoulder. "Let's go." We started toward the lounge.

It was dimly lit, with low-hanging light fixtures and windows blacked out by heavy curtains. There was a bar at the far end, busy even on a Wednesday evening, and plush red sofas and too-soft armchairs set in alcoves and conversation pits. I scanned the room and saw Craig sitting by himself at a raised table near the bar, poking at his comm and looking bored. There were a few empty seats scattered across the lounge—I claimed a conversation pit while Cy went to buy us drinks at the bar.

I sank into the red sofa and touched my earpiece. "We're in position."

Duke and Nakano were next to enter, taking a seat at another conversation pit across the room. Tatiana entered after, pulling up a chair at an empty table. All the seats were now occupied.

"*Coming in hot,*" Malia said. Sara giggled.

Sara strode into the lounge not long after. She was wearing a short black dress that showed off her legs, her blond hair pulled back into a high ponytail, and vibrant red lipstick. She swept her gaze across the room, taking everything in, the picture of cool confidence.

It reminded me of Angel, I realized with a start.

Sara dropped her purse onto the table and slid into a chair opposite Craig, as if she owned it. He looked up at her, surprised. "Mind if I sit here?" she asked.

"I'm waiting for my friends," he answered.

"And you look lonely," she replied with a sly smile.

"They'll be here soon," he said, almost defensive.

"I'm not judging," Sara clarified. "I got stood up by my friends too. But I'm already out here, I'm already squeezed into this dress, might as well have a good time, right?"

Craig looked like he was working through his options. Sara waited patiently, a hint of amusement in the arch of her eyebrows. There was always the possibility he would refuse—no matter how skilled the grifter, the mark always had the power to say no. But he would have a hard fucking time saying no to those gorgeous green eyes.

Finally, a smile spread across Craig's face. "I'd love to have a good time."

"Good." Sara sat back in her seat and crossed her legs. "Want to start by buying me a drink?"

"Only if I can have your name," he replied.

"Aria Monahan," Sara extended a hand. "And you?"

He took her hand. "Craig Burns."

"Charmed." Sara smiled. "Now how about that drink?"

"Absolutely," he said, rising. "What'll you have?"

"Whatever you're drinking."

"I'll be right back," he said, moving toward the bar.

"*Good job, Sara,*" Angel said. "*Keep him occupied until Tatiana can do the lift.*"

I had to admit, Sara was killing it out here. She took to naturally, and maybe she had more practice than I'd originally given her credit for. Things were going smoothly so far, which is more than I could say for my and Angel's first real job—a straightforward bar bill scam. I barely kept it together, but Angel never lost her cool. She was always good like that.

Craig returned a few minutes later with two drinks. He slid back into his chair and offered one to Sara.

"Thanks," she said, smiling gratefully.

"*Ask him about his work,*" Angel said. "*Men like him love to feel important.*"

"So what do you do?" Sara asked, taking a delicate sip of her drink.

"I'm a developer with Atlas Industries," Craig answered.

"Oh, wow! So you code and stuff?"

"I refine targeting algorithms for ship-to-ship weapons systems. Do you know what that is?"

"I don't, actually. What is it?"

"It means I make the guns in space more accurate. Better to shoot down the bad guys." He mimed pointing a gun at Sara. "Boom."

I dropped my head into my hands. What a huge fucking tool.

"*I'm gonna fucking barf,*" Tatiana groaned.

"*Is it too late to just murder this faka?*" Malia asked.

"Fo' real," Cy agreed.

"*Keep him talking about himself,*" Angel said, ignoring us. "*Should be easy enough.*"

"Wow, that sounds so hard," Sara said, awestruck. "How do you know what to hit?"

"Well, you see—" Craig gestured, knocking Sara's purse to the ground. "Oh, sorry. You got that?"

"Yeah, sure, I got it . . ." Sara grumbled, ducking below the table to reach for her purse.

"*Whoa, hold on,*" Tatiana said. "*He just put something in your drink, Sara. Don't touch it.*"

Cy and I made to stand.

"*Wait. We can work with this,*" Angel said.

"Angel—" I began, sharply.

"Sit down, Edie. She can handle this."

I glanced Sara's way. She was rooting through her purse, making sure nothing was broken, buying time to compose herself. Like a pro.

I wanted to knock that smug faka flat on his ass, and I knew Cy would support me. But I couldn't jeopardize this job. I had to trust that Sara knew what she was doing. That Angel knew what she was doing.

I took a slow, deep breath. Then I sat down.

"*Sara*," Angel addressed her. "*I want you to swap the drinks, on my mark. Nakano, provide a distraction. Everybody else, look interested. Now.*"

"You *bastard*!" Nakano shouted. I twisted in my seat toward the noise, along with Tatiana and Cy, and the entire lounge—including Craig—followed suit. Nakano stood abruptly, and even Duke looked shocked. Then Nakano threw her drink in her partner's face. The whole lounge gasped.

"*Do it now, Sara*," Angel said.

Sara swapped the drinks.

"Don't call me!" Nakano continued tearfully. "I don't ever want to hear your voice again!"

"Babes—" Duke began.

Nakano turned and rushed out of the lounge, crying into her hands. Duke remained, looking stunned.

"*Good*," Angel said. "*Now offer a toast, Sara.*"

"Wow, what a mess," Sara said, drawing Craig's attention back to the table. She laughed. "Hope I don't have to throw my drink at *you*."

Craig tugged at his coat. "Nah, of course not."

Sara raised her glass, inviting a toast. "To no more messy breakups."

"I'll drink to that," he said, clinking their glasses together.

Sara lifted the glass to her lips and drank, and Craig followed suit. Sara drank deeply, and he matched her with a surprised look.

"Don't drink that too fast," he said when they both put their glasses down.

"I'm tougher than I look, Craig," Sara said with a sly smile.

They chatted for about half an hour longer. Craig started to look pretty rough about fifteen minutes in, and by the time the two were nearly finished with their drinks he had to excuse himself to the bathroom. We all waited on edge. When he didn't come back in five minutes, Cy left to go check on him. He swung by Sara's table, and she surreptitiously passed him her purse.

"*He down,*" Cy said. "*Cloning da card and planting da bug now.*"

"*Perfect,*" Angel replied. "*Everyone, return to the rendezvous point. Let's get out of here.*"

Freed, Cy and I immediately went to Sara's table. We didn't even care if we were seen. Cy put his cybernetic arm around her trembling shoulders and we walked her out, Tatiana and Duke following close behind.

Angel, Malia, and Nakano were waiting at the van when we returned. By now, Kepler's sun had set, and Angel's silhouette was stark against the light of the van's interior. Nakano was the first to approach, pulling a visibly shaking Sara into her arms. "I'm so sorry, love," she said.

Sara sobbed into her shoulder.

We all crowded around her, taking turns holding her close. When she was in my arms, crying into my shoulder, all I could think about was the night ten years ago when Cy and I hauled Robbie Mattias out of the bar and kicked the shit out of him in the street, after Angel told us he'd tried to corner her on a job. I was so angry, I had half a mind to pull Cy in for a repeat performance.

Sara was calming down by the time I gave her a final squeeze and let her go. Cy held her next, his body so big that his embrace almost entirely enveloped her. "I going give that faka dirty lickins," he growled.

"Don't do that," Sara said, sniffling into his human bicep. "It won't make me feel any better. And he might call the cops, put them on our trail. He's already tasted his own medicine, it's better to just let it go."

"What if I drained his IRA and donated it to a crisis center?" Malia offered.

"That might make me feel better," Sara sniffed.

"Sara," Angel addressed her.

We all looked up at Angel, who until now had said nothing. She stepped down lightly from the raised van and approached Sara. Sara slipped out of Cy's arms, wiping her eyes. Angel met Sara's gaze, her expression inscrutable.

"You did a good job," she said. "I'm sorry I put you in harm's way. I didn't know that would happen."

"It's okay, you couldn't have known," Sara said.

"But I should have," Angel replied, so adamant it surprised me. "I'm the mastermind. It's my job to keep you all safe."

Sara smiled. And even through her running mascara, it lit up her whole face. She closed the gap between her and Angel and threw her arms around her shoulders, holding her tight. Angel stiffened in her embrace, but after a moment she relaxed and hugged her back.

"It's okay," Sara said. "Thank you for helping me get out."

Sara let Angel go, and Angel stepped back. She composed herself in an instant, straightening her blazer and schooling her face into her characteristic calm. "Good job, all of you," she said. "Go get some rest—I'm sure we all need it."

I touched Sara's shoulder. "Can I walk you home?"

Sara smiled. "I'd like that."

We started down the sidewalk. We passed Cy and Angel debriefing. Past Tatiana and Malia, who were crowded around Malia's laptop, searching for crisis centers on Kepler. Past Duke, whose face Nakano was dabbing with a handkerchief. "Did you really need to throw the drink?" she grumbled.

"Sorry, babe," Nakano said, though there was amusement in her eyes.

Ordinarily, we all took separate paths to and from the hideout. I didn't know where anyone lived, other than Cy, who had lived in the same apartment with his family all our lives. Sara directed me to a tower in Ward 2, which used to be home to the Garment District, where Cy and I would run errands for his tūtū. Sara told me it was transformed into a massive Atlas Industries warehouse about three years ago.

On the way home, Sara filled me in on some of the details between the lines of her dossier. She grew up in Ward 2, like me. Her mom sank all their credits into her gymnastics career in a bid to improve both of their lives. She had a hard-ass gymnastics instructor, who taught her that the sport was all about failure—all practice, all day, until you didn't fail any longer. She told me a friend confided in her about their coach's abuse, and after he made a move on her too, she blew the whistle and ended up on a blacklist—like me. She took a job at Venus after her endorsements fell through, because at least there she got to dance. She told me it was all worth it though, to seek justice for the other girls. That was what she really wanted out of this job: justice. The money helped, of course. When this was over, she wanted to spend her cut on opening her own line of gyms, the first in her old neighborhood. Her dream was over, but someone else's might begin there.

I listened all the way. It reminded me that all of us were here for different reasons, but all of us had a stake in this job. It reminded me that it wasn't just me and my family who would benefit, but families all across the station. All across the galaxy, if some of us had our way.

Sara had failed all her life, but it only prepared her to succeed. I only hoped that I could be a part of that and make this whole shit show worthwhile.

Chapter 14

WHEN I WALKED INTO THE HIDEOUT ON THURSDAY, IT WAS TO A COMpletely different room. Someone had rearranged the furniture while we were out—the tables had been pushed to the outer edges of the room, while the chairs and sofas had been arranged into a rectangle in the center, the leather cushions laid across the floor within. It reminded me of Casey's pillow forts.

I was standing at the edge of it, puzzled, when I heard the doors open behind me.

"Ho," Malia said, "you been busy, cuz?"

"Not me," I said, turning toward her. "Thought it might've been you."

"Why, 'cuz I'm the youngest?" Malia feigned offense. "You ageist, brah."

I shook my head. I dropped my bag on one of the armchairs and circled the fort. Malia perched on the back of a sofa, surveying the room.

"I bet you could do a flip onto those cushions and not hurt yourself," Malia said.

"Probably," I replied.

"I bet *you* could do a flip onto those cushions and not hurt yourself," she prodded.

"No," I said flatly.

"You not sked, are you?"

"No," I repeated.

"Would you do it for twenty credits?"

I considered it. Twenty credits could buy me a bodega haul and some cigarettes. It was tempting, I had to admit.

"Any particular reason the hideout looks like a fight club?"

I glanced behind me. Duke was strolling into the hideout, Nakano on her arm. She looked amused.

"No ask me," I said. "I have no clue."

Nakano approached the ring curiously and Duke moved to stand beside me. "You trying fo' scrap me?" she asked.

"What would I even scrap you for?" I asked her, annoyed.

"Your femme's honor," Nakano supplied.

"Two butches enter, one butch leaves," Malia said, voice pitched low.

I didn't have a femme, and I hadn't had one for a long while. I realized that the closest I had was Angel, but I crushed that thought into the darkness of my subconscious.

"Oh!"

We all turned toward the entrance, where Sara was standing in the doorway with a tray of coffees in each hand. She blinked her big green eyes and looked between us. "What's this for?"

I shrugged. "It was like this when we got here."

Sara placed the coffees on a table and approached the fort. She tested the cushion with one of her high-heeled feet, then looked up at me. "Is this a test from Angel?"

I frowned. "Why are you asking me?"

"You just seem closer to her than we are," Sara explained.

"That's one way to put it," Duke muttered.

"What's that—"

"Oh good, you here."

We turned back to the other side of the room, where Cy stood with his arms full of protective padding.

"You do dis?" I asked him.

"Yeah," he answered, crossing the room to dump the padding on a table. "Today's training day."

"Training?" Duke repeated, raising an eyebrow.

"Not fo' you, cuz." He jerked his head toward Sara and Malia. "Fo' dem."

"Me?" they both responded.

"You need to know how to protec' yoself," he explained. He gave Sara a stern look. "Las' night proves dat."

"But I had all of you," she replied.

"But what if nevah have us?" he challenged. "Den what?"

Sara tucked a loose lock from her braid behind her ear. "I don't know."

"And you—" He turned his sharp gaze on Malia. "What you going do if you no moa one computer?"

"First mistake: thinking I no moa one computer. You forget, brah, I get one up here," she replied, tapping her temple. "Second mistake: thinking you no can hack anything and everything." Malia grinned, sinister. "With the GhostNet, I never unprepared."

"What dat going do in one scrap, eh? You going DDoS me?"

I laughed. "You even know what a DDoS is, cuz?"

He shot me a glare. "Do *you* know what a DDoS is, cuz?"

I blinked. "Uh."

Cy narrowed his eyes. "Dat shit no work on me, das all dat mattahs."

I put up my hands.

"What about her?" Malia objected, gesturing at Nakano. "Why doesn't she have to train?"

"Because I've been practicing jiu-jitsu for ten years," she answered simply. Malia and I blinked at her. She shrugged. "It's in my dossier."

"She's multitalented like that," Duke said fondly.

"Anyway!" Cy said. He toed off his shoes and entered the makeshift ring. He gestured for Sara and Malia to follow.

Sara carefully slipped out of her heels and left them at the edge of the ring. She stepped onto the cushions, bouncing in place to feel their give. She grinned. "It reminds me of a tumbling mat!"

"Das da idea." Cy looked past her at Malia, who was still in her perch. "Wazza mattah? You sked or someting?"

Malia stiffened. "I not sked."

"If you not afraid, den why you sulking?" I challenged.

Malia shot me a dirty look. "I not getting paid to get bus' up by my own crew."

"I not going bus' you up," Cy said, exasperated. "I going teach you how fo' bus' up somebody else."

"It'll be good for you," Nakano encouraged. "It's always good to have something you can rely on, should your tech ever fail."

Malia looked put out. "But—"

"What the hell is this?"

We all turned toward the door again, where Tatiana stood, pulling off her sunglasses. "Did Angel do this?" she directed at me.

"Why does everyone think I know what Angel's up to?" I grumbled.

Cy ignored me. He pointed at Tatiana. "You need dis lesson too, cuz."

"What lesson?" she asked.

"Self-defense," he said. "I going teach you how fo' bus' a buggah up."

Tatiana looked offended. "Why you think I need to learn self-defense?"

"No offense, but you no look like you been in one scrap."

"Never been in one scrap!" Tatiana echoed. She reached into

her coat pocket and pulled out a switchblade. She snapped it open. "I'll cut a bitch!"

"Good!" Cy said approvingly. "Das da spirit." He gestured for the three of them to enter the ring. "C'mon, we no have all day."

Tatiana looked ready to object. But then Duke said, "C'mon, it'll build character."

"You sound like my dad," Tatiana grumbled.

"Is your dad always right too?" Duke asked with a grin.

Tatiana let out a long-suffering sigh. Then she pocketed the switchblade and moved to the ring. Malia, however, remained on her perch. "You're not coming?" Tatiana asked.

"Nope," Malia answered. "You no can make me."

"I'll do a flip if you do Cy's lesson," I offered.

Malia paused, considering. Then she grinned and hopped off the sofa. She kicked off her shoes and entered the ring.

"First ting," Cy began, "is dat scrapping is da las' resort, only if oddah tings fail." He gave Tatiana a pointed look. "No go looking fo' one fight."

Tatiana shrugged.

"Second ting," Cy continued, "is dat you not going win a fair fight. Save fair fighting fo' da ring. Some buggah try someting wit you, you scrap 'em dirty kine. Now try find someting to scrap wit."

Sara picked up one of her heels and brandished it like a weapon. Tatiana wrapped her wallet chain around her knuckles. "Good!" Cy turned his attention to Malia. "Eh! What you going do now?"

Malia screwed up her face in concentration. Then the lights flickered and went out.

"Get 'em!" Malia yelled.

The room erupted into a cacophony of yelling, laughing, and blows landing. Only the dim light of the Ward filtered in through the plastic sheets, and I squinted in the darkness.

I could make out the hulking figure of Cy and three smaller women. One was swinging a cushion at his head. One was hanging off his arm. The last—the smallest—was climbing up his back. The whole pile of them shook and swayed, until with a roar Cy bucked all three of them off and they hit the ground with indignant cries.

I bus' laughing at the sight. It reminded me of the scraps I used to get into as a kid. Most of them I couldn't remember who started it, what started it. But it felt important back then. It was always me and Cy against the world, for as long as I could remember. He always had my back, and I always had his.

At least until Kepler System Penitentiary, I did.

The thought was sobering. We talked story while I was gone, but there were always holes in Cy's side of the story. He lost his papa, and his tūtū was getting older. He transitioned and upgraded, putting himself in debt for it. He got out of the business, only to be pulled back in. How much of his life was I gone for? How many opportunities to stand by him did I miss? But before I could dwell too long, the lights flicked on.

"What's going on here?"

I blinked in the light. Cy was in the middle of the room, trying to wrestle a pillow out of Sara's hands. Malia had her comm open. Tatiana was lying dazed on the floor. I turned to the entrance, where Angel stood in the doorway.

Busted.

"Cy's teaching us self-defense," Sara said cheerily. Cy let the pillow go and she stumbled backward with a yelp.

"Self-defense," Angel repeated.

Malia grinned. "We learned a lot."

Tatiana raised a thumbs-up from the floor.

"Well. If you could take a break from your . . . lessons, Cy, you should be receiving a phone call from recruitment any minute now," Angel said.

"Shoots," Cy replied. "We go clean up while we wait."

The four of them started clearing the floor of cushions and dismantling the ring. I hopped off the table to help, followed by Duke and Nakano. We were in the process of heaving a sofa back into place when Cy's comm rang.

We all went quiet as Cy opened the line. "Hello?"

"*Hello, Mr. Iwata?*" A low voice greeted him.

"Dis him," Cy answered.

"*Mr. Iwata, this is Adam Alba, of Atlas Industries Security. Do you have a moment to talk?*"

"Yeah, whaz up?"

"*Good. All of us at Atlas Industries were very impressed with your resume, and we all appreciated your attitude toward the work. We'd like to offer you a position in our organization.*"

"Ho, much mahalos!" Cy exclaimed. "I take 'em."

"*Excellent, I'll forward you the offer now. Your start date is tomorrow. Meet me at the front desk of the Ward 5 tower at 0800.*"

"Rajah dat."

"*I look forward to speaking with you again, Mr. Iwata. Goodbye.*"

"Aloha." He closed the line, then fixed us all with a grin. "I get one job."

The room cheered. Even Angel looked pleased. Though I couldn't be sure if it was happiness for her friend's success or satisfaction that her plan was working.

"We go celebrate," Cy said. "We go inu and get some pūpūs."

We all agreed heartily to that, though Angel declined. We put the furniture back in its place and packed up. Tatiana and Cy led the way, bickering good-naturedly about where to eat. Duke and Nakano followed, holding hands and laughing to themselves. Sara walked just behind them, finding directions on her comm. I brought up the rear, Malia jogging up to catch up.

"Eh," she said, pausing at my side. "You still owe me one flip."

I opened my mouth to protest, but she was already dashing forward to join the argument between Cy and Tatiana.

Fair's fair, I guess.

* * *

On Friday, Atlas called up Nakano for a meeting. Sans Duke.

Everybody else crowded around the screen in the hideout, watching through the button cam on Nakano's blouse and listening through our earpieces. This was Nakano's moment. Atlas was on the hook, it was just a matter of reeling him in. And with time in his office, she could give Malia access to the files on his computer—the personal files even Angel couldn't touch. It was a big deal. Duke and Nakano's whole con hinged on this.

"You got this babe," Duke encouraged. "Don't worry."

"*I never worry,*" Nakano teased. She climbed the steps up to Atlas Industries' Ward 7 tower and strode inside. "*Going in now.*"

Malia switched from Nakano's button cam to Atlas's security feeds. The inside of the tower was quintessential Ward 7 luxury. Bright tile floors, designer furniture, and a chandelier of hanging glass rods that refracted Kepler's light in rays across the room. Upon entering, Nakano shrank into character, walking uncertainly into the foyer.

Angel was there to meet her. Dressed in her uniform of a black pencil skirt and a flowing white blouse, her blond hair immaculately styled, she looked the picture of an exec. She extended a hand. "*Dr. Abe. My name is Angel Huang, Mr. Atlas's chief of security. It's a pleasure to meet you.*"

"*We met, briefly,*" Nakano replied. "*Though it's good to make it official.*"

Angel nodded. Wasting no time on pleasantries, she turned and walked with purpose toward the elevators. "*Mr. Atlas is waiting for you in his office. Please follow me.*"

Malia changed feeds to the camera in the elevator. There, the two women stood side by side. It was quiet for a moment, before Nakano asked, "*How long have you worked for Mr. Atlas, Ms. Huang?*"

Angel briefed Nakano before the meeting. Atlas had a habit

of listening in on the elevator in case his business partners talked stink behind his back.

"As a part of the company? Four years. As Atlas's chief of security? Almost two."

"That's quite a rise in rank."

It was. Angel told me that she took a job at Atlas Industries after college, but how she rose from entry level to exec in two short years, I had no idea. Whatever con Angel was pulling, it was definitely working.

"I had an apprenticeship, of sorts, with the previous chief of security."

Nakano gave Angel a sidelong glance. *"You seem very . . . hands-on."*

"Mr. Atlas likes to keep me close," Angel said neutrally.

"He must trust you to take care of things, then."

"You could say that."

Nakano gave Angel another glance. But before Nakano could press—and satisfy the group's collective curiosity—the elevator doors opened to the executive offices. Angel led the way and Nakano followed.

Malia shifted the feed to Nakano's cam as she walked. The executive offices were all clean white walls, expensive-looking art, and plush geometric carpet in shades of gray. Angel took Nakano to a door at the end of the longest hallway and knocked. A muffled voice called, *"Come."*

Angel pushed open the door and stepped inside, Nakano close behind. Atlas sat at a wooden desk—heavy, real wood—his back to a floor-to-ceiling window that let in the light and looked down on the Wards below. He turned away from the monitor on his desk and smiled. *"Dr. Abe. It's so good to see you again."*

"And you as well," Nakano replied. She clasped her hands in front of her. *"I wasn't expecting you to reach out, after . . ."*

Atlas waved dismissively. *"Don't worry about that. It's not the first time an offer of mine has been rejected."* He smiled again. *"And it's not the first time I've had to be creative about an offer."*

"Creative?"

Atlas leaned back in his chair. *"Dr. Abe. I couldn't help but notice that Clairvoyant wasn't meeting your needs. You have potential. I hate to see it wasted."*

"Thank you?" Nakano replied, her voice pitching up in a question.

"What if I told you that I could fulfill your potential? Here, at Atlas Industries. You would have the expertise of my team in R&D, all the funding you could ever need, and my full support. No restrictions, no strings."

Nakano paused, astonished. *"That's very kind, Mr. Atlas, but I'm afraid I'm committed to Kalei and Clairvoyant. I wouldn't be able to leave."*

"That's the thing," Atlas said, leaning forward on his desk. *"What if I could offer you a way out?"* He chuckled. *"Or a way in, so to speak."*

"I don't understand."

"Sell to me. You wouldn't be leaving Clairvoyant—Clairvoyant would be coming to us."

Nakano sucked in a breath. Through the camera, I saw the anticipation on Atlas's face. All of us watching in the hideout, we were feeling it too—leaning forward in our seats, completely silent, barely breathing. He was buying it. And Nakano was really selling it.

"What do I need to do?" Nakano said, finally.

Atlas sat back in his chair again, a relieved grin on his face. *"You and Kalei are partners in Clairvoyant, each of you with forty percent of the shares. If you could persuade a mere eleven percent of your shareholders to sell . . . well. There would be nothing we couldn't do."*

"What about Kalei?" Nakano asked, wringing her hands.

Atlas smiled. *"What Kalei doesn't know won't hurt her, will it?"*

"But I can't keep it from her forever—"

"Which is why we need to move fast. Faster than what is entirely customary. You find the votes, and I'll find the funds."

"*Where exactly will you find these funds?*" Angel interrupted.

Atlas tore his eyes away from Nakano to glare at Angel. "*I don't see how that's your concern.*"

"*It's my concern because I'm a member of the executive board. Same as you, Mr. Atlas.*"

Atlas stood abruptly. "*Then let's discuss, fellow member of the executive board.*" He rounded his desk and stalked across the room. "*Come with me.*"

Angel followed him out, leaving Nakano alone.

"You're up, sis," Malia said into her comm. "Now plant the keyboard recorder, just like I showed you." With it, Malia would have access to Atlas's passwords—and a way into his personal files.

Nakano reached into her purse and withdrew a small data chit. She moved purposefully across Atlas's office to his desk and plugged it into his computer.

As she did that, Malia glanced at us. Then, nīele as ever, she turned up the volume on Angel's feed.

"*—I represent the interests of the shareholders, same as you,*" Angel said. "*And I would be remiss to not express my concerns about this merger—*"

Atlas cut her off. "*Your concerns have been expressed and duly noted, Angel. Between the SSA investigation and the lawsuit, acquiring Clairvoyant is in our best interests. And as CEO—and founder, I might add—there is no one with greater investment in this company. No one more equipped than me to lead this company.*"

"*I'm not questioning your competence,*" Angel said coldly. "*I'm questioning your judgment.*"

"*There's no need to. I know the shareholders, and I know what they want. Besides—*" Atlas's voice suddenly became closer. "*It's better to ask for forgiveness than permission, isn't it?*"

My stomach turned with disgust. I could barely stand the man from afar. How Angel had managed to work under him for four years, I had no idea. It made her plan make a little more sense, at the very least. In the beginning, she asked me whether I wanted to destroy a man like Atlas. At the time I said no. But the more time I spent on this con, the faster I came around to the idea.

The line was silent for a long time. Even through the transmission, I could sense the chill in the air.

"*I thought so,*" Atlas said, smug. His voice retreated. "*Someday you'll learn not to question me. I look forward to that day.*"

Nakano was standing right where they left her when Atlas and Angel reentered the office. Atlas smiled at her broadly. "*Well? What do you think?*"

Nakano took a shaky breath. Then she said, resolutely, "*I'll do it.*"

"*Excellent!*" Atlas crowed. "*Then we have an agreement!*"

Angel said nothing.

"*Get me eleven percent of the vote, and I'll take care of the rest,*" Atlas said. "*Are you available next Saturday?*"

"*I can be,*" Nakano replied.

"*Good. Meet me here at 2000. Atlas Industries is hosting a charity gala for the Outer Worlds Cultural Fund, I'd love to talk to you more. Perhaps you can show me some of your research findings.*"

"*That sounds wonderful, thank you.*"

"*The pleasure is mine, Dr. Abe,*" Atlas said, a warm smile on his face. "*You're making the right decision, I can assure you.*"

"*Yes,*" Nakano said, and I could envision her sweet smile. "*I'm sure I am.*"

I was in charge of the kids that night. Andie went straight to bed after dinner, and the kids pleaded with me to stay up past their bedtime. Which I foolishly allowed.

Casey was already asleep on the couch, his cartoons still playing. I was sitting backward with my arm draped over the table, facing the kitchen. Paige sat beside me, busy at work with her markers. Fifteen minutes ago, Paige said that my tattoos were nice but would look prettier with color. I challenged her to do better. So now my thirteen-year-old niece was turning the spiderweb on my elbow into a rainbow.

Served me right, I guess.

"Why did you get this?" Paige asked as she colored in the center of the web.

"I got it in prison," I explained. "Means I've been there for a long time."

"That's depressing," she replied.

"Well, it's a prison thing. Lots of people have them."

"So you got it because everybody else had one?" she said, incredulous.

"No," I said, only slightly defensive. "I got it because it's important to me. It shows where I've been, what I've been through. Who I am because of it."

"Hm." She seemed to accept that.

"And I thought it'd make me look cool," I added. Paige snorted, which made me grin.

"I want to get a tattoo," she announced.

"Oh yeah?"

"I want a tattoo like the Eluin in *Spirit of the Forest*."

"That's the one with the talking dragon, yeah?"

"Not all fantasy has dragons in it, Aunty," she said, exasperated.

"Sorry, didn't mean to stereotype."

"Eluin have tattoos all over their bodies," she explained, exchanging her purple marker for a green one. "And they use them to activate their spirit magic."

"And you want one just like them?"

"Yeah."

"I'm sure your mom will love that."

"Mom says I need to wait until I'm eighteen," she said, and I could sense her rolling her eyes. "But I'm already a teenager."

"Thirteen," I corrected.

"It has *teen* in the word," she replied irritably.

I laughed. "And you can't wait until you're eighteen?"

"No."

"Why not?"

"Because I might not make it to eighteen."

I felt a jolt of pain go through my heart. She said it so matter-of-factly, it shocked me. Whenever I thought about Paige's treatment, I thought about it in the context of finding her better care, or paying off the debt when she was better. I never let myself think about what might happen if it didn't work.

"You don't really think that, do you?" I asked softly.

Paige shrugged. "It's better to be realistic."

I shifted in my seat. Better for whom? I wondered.

"But isn't it scary?" I asked.

"Of course it's scary," she answered. "But I don't like being lied to."

". . . Yeah, I get that."

Paige was quiet for a moment while she sat back to scrutinize her work. Satisfied, she went back to coloring. "I don't want to die," she said plainly. "But if I do, I know that I'll be with Papa and Tūtū."

I felt another stab of pain go through my heart. I should have been comforted knowing that Paige would be with family, but all I could think of was the void she would leave in our lives, after the loss of both my parents.

"The ones we love are never truly lost," Paige said. "We find them every day, in every joyful memory."

I laughed. When did this thirteen-year-old get to be so wise? "That's profound."

"It's from *Way of the Sword*," she explained.

"*Way of the Sword*. That's the one with the talking dragon."

Paige smiled. "Yup."

"Listen," I said, twisting in my seat to face her. "You know I would do anything for you, right?"

Paige looked a little surprised. "I know, Aunty."

"I mean it. I'd do anything for you, and your mom, and your brother. Anything at all."

"Why are you telling me this?"

I paused. Why *was* I telling her this?

I passed my free hand through my hair and sighed. "I just wanted you to know."

In case something happens.

She smiled again. "I know, Aunty." She gestured for me to turn around again. "I'm almost done."

I smiled at her, then turned back around in my seat. Paige went back to work with her markers, filling in the gaps in the web with all the colors of the rainbow. At the end I looked like I'd been attacked by a lesbian black widow, but I didn't tell Paige that.

It was slow in the shop the next day. Paige lent me one of her books—foisted it into my hands when I complained about being bored—which I was surprisingly grateful for. The writing was nice, and I could get behind the main character. Didn't think the book needed so many people on the family tree at the beginning, though.

I was leaning back in the chair behind the counter when the bell on the door rang. I glanced over the edge of the book. Filing through the door were three haole guys in shades and pressed suits. They were more than a little out of place crammed between the aisles of our Ward 2 shop.

I had a bad feeling about this.

I set the chair back on its legs and closed the book. "Can I help you?"

One of the haole guys flipped the switch on our neon sign. The word Open flickered and died.

I had a *really* bad feeling about this.

I was about to say something when the wall of haole guys opened to let someone pass through. She was an older woman dressed in a sharp pantsuit, with crisp creases and shiny black patent leather heels. Her brown hair was pulled back into an immaculate bun, graying at the temples. She had sharp brown eyes and light skin, and her expression was no invitation for bullshit.

"Can I help you?" I asked again.

The woman smiled. "I certainly hope you can."

My eyes flicked between the woman and the three haole guys. My mom made my dad put a bat under the counter in case there was ever a robbery, and as far as I knew it was still there. But I was never the hitter in a crew, and I doubted I could take down all three of these guys. And I didn't know if they were armed.

"Who are you?" I asked.

"I'm Special Agent Leah McKay," she said, showing the badge pinned to the inside of her blazer. "System Security Administration, Financial Crimes Division."

Feds.

Fuck, I was really in it now.

I had no clue how the SSA found me, let alone how the SSA connected me to Angel and her heist. But here they were, standing in the place I always felt the safest. It felt violating, in a way. Was this what I'd invited into my life? My family's life? Did I just ruin the fragile peace we'd been living in, destroy the last shred of normalcy we had? Ended it all, on Angel's word?

No, I couldn't let it go down like this. I couldn't let it end this way.

My hands tightened into fists at my sides. Time to lie my fucking ass off.

"What do you want with me?" I asked.

Agent McKay regarded me coolly. "Mx. Morikawa, as I understand it, you're a felon on parole. What was your crime?"

"Shouldn't you already know that?" I said through my teeth.

"I'd like to hear it from you."

I let a cold beat of silence pass. "Grand larceny, breaking and entering, trespassing, fraud, assaulting a police officer, and obstruction of justice. Tack on some time for bad behavior, and you get eight years of prison time."

"And violation of your parole," Agent McKay added.

"I'm sorry?"

"Associating with known criminals," she said, matter-of-fact. "You've been in contact with Angel Huang."

"Angel's not a criminal, the charges were dropped."

"That's true. At your expense, no less."

"You still haven't answered my question: what do you want?"

Agent McKay wandered through the aisles, taking in all the tidy shelves as if she were browsing. "The last time you and Angel Huang were seen together, it was in conspiracy to defraud and steal from Joyce Atlas. Just like you defrauded and stole from countless others." She shifted her gaze back to me. "I believe that old habits die hard."

"What's your proof?"

She shrugged. "I have none."

"Then you should leave," I growled.

"Let me explain: Joyce Atlas has been defrauding his investors for years, and Angel Huang has been covering his tracks. The case is not against you, it's against them."

Of course it was about his investors. It was always about the big money. What did the SSA care about the people with Atlas's boot on their necks? Nothing at all, as long as the money kept flowing. But when Atlas fucks with his investors . . . that's when they care.

So, what did I owe them?

I scoffed. "What do I care?"

"I also understand that your family is in a significant amount of medical debt. To the tune of thirty thousand credits. *And* you're three months behind on rent payments." Agent McKay tutted. "It's not a good look to have debt collectors constantly calling."

"Why would the SSA care about my family?"

"The SSA values its informants," she explained. "Whatever we can do to keep them safe and secure . . . well. Let's just say we have a lot of sway in the financial world."

Informant. It sounded like a dirty word. But like a kid learning dirty words, I wasn't sure what it would entail. And I couldn't contain my curiosity.

"What would you even want from me?" I asked cautiously.

"You have access to Joyce Atlas's personal records. With those, we could build a case against Atlas and Huang."

"But why me, specifically? You could have contacted anyone else."

She smiled. "Because you're motivated."

Safety and security. I could admit that it was appealing. No more begging the landlord for another month's grace. No more relying on charity. No more debt collectors calling at all hours. How good would it feel to have that lifted from my back? And all without falling back into my old life, my old habits. I could go straight. I could leave Angel and her betrayal far behind me. I could move on.

But I couldn't. I couldn't turn on the crew like that. I wasn't a snitch.

As if she could read my thoughts, Agent McKay interrupted. "If that isn't enough incentive, perhaps this might motivate you: I understand that your sister, Andrea, is in quite the tough spot. Splitting all her time between two jobs, a baby on the way, putting food on the table, watching the children, maintaining the house . . . It makes one wonder, is she really the best person for them to be with right now?"

A snarl split my face. "Andie's not involved. This is between you and me."

"I think this is far beyond just you and me, Mx. Morikawa."

In all my time in the business, I'd managed to keep Andie out. I never wanted to drag her into this life, never wanted her to be in harm's way. It was my greatest fear, even beyond getting made and going to prison.

But was this an empty threat?

I searched Agent McKay's face for any clue, any tell, but found nothing.

"Whatever you're planning with Huang, it won't succeed," Agent McKay said. "And I can promise you, *when* you're caught, you will be prosecuted to the fullest extent of the law. And there will be no possibility of parole, not this time."

Suddenly, it felt like the walls were closing in around me. I was done being threatened.

"I think we're done here," I said, voice low.

Agent McKay sighed. "Very well." She touched her comm, and mine beeped in acknowledgment. "I'm giving you my number, should you ever find yourself in trouble and more amenable to talking."

The haole guys filed out of the shop, leaving Agent McKay. She studied me one last time: "Think carefully, Mx. Morikawa. You have time now, but that time will run out eventually."

She flipped on the switch of our Open sign and let the door close behind her with a jingle.

I dropped my head into my hands and groaned. Fuck everything about this. How did the SSA find me? How did the SSA connect me to Angel? At least I knew better than to spill my guts or lose my cool, especially when they had no evidence connecting me to the heist. The other threats, I wasn't so sure. Big money was involved, and the full weight of the SSA was behind this investigation. Fucking over a nobody like me? It would be easy. I couldn't be sure whether this was all a bluff.

For 125 billion credits, I had to bank on it.

I'd been so careful all this time. Never taking the same

route to the hideout twice, keeping my interactions with Angel short in public, keeping up appearances with the shop—I didn't know where I'd made the mistake.

I thought of what Tatiana said to me, about the uncertainty around my place on this job. Would Angel forgive this mistake? I couldn't be sure. And this was my one shot at everything I'd ever worked for. My one shot at the life I'd always wanted. I couldn't lose it now. I couldn't throw away that chance in exchange for a simple existence like the one Agent McKay offered me. Not when I was so close to something more.

I couldn't tell Angel. I had to figure this out on my own.

I closed the shop early and turned off the lights.

Chapter 15

"WHY DON'T I GET TO DRESS UP?" MALIA WHINED.

Atlas's charity gala was in two hours, and each of us were in various stages of getting ready at the hideout. Angel wanted all hands on deck for this part of the job, but not all hands were getting a fancy dinner.

"I'll be right there with you," Duke said, sitting on the couch beside a sulking Malia. She laughed. "I'm on Atlas's shitlist, so I'm stuck in the van too."

"But you at least get to wear a suit," Malia argued, pointing at Duke's tasteful navy suit. "I'm stuck in my hacker-who-doesn't-see-the-light gear."

"At least you not service staff," Cy grumbled, straightening his tie. I laughed, and he shot me a glare.

"What happened to not wanting to be perceived?" I asked.

"On the *job*, yeah! I'm the Obake, I work my magic from afar." Malia scowled. "Doesn't mean I can't look good doing it."

"Nobody said you can't dress up in the van," Tatiana said, lining her lips in a deep wine red.

"And wear what?" Malia snapped back. "Angel didn't bother to buy me a fit."

"This!"

We all turned toward the front of the room. Sara was holding a dress bag, triumphant.

"What you got there, cuz?" I asked.

Sara crossed the room, a grin on her face. "Angel gave each of us some discretionary funds," she explained. "I wasn't going to use mine for anything, really, so I splurged a little." She offered the dress to Malia. "When I heard you weren't going to come with, I didn't want you to feel left out!"

Malia took the dress bag eagerly. She unzipped it, and her expression lit up with delight. She withdrew the dress and we all crowded around to see it: a black illusion dress of sheer tulle with a full skirt, embroidered with shining stars and shimmering galaxies.

"I thought I'd get you a full skirt, in case you need to run!" Sara said cheerily.

Malia fixed Sara with a grin. "Mahalo, sis! This is sick!" Then she looked somber. "I'm sorry for catfishing you on Sporty Singles."

Sara's eyebrows shot up. "Sorry for what, now?"

Malia frowned in concentration. "Now, how am I gonna do my makeup?"

"I can do it," Nakano volunteered. "Go get changed and I'll beat your face."

Malia leapt to her feet. "Try wait just a minute!" Then she dashed out of the room, the dress trailing behind her.

I grinned as she went past. Preparation for a fancy job always felt like prom night, and I had to wonder how Malia's compared. There was always a sense of excitement about the glamour, nervousness about the stakes, with the undercurrent of danger running through. Angel always liked these jobs—she loved to turn heads, break hearts. I liked them too. If only to witness Angel in her element.

"Edie."

I twisted around in my chair toward the entrance, where

Angel stood, looking expectant. "I need to speak to you," she said.

I stood, buttoning my coat. Duke glanced my way as I walked past. I had a brief moment of panic as I crossed the room—did Angel know about the SSA contacting me? Would she say anything if she did? Or would she let me flounder in my own lies, until she finally cut me out?

I squared my shoulders and straightened my coat. If I had to lie, I'd do my damnedest to make it look good.

I followed Angel out of the common space and into an adjoining room she'd claimed as her own. Her things were laid out on a card table: expensive makeup, a change of clothes, and a long, shining silver necklace.

"I need to ask you something," she said, picking up her necklace.

Here we go.

Angel wore a red dress. It was long and fit to her slender curves. The fabric was vermilion silk, with long sleeves and a high neckline. Almost modest—save for the open back that went all the way down to the base of her spine.

I lifted my gaze. She was watching me over her shoulder, impassive.

"Help me with this," Angel directed, holding both ends of the necklace in her hands.

I approached warily. "I'll be engaged with Atlas and the other guests for most of the night," she continued. "I need you to be my eyes and ears on the ground."

I relaxed. That I could handle.

I threaded the hook on one end of the necklace through the eye on the other. I untangled the necklace as it ran through my fingers, lengths of silver set with dewdrops of crystal that cascaded down her back. My knuckles brushed Angel's spine and she shivered under my touch, almost imperceptibly.

"You're really letting me take the lead?" I asked.

"Not taking the lead," Angel corrected. "Executing my directions."

"Delegating? That's not like you." I grinned. "Must be getting lazy, A."

"Don't doubt my dedication to the job," Angel said. She turned to meet my gaze, her dark eyes burning with conviction. "I've been planning this for years. I would do anything to see it through."

"Sorry," I said, taken aback.

"I'll be in the meeting between Atlas and Nakano," Angel said. "You'll need to keep Malia and Tatiana on task while they gather the retinal scan and access Atlas's personal files."

"Oh, so I'm babysitting the teens." I paused. "What makes you think they'll listen to me?"

"They like you, but they don't respect you."

I frowned. "Thanks."

"Be authoritative with them. Be firm. Demonstrate that you're worth respecting, and they'll listen."

I considered that. I never had issues with Andie's kids, or any of my other nieces and nephews. But truthfully, I never really had to lay down the law like their parents did—I was the cool aunty, and it was a point of pride. Who knew that on this heist I'd learn what it meant to parent a teen.

"I can do that," I said.

Angel nodded. "Good. And of course, you're gathering Atlas's fingerprint—I trust you to do that on your own."

"Trust me?" I repeated. "You sure you're feeling all right?"

Angel looked annoyed. "I've never doubted your abilities, Edie. You're good at what you do—maybe the best. That's why I picked you. And I know that you'll do anything it takes to get the job done." She paused. "You've always been impossible, that way."

I was taken aback again. The teens didn't respect me, but

it was weird to think that Angel did. After all these years, she still did.

Maybe Tatiana was wrong.

"Thanks," I managed.

Angel checked the time on her comm. "I need to go inspect the security measures at the gala. Will you make sure everyone is ready and in position by 1900?"

"Yeah, I got it."

"Good." She looked up from her comm to meet my eyes. She held my gaze, her dark eyes searching mine. I didn't know what she was looking for. Hesitation, maybe? Nerves, maybe? She wouldn't find any of that. Like she said, I would do anything it takes to get the job done. In our good times, she called me too determined to lose. In our bad times, she called me too stupid to fail.

Where we were this time, I wasn't sure.

She must have found what she was looking for, because finally she said, "Good luck, Edie," and moved past me toward the door.

"You know me," I replied, watching her go. "Always lucky."

She paused in the doorway. "That's part of why I picked you too," she admitted. She gave me a last, parting glance. "Because we could use it."

Then she walked out of the room, leaving me in charge.

The charity gala for the Outer Worlds Cultural Fund was held in Atlas Industries' Ward 7 tower. In the years since its founding, the headquarters for the technology giant had gradually climbed up the tower. From the R&D labs housed in Ward 1, to the developer workspaces in Ward 5, to the corporate offices at the peak of Ward 7, upward until it took over the whole thing, pushing out the lesser businesses and cheap apartments that lived there before. A microcosm of what the corporation was doing to Kepler itself.

The lobby of the tower had been completely transformed overnight in preparation for the gala. Its bright tile floor was cleared of uncomfortable geometric furniture to make space for card, roulette, and craps tables covered in pristine red velvet. Dark curtains partitioned the space, and the walls were hung with lights. What hadn't changed was the chandelier of clear glass rods that caught the low light of the room.

If the space itself was spectacular, it had nothing on the guests within.

Everyone was dressed in the latest fashions of the inner worlds: pressed suits and long gowns of shimmering silk, cut tastefully to expose the wearer's skin. And it wasn't just the clothes that were trendy—the mods were too. Bioluminescent tattoos, subdermal LEDs, biofeedback jewelry. The whole crowd was a mass of light and color, shifting and changing with the whims of the guests.

Showing the guard my invitation on the way in, I felt like a liar. Dressed to the nines in a black suit threaded with strands of shining silver, I felt like I was wearing someone else's skin. Rattling the casino chips in my jacket pocket, I felt like a fraud. A fraud because the only way a lowlife like me would end up in a place like this was to lie and steal—there was no place for me here.

So that's what I was going to do: lie and steal.

Duke and Malia were in the van, parked a few streets over from the tower. Sara sat at the bar in a delicate pink dress with waves of soft chiffon. Tatiana was a few seats down, wearing a plunging halter dress of deep indigo, the shimmering fabric catching the light. The bartender was completely entranced by Sara—to the chagrin of the other patrons at the bar. Cy patrolled the upper floors, ready to run interference. I stood at a cocktail table at the back of the room. Angel was with the executive board and their wives, listening to a story from the chief operations officer. She stood beside an older man, maybe midsixties, with light skin, close-cropped gray hair, and a lined face. The group laughed, and he leaned close to speak quietly in her ear.

It made my skin crawl, though I couldn't say why.

I pushed it out of my mind. I said into my comm, "Everyone is in position. You're good to go."

"*Heard,*" Nakano replied. "*Making contact now.*"

I looked toward the front of the room, where Nakano ascended the stairs. She was a vision in white silk, her full skirts printed with blue chrysanthemums.

"*You look gorgeous, babe,*" Duke said, awestruck.

Nakano smiled. She reached into her clutch for her invitation, but Atlas quickly excused himself to meet her at the door.

"Dr. Abe," he greeted her with a kindly smile. Nakano looked up from her clutch, affecting pleasant surprise. "I'm so glad to see you."

"I wouldn't miss it for the world," Nakano replied. He gestured to the security officer checking invitations, then offered his arm. Nakano took it and followed him into the building.

"Can I offer you a drink?" Atlas asked. He chuckled. "It's on the house."

Nakano laughed politely. "I would love one."

"They're on their way to you, Sara," I said, just as Atlas stopped at the bar, in the empty space next to Tatiana.

"That's so interesting!" Sara said, swirling the straw in her drink. "Were you, like, the bartending valedictorian?"

"Not quite, but I would have been really close," the bartender said eagerly.

Atlas drummed his fingers on the bar top, looking annoyed. Tatiana twisted in her seat to give him a grin. "None of us have been able to stop him, it's been like this for almost an hour."

She lowered her voice, conspiratorial. "But maybe you have more pull than we do."

"You would be right," Atlas said. He leaned forward on the bar top. "Excuse me!"

Startled and scared for his job, the bartender excused himself from Sara and rushed to take Atlas's order. The other patrons jostled forward, trying to get their orders in as well. Tatiana fixed Atlas with another grin. "Thanks. Your help is always appreciated, Mr. Atlas." She extended her hand.

Atlas took her hand with a laugh. "Anything I can do."

"*Got his RFID*," Malia said.

Tatiana gave Atlas's hand a firm shake, smiling. Then she slipped off her barstool, drink in hand, and walked casually to my cocktail table.

"Nice work," I said. "Right according to plan."

"I know," Tatiana said breezily, sipping from her drink. "We only went over the plan three times on the way over."

I bit back a snarky comment. That wasn't how to gain her respect.

A few minutes later, Atlas guided Nakano to where the COO was still regaling the group with details of his trip to the luxurious beaches of Elysium, untouched by the pollution that drove us from Earth. But he shut up at Atlas's expectant look.

"This is Dr. Ella Abe," Atlas said to the group. "Sure to be one of the greatest minds in transhumanism of our generation."

Nakano blushed. "You're too kind."

I tuned out as Atlas went around the group, introducing the board. I was focused on Angel, and the man beside her. Atlas introduced her as "Angel Huang, my current chief of security." He gestured toward the older man. "And this is Raleigh Hodson, my previous chief of security and dear friend."

"Previous chief of security?" Nakano asked. Thank God for that, because I was burning with interest.

"Previous and first," Atlas said with a laugh. "Hodson was with me from the very beginning."

"And he's sorely missed!" the COO chimed in.

Hodson chuckled. "I miss the job, but retirement is treating me well. Besides"—he elbowed Angel—"I'm sure my successor is doing a fantastic job."

"She certainly tries," the CFO said.

I glanced at Angel. Her expression was stoic—unreadable.

"Her knowledge is irreplaceable," Hodson said. "It's not often you get perspective from someone on the other side of a security system." He laughed. "Hers was quite the introduction to the company."

Begrudgingly, I had to admit that I liked this guy.

"Yes, she certainly has a storied history," Atlas said, looking Angel up and down.

I felt hot under the collar. I hated this guy.

"Anyway!" Atlas clapped his hands. "I need to borrow the board for a moment. Would you all accompany Dr. Abe and me to the boardroom?"

"Of course, sir," Angel replied, putting aside her drink.

"Be ready to follow," I said to Tatiana.

The group of them made their way to the lifts together. The board took the first elevator, while Atlas, Angel, and Nakano took the second. Atlas held his hand to the sensor inside and pressed the button for the top floor, and the doors closed behind them.

"Go," I directed. Tatiana locked my gaze, then knocked back the last of her drink. "You cheeky little fucker—" I started, but she left the table before I could finish insulting her.

"*Truthfully, I was surprised to hear from you,*" Nakano said, their conversation coming in through the comm.

Atlas chuckled. "*You shouldn't be. You're an incredible woman, Dr. Abe.*"

"*Ugh,*" Malia said. "*What a creep.*"

"*I brought some of my research findings,*" Nakano said. "*I have them on my datapad—I'd be happy to show you.*"

The datapad was fitted with a scanner, courtesy of Malia. It would capture Atlas's retinal scan while he read the documents. Most of them were fabricated, also courtesy of Malia. But I certainly couldn't tell the difference.

"*I would love to see it,*" Atlas said. "*I hope you don't mind that my chief of security is with me—it's not that I doubt your legitimacy, it's that—*"

"*—she doubts my legitimacy,*" Nakano finished.

"*It never hurts to be cautious,*" Angel said evenly.

"*Right. Of course not,*" Atlas replied.

As the lift doors opened on the executive suites, Tatiana stepped into the lift on the bottom floor and touched her spoofed RFID to the sensor. The doors closed behind her.

"*If you'll follow me, Dr. Abe,*" Angel said. "*The boardroom is right here.*"

I heard the beeping of a keypad, then a door opening.

"*Thank you all for taking the time to meet,*" Atlas greeted the room. "*I'm so pleased to introduce you all to Dr. Ella Abe.*"

"*Hello,*" Nakano greeted the room timidly. "*I've brought some of my research findings. Here, let me share my datapad—*"

The conversation abruptly cut out.

"They're in the boardroom," I said. "No outgoing signals. Cy, if we don't hear anything from them in the next five minutes, swing by."

"*Rajah,*" he responded.

"*I'm at Atlas's office,*" Tatiana said.

"*I cover you,*" Cy said in response. "*My pahtnah stay on da west side.*"

"*Sweet.*" The door chimed as Tatiana pressed her hand to the sensor. "*I'm in.*" The door creaked open. "*Aight, if I were a multitrillionaire tech god, where would I hide a high-security safe?*" Tatiana mused aloud.

"*Hidden bookshelf is a classic,*" Malia said.

"What's he got in his office?" I asked.

"*Fancy desk, big bookshelves, haunted painting—*"

"*Haunted?*" Duke asked.

"*It's a pretty shoreline, but there's this big creepy cave in the middle.*"

"*Yeah, sounds haunted,*" Malia agreed. "*Like da kine on dat one ghost-hunting show.*"

"*Brushes with the Paranormal?*"

"*Das da one! I can show you the episode after if you want—*"

"Focus," I interrupted. "Check the floors. Any mismatched carpet? Uneven flooring?"

I heard the dull *thump* of high heels on carpet as Tatiana checked the floors. "*Ah! This bit sounds different.*"

"Check the carpet, it should have a seam."

"*Yup!*"

"Pull it up. The safe should be under there."

"*Ugh, I'm gonna wrinkle my dress,*" Tatiana grumbled. I bit back another snarky comment. Respect.

"*It's manual,*" Tatiana said. "*Looks like an Ironside 450. Who knew he was into vintage security.*"

"You familiar with it?" I asked.

"*It's a twenty-year-old model.*"

"So, no."

"*Not like there are many of these anymore, in modern times,*" she said, defensive.

I ignored her again. "Ironsides have an exploit," I said. "They have manual keys as a backup in case you forget your combination. It should be under a panel on the underside. It's easier to pick the lock than cracking the combination by feel."

Tatiana went quiet, and so did the others. I let the line stay silent. She had to pick the manual lock to get the safe open—a drill would be too loud, an autodialer too slow, and any visible damage to the safe would put Atlas on our trail. I would have preferred to crack it myself, but Angel trusted me as shot caller. At least for now. She never would again, if I blew it with my hubris.

We waited for another long minute. I heard Malia drawing in a breath to say something when the safe popped open and Tatiana crowed in victory. "*Got it!*"

"*Nice one, cuz!*" Malia said.

"Get to scanning," I said to Tatiana.

"*Aw, man,*" Tatiana said, accompanied by the sound of paper rustling. "*There's choke files in here, it'll take forever.*"

"Cy, swing by the boardroom and make sure Atlas is still engaged. If you need to, pull Angel aside and tell her something's wrong. Atlas is a nīele faka, he'll follow."

"*Shoots,*" Cy replied.

"*Ho,*" Malia said. "*Some of these files look like they're from early trials of AXON.*"

"*Why's Atlas keeping them separate from R&D, then?*" Duke asked.

"*Dunno,*" Malia replied. "*These aren't public record though, garans.*"

"Keep scanning," I directed.

"*Atlas wrapping up wit Nakano,*" Cy said. "*I going to you, Tati.*"

"*—I'm glad we could have this chat, Dr. Abe,*" Atlas's voice cut in. "*It was an honor to see your research.*"

"*I'm happy to share, particularly with like-minded people,*" Nakano replied.

"*Atlas's retinal scan is coming in now,*" Malia said. "*Nice work to you too, sis.*"

"*Shall we go back to the party?*" Atlas asked.

"*I'd love to,*" Nakano replied.

"Finish scanning those files," I said to Tatiana. "I'm getting in position."

I pushed off from the cocktail table and scanned the floor for a table in Atlas's path. My gaze settled on a poker table with two open seats, not far from the elevators. I picked up my drink and made my way over, moving smoothly between well-dressed patrons. A game had just started by the time I slid into one of the empty seats. I watched, though my attention was focused on the elevators in my periphery.

My ears pricked when the doors slid open.

The executive board filtered out of the first car. A moment later, the other three exited the elevator and moved deeper into the foyer, Angel subtly leading the group toward the card table I sat at.

"I'll run the files through our system," Angel said, turning to address the other two. "I'm sure everything will be in order, but—"

"—but it doesn't hurt to be cautious," Nakano finished, amused.

"Yes, if anything you've always been thorough," Atlas said, similarly amused.

Angel gestured at the poker table, where the current hand was just wrapping up. "I can meet you here after I've finished scanning the files, if you like."

Atlas moved to stand beside Angel, observing the game. He smiled. "That sounds like a fine idea, Angel."

As he spoke, he brushed aside the strands of necklace and spread his fingertips across the small of Angel's back. She didn't react.

I sat up straighter.

"Tell me when it's done," he said to her.

Angel shifted, removing Atlas's hand from her back. "Of course, sir."

She brushed past me on the way to the cocktail table where the executive board resumed mingling. I caught her eye as she left. There was determination smoldering in her dark eyes, the same I'd seen earlier that night.

Eventually she let her gaze slide off me, and she turned to the board.

Atlas chuckled from beside me. I turned my head to face him. He must have noticed my lingering gaze, because he gave me a conspiring look. "You hate to see her go, but love to watch her leave."

"*Oh, gross,*" Malia said.

A flash of anger went through me. If I didn't hate this guy before, I hated him now. How dare he treat Angel like that. How dare he touch her like that. I wanted to break his hand, but instead I forced a laugh. "You've got that right."

If I couldn't scrap him, at least I could kick his ass at poker. I'd always been a mean card player, and developed a reputation as a hustler while in prison. My dad taught me to play when I was a kid, and I couldn't count how many games I played with my uncles around the kitchen table. I was relying on that knowledge now, twenty years later. But the stakes had never been higher.

Atlas clapped his hands. "Shall we play?"

"The blind is one hundred credits," the dealer said.

Atlas whistled. "High stakes."

I smiled. "It's for charity, isn't it?"

He met my smile. Then he reached into his pocket and threw a one hundred–credit chip into the center of the table. There was no need to, he was a new player at the table. But I guess he needed an excuse to throw his money around.

The big blind fell to me. I tossed in two one hundred–credit chips. The dealer dealt our two hole cards, and we each took a peek. Mine were trash—the two of diamonds and the ten of spades—but I wanted to see firsthand how Atlas played. Feel him out first.

The player to my immediate left folded. The next called. The last raised by two hundred credits. When the bet came back to Atlas, he peeked at his cards briefly, then raised another five hundred credits.

My poker sensibilities were screaming at me to fold, but I was still on my reconnaissance mission.

"I call," I said, pushing in three one hundred-credit chips and one five hundred-credit chip.

The other two players folded, which was probably the sensible thing to do.

Atlas raised on the flop, turn, and river. I was lucky that Angel bought me so many chips—this man was going to break me. But I held out. Either he had pocket aces, or this was all a huge bluff.

When it came time for the showdown, I revealed my cards: a pair of twos. Atlas revealed his: a pair of fives.

Big fucking bluff.

But it paid off, because Atlas smugly gathered the chips in the pot and consolidated them with his pile. "I'm still impressed by your bravery," he said to me. "All you need is a little more luck."

I forced another laugh. "We'll see if it turns."

The next several hands were the same as the first, but this time I played more cautiously. Atlas played almost every hand and raised on almost every round. It was enough to bully most of the players into folding, and a few into leaving the table entirely. I managed to win back some of my losses on the hands that Atlas folded, but even so, Atlas had the lion's share of chips at his place. It took all my concentration to keep my head in the game, despite the peanut gallery chattering and offering commentary in my ear.

Another hand was being dealt when Angel's voice cut through the noise: "*Edie. I'm almost done running the files, I need Atlas's fingerprint soon.*"

"*Yeah, I'm almost out of here too,*" Tatiana chimed in.

Almost on cue, Atlas flexed his hand to check the time. "I think this will be my last hand." He smiled at the table. "Let's make it a good one, shall we?"

"*I hate this guy,*" Duke said.

"*Good thing we're robbing him!*" Sara said cheerily.

I smiled. "I'll give it a try."

The two players to my left put in the blind and big blind. The dealer dealt the hole cards and we all took a peek. I had a better start this time: the queen of diamonds and the eight of clubs.

The third player called. And, as he always did, Atlas raised. "Two hundred credits," he said, carelessly tossing two chips into the pot.

I considered my cards. "I call."

Surprisingly, the other players called too.

Atlas's smile broadened into a grin. "Good! Let's make it interesting."

The dealer dealt the flop cards: the eight of hearts, nine of clubs, and king of spades.

The first player on my left checked. The second checked. The third raised two hundred credits. Atlas, the smug fucker, raised another three hundred to make it five hundred.

"*The others will fold, if not now, then in the next round of bets,*" Angel said. "*Put the chip in the pot and fold.*"

I reached into my pocket. Malia had loaded a chip with a fingerprint reader—all I needed to do was get Atlas to touch it.

"I call," I said, putting five hundred-credit chips in the pot, the loaded one among them.

The first player called. The second folded. The third called.

The dealer dealt the turn card: the eight of diamonds.

My heart pounded. Three of a kind wasn't a bad hand. But my job wasn't to win, it was to get the chip in Atlas's hands.

The first player folded. The third player raised another two hundred credits right off the bat. Atlas, amused, called. I was about to fold, but the expression on the third player's face made me pause. His mouth was tight, and he kept checking his cards even while I considered my bet. He had a good hand. He must, if he was willing to raise against Atlas.

I needed to spook him.

"*Fold, Edie,*" Angel said.

"I raise," I said. "Five hundred credits."

"*Ho, shit!*" Malia and Tatiana said in unison.

"*What are you doing?*" Angel hissed. "*This is Atlas's last round, you can't beat him here.*"

"Taking some risks, are we?" Atlas said, taking in my shrinking pile of chips.

I smiled back, resisting the urge to bare my teeth. "What's life without a little risk?"

The third player glanced at his cards again. Then he called. The bet came back to Atlas.

Atlas peeked at his cards again. He raised his brows, then tossed a one thousand–credit chip into the pot. "I raise."

"*How much is in that fucking pot?*" Duke asked.

"*Six thousand one hundred credits,*" Malia answered instantly.

The bet came to me. Atlas was watching, amused interest in his electric-blue eyes. I kept my face impassive as I checked my cards again.

"I'll call," I said, throwing another chip into the pot.

The third player called.

"*Edie, I'm ordering you to fold!*" Angel said sharply.

I ignored her.

By now a small crowd had gathered around the table. The executive board were gathered around Atlas, Tatiana, Sara, and Nakano beside me.

The dealer dealt the river card: the queen of hearts. I fought to keep my hands steady and kept my face impassive.

The third player checked. Atlas kept his eyes on me as he threw three thousand–credit chips in the pot. "I raise."

"I call," I said, stacking my chips.

"*Edie!*" Angel snapped.

Atlas chuckled. "Most people would be intimidated."

"By what?" I asked.

"By me." He leaned forward on the table, looking at me askance. "But you're not."

I met his eyes. "I'm not afraid of much."

"Yes, you seem like someone who contends with danger."

I held his gaze. Then I stacked two more chips on the pile and slid it into the pot. "I raise, two thousand credits."

The third player folded.

Atlas laughed outright as he threw two more chips into the pot. "You really think you can win?"

I could almost hear Angel's voice in my head. I wondered what she would say to me now—too determined to lose, or too stupid to fail?

"You don't have the nuts," I said.

"*The nuts?!*" Malia screeched.

I showed my holding. "Full house, queens over eights."

"Yo!" Tatiana exclaimed from behind me.

A slow smile spread across Atlas's face. My palms were sweating in my fists.

He showed his holding: two pair, kings high.

"*Yooooo!*" Tatiana crowed. The crowd lightly applauded.

Atlas chuckled. "Lucky."

"Always have been," I said.

I reached for the pot, plucking the loaded chip from the pile. Atlas watched my hand as I made it walk across the tattoos on my knuckles. Then, I flipped it in his direction. "A consolation prize."

Atlas caught it in his hand. Then he turned it over between his fingers before handing it back to me. "This is a charity gala, but not for me."

"*Got the fingerprint*," Malia said gleefully.

I expected Angel to scream at me over the comm, but she was notably silent. The click of high heels drew my gaze over Atlas's shoulder, where Angel was approaching with a datapad in hand. Her face was an icy mask. "I have the files for you, sir."

"Thank you, Angel," Atlas said. He gave her a long once-over, then smiled at me. "As you can see, I don't need luck."

I felt a flush of heat spread beneath my collar.

Atlas tipped his glass toward me, inviting a toast. I wanted to smash my glass over his head. But I swallowed down the rage building in my throat and touched the rim of my glass to his. "To your continued prosperity," I said.

Atlas laughed. "And to yours."

He rose from the table, then gestured for Nakano and Angel to follow. "Let's go review those files."

Sara and Tatiana immediately closed in, grins on their faces. "Let me help you carry that," Tatiana said as she scooped up piles of chips and loaded them into her purse.

Sara, Tatiana, and I made our way to the front of the foyer. I cashed out: over sixteen thousand credits. Even split among the eight of us, it was enough to cover a month's rent.

As the attendant swiped my credit chit to transfer the money to my account, I swept my gaze across the gala, taking it all in before I left. The opulent decor. The beautiful clothes. The indulgent mods. I didn't belong here. But at that poker table, I felt like I did. I felt like I *could* belong here, if only I had a way in.

As the reader chimed and the attendant handed back my chit, I knew that I wanted to, more than anything. And I would do anything and everything to get there.

Even if it meant lying to Angel, just a little longer.

"Everyone, meet at the rendezvous point," I said into my comm. "Hold until Nakano, Cy, and Angel can join us. We'll debrief then. Good job, everyone."

"*And you too, cuz!*" Malia said over the line. "*That was sick!*"

"Yeah!" Tatiana agreed. "We knew you had it in you!"

I bit back another snarky comment. If I had their respect now, I would lose it then. But even so, I grinned as they broke into chatter over comms. I remembered when I was young, breaking into the business for the first time. I remembered being the kid of the crew, the young upstart with something to prove. I remembered being hungry for more—riskier jobs, bigger payouts, higher profiles. And through it all, Angel was at my side.

I wondered what those kids would think of me now, after my first job as mastermind.

Chapter 16

IT WAS LATE WHEN WE GOT BACK TO THE HIDEOUT. WE FILTERED IN OVER the course of an hour, after the charity gala ended. Duke and Malia were first to arrive, followed by me, Tatiana, and Sara. Nakano came next, and Cy and Angel would be last after closing the gala and debriefing the security team.

We changed into our street clothes, but the excitement of the night remained. The team chattered animatedly the whole time, the teens most of all. I didn't know how to feel. The adrenaline high had worn off, and I was left with the uncertainty of how Angel would react to my off-script play. I wasn't sorry, I knew that, but I wasn't sure if the tension in my body was due to my own defensiveness.

I got the print and walked away with sixteen thousand credits. Did it really matter how?

"And then Atlas was like, 'Do you also disrespect women, bro?'" Malia mimicked, pitching her voice low. "And Edie was like, 'Hell yeah I do!'"

I scowled. "I never said that."

"With your eyes, brah. You said it with your eyes."

I ignored her. "I don't know why he thought I was a scumbag."

"Because you look like a scumbag, E," Tatiana said, gesturing at my tattoos.

"I *don't* disrespect women!" I said, annoyed.

"When you're looking at Angel, you do," Duke said quietly.

I shot her a glare. "What the fuck is that supposed to—"

The sound of a door opening put a stop to the conversation, as Cy and Angel appeared in the doorway.

The team broke into applause.

Angel had changed back into her street clothes, businesslike as ever. She smiled, but even I could tell it was false. She strode to the front of the room and turned to address us. "Good job, all of you," she said. "Atlas is on the hook and will call Nakano for a final meeting soon. We'll break into the vault on the day he signs the papers for the merger. And with the biometrics secured, all we need to do now is wait."

"*And* we get to walk away with sixteen thousand credits!" Malia exclaimed. The crew broke into more applause, and Tatiana let out a whoop. Duke clapped me on the shoulder, and I grinned. Not a bad haul for my first job as mastermind.

Angel's smile turned into a frown. "I'm afraid that's not possible."

My grin slipped. "Wait, what?"

"I canceled the credit transfer," Angel explained. "It could lead Atlas to your accounts, and then to your identity. I couldn't risk this job on a small payout like this one."

"Small payout?" I repeated. "That was a month's rent, Angel!"

"Sixteen thousand credits is nothing compared to the payout at the end of this," Angel said, annoyed. "Be patient."

"*Patient?*" I repeated, my voice hot. The crew exchanged uneasy glances. "We're at the mercy of our landlord right now," I continued angrily, "and you expect me to just let this money go?"

"Yes," Angel said, coldly.

"You can't—"

"That's enough, Edie," Angel cut me off. "We'll discuss it more when we debrief. Alone." She swept her gaze across all of us. "Everyone else, get some rest. You all deserve it. I'll see you in the morning."

The others started gathering their things and filing out of the room, exchanging goodbyes. I remained, stewing in my anger. What the fuck was Angel's problem? I won those credits fair and square, there was no reason for anyone to suspect I was in on this job. And if Atlas did, it was easy to launder the money so it couldn't be traced—Malia could do that in her sleep. I felt like I was being punished—for going off plan, for disobeying her orders. If she trusted me before, she wouldn't trust me anymore.

She could punish me all she wanted, but this wasn't about me. This was about Andie and the kids, and keeping them off the streets. I wasn't sure if Angel was too consumed with the job to know that, or if she just didn't care.

Angel gestured for me to follow, and I left my things and followed her out of the room, ignoring Duke's pointed look.

We walked briskly to her room. I brushed past her, taking it all in. In the darkness of Ward 1's night, the only light that penetrated was the flickering neon of the signs outside.

My gaze was pulled away from the room and back toward the entrance as Angel slammed the door behind me. "Never, *ever* disobey me like that again," she snapped.

"Disobey you?" I barked out a disbelieving laugh. "If I obeyed, you could have blown the whole operation."

"I had everything under control."

"You weren't at that table!"

"I had everything under control," she said through gritted teeth.

"You like to think that, don't you?" I took a step toward her. "You like to think you've got everything under your control, everyone under your command. But you don't control me,

Angel, you never have." I took another step toward her. "And it drives you fucking insane."

She didn't move, staring me down. "We're not children anymore, Edie. I'm the mastermind now, and you'll do what I say."

"And you'll do what if I don't?"

"I'll cut you out."

"Is that the worst you can do?"

Her dark eyes smoldered in the low light of the Ward behind us. "You know it's not."

My face twisted in anger. "Fuck you, Angel."

"No, fuck *you*, Edie," Angel snapped. "Fuck you for dragging me into this life. Fuck you for playing with my feelings. Fuck you for everything you've put me through."

"You ruined my life for it," I said, my voice low.

"And what will you do about it?"

I felt adrenaline surge through my body, hot and wild.

I lunged forward, bracing my forearm across her neck and crowding her backward into the door, fast enough to knock the back of her head against the frame. She let out a startled gasp as I pinned her to the door, her eyes wide.

"You know what we do to snitches in prison?" I growled.

Angel's pretty face twisted into a snarl. "Are you threatening me?"

"Damn right I am," I snapped. "I ought to kill you for what you've put me through."

I could feel Angel's breath on my face, her pulse pounding beneath my grasp. "You're no killer," she said. "You never have been."

"I've changed, A. Prison changed me." I renewed my hold on her, and she sucked in a breath. "*You* changed me."

"Have I?" she asked. "Because I've been watching you, E, and you're the same person I've always known." Her eyes searched my face. "And I know you better than anyone else."

"I've been in prison for eight fucking years. You have no idea what I can do."

Angel met my gaze again, dark eyes blazing with defiance. "Then do it."

My heart pounded in my chest, my breath hot in my lungs. I'd never seen her like this—the blue ring of her mod cutting through the near black of her blown pupils, vermilion lips parted and her breath coming in pants, clutching my arm with her slender hands. I felt another surge of adrenaline, this one burning through my veins, lighting fires deep within me.

She gasped when I pushed her harder against the door, closing the gap between us, pressing our bodies together.

Then I kissed her. Hard.

And she kissed me back.

Just as hard.

Just as hungry.

I pressed our bodies closer, spreading her legs with my knee and hiking her skirt up around her waist. She moaned into my mouth as I ground my thigh against her. I felt the fires burning hotter, stoked by the way her body responded to my touch, hips rolling into the pressure between her legs.

She pushed my jacket off my shoulders. I shrugged out of it and tossed it to the side. She followed up by sliding her hands beneath my shirt, and I broke the kiss to pull it over my head. I threw it vaguely in the direction of my jacket. Her nails dug into my bare shoulders as I kissed her again. The pain made me ache in my jeans.

I smoothed one of my hands across her cheek, spreading my fingers through the blond hair at the back of her head. I made a fist, and pulled. She cried out in pain, her head tipping backward to expose her throat. I pressed my mouth to her neck, and I could feel her pulse racing beneath my lips. My heart was pounding just as hard, just as fast.

I sucked hungrily at the tender skin of her neck, raking my teeth across her throat, with the knowledge that her pale skin would bruise. The thought of leaving my mark on her sent a thrill through me.

I worked my way down her neck to her collarbone, then grasped the collar of her blouse and wrenched it open, popping seams and sending buttons scattering to the floor. I thought she might yell at me for it, but she only let out a thrilled gasp. My hand slipped into her open blouse, sliding down her chest and then into the cup of her black satin bra.

Her moans were becoming more urgent, her grinding against me more desperate. I could feel the heat of her skin, the rising and falling of her breath, the beating of her heart. Her body was telling me what it wanted, and mine was happy to give it every single fucking thing.

But that was how we always were—in sync, now more than ever.

I kissed my way down her chest, down her belly, until I was kneeling on the floor. I pushed her skirt up higher, revealing the garters holding up her stockings. Seeing them sent a bolt of heat straight through me, all the way down.

I slipped my finger into one of the bands and snapped it. She yelped in response. I snapped it a second time, and elicited a moan.

I reached up and hooked my fingers under the waistband of her panties. I drew them down her long legs and she stepped out of them, careful not to catch her heels on the lace. They were soaking wet. I'm sure I was in a similar state.

I smoothed my hands up her thighs, slowly, savoring the feeling of her nylon stockings that gave way to the softness of her skin. I kept my eyes on her face, her expression shifting from anticipation, to desperation, to frustration.

"Edie—" she said, an edge to her voice.

"Tell me you want it," I interrupted.

"Edie—" she said, even sharper.

"Tell me. You want it." I grit out.

Angel looked furious, the way she always looked when I teased her and went too far. It was funny then. It was hot as hell now.

After a long pause, she whispered, "I want it."

I dragged two fingers through her folds, drawing from her a breathy moan. They came away slick. "Again."

Her lip curled. "I want it."

She drew in a sharp breath as I eased my fingers inside her. "Louder."

She squirmed against my hand, seeking friction. Unable to find it, she ground out, "I want it."

"Now say it like you mean it, A," I growled.

"Just fuck me already, E," she snarled back.

I didn't need to be told twice.

I sat up on my knees, my fingers plunging into her as I pressed my mouth into her folds.

Angel cried out as I moved, mouth working and fingers stroking. She grabbed a fistful of my hair, and I grunted when she pulled. It didn't stop me, though. If anything, it made me want her more—more of her desperate moans, more of her pleading cries. She wanted it so bad, and I wanted it too. For so long. Forever, maybe. There were women before her—girlfriends and one-night stands and prison hookups. But it wasn't the same. Because this was Angel, *my* Angel. And I knew when she screamed my name, there was never anybody else.

She came hard against me, doubling over as her climax overtook her. I slowed my pace when she stilled, putting a hand on my shoulder to steady herself. I stood, then took a look at her face. Her lipstick was smeared, her hair tangled, her eyes soft and unfocused. I kissed her, hard, wanting her to taste herself on my mouth.

Gradually she came back to her senses, and she kissed me back. I grunted in pain when she bit down on my lower lip. Before I could recover, her hands found my belt. With the deftness of a thief, she undid my belt and fly and slid her hand into my jeans.

I groaned into her mouth as her hand slipped into my underwear and between my legs. I teased her—but Angel wasted no time teasing me. Direct and to the point, as she always was.

I braced my arm against the door as she stroked me, breathing hard and fighting down a moan. I let it out in a curse instead. The fire inside me was burning hotter and hotter, enough to make the sweat stand out on my skin. It spread through every muscle, lighting up every nerve ending. My whole body tensed, my hand curled into a fist on the door, only for something to snap and the whole of me to come undone. This time I did moan—loud, guttural, shuddering, primal. I think I blacked out.

When the world came back to light, the first thing I saw was her.

Watching me with those dark, nearly black eyes.

We stood still for a long time, foreheads touching, just watching each other as our heartbeats slowed and our breathing fell into time. I could feel her soft breath on my face, the warmth radiating off her skin, her body trembling just slightly against me.

After a while she asked me, softly, "How long have you wanted to do that?"

"Since tenth grade," I answered. "I saw your tits once in gym. Haven't stopped thinking about it since. You?"

She paused for a moment. "I think I always knew it would be you and me, in the end."

"Well, now I feel like an asshole."

She actually laughed. "Don't."

We fell silent again, watching each other, listening to each other breathe. I realized then that these were the moments I missed the most. There was always laughter, always fights, but between them were thousands of little moments just like this one. Listening to music on the bus. Sharing lunch in the Common. Lying in silence on my bed. How many moments had we lost, over these past eight years? How many opportunities to do what we really wanted, say what we really meant?

"Why did you do it?" I asked quietly.

The question hung between us, heavy in the air. Angel kept her dark eyes on me, searching my face. For what, I didn't know.

"It doesn't matter anymore," she said to me. "What's done is done. All that matters is this job."

"And what happens after this job?"

"You do whatever you want. You'll be free of me, and I'll be free of you. We'll never have to see each other, ever again."

I didn't know why, but that hurt like hell.

"You never want us to see each other again?"

"Do you?"

I didn't have an answer for that. She was a part of my life for so long, I never got used to not having her in it. Not at all, in those eight years. The idea of Angel leaving my life forever—it sat strangely in my gut.

Taking my silence for an answer, Angel put her hands on my shoulders, pushing me off her. I stepped backward out of her space, standing dumbfounded as she pulled up her panties and straightened her clothes.

I blinked out of my stupor as she picked up her coat and bag. "Angel—"

"There's nothing left for us, E," Angel said. "Not anymore."

Then she left me in her room, shutting the door behind her.

Chapter 17

IT WAS DEEP IN THE EARLY MORNING HOURS WHEN I FINALLY GOT BACK home. I told Andie I'd be home late, but definitely not this late. She was disappointed—she hoped that we could have a movie night, just the four of us. I was disappointing her a lot, lately.

I opened the door to the dark apartment. As I toed off my shoes and headed toward my room, I realized I was starving. Too keyed up to eat at the gala, the last thing I ate was a bodega bento.

I made my way to the kitchen and opened the refrigerator. Inside, front and center, was a plastic container of chicken katsu with a note on top that read *Edie :)*.

A swell of affection washed over me, and a smile rose on my face. I took the container and quietly shut the fridge. I rummaged through the silverware drawer and picked out two mismatched chopsticks, then sank into a kitchen chair.

For a few minutes I ate in peace, my mind completely enraptured by the cold yet still-crunchy katsu. But as the growling of my stomach settled into a low grumble and I started to eat at the pace of a civilized human being, all the thoughts I'd tried to keep from my mind during the monorail ride home came creeping back.

I didn't know what to do about Angel. It was clear to me now that I wanted her, had always wanted her. What wasn't clear was what to do with that want. Every option felt too messy, too painful. I never expected to see her again after what she did to me, and I'd made my peace with that. Or as close to peace as I could get. I was ready to move on.

So what the fuck was I doing on her team?

My head sank to the table at that thought. What the fuck *was* I doing? A month ago, I had a fresh start ahead of me: released on parole, a possibility I'd never really entertained. And I threw it away on Angel's word. But what choice did I have? Blacklisted and indebted . . . There was nowhere else for me to go.

At least that's what I told myself.

Because after the fight, after the kiss, after the sex—I knew now there was a secret, deeply shameful part of me that always wanted her back.

The soft shuffle of tiny footsteps made me raise my head. Casey was standing at the other side of the table, a plush unicorn held in his arms.

"Hey, Casey," I greeted him. "What are you doing up? Couldn't sleep?"

He nodded his head.

"Nightmares?" He shook his head. "Too much sugar?" He shook his head. "Out being a superhero?" He giggled but shook his head. I thought about it a bit more, then my expression fell. "You weren't waiting up for me, were you?"

He nodded.

A wave of guilt washed over me, and I dropped my face into my hands. "I'm sorry, kid. I got caught up at my job."

Technically, I was fucking my boss—which only made me feel worse.

I peeked through my fingers at my nephew. Maybe I was projecting, but I thought I saw disappointment on his face.

"I'm sorry I haven't been around," I said. "I wish I could spend more time with you all."

Casey shrugged.

"Would you believe me if I said it'll all be worth it? That in a few weeks, we'll have all the time in the world? I'm going straight, Casey."

Casey smiled. Maybe I was projecting again, but it felt like he didn't believe me. And he was right not to, honestly. I was lying to his face. I was letting him believe that I had a job, that I was going straight, that everything was all right.

I hated to lie when I didn't have to.

What was my silent nephew going to say?

"I really am," I said. "After this last job, I really am."

Casey cocked his head, confused.

"Your mom said I was a bad influence on you," I continued. "I think she was joking, but maybe I am. The things I've done—the things I'm *doing*—I wouldn't want you to be like me either. But everything I'm doing, it's for all of you. And when it's done, I won't have to do it anymore. Your mom won't have to work anymore. Paige will get better. We won't have to struggle anymore. It'll all be worth it."

I said it for me as much as for Casey. I had to believe all of this would be worth it. I had to believe that the job would work out. That Angel's betrayal would stop hurting. That Andie's disappointment would fade. That the kids wouldn't grow up to be like me.

My head sank into my hands again. I cursed under my breath. I had to believe. I couldn't bear to think of the alternative.

"It's okay, Aunty," a little voice said.

I jerked my head up, looking toward the sound. Casey was still watching me, a sympathetic look on his face. "It's going to be okay," he repeated.

I stared at him. "You—you talked."

Casey moved to the kitchen table. He climbed into a chair beside me, plopping his stuffed animal on the table. "I wanted to."

"But what about your vow?"

Casey shrugged. "I think it's over."

"Because I told you my secret?" I asked, uneasily.

"No," he replied. "Because my wish came true."

Despite my roiling thoughts, I smiled. Of course it was a wish. "What was your wish?"

"That everyone will be together again," he explained. "You're here, and you said that Mom will stop working and Paige will get better. That's what I wished for."

My smile softened. "And you believe me?"

Casey smiled and nodded.

I'm not sure why, but that really got me. I lifted the little boy out of his chair and pulled him into my lap, holding him tight. Inexplicably, I laughed. My nephew trusted me, believed me, took me at my word. My nephew who had only met me once in his six years. My nephew who always seemed so happy to see me, even through a grainy feed. My nephew who loved me through miles and miles of distance and time.

I released him, then drew back to regard him somberly. "You won't tattle on me, will you?"

Casey shook his head vigorously.

"You'll keep that vow going, just for a little bit longer?"

Casey nodded vigorously.

I grinned and tousled his hair. "Thanks, kid. I'm gonna buy you a zoo of Plushie Pets."

Casey pushed his hair back into place. "I want the tiger first," he said.

"Done," I said. I gave him a final squeeze, then put him on the ground. I shooed him toward his room. "Go to bed, you need some sleep. I'm going to bed after I eat this."

"You promise?"

"I promise."

"Okay, Aunty." Casey picked up his stuffed animal and started toward his bedroom.

"I love you," I said to him.

"I love you too," he replied.

As the door shut behind him, I was left alone with my cold katsu again. But as I ate, my mind was at peace, and by the time I finished the food and put the container in the sink, the late hour finally caught up with me. I trudged to my room and dropped into my bed, and before long I was fast asleep.

I woke up early to spend the morning with Andie, Casey, and Paige. The kids and I handled breakfast, and even if the eggs were a little undercooked and the bacon was a little overcooked, Andie was appreciative. I told Andie I was picking up an extra shift today, but I would try to be home for dinner. Casey, to his credit, looked completely at ease keeping my secret. Kid could've made a professional liar. It was almost a shame we were getting out of crime.

I was last to the hideout. When I got to the common room, everyone was crowded around one of the card tables. I made my way over. The low conversation stopped when Sara spotted me, and she waved me over enthusiastically. "Edie!" she called. "Edie, we're playing poker!"

I grinned. Of course they were playing poker. "You know how to play?"

"Malia is teaching us!"

". . . Malia knows how to play?" I asked, incredulous.

"I do now," she said, tapping her temple.

"Shouldn't you be reviewing those files?" I asked.

"No worries, brah, I get 'em running in the background," she said. She gestured at her laptop, sitting on an armchair. The screen flickered as each of Atlas's personal files passed through it. It made me uneasy. I didn't think I would ever get used to that.

"One thing the Net can't teach you, though," Nakano said, drawing my eyes back to the card table, "is how to play the social game."

"You're not supposed to bet on every hand," Duke grumbled.

"It's more fun that way!" Tatiana protested.

"All right, well, move over and I'll teach you," I said.

It didn't take too long to figure each of them out. I already knew that Cy's cybernetic eye started to twitch when he had a good hand. Tatiana bet on every hand—she argued that it threw people off—but it was easy to call her bluff when she bounced her leg under the table. Malia was a little more reserved but had a tendency to bet big with a middling hand. Sara was a timid player, so when she bet, it was easy to tell that she had a good hand. Duke and Nakano were more difficult—I couldn't find their tells, and their bets were more reserved. Where they stumbled were the odds, which only took practice.

I robbed them all.

After a few hands, the group shooed me away to play among themselves. I sat on the couch a little ways away, opening my comm to poke at my messages. I wasn't sure what I was looking for—nobody except Andie and Angel called me, anyway.

I was scrolling aimlessly when Duke folded and stood. She came to sit beside me on the couch. She looked amused.

"What is it, Duke?" I asked.

"I wanted to ask how things went with Angel last night," she replied.

"She reamed me for going off plan," I said, opening and closing a three-week-old message from Andie. "That's about it."

"You sure?"

I frowned. "Why wouldn't I be sure?"

"Because you have a hickey on your neck."

I clapped a hand to the side of my neck, and my comm's haptic screen snapped closed. I felt a flush of heat creep up my collar. "How long has that been there?"

"Probably since you made out with Angel," she said, smug.

"I didn't make out with Angel," I lied.

"No, it's a good thing," she said. "Did you get it out of your system?"

"Get it out of my system?"

Duke raised a brow. "Repeating back the question to stall for time? That's grifting 101, E. You know exactly what I mean."

I glared at her. "No, I don't."

Duke sighed. "Can I level with you, E? Butch to butch, wife guy to wife guy?" I scowled. She continued anyway. "You know what they say about little kids who pull little girls' hair?" I didn't answer. "You like her, E."

"I definitely don't."

"You're telling me that you can ignore all those years of history?"

"Yes, easily."

"I'm not convinced."

"Good thing I don't give a shit if you're convinced."

"Oh, but it's not just me. There's a pool running about when you two kids are gonna get together." She grinned. "And by the looks of it, I might've just won the pot."

"I am not pulling Angel's hair," I snapped.

The chatter from the card table went silent suddenly, letting my words ring out in the common room. I felt the flush under my collar deepen.

Duke spread her hands. "Hey, what you do in the bedroom is none of my business."

Tatiana looked like she was going to make a smart-ass remark, but she was cut off by Malia standing abruptly. She tossed her cards onto the table and walked to her laptop, which had paused on a single document.

"What's up, Malia?" I asked.

She didn't immediately answer me. The laptop flickered through a few more documents before coming back to the original, Malia's eyes running across the lines of text. She looked over at me—I couldn't be sure, but it might have been worry. "Try look at this," she said.

The big screen beside her flashed to life, and with a glance Malia projected the array of files across it. The group of us crowded around the screen, squinting at the writing.

"Most of the files are your typical shady business shit. Kickbacks, bribes, insider trading—the usual," Malia explained. She pointed at the screen, and it zoomed into a list of account numbers and credit amounts. "These are transactions from six years ago, after the conclusion of AXON's first round of clinical trials. Millions of credits, paid out to the original test subjects and their families."

"Separate from compensation for the trial itself?" Nakano said.

"Separate, and way more," Malia answered. "I searched the R&D files and found the records of the first trials. It was pretty fucking grim, brah." The screen spread out an array of medical records, all of it de-identified. "Almost all of the OG test subjects ended up with some kind of side effect—migraines, ataxia, memory loss, cognitive decline—some of it permanently disabling." She paused. "A lot of 'em died. If not right away, then years later after the conclusion of the trials."

"It was hush money," I said, my voice low. It made me livid. All those people—*my* people—who signed on to the trials hoping for a payout, for a chance at a better life for their families. I couldn't imagine losing my mind, my body, my ability to care for them on that hope.

Malia gave me an uneasy look. "Atlas recruited heavily from Wards 1 and 2. I hacked into the database of test subjects and cross-referenced it against the medical records and payouts, and . . . I found something."

Three documents filled the screen. A medical record, a list of names and ID numbers, and the list of transactions. The medical record detailed a successful implantation of the mod, but debilitating side effects of ataxia, amnesia, and cognitive decline. The ID number on the record matched to *Huang, Daniel.* The highlighted payout was made to his surviving child: *Huang, Angelica.*

The floor lurched beneath me, and even though I was sitting on the couch, I thought I might topple over. Duke put a steadying hand on my arm. I put my head in my hands, trying not to be sick.

I knew Angel's dad was into some shady shit, had a tendency to get in over his head. Desperate times and all. But I never would have expected him to take Atlas's bait. I thought he had stronger self-preservation instincts than that.

But then again. Desperate times.

The couch shifted as Cy sat beside me. "Did you know?" he asked quietly.

"No," I answered. "I only knew what Angel told me. Which wasn't much."

"She didn't tell any of us," Duke growled.

"But does it really change the plan?" Tatiana said.

"What do you mean?" Nakano asked.

Tatiana shrugged. "I mean, everything's still the same, isn't it? Maybe Angel's got more skin in the game than we thought, but the plan hasn't changed."

"This changes everything," Duke objected. "What about when the job is done? What will we do with the tech when this is all over?"

"Isn't the plan to ransom it?" Tatiana asked.

"We can't give it back now," Nakano said.

"I'm sorry, what did you say?" Tatiana asked, appalled.

"We can't give it back," Sara repeated instead. Everyone looked from me to her. "If it's so dangerous, and Atlas is using it to control people, we can't give it back. We can't let him harm any more people."

"Then what do we do with it?" Tatiana pressed.

"Destroy it," Duke answered.

The crew fell into stunned silence. Destroy the tech? What the hell would that mean for us, if we destroyed the tech?

Cy was first to respond. "No." All eyes went to him. He looked grim. "We do dat, we put one tahget on our back. Atlas nevah stay giving up on dat."

"But would it be so different than what we already have planned?" Nakano asked. "We're all good at keeping a low profile, and Angel's taken care of the payout."

"Cy's right," Malia said, uncharacteristically subdued. "Atlas will pay out a ransom, but we don't know what he'll do if his tech is destroyed."

"But does it really matter?" Duke said, agitated. "Who would we be if we let this go? If we let Atlas keep killing and imprisoning people?"

"We'd be thieves," Tatiana responded, defensive. "We're not vigilantes."

"But maybe we should be," Sara said.

"No," Cy repeated. "It too dangerous. We take da money and run."

"And be cowards?" Duke challenged.

"I not a coward—" Cy said, raising his voice.

The crew broke down into overlapping arguments. I had no idea what to think. If Angel had a vendetta against Atlas, would it get in the way of our job? Would she really ransom the tech, like she told us from the outset? The Angel I used to know always kept her word—to me, at least. What this Angel would do, I didn't know.

It made me wonder what *I* would do, given the choice. What

was best for the Ward, I think. But what *was* best for the Ward? Atlas Industries was the number one employer on the station and had its claws in every industry and every market. Would destroying it from within be worth the cost?

The crew were still arguing when I came back to the present. "That's enough," I interrupted. "What we do with the tech at the end doesn't matter right now. What matters is pulling off this job to get the tech in the first place. If we're at each other's throats, that's not gonna happen."

The crew fell into begrudging silence.

"I'll talk to Angel," I continued, rising to my feet. "Get a read on what she's planning, where her head's at. Maybe then we can decide what to do."

The room remained silent as I walked toward the entrance, crossing the threshold into the unfinished hallway.

I was still reeling. How could I not have known? How could she not tell me? We told each other everything. From the smallest, most mundane details of our days to the events that defined us. Firsts and lasts. Joys and sorrows. Secrets and lies. She knew everything about me, all my ugliest truths. How could I have not known her?

Maybe I never knew her at all.

Light footsteps on the concrete made me pause. I turned and saw that Malia had followed me out.

"What is it, Malia?"

"I—" She looked surprised, as if she wasn't sure why she followed me. She was fiddling with her comm. After a long pause, she asked, "I was wondering about Angel's dad."

"What about him?"

"How did he die?"

I raised my brows in surprise. "I don't know, I was in prison. You probably know more than I do."

"Oh. Yeah." Malia twisted one of her locs around her finger. "I'm a superhuman, right."

"Why?"

Malia opened her mouth, then closed it. She looked conflicted, like she was choosing between a smart-ass remark or . . . something else. I didn't know what.

She sighed.

"I got these mods super young," she said. "Way before the recommended age of implantation."

"How young?"

"Fourteen."

I tried to hide my shock, but based on Malia's downcast gaze, it must have shown on my face. I couldn't help it. Fourteen years old with a mod in your brain? If I wasn't sick before, I was now.

"How'd you manage that?" I asked, schooling my face back into calm.

She didn't meet my eyes. "I'm the Obake, E. I was made for this."

"Oh."

I didn't really understand. But I knew well enough not to press.

"Anyway. I thought that, maybe if you knew something, about Angel's dad I mean, you might be able to tell me—" She paused again.

My expression fell. "You want to know if it'll happen to you."

Malia's cheeks took on a darker hue. "I'm not sked, though. Just interested. 'Cuz I'm nīele."

"Yeah," I said. "I wouldn't think so."

A brief silence fell as I collected my thoughts. I had no idea what the hell to say to her. I was never one for comfort. When one of the kids started crying, I passed them back to Andie. And that was what Malia was, really—a kid. A kid who looked scared as hell, despite her brave face.

I passed a hand through my hair and sighed. "Angel's dad

got his mods ten years ago, in the first wave of trials. The mods have changed a lot since then. They're a lot safer now. And even if something goes wrong, people know how to fix it. Your situation is different. You have people to support you—he didn't."

Malia nodded, slowly, processing. It was weird. Nothing about Malia was ever slow. But I kept my body still, my stance confident. I needed to look like I knew what I was talking about. I needed to look like an adult.

Finally, she gave a definitive nod. "Cool. Good to know. Thanks."

"Yeah," I said. "Anytime."

"I'm gonna scan the files some more. Tell me what Angel says about the tech."

"I will."

Malia flashed a halfhearted shaka, then turned back toward the common room. "Shoots."

I watched her go. "Shoots."

I found Angel in her room, poring over some documents spread out on the card table. I knocked on the door frame.

"Come in," she answered.

". . . Hey," I said, cautiously. She lifted her gaze. I thought I saw a flicker of surprise, but it was gone by the time she turned to face me fully. She was wearing a high-necked blouse, but even through the pale fabric I saw the marks I'd left on her. An electric thrill went through me at the sight.

"What is it, Edie?" she asked.

I pushed away the distraction. "Malia went through Atlas's files," I said. "She found your name among the beneficiaries of Atlas's payouts. Your dad was one of Atlas's test subjects, we know that now."

Angel remained impassive. "And you have questions."

"Lots of fucking questions."

She crossed her arms. "Then ask them."

I wasn't sure where to start. I began with "How long have you known?"

"That he was a test subject? When the seizures started. He played off everything else as stress, but the doctors told me about the mods when I took him to the hospital. He was deeply ashamed."

In over his head again. I would be ashamed too.

"Why didn't you tell me?" I asked quietly.

"Dad was using the money to pay off his debts," she explained. "Banks, loan sharks, friends and family . . . even Uncle Rich."

"We could've helped, though," I said. "We could've done something—"

"—Could you? There was nothing to be done, E. He begged me not to break the NDA. He said that if I did, we'd all be ruined." She paused. "It was his last wish. I needed to honor that."

There was a long beat of silence between us. My heart hurt for Uncle Daniel. My heart hurt for Angel. I couldn't imagine the pain she must have felt. I lost my dad, suddenly and unexpectedly. I couldn't imagine what it would be like to watch him unravel, slowly, with nothing to do but watch.

"When did you start planning this job?" I asked.

"Not long after I found out. It's been a little over eight years. But I didn't know how to get close enough to Atlas to do it. When I ended up in that holding cell with Hodson—after your idiot plan fell through—I knew I had a way in."

"Hodson?" I repeated. "The chief of security for Atlas?"

"That's right. He offered me a deal."

I knew the facts of what happened. I learned as much from the police, through my trial. But hearing it from her—it was different. I knew there was a wound there, but I didn't know just how much more it could open. It hurt like hell. But mostly, it made me angry.

"And what was the deal?" I said in a low voice.

"He offered to drop the charges, in exchange for my cooperation."

"That's pretty fucking generous."

"It's not just that. He was impressed with my abilities, my knowledge of his security system. He offered me a place in the organization. Promised to bury my connection to my father, if I would just straighten out and get a college degree."

"So that's why you sold me out," I growled. "It wasn't just about the deal—it was about getting close to Atlas."

"I sold you out because you would have done the same to me. Don't lie and say you wouldn't."

"I wouldn't, and it's not a fucking lie," I snapped.

"You were in prison for eight years, Edie. Would you really go back to save me?"

"Eight years ago, yes!" I said vehemently. "Back then, I would have done anything for you, anything for you or Andie. You were *family*, Angel." I couldn't help the way my voice wavered. "You were family, and we could've been—"

We could've been so much more.

Angel's eyes widened, just slightly, like she was surprised. Like she didn't know. Why didn't she know? She couldn't fathom caring about me the way I cared about her. Maybe because she didn't understand *how much* I cared about her. Maybe because she didn't understand how someone *could* care about her so much. Maybe because she didn't understand how *I* could care about her so much.

White-hot anger spread through me at that. Did she really think so lowly of me that I would betray her trust, the same way she betrayed mine? Blood or not, she was my family. Who would I be if I betrayed her that way?

"You were my family, Angel," I repeated. "I would do anything for my family, I would never betray my family—but I'm not a lying snake," I spat.

Angel's eyes widened again. I knew I was out of line. I knew I was saying things I would regret. I understood her well enough to know what would hurt her most—where to cut, where to bruise. Deep down, I knew it was wrong. But that wound was raw and open, and beneath the anger, it hurt so bad. And this felt good. This felt really good.

"What did you call me?" she asked, her voice dangerously quiet.

"I called you a snake," I said, louder. "I called you a snake, for what you did to me, for what you did to all of us."

Angel's face twisted into a snarl. "I'm not a snake."

"You are! We took you in, we cared for you, we treated you like family, and this is what you did to us? I should have known you would keep that money from me—you never cared about us, not really. You never cared about Andie."

"That's not true," Angel said hotly.

"Then why did you leave her? Why did you abandon her? For eight years she's struggled, getting by on other people's charity. You left her behind. And for what?" I scoffed. "To be rich? Famous? To play pretend that you're worth more than what you are? Because you're fucking trash, Angel. You're trash, just like me, and you'll never be more than that."

"I did what anyone else would have done!"

I barked out a disbelieving laugh. "And that's your fucking problem. Because not everyone is like you, Angel. Andie's not. I'm not. Everybody else on this crew is not." I paused. "But that's good for you, isn't it? If things go south, you know none of us would turn on you. Better to stab us in the back if it does."

"How dare you," she hissed. "I would never betray this crew."

"Then why did you betray *me*?" I shouted. "Why me? Why me, you heartless *bitch*!"

Angel looked like she was ready to scream. Her lips were

trembling, eyes shining, whole body quaking. I'd never seen her like this. And even through my anger I could feel my heart ache for her. I wish it didn't. I wish I could have let her go, felt nothing for her, but I couldn't. It was Angel. I couldn't.

"Get out," she whispered.

"Angel—" I began.

"I said *get out*!" she screamed.

She shoved me backward, through the door. I stumbled to a stop outside.

"Angel—"

Then she slammed the door in my face.

I stood outside her door, chest heaving, eyes stinging, whole body trembling with rage and hurt. I didn't know what to do with all of this, all that I was feeling. I didn't know what to do about anything.

Just then, my comm began to chime. I checked the number and saw that it was Tyler. Most of me wanted to let it ring, but part of me wanted a target to direct all that pain at.

I opened the line.

"What do you want?" I snapped.

The line was silent for a beat, Tyler clearly stunned. After a moment, he said flatly, "Andie's in labor. We're at the hospital. Hurry your ass over here." Then he hung up.

Chapter 18

GROWING UP IN THE DARK, DAMP, AND HEAVY PULL OF THE LOWER Wards, it was easy to get sick. If you saved enough credits, you could travel up, find a private doctor, pay out of pocket for the medical care you couldn't find down here. Not like the people of the Upper Wards needed it, in their clean air, bright light, and Earth-standard gravity.

But if you grew up in a family like mine, you went to Progress General Hospital, which serviced all the Lower Wards. Dad was born there, I was born there, and Andie was born there. I went there with Mom when I broke my wrist falling out of my window. I took Cy to the ER after a bad scrap when someone pulled a knife. I brought Paige to the oncology unit, sat with her while the doctor explained her treatment to both of us—Paige knew more than I did.

Now Andie was having her third child there, and I was thirty minutes late.

I wove through the lobby to the elevators, jabbing at the up button impatiently. Alone in the elevator, I paced until it stopped at the seventh floor. I rushed to the maternity ward, throwing open the doors to find Tyler and the kids sitting in the waiting room.

Tyler scowled at me. "You're late."

I scowled back. "Derailment on the Main Line, I was stopped for twenty minutes."

Tyler shrugged, as if he didn't accept my excuse.

I moved to stand by the kids, laying my hand on Casey's shoulder. "How's Mom doing?"

"She's fine," Tyler answered for them. "She's three kids in, she knows the drill."

"With your unflagging support, it must be easy," I said coldly.

He met my gaze, disdain in his blue-ringed eyes. "I've been here for every one. Which can't be said for all of us."

I wanted to ask him what that meant, but he turned away to flag down a nurse. "Excuse me! I'm Andrea Morikawa's partner, could you take me to her?" At the nurse's agreement, he turned his eyes back to me. "It'll be another three or four hours. Take the kids to get some dinner, will you?"

"Sure," I said through my teeth.

He gave me a nod. "Listen to your aunty," he directed at the kids. "I'll call you when Mom's ready." He followed the nurse down the hall and out of sight.

I let out a slow breath, passing a hand through my hair. I always hated Tyler. From the first time I saw him making a pass at Andie in the shop, I hated him. He always acted like he was better than me, better than all of us. Like Andie should be grateful to him for pulling her out of this life. The smug fucker.

But look where he'd left her now.

Casey and Paige's watchful eyes brought me back to the present. "How are you both?" I asked.

"Good," Paige answered, closing her book. "Casey's nervous, but I'm okay."

Casey scowled at his sister.

"Nervous?" I asked, crouching down to meet Casey's eyes. "What're you nervous about?"

"Mom," Paige answered for him. "But she seemed pretty calm when she went back."

"It's pretty hard to shake your mom." I smiled. "She'll be okay. I promise."

Casey met my smile, seemingly reassured.

"He's never had a younger sibling," Paige explained. "He's never been around someone being born."

"Do you remember Casey being born?"

"A little. I was with Tūtū for most of it."

Right. Mom was still around then.

"Mostly it was really boring," Paige continued. "But they let me watch cartoons on the TV, which was nice."

"Well, I'll try and convince them to let you watch your show," I promised. "Meantime we go kau kau, yeah?"

Casey nodded and hopped off his chair. I took his hand and started toward the elevator, Paige following close behind.

"Are you excited to have a younger sibling, Casey?" I asked, looking down at Casey by my side.

The little boy grinned and nodded.

"What about you, Paige?" I asked, looking to my other side.

"Sort of," she answered, pressing the down button for the elevator. "I'm probably gonna have to help with the baby, now that I'm a teenager."

"Thirteen," I corrected.

She shot me a glare. "Mom said she had to help Tūtū with you and Aunty Angel."

I shuddered at that. Aunty Angel sounded awful. I was certain she'd hate it too.

"Yeah, but your mom's only three years older than me," I replied. "She just liked to act like she was older and wiser."

"So, she *didn't* have to fly you home from detention every weekend?" Paige asked, incredulous.

"It was *not* every weekend." I paused. "Most weeks Angel got me out and we took the bus."

The elevator doors opened, and we stepped inside. I let Casey hit the button for Ward 2.

Paige gave me a deadpan look. "So, Aunty Angel took care of you too?"

"Nobody 'took care of me,'" I said, defensive. "I was very independent."

She opened her book again. "Okay, Aunty."

"I'm serious!" I protested. "It was me, your mom, and Angel most days. She 'babysat,' but really we were all doing the same thing."

"And what was that?" she asked, turning a page.

I shrugged. "Cruising, mostly. But that was before you got auto-fined for loitering."

Paige squinted at me. "That's all you did? Cruise?"

"Hey, cruising is great when you're a broke teenager with nothing else to do."

Never mind the little confidence tricks and petty larceny, but I left that unsaid.

Andie and I were always close, closer than I was to most of my friends—other than Angel. It was always the three of us sharing toys, talking story, and cruising around the neighborhood. Until Andie suddenly grew up. Being a teen mom does that. And I resented Tyler for it. He stole Andie from me thirteen years ago, when I needed her most. Maybe if she were there, things would have turned out differently.

"Well, we have four hours to kill," I said as we stepped out onto the street. I grinned at them. "Let me show you how to cruise."

We cruised for almost four hours. First, I took the kids out for lunch at Aunty Selene's diner that I promised had the best loco moco in the Ward. Then we walked to Uncle Pedro's hole-in-the-wall ice cream shop, which had my favorite shave ice. I let Paige loose in a secondhand bookstore, and she read until Mx. Yanagi gave us stink eye. After we were done with the bookstore, Casey was hungry and Paige was tired. We picked up dinner at one of the galactic chain burger joints, then sat under the scraggly trees in the light between skybridges. By the time we were finished, I had a message on my comm from Tyler: The baby was coming.

We rushed back to the hospital, but even then, there was more waiting. Paige read from her book haul, Casey watched cartoons on the TV, and I paced restlessly around the waiting area. Somehow, I was just as nervous now as when the other kids were born.

Andie was in labor for nine hours. At 2207, the baby was born.

The room was quiet when the nurses finally called us in. Soft music was playing while Andie and Tyler talked in hushed tones. They glanced up as we entered the room—Andie looked exhausted, but her face lit up when she saw us.

"Hey, you," she said. "Come say hi to the baby."

I let Paige go first and picked up Casey so he could see into the tall hospital bed. We crept across the room, coming to stand at Andie's side. She beamed up at us, shifting so we could better see the baby in her arms. "Meet Madeline."

Madeline. Baby Maddie. She was fast asleep in Andie's arms, and I watched her in awe. She already had wisps of soft dark hair, and when her lashes fluttered, I saw her clear blue eyes. She was so small, so beautiful, utterly perfect. A broad smile rose on my face, and tears prickled at the corners of my eyes.

"Do you want to hold her?" Andie asked me.

"If that's okay," I answered.

She laughed. "Of course it's okay."

I set Casey down. Carefully, she placed the baby in my arms. The baby cooed as I shifted her into a more secure position to support her head.

As I held her, I felt warmth spread through me. Affection, care, awe. I loved her so much already. As I looked at her tiny face, I knew immediately that I would do anything for her. Anything for her, or Andie, or Paige, or Casey. Anything at all.

"You're a natural, E," Andie said affectionately.

"I've had practice," I deflected. "I was around when Paige was born, remember?"

"And hopefully you'll be around for longer, this time," Tyler added.

The comment broke the spell Maddie had over me, and all those warm feelings went cold. I glared at him. "What's that supposed to mean?"

Tyler shrugged. "You've been in prison for eight years. Paige was just starting kindergarten when you left, and now she's in middle school. That's a big chunk of her life where you were gone. You've missed a lot—it's just a fact."

"I'm making up for it now," I said hotly.

"Is that really something you can make up for?"

"Tyler—" Andie tried to interject.

The baby started fussing in my arms.

"I'm just stating the facts," Tyler said evenly. "Paige won't get those eight years back, and neither will you."

"If you have some kind of problem with me, we can take it outside," I growled.

"Edie!" Andie tried again.

"You'd like that, wouldn't you?" Tyler replied. "Once a thug, always a thug."

The baby started to cry, startling me out of my anger. I tried to soothe her, but Andie impatiently gestured for me to give her back.

"That's enough," she said, settling baby Maddie in her arms. "You're grown adults, I would expect you to keep it together in front of the children."

I glanced at Paige and Casey, who looked uneasy.

"One of you, go outside and cool off," Andie said firmly.

"But—" I protested.

"I'm your husband—" Tyler argued.

"One of you, *out*," Andie commanded.

Tyler looked at me expectantly. Scumbag or not, he was Maddie's father. It didn't sit right with me to separate them, at least not now.

I made a frustrated noise.

"I'll go," I said, shrugging into my coat. "I need a cigarette, anyway."

"Those'll kill you, you know," Tyler said coolly.

"Hey, kids," I said to Paige and Casey. I pointed over their shoulders. "What's that over there?"

They both turned to look out the door. Out of their sight, I threw up my middle finger at Tyler.

"Edie!" Andie said sharply.

"I'll be back," I said, stalking out the door.

I fumed to myself on the way down to street level. Tyler had no right being so self-righteous, not after he abandoned his kids, left Andie in the lurch. I was doing more for the family now than he'd ever done. Would ever do. With 125 billion credits in our accounts, Andie would never have to see his face again. That made up for it, right?

I blew out a sigh. I knew it didn't. The worst part of all of this was that Tyler was right: he was here when I wasn't. There was no way for me to get those eight years back. Money couldn't buy me back that time. And that hurt so fucking bad.

I exited the hospital onto the streets of Ward 2 and stormed my way to the closest store: a colorful little bodega owned by a yobo family farther up the tower.

"Edie!" Aunty Yeo cried as I walked through the door. "I heard you were back!"

Despite my shitty mood, I smiled at her. I used to frequent her shop a lot, accompanying Andie to her obstetrician visits when she was pregnant with Paige. "Hey, Aunty."

"You here with Andie?" she asked. "Last time I saw her, she was so hāpai she was about to pop!"

"She just did," I said, leaning on the counter. "Baby girl."

"Ho, so sweet! Here—" She ducked behind the counter, picking out a little plush cat charm from the case. "For the baby," she said, pressing it into my hands.

"Thanks, Aunty."

"Anyting else you need?"

I nodded at the cigarettes behind the counter. She glanced behind her, then sighed heavily. "Those are going kill you, y'know."

I grimaced. "So I hear."

Aunty Yeo tutted to herself as she rang up the cigarettes. I paid with my credit chit. I was certain I'd pay it off with some to spare soon.

As I paid, an impatient-looking haole guy came up behind me, a single pack of chips in hand. A second was lingering by the entrance. My eyes flicked between the two of them. More suits and shades.

Something was wrong.

I smiled at Aunty Yeo as she gave me back my credit chit. I turned to leave, a little too close to Haole Guy #1 behind me. He stepped backward into a shelf, knocking a stand of chips to the floor. Aunty barked at him in Korean, pointing at the chips on the ground. Haole Guy #1 bent to pick up the mess, and I brushed past him toward the door and out into the street as Haole Guy #2 looked between me and Haole Guy #1.

I pulled up the hood of my jacket as I exited the bodega, moving into the crowds and weaving between pedestrians, trying to vanish. I heard hurried footsteps behind me, then someone calling out to their partner. I ducked between towers, into an alley blocked off by a chain-link fence.

Someone shouted at me to stop, spurring me into a run. I sprinted down the alley and leapt onto a closed dumpster alongside the tower. I jumped, vaulting over the fence and dropping into the alley on the other side. Haole Guys #1 and #2 hit the fence behind me, struggling to climb it.

I turned and ran, only to be stopped in my tracks by two more haole guys in suits.

"Edith Morikawa?" Haole Guy #3 said.

"Fuck, it sounds so much worse when you guys say it," I replied.

They exchanged a glance.

"Come with us, please," Haole Guy #4 said.

I scowled at them both. "Am I being detained?"

"Let's just say you'll *want* to come with us," Haole Guy #3 said. "The other options are less appealing."

I looked between them, searching for a means of escape. I thought briefly of fighting my way out, but then I heard Haole Guys #1 and #2 drop to the ground behind me. I was outnumbered.

". . . Fine," I said.

Haole Guys #3 and #4 nodded, then led me out into the street. Haole Guys #1 and #2 came up close behind me, still panting with exertion. The whole group of them escorted me to a sleek black flyer parked alongside the street. I noticed it had government plates. Feds again.

One of the Haole Guys opened the back door for me. I glanced down the street, toward the hospital. I thought of what Tyler said to me, about making up for lost time. What if I never even got the opportunity? What if I'd already blown my chance? What if Angel's heist had destroyed my future with my family?

No. I couldn't let it end here. There was too much at stake.

I steeled myself and ducked into the flyer. Haole Guy #3 shut the door behind me.

The flyer was nice, with leather seats and a paneled interior—it even smelled new. A flyer this nice wasn't some midlevel bureaucrat's. I was in some deep shit.

"Mx. Morikawa," a woman's voice greeted me.

I turned toward the voice. Agent McKay was sitting across from me, just as professional and put together as the last time I saw her.

"Oh, it's you again," I said.

Agent McKay smiled. "It's good to see you, Mx. Morikawa."

"Likewise," I said flatly. "Am I being detained?"

"No," she answered. "At least, not yet."

"Then what do you want?"

Agent McKay crossed her legs. "I'm here to repeat my offer: Give me Atlas's personal files, and I will take care of your family's debt." She smiled. "I'll even throw in immunity for your trial."

"Nothing's changed," I said. "No deal."

"Oh, but something has changed," she replied. "My team has found something that may interest you."

With a gesture, a single haptic screen flew from Agent McKay's comm to hover between us. She gently brushed it forward, close enough for me to see. It was a voice recording, and the visualizer came to life as a voice began to speak.

"I have a new addition to the list," a woman's voice said. *"I'm forwarding you the information now."*

I startled at the sound. Even through the crackle of the recording, it was a voice I would recognize anywhere. The smooth, even, pleasant voice of Angel Huang.

"Edith J. M. Morikawa. December 20th, 2141. 760-04-1720. Get this out to our contractors ASAP. They're actively searching right now—make sure they aren't let in. Or if the hiring process has started,

terminate it immediately. No need to be coy about why. The blacklist is an open secret, they'll figure it out eventually."

The blacklist? Atlas's blacklist? What was Angel doing with Atlas's blacklist? I guessed that as a matter of security, it would fall under Angel's purview.

But why was she putting me on it?

"Thank you. That's all I need. Let me know if you run into any complications and I'll take care of it."

The recording cut out.

I stared at the screen. It was true that the blacklist was an open secret. Everyone knew about it, but it felt wrong to talk about it. I wasn't the first one to be driven off the station because of it, but maybe the only one to find a way around it. I joined Angel's heist for that reason—I couldn't stand to leave, so I took the job out of desperation.

It hit me then. Angel put me on Atlas's blacklist. At that realization, everything started to unravel. She'd been manipulating me the whole time. She manipulated me into joining by eliminating all my options, until only she was left. She manipulated me by leveraging my family, my love for them, how I would do anything for them. She manipulated me by messing with my head, my heart, my feelings for her. I wondered how she'd manipulated the others, whether it was with wealth, or status, or justice. We all took the bait. I took the bait.

My hands balled into fists on my knees. I took the fucking bait.

Agent McKay gestured again, beckoning the screen back into her cuff. She regarded me coolly. "Angel Huang betrayed your trust, Mx. Morikawa. She sacrificed you to achieve her own ends, just as she did eight years ago. And I have no doubt that she would do it again, given the chance."

"Why did you show me this?" I asked, my voice low.

"Because you deserve to know the truth. You deserve to have

all the information before you decide. So I must reiterate"—she leaned forward in her seat—"if you give me Atlas's files, I will grant you immunity in your trial. I will erase your family's debt." Her brown eyes searched my face. "And I will put Angel Huang away for a long, long time."

I went silent, barely constraining my fury. How could Angel do this to me? How could she meet my eyes, lie to my face, tell me she trusted me, knowing what she did? How could she kiss me, fuck me, play with my feelings, after destroying me again and again? In that moment, I hated her. I hated her with everything in me.

I almost said yes, in the heat of that moment. But then my comm chimed, and I glanced at the message. It was Andie, inviting me back to the room. And beneath that, unread, was a message from Duke, asking me where I went. I realized then I'd left without a word. I'd left them waiting.

The moment passed, and all that was left behind was the pain of knowing what she'd done.

I looked up from my comm. Agent McKay was watching me expectantly. Waiting for an answer.

"I need time," I said instead.

To her credit, Agent McKay seemed unfazed by my nonanswer. "If you need the time, I will give you the time. You have my number. I'll be waiting."

I opened the flyer door, and Haole Guy #1 stepped aside. I ducked through and stepped into the street. Agent McKay called out to me one last time: "I've been following your case, Mx. Morikawa, even before your imprisonment. I know you, more than you would expect." Her brown eyes shone in the dim light of the flyer. "I know that you would sell your soul if it meant saving your loved ones. I only ask that you consider who you're selling your soul to."

I slammed the flyer door shut behind me. Haole Guys #1 through #4 looked at me with various degrees of disapproval, then all climbed into the flyer. They lifted off the sidewalk to rejoin the traffic above, and I watched them go.

Angel betrayed me. Twice. And there was no guarantee she wouldn't do it again. I didn't trust her. I never should have trusted her—and now I had even more reason not to. I had no doubt that if push came to shove, she'd let me take the fall. Like she always did.

But even with that knowledge, there was a part of me that couldn't stand the thought. I wasn't a snitch. I wasn't a traitor, like Angel. Despite what she did to me, it didn't sit right with me to do the same. And that was without considering the crew—I couldn't let them down. I couldn't betray them either.

There was that, and there was a lingering part of me that wasn't ready to give up on the dream of success. Agent McKay was offering me security, safety, comfort. But Angel was offering me wealth, status, power. Almost limitless. Could I throw that away too? Could I let go of that dream, after wanting it so badly for so long?

I stalked back to the hospital with my hands in my pockets.

"Edie," Andie said gently.

I roused from my sleep, drawing in a deep breath and blinking my bleary eyes. The lights in the room were low, and I was slouched in the big, heavy armchair on the far side of the room. Paige was nestled in the crook of my arm and Casey on my chest. They didn't even stir when I shifted into a sitting position.

I groaned. My neck hurt like a motherfucker.

"It's almost 2400, you should go home," Andie said, smiling at me from the bed. "I'll be okay overnight."

"Maybe," I conceded, scrubbing at my face with my hands.

"Can you take the kids with you? Maybe watch them tomorrow?"

I paused, face in my hands. "Fuck. I can't."

"Oh?" Andie sounded surprised.

I met her eyes. "I'm on call at work. They could call me in any minute."

"Work? You have a job?" Tyler asked, striding into the room with a cup of water. He handed it to Andie. "That's a pleasant surprise."

"Edie's working at Atlas Industries," Andie said proudly.

"*You?*" Tyler's blue eyes widened in disbelief. "Why would someone like Joyce Atlas invest in someone like you?"

"I'm just lucky, I guess," I said flatly.

I wanted to tell him it was a pleasant surprise he still remembered his kids' names, but Paige stirring made me bite my tongue.

"I'll take them," Tyler said. He leaned down to kiss Andie's forehead. "I'll take the day off."

"Thank you," Andie said with a smile. "I really appreciate it."

"You focus on healing up," he said. "Don't worry about the kids."

He glanced my way, his light eyes smug. I clenched my jaw but said nothing.

"C'mon, you two," he said, taking Casey from me. The little boy nestled into his father's neck. Paige slid out of the chair, rubbing her eyes. She took her father's outstretched hand and followed him toward the door.

"Goodnight," I called after them.

Paige waved at me over her shoulder. Casey didn't stir. Tyler and the kids walked out the door and left for home.

I leaned forward in the chair, dropping my face into my hands. I took a deep breath and let it out in a sigh. "I'm sorry."

"It's okay," Andie said. "You can't help it."

I tried to swallow my guilt. I tried to remember that this was just for today, maybe tomorrow. Once I got Angel's call, everything would change. I'd have all the time in the world after that.

"Edie?" Andie said.

"Yeah?"

"What's going on with you?"

I met her eyes again. She looked solemn. "What do you mean?"

She was silent for a moment. "It's been eight years, but you haven't changed at all, E."

"Oh yeah?" I asked, surprised.

"Yeah. I've been thinking about it a lot, lately. The way you talk, the way you move, the way you act . . . it's all the same."

I smiled at her. "That a good thing?"

She went silent again. "Mostly."

My smile faded. "Mostly?"

"Did you really think I wouldn't notice?" she asked. "The late nights, the sneaking out, the lies . . . Mom could never read you, but I could."

My stomach dropped, heavy with guilt and fear.

"It's not what you think," I said quietly.

"Then what is it, E?"

I stared at my palms. Angel and I had come up with another lie in case Andie saw through the first one. And like all good lies, it was based in a scrap of truth.

"I'm working with Angel," I said. "I'm helping her move Atlas's assets around—she needs a consultant. It's all under the table, and I'm not entirely sure whether it violates my parole. But we need the credits, so I didn't ask any questions." I met her eyes again. "I didn't want to make you worry."

Andie's mouth tightened as her eyes searched my face. "I don't believe you."

I stared at her. "It's the truth."

"I wish I could believe you. I wish you trusted me."

"I do trust you," I protested. "But I knew you would try and talk me out of it."

"Because I don't want to see you back in prison!" Andie exclaimed.

We both jumped at the sound, looking toward the bassinet. Maddie was still asleep.

"What good would I be if I didn't try and *do* something?" I asked in a hushed voice, turning back toward Andie. "I might as well have stayed in prison."

"You don't need to *do* anything to be good for us, Edie," Andie shot back.

"We deserve better, Andie. We deserve so much more than what we have. I just want us to be happy."

"So you'd sell your soul to make us happy?" she demanded.

I started at that.

"You'd sell your soul, and for what? To make it big? Strike it rich? We don't need that kind of money, Edie. All I want is to have you here. All I want is to have you with us. That's enough. For all of us."

I stared at her again. I had no idea how to respond.

Andie broke the silence. "You're a grown-ass adult, E. I can't tell you what to do. But whatever you're doing, think very hard about whether it's worth it. Whether it's worth the risk, worth the cost."

I stayed silent. I didn't have a response for her.

She sighed, exasperated. "I'm tired. And I don't think I have anything else to say."

"Yeah," I said softly. "Me neither."

I rose from the chair, picking up my jacket and bag. Andie watched me closely as I crossed the room. I paused in the doorway.

"I'm sorry, Andie," I said.

"I know," she replied. "You always are."

My whole body felt heavy with guilt. I could feel her eyes on me as I left the room.

All my life, I'd wanted more for us. I'd given up so much—eight years of my life—just trying to make a better life for us. And now I knew that everything I gave up wasn't worth it. Not to Andie. All she wanted was time for herself, for her family.

Time that I could never give back.

I paused outside the hospital's entrance to fish my pack of cigarettes out of my pocket. I tapped one out of the pack and lit it, taking a long drag before setting off toward the monorail.

I'd convinced myself that with this last big score, I would have all the time in the world with them. I'd convinced myself I could make up that lost time—enough money could buy you anything, right?

Despite the thief's instinct screaming in my head, I couldn't help but think about what Agent McKay said in our shabby little shop. What if the heist did fail? What if everything went wrong, just like last time? What if I went back to prison, with no way out? What if I lost all that time, the time Andie desperately wanted with me?

And for what? For Angel?

I thought of what Angel said to me last night: there was nothing left for us. Nothing left of the past, no hope for the future. No longer friends, no longer family . . . We were strangers now. I thought of what I said to her earlier that day: I wasn't like her. I would never turn on my family, my friends. Eight years ago, I would never have turned on her either.

But would I turn on a stranger?

Would I turn on an enemy?

Because after the blacklist, there was nothing else she could be to me.

I had a choice now. Choose Angel and potentially lose

everything—the money, the kids, my freedom—or choose Andie, and sell Angel out the same way she sold me out.

My comm chimed as I approached the station. I stopped near the doors and checked the number—it was Angel.

I opened the line. "Yeah?"

"*Nakano is meeting Atlas on Tuesday, at 1000. Be ready at 0600.*" Despite the anger between us, I could almost hear her smile. "*It's time.*"

SOMEWHERE, FAR ACROSS THE GALAXY, IT WAS A COLD WINTER MORNING on the homeworld. The only winter I'd ever known was when the Rock got even colder, when it was cold enough to penetrate the prison walls and make me shiver in my bunk. When the prison yard was heaped with dirty slush. When the banging of the HVAC got so loud it was hard to sleep.

I heard once that winters on Earth were beautiful, with snowcapped mountains, frosted trees, and dark skies lit with stars. Kepler had no pretty winters. It had no passing seasons. And aside from the rising and setting of the simulated sun, there was no real variation between days either.

So when I woke up at 0500 on the day of the heist, it could have been any other day of the year. It could have been any other day of my life.

Everything was the same, except for a message from Angel on my comm:

> Good luck, E.

Her words felt incongruent with the way we'd left things two days ago. It felt incongruent with what I knew about her now. Was she really wishing me well? Or was she worried about her own skin? We were in this together, and if I went down, I'd take her with me.

There was so much that could go wrong, it would be easy.

I put my head in my hands and spread my fingers through my hair. I still didn't know what to do. Two days of thinking—about the sex, the fight, the blacklist—and I was no closer to an answer. I was weighing the success of the heist against Andie's disappointment in me. Against Agent McKay's promises and threats. Against Angel's betrayal, and the prospect of revenge.

Who are you selling your soul to?

Despite everything she did to me, thinking about betraying Angel, going back on my word—it felt like bachi. Bad luck.

I dressed carefully in the dark, in a suit that Angel bought me—classy and chic, but not loud enough to attract attention. Black pants and a matching coat, a muted shirt of cerulean, and a tie in a complementary shade of darker blue. I don't know when Angel got my measurements, but the suit fit me perfectly. As I straightened my tie in the mirror, I smiled, despite my nerves. I looked like a million bucks.

Or 125 billion, if everything went to plan.

I took a deep breath, then stepped outside the apartment, closing the door quietly behind me.

The crew's van was hovering at the curb when I stepped onto the street. I opened the door and climbed in, settling into the seat. Cy sat on the pilot's side. The others were still at their homes in the other Wards, waiting to be picked up.

"Jus' like ol' times," Cy said.

"Yeah," I agreed. "Jus' like ol' times."

He studied me for a moment. "Eh. You worried, cuz?"

"No," I lied.

"You big liah," he said. "You look like you going trow up."

I scowled at him. "I fine. No worries."

"Nah, I no believe you. You nevah worry about one job befo'. Waz going on?"

"I jus'—" I paused. Cy was one of my oldest and closest friends. How could I lie to him?

I had to.

I sighed, passing a hand through my hair. "I nevah worry li'dis 'cuz we never been on one job li'dis. It's choke credits, cuz. Change yo' life kine credits."

"Yeah," Cy agreed. "But we got dis, cuz." He reached over to clap his metal hand on my shoulder. "You da bes'. We all da bes'. Angel wen plan dis fo' a long time—and you know she hate losing. You remembah one time she stay losing to Mikey at chess, and she go learn 'em so good she nevah lose again?"

I laughed. I'd forgotten about that. The fact that it was Mikey only added insult to injury.

"Iz li'dat," Cy continued. "Angel nevah let us lose, cuz."

Angel never let us lose. Not unless it was intentional. Not unless she had something to gain, if you had something to lose.

Who are you selling your soul to?

"No," I said quietly. "She nevah would."

Cy was first on the scene: Malia did some shuffling, and he was scheduled to patrol the vault beginning at 0600. Angel was next, biding her time in her office until Atlas arrived with Nakano. Nakano would arrive at 1000, to seal the deal with Atlas. As the deal went down, Tatiana, Sara, and I would use the stolen credentials from Yusef, Vera, and Craig to enter the building and make our way to the vault, to rendezvous with Cy. From there it was a matter of breaking through Atlas's security system—hacking the firewalls, crossing the floors, and cracking the vault.

Easy.

"*Eh, E*," Malia said in my ear.

"What?" I responded, crossing the street to Atlas Industries' Ward 5 tower.

"*Why you nervous?*" she asked.

I scowled. "I'm not nervous."

"Your comm thinks you've run three miles. You're definitely nervous."

I held the door open for Sara and Tatiana to pass me. Tatiana looked me up and down. "You look like you're gonna puke, dude."

"*Pull it together, E*," Duke said. "*Check your pressure point.*"

"I'm fine," I snapped. But I squeezed the pressure point between my thumb and forefinger anyway.

Sara greeted the woman at the front desk pleasantly as she strode up to the security checkpoint, flashing her forged badge. Both she and Tatiana handed over their bags and I laid my briefcase on the scanner.

Malia continued needling me. "*You haven't been worried about nothing this whole time, brah, what's up?*"

I didn't respond.

Sara and Tatiana walked through the metal detector without incident. I followed, and immediately the detector made a grating *beep*. The guard frowned in my direction, and I feigned surprise. I patted down my pockets, then withdrew my wallet with its chain. I met the guard's impatient expression with a sheepish grin. "Sorry, forgot this."

I tossed the wallet on the other side of the scanner with Sara and Tatiana's cleared bags. The guard gestured me through the detector again, and this time I passed through without incident.

I picked up my wallet and chain—my lockpicks tucked safely within—and started deeper into the building with Tatiana and Sara.

Tatiana flashed me a grin as we left the security checkpoint behind. "It's okay if you're nervous," she said, "everybody gets nervous sometimes. I mean, *I* don't, but I've heard it said."

I was ready to snap back, but Duke beat me to it. "*You should be nervous,*" she said. "*A healthy dose of nerves is what keeps you alive in this business. Only rookies think that nervousness is a sign of weakness. Overconfidence gets you killed.*"

Tatiana pouted. "I guess."

"I'm glad you said that," Sara said quietly. We both glanced her way. She tucked a strand of hair behind her ear that had escaped from her pristine bun and gave us a small smile. "I'm very nervous and was starting to feel bad about it."

"*See, you made Sara feel bad!*" Malia scolded. "*Shame, cuz!*"

"Shame?" Tatiana repeated, affronted. I shot her a warning look, and she lowered her voice to a hiss as we wove through the maze of cubicles in the general offices. "*You* started it!"

"*It's not about who starts it, it's about who finishes it.*"

"That doesn't even make sense!"

"*Listen, cuz—*"

I gritted my teeth and squeezed the pressure point on my hand again.

"*Quiet on comms,*" Angel commanded. "*Nakano is here.*"

Blessedly, the line went silent.

"*Mr. Atlas,*" Nakano said, her voice breathy with excitement, "*it's so good to see you again!*"

"*The pleasure is always mine, Dr. Abe,*" Atlas replied. "*If you could come with me, we'll take care of business first and then move on to pleasure.*" He chuckled. "*So to speak.*"

Malia retched on the comm.

"Oh God, now *I'm* gonna puke," Tatiana groaned.

"*Doesn't this piss you off, Duke?*" Malia asked.

"*To no end,*" Duke growled.

Sara, Tatiana, and I paused at a door across from the general offices. Sara tapped her keycard to the sensor, input Vera's PIN, and we passed into the R&D labs.

"I'm so pleased to hear that Clairvoyant will be joining us," Atlas said. *"You met the board briefly at the gala, but I'd like to introduce you more formally."*

"I would love that," Nakano replied.

"I need you to move faster, E," Angel said.

"I can do that," I replied, and we picked up our pace.

We walked briskly through the hallways of the R&D labs, moving with purpose, as if we belonged here. I tried to channel the me that could have been—the me that was born high up in the Upper Wards, the me that never fell into this life. The me who had everything they needed, everything they wanted. I'd gotten better at envisioning that person lately.

At the far end of the office space was the lift that would take us down into the restricted areas of Atlas Industries' tower, where the more sensitive technology—including the vault—was kept. I tapped my keycard to the sensor, then input Craig's PIN. The doors to the lift slid open, and the three of us walked inside.

"We're at the lift," I said as I hit the button for the basement floor.

"Cherreh," Malia said. *"Try wait just a minute."*

The lift began to move. Shortly after, it hitched in its descent. "Whoa."

"I'm in da system. Slowing it down and looping the cameras."

I loosened my tie, then pulled it over my head. I shrugged out of my jacket while Sara shimmied out of her skirt and Tatiana pulled up her dress. We changed quickly, out of our business getups and into gear fit for thievery. Tatiana crushed her curls under a beanie while Sara re-secured her bun, and I stuffed all our clothes into my briefcase.

I nodded at Sara, then braced myself to give her a boost. "Ready?"

She stepped into my cupped palms and reached for the ceiling of the lift, popping off a panel before pulling herself up through the opening.

I scowled at Tatiana as I reset. "No bullshit."

Tatiana put a hand to her chest, affronted. "Me? Bullshit?" She grinned, then stepped into my palms. I boosted her up and Sara helped pull her through the opening.

I tossed the briefcase up through the opening to a waiting Tatiana as Atlas spoke in my ear again. "*Ah, Angel!*"

"*Good morning, sir,*" Angel replied.

"*I'm glad to see you—I have news. It's related to our Dr. Abe, as it happens. Let's go to the boardroom and discuss.*"

"*Of course, sir.*"

I braced myself, then did a wall jump off the metal side. I grabbed the open panel and pulled myself up onto the top of the lift.

Tatiana blinked at me. "Ho," she said simply.

I ignored her. "Angel's in the boardroom, no outgoing signals," I said. "Cy, it's time fo' crack some heads."

"*Hehe,*" Cy chuckled. "*Shoots, brah. Eh!*" He addressed someone on his end. "*Eh! Boddah you?*" Then the line went quiet.

"*I get you near the bottom now,*" Malia said as the lift came to a stop. "*You're between floors, the service tunnel is straight ahead.*"

I moved cautiously across the top of the lift to the side of the shaft. Beyond the secured grate there was a low passage, just tall enough for me to crawl through, that led deeper into the tower. I took out my tools and started unscrewing the grate. Tatiana helped me pull the grate off and lay it over the top of the lift, while Sara re-secured the panel.

"All right," I said to the two of them. "Let's hele on."

We entered the passage, and just behind us the lift descended again.

"*Ho! Cy really get 'em, eh?*" Duke said, obviously impressed.

"*It no help dat da cafeteria coffee get skosh sedative in 'em,*" Malia said.

"What the fuck, Malia," Tatiana replied.

Malia cackled.

The sounds of blows landing became more pronounced as we made our way through the service tunnel on hands and knees. I heard someone shout into their comm, but there was no answer. Malia was already in their system, and communication was blacked out. The noise reached a peak when we came up on a grate in the floor of the tunnel, and Sara paused above it to exclaim, "Oh!"

Tatiana, Sara, and I crowded around the grate. Cy was circling two guards, mismatched eyes narrowed and flesh and metal fists up. There was a sheen of sweat on his bald head. One of the guards lunged forward with a weighted baton, swinging it in a sloppy arc at Cy's head. He caught the guard's arm and wrenched it forward, cybernetics whirring, twisting until the guard yelped and dropped the baton. He shoved the first guard back into the wall, resettling into his stance as the second guard sprinted forward with a flurry of blows. Most of them Cy was able to block or deflect with a clanging of metal, until a break in the guard's assault let him retaliate with his own. One loaded punch to the face sent the guard staggering backward, and the second sent him reeling into the other guard.

Cy wiped the sweat from his brow, resetting for another round. But a third guard came pounding around the corner of the corridor, and with a roar he rushed Cy and tackled him to the ground.

Tatiana gasped, Sara cried out, and I cursed. I fumbled for my tools and started unscrewing the grate. I threw one of my screwdrivers to Tatiana. "Help me with this!" I barked.

Cy managed to throw off the third guard and stagger to his feet, but now he was surrounded—one of the guards was apparently not a coffee drinker. They circled him slowly, waiting for an opening. One still had his baton, the second had drawn a taser from his belt, and the third had raised his fists. All three of them surged toward Cy, and Sara cried out again.

I removed the last screw and the three of us cleared the grate. With a grunt I threw my body weight onto it, and with a groan the metal gave way. I fell through the floor, riding the grate, and landed squarely on the second guard and his taser.

I leapt to my feet as the first guard staggered to his. He raised the baton, and I raised my fists.

The first guard swung at me and I ducked the blow. I answered with a hit to his abdomen. He swung again, and again I answered. The third swing was even sloppier than the first—this guy was bus' the fuck up and half-asleep. I blocked the swing and twisted his arm, and he dropped the baton. The guard fell to the floor when I kicked his leg out from under him. I picked up the baton and cracked him across the head with it, and he stayed down.

I turned on my heel to see Cy was struggling in a grapple, and the second guard rousing beneath the grate. He reached for the taser, and I started toward him.

Sara dropping heavily onto the guard made him fall to the ground again, followed by Tatiana. She grabbed for the taser while Tatiana kept her weight on the prone guard. Sara darted across the hall and, with the athleticism and grace expected of a gymnast, leapt onto the third guard's back and jammed the taser into his neck, making him shudder and shake and the whole pile of them topple to the ground.

I rushed over to them, kneeling beside Sara as she soothed a coughing Cy. "You okay, cuz?"

I helped him sit up. He took a few wheezing breaths, then fixed me with an amused smile. "Good ting you moke'd up, eh, cuz?"

I blinked at him. Then, inexplicably, I laughed. Harder than I should have.

Cy gave Sara a fond smile. "You did good too, sis."

Sara beamed. "It's all those self-defense lessons."

"I helped too!" Tatiana called.

"Das right," Cy agreed. I helped him to his feet, and we moved to where Tatiana was still standing on the second guard. Cy extended a hand and helped Tatiana step down onto the floor. I shoved the grate off the guard's back with my foot, and Cy gave him a swift kick in the head.

I blew out a breath and ran both my hands through my hair. "Good job, everyone. Let's get these buggahs tied up and we can head for the vault."

We made short work of the guards, binding each of them tightly with cord and leaving them in a utility closet without their comms. From there, Cy led us at a jog to the vault.

"*—it would be good for us to discuss this privately,*" Atlas's voice cut in.

"*Yes, I would appreciate some clarification,*" Angel replied coldly.

"*Must be out of the boardroom,*" Malia said. "*Dunno why, though.*"

I listened uneasily. I felt like I was about to cash in on all that bachi.

"*I'm sure you have questions,*" Atlas said.

"*I do,*" Angel replied. "*Let's start with why Hodson is here.*"

I felt the hairs on my nape rise. What was Hodson doing here?

"*To take your job,*" Atlas said simply.

"*What?!*" Malia screeched.

Angel didn't react. "*You're firing me.*"

"*I am.*"

"*With what cause? I oversaw the installation of Casius II, the recruitment of a new caliber of security, and record profits with minimal losses to 'incentive payments.'*"

"*Yes, you're very competent,*" Atlas replied, amused.

"*Then why?*"

Atlas's voice became very close. "*Because you don't respect me. Not the way you should. Not the way I want you to.*"

"*Respect?*" Angel said, disgust in her voice.

"I'll give you one last opportunity. I could tell Hodson to go home, that he's not needed. He'd happily return to retirement. If you'll only give me what I want."

The line was silent for a long moment. My heart was pounding in my throat, my whole body shaking with rage. I would have given anything to be in that room. Given anything to show that man the type of respect he deserved—a beating to end all beatings.

"*No,*" Angel said, her voice dripping with disdain. "*You're a disgusting little worm playing at greatness, throwing money around as if it's a substitute for wit or power. You have no power over me, and you don't deserve my respect.*"

"Ho, shit!" the crew said in unison.

Atlas was apparently shocked. I guessed nobody ever spoke to him like that. "*What did you say?*" he said, dangerously quiet.

"*I said that every ounce of power you wield, you bought or stole from someone else. Hodson, me, all your scientists in R&D—they're the real people who built Atlas Industries. You're just a front. A face. A fraud. I don't owe my respect to someone like that.*"

"*Collect your things,*" he snarled. "*Security will see you out in thirty minutes.*"

There was another silence. I felt a mixture of pride and panic. Angel just brutally took down Atlas and man, did I love to see it. But what did that mean for the job? Did we just lose our chance at the vault?

". . . Angel?" I asked cautiously.

"*This is just a setback,*" Angel responded. "*Atlas will have changed my credentials to the vault. Duke and Nakano, I'll need you to create a distraction. I'll gather Hodson's biometrics.*"

"*On the fly?*" Duke asked, shocked.

"*I can do it,*" she said, firmly.

Duke sighed. "*All right. Give me five and I'll head over.*"

"*Good,*" Angel said. "*Everyone else, work with what you have.*

Some improvisations will have to be made, but I have full confidence you can pull it off. You're all the best, remember, that's why I picked you. That's why you're here. We can still do this."

Angel sounded so sure, so certain. I wasn't. We had thirty minutes to improvise our way into and out of the vault. After that, without Angel to run interference, Atlas could catch us at any moment. Our chances at the 125 billion had just narrowed, and my chances of getting sent straight back to Kepler System Penitentiary had skyrocketed.

But I still had Agent McKay's number. I still had a way out.

"And Edie?"

I started out of my thoughts. "Yeah?"

"Now would be a great time to bring us some luck."

". . . Yeah. I can do that."

I shook my head. Bachi.

Cy led us to a metal door set behind a security station—now unmanned, thanks to our violence. The first of the three doors we needed to pass through, it looked as unassuming as any other—except for the dual-custody manual locks, keypads, and the glaring sign reading Restricted Access.

I touched my earpiece. "We can't progress without the codes, Angel."

"You have Atlas's," Angel replied.

"What about Hodson?"

There was a brief pause on the line, Angel considering. *"Try 210357."*

"You sure about that?" I asked. "We've only got three tries."

"Do it. I'm certain."

I raised a brow at Tatiana. She shrugged.

We took our positions on either side of the door, kneeling to access the manual locks. I withdrew my lockpicks from my pocket. I nodded at her, and we went to work. The dual-custody keys needed to be unlocked within ten seconds of each other. We made quick work of the locks, then stood to input the codes. I typed in Hodson's: 210357.

The keypads beeped affirmatively, and the lock disengaged with a *click*.

"Code's good," I said, pulling open the door. I held it as Cy, Sara, and Tatiana passed through. "How'd you know it?"

"*It's a date,*" Angel explained. "*When Hodson started working with Atlas.*"

"*Ugh, sentimental,*" Malia said.

"What's wrong with sentimental?" Sara asked.

"*It makes your codes easy to guess, sis.*"

The door in the next room was far more imposing, befitting a high-security vault. A hulking mass of metal, I knew from the plans that it was a three-ton door held in place by a five-ton mag lock. I also knew that I'd planted an EMP forty feet below, taped to the bottom of the door's power supply.

Almost died for it too.

"I'm priming the EMP," I said, unslinging my bag from my shoulder. "Gonna need those biometrics in the next room though, Angel."

"*I'm on it,*" she replied. "*I have the datapad with the retinal scanner, that's easy enough. Can you get me something that can read a fingerprint, Malia?*"

Malia hummed to herself. "*If you could get Hodson's comm, I could reconfigure its IR scanner to work like a jerry-rigged fingerprint reader.*"

"*Understood. Stand by.*" Another pause. "*Hodson,*" she called.

"*. . . Angel,*" came Hodson's voice. "*I wish we were meeting under better circumstances.*"

"*It is what it is,*" Angel said neutrally.

"*Is it?*" he pressed. "*You gave up a lot to be here. Burned a lot of bridges. Some of them you were better off without, but it was a loss all the same.*"

"I came out better for it," Angel replied. *"I cleaned up, straightened out. Even without this job, it was worth it to burn those bridges."*

I went rigid at that. The others glanced at me uneasily. I went back to rifling through my bag for the primer.

"Attagirl," Hodson said warmly.

"I have my resignation letter," Angel continued. *"Here, on this datapad. I would appreciate it if you disseminated it for me. I've had my access revoked."*

"Revoked?" Hodson sounded surprised. *"Already?"*

"Atlas and I are not parting on amicable terms," she said, keeping her tone carefully neutral.

"Why?"

"We—" Angel hesitated, just long enough to be noticeable. *"—We've discovered some irreconcilable differences."*

"Sounds like my divorce," Hodson joked. There was a somber pause. *"Would you like me to talk to him about it?"*

"I'd rather not get into it," Angel said. She sounded defeated. It was a bizarre sound. *"If you could just give him my resignation letter."*

"Here, let me see."

I pulled out the primer and set the controls. "I'm ready to blow the door, as soon as we have the biometrics."

"The retinal scan is coming in!" Malia announced.

"It's very... brief," Hodson said, diplomatically.

"It's the most I could do with five minutes and a datapad."

"Are you sure you don't want me to speak to him?"

"I'm sure. But I appreciate it anyway, Hodson. It's been a pleasure."

Hodson laughed. *"A handshake and a goodbye? You say that as if we won't see each other again."*

"Will we?"

"Your star is on the rise, Angel. I'm sure no matter where you end up, we'll meet again."

"We can hope so."

I scowled at the primer.

"Goodbye, Angel."

"Goodbye, Hodson."

"You get the comm? Try put it closer to yours, Angel. Cannot connect." Another pause. *"Get 'em! You're good to go!"*

"*Hodson,*" Angel called out. "*You're missing something.*"

"*You—*" He laughed. "*Once a thief, always a thief, I see.*"

"Old habits die hard."

Even eight years later, Angel still knew how to do a lift. I felt another weird surge of pride.

"*Here comes the print!*" Malia exclaimed.

"*Atlas really doesn't know what he's losing, does he?*" Hodson mused.

"*No,*" Angel said softly. "*He doesn't.*"

"*Nice one, brah!*" Malia crowed. "*Forwarding the biometrics to you, Sara.*"

"I'm blowing the door," I said. "Comms will be out for thirty seconds in three . . . two . . . one . . ." I hit the primer button.

My comm went silent, the lights flickered, and the lock disengaged with a *thunk*.

Cy and I swung the door out on its hinges, and we hustled inside before the backup generator kicked in. Before us was a field of lasers in a harshly lit room. I came to a rigid stop at the edge of it, scanning the room uneasily. The lights should be down, the IR cameras off. Something was wrong.

"—like one airlock, brah!"

I touched my earpiece. "What's going on?"

"*We can't shut down the IR cameras or disable the pressure sensors without my access,*" Angel explained.

Sara paled, looking out over the field of lasers. "I can't move fast enough to trick a motion sensor."

"What about Malia?" I asked.

"*I already said, this security system is airtight,*" Malia replied, aggravated. "*Everything is on a discreet network—new firewalls, different algorithms, unique passwords. They pushed an update in the last hour, just in time for Angel to get shut out.*"

"Can't you break the new algorithms?" Tatiana asked.

"That's what I'm trying to say—I cannot, there's not enough time!"

I sucked in a breath through my teeth. "So we're blown."

I was right. There was no way out of this. And now I might have lost my chance with Agent McKay. Andie would lose the kids. The crew would be arrested. I would go to prison. It was over.

Malia was quiet for a moment. "*Not if I brute force it.*"

"*You're not brute forcing it,*" Angel said sharply.

"I've got the computing power, if I just overclock the mod."

"Overclock?" I echoed, horrified. "That's your fucking *brain*, Malia!"

"You only get one of those!" Tatiana agreed, similarly horrified.

"*With 125 billion credits, I can buy a new one!*" Malia laughed, but it sounded borderline deranged.

"Malia, I'm ordering you to stand down. We'll find another way."

"*There is no other way!*" I could hear Malia's breathing on the line. "*So make it worth it, yeah?*"

"*Malia!*" I shouted.

"*Cheeeee hoo!*" Malia whooped. Then, all the lights went out.

Chapter 20

IT WAS DARK, THE ROOM LIT ONLY BY THE CRISSCROSSING LASERS THAT divided the floor. It was quiet too, with only the sound of our labored breathing. The silence was heavy in the air.

"Malia?" Tatiana called, her voice thick. "Malia?"

There was no answer.

I touched my earpiece with shaking hands, straining to hear her. She had to be there. She had to. Anything else was unbearable to think about.

"*We don't have much time,*" Angel said, breaking us out of our collective daze. "*Sara, you need to cross the floor.*"

"But what about Malia?" Sara asked, her voice quivering.

"*I'll go find Malia,*" Angel promised. "*But if you don't go now, we'll lose the chance she gave us.*"

"Okay," she said, letting out a shaky breath. She took a moment to breathe, resettling herself into calm. "Okay," she said again.

"You got this, cuz," I said.

"We're here for you, cuz," Tatiana agreed.

"Go get 'em, sis," Cy said gently.

"Thank you," Sara replied with a smile. Then she extended a leg in between the first pair of lasers and slipped into the maze.

Sara ducked below one pair, slid on her belly for another, stood on her hands and tumbled over the next. Her movements were fluid, graceful, and quick. She needed to be, so as not to trip the pressure-sensitive floor. We held our breath as she traversed the grid, as though we might break her balance if we moved.

Sara was in a handstand, carefully lowering her legs down on the other side of the last set of lasers, when the lights flickered back on.

Tatiana let out a sharp gasp.

"Nobody move!" I commanded.

We all froze—including Sara, still midway between lasers.

"Stay steady, cuz," I called out to her.

Sara grunted in response.

I don't know how long we stood there, frozen in fear. Malia took down the IR cameras when she brute forced the codes, but it looked like the security system was fighting back. Sara's limbs were trembling with exertion, her balance wobbling. I knew the pressure sensor was counting down to when it would trigger the alarm, Sara's weight activating the mechanism within. I didn't know how much time Malia had bought for us.

"Angel—" I began, but just as I was about to call it, Malia broke through and the lights went out again.

Sara released her handstand with a gasp, dropping upright to the far side of the laser field. Cy let out a whoop. Sara turned to flash us a broad grin and a shaka.

"*Nice work,*" Angel said. "*Now input the biometrics to deactivate the lasers.*"

Sara did as she was told, moving to the door. Out of her pocket she drew four squares of agar gel, freshly loaded with Atlas and Hodson's fingerprints and retinal scans, courtesy of Malia. She placed a square on each of the scanners. Then, carefully, she extended one arm and one leg to activate the scanners on opposite sides of the vault door.

The sensors beeped in response, and we held our breath as it read the fabricated biometrics.

After a long moment, the sensors beeped again and flashed green. The lasers went out, and the door opened.

"Let's go," I said, and we crossed the room in a hustle.

The next room was the vault itself, and it was like nothing I'd ever seen.

The walls were lined with shelves, all of them holding priceless treasures. Lockboxes filled with outer-world bearer bonds. Experimental technology, their uses totally unknown to me. Pieces of artwork. I even saw a few bars of what appeared to be pure gold. The four of us stopped to take it all in, eyes wide and mouths open in awe. I thought about all the things I could do with wealth like this. Big houses, fast flyers, expensive clothes. I could have it all. I just needed to reach out and take it.

But what was on those shelves wasn't what we were here for. We were here for the hulking manual safe in the center of the room: the Liberty 1890.

Tatiana approached the safe, rifling through her bag. She pulled out her autodialer and started affixing it to the safe. "I'm setting the autodialer," she announced. "Fifteen minutes until we can crack it."

"Do it," I said.

As Tatiana fussed with the autodialer, Angel's voice came over the comm. "*Security is here*," she said. "*Stand by*." There was a beat of silence. "*Atlas*," Angel said. "*I'm surprised you're here to escort me personally*."

"What's Atlas doing there?" I asked aloud.

Tatiana shrugged.

"*I wanted to make sure you were really gone*," he replied. "*I don't want to see you try anything*."

"*Try anything?*"

"*You know this security system better than anyone. I didn't want to give you any opportunity to take advantage of that*."

"Is that why you had all my access revoked?" she asked. *"I'm not even able to send an email, Atlas."*

"And I'd like to keep it that way."

"Come with us, ma'am," a man's voice said.

"An armed escort? Is all this really necessary?"

"For you? Yes, it is," Atlas growled.

"Fuck!" Tatiana exclaimed.

We all jumped. I turned my attention to her. "What? What is it, Tati?"

"My autodialer," she said. She had the machine in her hands. "It's all fucked up. I think the EMP might have fried it."

"Then what do we do now?" Sara asked, alarmed.

Tatiana stared at the autodialer in her hands, working through her options. We only had a few precious minutes left before Angel lost Atlas's attention, and the autodialer would take longer than that to reset. Then Tatiana met our eyes in turn, her jaw set in determination. "I'll crack it by feel."

"You can do it?" I asked her.

She nodded. "I can do it."

With Angel engaged, the call fell to me. This was the biggest score of my life—of any of our lives. Let alone Tatiana, the snotty teenage thief. I almost refused. I could crack a safe, I'd been cracking safes my whole life. But I'd gone eight years without touching one, let alone a Liberty 1890. Angel put her faith in Tatiana. And I put my faith in Angel.

So I sighed, then stepped aside.

Tatiana moved past me, pulling a pair of earbuds from her bag. She attached the earpieces to her mod, then placed the other end on the door of the safe. She laid her fingers on the dial delicately and began to turn. I touched my earpiece. "Duke, Nakano? I need you both to buy us some time."

"I see Atlas and Angel. I'm on it," Duke replied. There was a pause on the line. *"Hey. Hey!"* she shouted.

Nakano gasped. *"Kalei—"*

"You have some fucking balls, Atlas!" Duke continued. *"You have some fucking balls going behind my back like this!"*

"I did what needed to be done," Atlas said evenly. *"I offered Dr. Abe what you couldn't: all the resources she could need, the respect she deserves, and"*—he laughed—*"a sizable pay raise. That certainly helps."*

Tatiana scribbled a number in pen on the safe door: 14.

"I'm sorry, Kalei," Nakano said softly.

"Snake!" Duke snarled. *"I gave you everything, Ella. And this is how you repay me? We were in this together! We were going to do something great, finally be people worth knowing! And all we needed was a little more time—"*

"Your time ran out," Atlas said coolly. Then, I could almost imagine his smug smile. *"Now she's moved on to greener pastures."*

Tatiana wrote down another number: 79.

"I'm sorry, Kalei," Nakano said tearfully. *"I really did care about our research. About you. About us."*

"Did you?" Duke snapped back. *"You sold me out! You ruined everything! Now what am I going to do? Now where am I going to go? You ruined me, and for what? To put yourself ahead? I regret ever giving you a chance!"*

"Kalei—"

"No! It's over, Ella. It's too late."

Tatiana wrote down the third number: 56.

"It's not too late," Angel cut in.

We all started at that. What was Angel doing, improvising on Duke and Nakano's con?

"What did you say?" Nakano asked.

"It's not too late," Angel repeated. *"It's not too late to go back. To say no. To make amends. It's never too late."* She paused. *"At least, I'd like to believe that."*

In the beat of stunned silence, Tatiana wrote down the last number: 28.

"Dr. Abe," Angel addressed Nakano. *"You're making a mistake.*

And you have no idea how much this mistake will cost you. You won't know, until it's all gone. Believe me when I say it's not worth it. Not for this man."

"*Angel, what are you doing—*" Atlas began, sharply.

"*Please,*" Angel pleaded. "*Please do the right thing.*"

Another long beat of silence.

"*Mr. Atlas,*" Nakano said finally. "*I think I need some time to think.*"

"*What?!*" Atlas said hotly. "*The contract you signed was binding!*"

"*I'm sorry. I just need a little more time. May I call you in the morning?*"

"*Fine!*" he snapped. "*Take some time, if you must. I know that you'll make the right choice—and I'll be here when you do.*"

Just then, the safe cracked open and Tatiana cried out in victory.

"*Goodbye, Mr. Atlas,*" Nakano said.

"*I'll see you again soon, Dr. Abe,*" Atlas replied.

Sara, Cy, and I rushed to the safe as Tatiana swung the door open. We crowded around the door. Inside the safe were a dozen data chits containing sensitive proprietary information and half a dozen small black boxes of different sizes. I opened the smallest box—about the size of my hand. Held within was a mod shaped like a wishbone, flexible wires coiled around it in the plush foam. AXON.

It was smaller than I imagined, more delicate too. How much had gone into making this single piece of tech? It was strange to think about. How many people's lives were spent researching it? How many people's lives were lost testing it? I thought of Daniel Huang, and Angel's last days with him. I thought of the way this mod destroyed his mind, and I had the wild urge to crush it in my fist. As retribution. For him, for all of us.

"*We're clear,*" Angel said. "*On our way back to the rendezvous point.*"

"And Malia?" I asked.

"*We'll make sure she's okay. What's your status?*" Angel asked.

"We have the loot," I said, closing the box and passing it to Cy. I reached into my bag, pulled out a coil of wire, and started unspooling it. "I'm about to blow the floor." I gestured at the other three. "Load up. Everything you can carry."

I unspooled the wire as the others filled their bags with Atlas's treasures—money and trinkets and tech. When we finished, we backed away into the far end of the room. I pulled out the ignition trigger from my bag. "Blowing the floor," I said. "Don't look into the light."

One end of the wire sparked alight. Fire spread along the length of the wire until the safe was encircled in light and smoke. I had to raise my hands to shield my eyes from the light as the temperature in the room spiked. The wire burned deep into the floor until the room was filled with the sound of metal groaning and giving way. The floor dropped out from beneath the safe, and everything went crashing into the catacombs below. The air around us rushed into the tunnel, equalizing with the thin atmosphere.

Alarms started blaring. The lights shifted to red. People started shouting.

I turned to the other three. "Let's get the fuck out of here!"

I leapt into the tunnel and landed light on my feet, Cy following close behind me. The two of us caught Tatiana and Sara as they jumped in behind us, and the four of us took off down the tunnel at a run.

I led us through the winding passageways, past cracked panels, fraying wires, broken lights, and empty pipes. Distantly I heard commotion coming from the vault, but it receded and was overcome by the sound of our pounding footsteps and ragged breathing.

The air grew thinner the closer we got to the blown airlock. Leeway was compromised, and while the tunnels hadn't been voided entirely, the atmosphere was steadily leaking out into space. In the planning stage, Malia did the calculations for us: at a run, we had fifteen minutes of air.

It was not a comforting number.

I picked up my pace.

We wove through three more corridors on our way to Leeway's last intact airlock. The thieves' cant on the walls indicated an escape route ahead, and it was just as we were rounding the bend that a Klaxon began to sound. I glanced behind me and saw that the blast doors behind us were slamming closed, one by one.

"Go!" I yelled, breaking into a sprint.

We pounded down the corridors, our footsteps echoing loudly off the walls. I was sweating despite the cold air, panting hard in the thin atmosphere. The airlock door came into view, crisscrossed with caution tape. I nearly slammed into it, my hands shaking as I tore open a panel and overrode the lock. The door opened with a gasp of hydraulics, and I waved the others through. Cy ran past, pulling Sara along by the hand. I looked farther down the tunnel for Tatiana—she was struggling down the path, breathing heavily and unsteady on her feet.

I cursed and ran back for her.

"No—" Tatiana groaned. "No, don't—"

"Shut up and move!" I snapped back, slinging her arm over my shoulders to support her weight. We hobbled down the corridor, the crashing of the blast doors growing closer and closer.

My head was swimming, my vision narrowing as we trudged down the corridor. The airlock was in sight. Cy and Sara were in the doorway, screaming our names. The last door slammed shut on our heels.

We weren't going to make it.

With the last of my strength, I lurched forward, half hauling and half throwing Tatiana into the airlock. She landed hard on her stomach. She turned over to look at me, and our gaze met. Her eyes were wide. "Edie—"

Then the blast door slammed shut, cutting off the end of her sentence.

My momentum carried me forward and I hit the blast door with my full weight, sending a shock through my body. I slumped down to the floor, trembling and gasping.

"*Edie!*" Cy yelled into my ear. "*Edie, we going get you out!*"

"No," I croaked back. "Atlas engaged the emergency protocols—you can't disengage them without access to Kepler's core systems. There's no manual workaround."

"*We not leaving you—*"

"You have to," I argued. "You have the tech, and Atlas is on his way. If you don't go, we'll all be made."

"*E...*" Tatiana whispered.

"Go," I said. "Finish the job."

The line fell silent.

I turned over so that my back was resting against the blast door. I took in a deep, shaking breath. My lungs burned. "Cy?"

"*... Yeah?*"

"Just make sure Andie's taken care of, yeah? That's all I ask."

"*Edie—*" he began.

"Make it worth it," I said softly. "Go."

Fifteen minutes of air at a run. I wasn't sure how much more I had left. I didn't bother counting.

I should have known better. I didn't respect Kepler, not the way it demanded. I trespassed on its wounded tunnels, blew open its silenced systems. A lifetime ago, I was going to dedicate my life to maintaining it, healing it. It didn't take me when I turned away from that path, but it would take me now. Just like it took Dad.

Maybe I lost my connection to Kepler somewhere along the way. Kepler would be within its rights to take me for my stupidity, for my hubris.

But wasn't that how I always was? Always reaching too high, pushing too hard, only to have it all come crashing down? I got so caught up trying to build something different, build something better, that I'd lost touch of what was truly important, what truly mattered. My family, my friends, the Ward... it all fell away in pursuit of being someone I wasn't, someone I would never be.

And Kepler was punishing me for it.

Even if Kepler didn't take me, Atlas would catch me. Last time I drew his ire, he put me away for almost a third of my lifetime. And that job was nothing in comparison to this one. There was no telling what he'd do to me this time.

Trapped in this tunnel, my life was over—one way or another. That was just the way the cards fell.

But I had one ace in the hole.

I opened my comm. Agent McKay's number was in the middle of my contacts list. My finger hovered over the call button. If I called, I could give her my location. SSA could override the doors, pull me out. If I testified, I could get immunity in my trial. It wouldn't matter if I was caught. I could protect Andie, care for the kids, erase our debt.

I could do all of that, it only took one call.

Who are you selling your soul to?

An incoming call filled my comm's interface.

It was Angel.

Part of me wanted to decline the call. I was still hurt, still angry. Part of me never wanted to speak to her again. Part of me wanted to see her behind bars, the bitter taste of her own medicine on her tongue.

Part of me knew that if I spoke to her, my resolve might waver. I might be swayed, change my mind.

But more of me wanted to hear her voice. Say goodbye.

I opened the line.

"*Edie?*" Angel said, her voice cracked. "*Edie, are you still there?*"

"Yeah," I said. "I'm here."

"*Thank God,*" she whispered.

"Were you worried about me?" I barked out a laugh, my breath visible in the frigid air. "That's not like you."

She was quiet for a moment. "*I always worry about you. Every time you go into the catacombs, I worry.*"

"Why?"

"*Wouldn't you? After Uncle Rich died?*"

I smiled to myself. "I used to be. Until I had everything to gain, and nothing left to lose."

"*You have a lot to lose.*"

"Do I?"

"*You always talked about doing anything for us—all we wanted was for you to be here with us.*"

I pulled my coat closer to my body. "Who is 'we'?"

"*Your parents. Andie. Me. All we wanted was for you to be in our lives—we didn't need money. We didn't need status. We just wanted you.*"

I laughed bitterly. "You have a real fucking funny way of showing it."

"*Why do you think I sought you out for this job?*"

"Because I'm an easy mark?" I answered. "Because I'm easy to control, easy to manipulate? I know what you did, Angel. I know you put me on Atlas's blacklist. I know everything now."

"*You don't know everything,*" Angel said softly.

"What don't I know, then?"

"*I could have had any runner, but I wanted you, E,*" she said. "*I told myself it was for practical reasons—that you were the best, that we worked well together, that you could be trusted . . . that you could be controlled.*" She paused. "*But really, I just wanted you back in my life.*"

I scoffed. "You shut me out of your life pretty solidly, A."

"But I'm trying to make amends."

"Oh yeah?" I challenged. "By leaving Andie alone? By abandoning your niece and nephew? That's how you make amends?"

She went quiet again. After a long while, she asked, *"Do you remember the Caduceus Cancer Fund?"*

"What? Yes. Why?"

"It's not real," she said. *"It's a front, bankrolled by me."*

I stared straight ahead. "You—why? Why all the trouble? Why didn't you just tell Andie?"

"I needed . . . distance."

"From me?"

"Yes."

"Why?" I asked. I found myself asking that question again and again. "Why did you shut me out?"

There was a long silence on the line. I almost thought I'd lost her. Then she said, *"After I was caught, when your plan fell through, Hodson said that you had already betrayed me. He said that you chose Andie—your family—over me. I technically hadn't committed any crimes, at least not yet. He told me that if I turned you in, he'd take care of everything. A job offer. Medical care. A way out."*

"And you believed him?" I asked.

"*. . . Yes.*" She sounded ashamed.

The prisoner's dilemma. It was the logical choice, and Angel was always logical. I just would have thought her loyalty to me would have won out over her logic. It would've won out over mine.

Then again, I was never known for my logic.

I sighed, then drew another breath. It felt insubstantial.

I slumped against the blast door. "I would've thought you were smarter than that, Angel."

"I . . . I was desperate," she explained. *"I was going to lose my father. I was going to leave him alone. I finally had a chance to find my revenge, and I couldn't let it go. Not even for you. Hodson convinced*

me—I convinced myself—that you would do the same. That all I had was my father. That no one in my life was trustworthy. That I was alone. I believed you would betray me too. You never cared about me the way I cared about you."

I took another thin breath. "What do you mean—what do you—" I squeezed my eyes shut and tried to concentrate. "What do you mean, 'the way I cared about you'?"

"Don't make me say it."

"No," I said firmly. "Say what you want to say, Angel."

There was a long silence on the line, with only my ragged breathing punctuating it.

Then, so quietly, she said, *"I loved you, E."*

I felt lightheaded, dizzy. My heart fluttered in my chest. I wasn't sure if it was the lack of oxygen, so I asked again, "What did you say?"

"Now you're being unkind."

"No, I literally—I'm asphyxiating here, Angel. What do you mean?"

"I mean, that you were never just my friend. You were so much more than that. There was never anyone else like you. Not in eight years. Not in the twenty years before that."

What the fuck.

"How—how long?"

"That's what I'm trying to say—it's always been you, E."

I didn't know what to say to that. All this time, all these years, and she was right in front of me, the whole time.

What the fuck.

"I was wrong," Angel said. *"I was so wrong. I got so caught up trying to avenge the dead I forgot I had people to live for. It cost me everything."* She took in a deep, shuddering breath. *"I have nothing, E. No family, no friends . . . and now, no purpose. You were the only thing I had left."* Her voice wavered, then broke. *"I'm nothing without you."*

"Angel—"

"I'm sorry, Edie," she sobbed. *"I'm so sorry."*

I had no idea what to think about all of this. All I knew was that I needed time—more time than I had left. More time with her, more time with Andie and her kids, more time with the crew.

I needed to live.

I grit my teeth and struggled to my feet. I didn't know how, but I needed to live.

"Edie?" Angel asked.

"I hear you," I answered, swaying on my feet. "I hear you, and we're gonna talk about this. I'm gonna get out of here, somehow, and we're gonna have a long fucking . . . talk . . . about all of this."

Angel sniffed, and I could tell she was smiling. *". . . I believe you."*

"Good." I coughed. "Now would be a good time for you to reveal your master plan, though."

"Eh . . . E?" a soft, high voice said in my ear.

Angel and I went silent.

". . . Malia?" I said. "Holy shit, Malia, are you okay?"

"Been better," she said with a shaky laugh. *"Blew a few synapses, probably. Knocked a few points off my stupid-high IQ. But it was sick, yeah?"*

"We're gonna talk"—I coughed—"about that later."

"Yeah, yeah, yeah," she said. *"Try do 'em at the hideout."*

The blast doors sprang open.

And Cy, Sara, and Tatiana were still there.

"Chee—" I began, but my whoop broke down into a coughing fit.

"Conserve your fucking oxygen, brah!" Malia chastised. *"Now go!"*

Cy slung my arm over his shoulders, supporting my weight. He grinned at me. "Lead da way, cuz."

I pointed down the passageway to the left. "This is the fastest route. Let's get out of here."

Together, the four of us hobbled out of Leeway and deep into the catacombs. Not such a clean getaway, but it was a getaway all the same.

Chapter 21

SARA, CY, TATIANA, AND I WERE THE LAST TO MAKE IT BACK. WE POPPED out of a manhole in an alley near the hideout, then trudged wearily to the unfinished building. When we entered the common room, we were met with applause from Duke and Nakano. Malia was sitting in an armchair near the screen, and she winced at the noise but joined in anyway.

I grinned as the four of us shuffled into the room.

"We did it," Malia said. "We fucking did it."

"We did," I agreed, walking toward her. I crouched down to meet her eyes. "Are you okay?"

"Yeah, brah," she said, her words a little slurred. "We just pulled off the greatest heist of my life, I'm more than okay."

"Of your life? You're seventeen," I said, amused.

"You think I going top this?" Malia laughed. "I going retire after this, brah."

Somehow, I didn't believe that.

"Edie," Duke said, drawing my eyes up toward her.

I stood, turning to meet her gaze. She extended a hand. I grinned and took it, and she pulled me in for a hug, clapping me on the back. "You did good, E."

"You too," I said, pulling back. "That fight with Atlas was inspired."

"Had some inspiration from you," Duke said coyly.

I was about to interrogate that when Nakano came in for a tight embrace. "I'm so glad you're okay."

"I'm okay," I reassured her. I pulled back to smile at her fondly. "We couldn't have done this without you two."

"Maybe not," Nakano said, matching my smile. "But you brought us all together. We owe you that."

The grifters moved off to congratulate the others as Sara approached me, a broad smile on her face. She threw her arms around my shoulders, and I held her close. "We did it! We're criminals!"

I laughed. "And you're a good one too, cuz!"

"I never thought I would be!"

"You're a natural."

As she stepped back, Cy stepped forward to put his metal hand on her shoulder. "You did good, sis."

"We all did good," she replied, laying a hand on top of his.

Cy directed his attention to me. "You no need me to take care of Andie. You going be around fo' a long time."

"Yeah." I smiled at him. "Appreciate it anyway."

"Anytime, cuz. Anytime."

The two of them left to talk to Duke and Nakano. Tatiana was sitting beside Malia, talking in low tones, when she caught my eye. She excused herself, then moved to talk to me.

"So," she said.

"So," I replied.

"You almost died back there."

I shrugged. "I've almost died before."

"Yeah, but . . ." She pushed a curl out of her face. "You almost died for me."

"Any one of you would've done the same," I deflected.

"But the others haven't been a huge dick to you," she said. "Talking about how they're younger, smarter, better looking—"

"If this is an apology, it's not a very good one."

"I'm sorry," Tatiana said. "I'm sorry for being a huge dick. And thank you. Thank you for saving my life."

I smiled. Then I held out my hand to shake. Tatiana took it and met my smile.

"You're welcome," I said. "Anytime."

"Eh, Tati," Malia called, waving her over. "Try look at this."

Tatiana left to sit with Malia again. I moved away from the group, dropping into an armchair with a sigh. I watched them all, chatting and laughing and congratulating each other on a job well done.

Most crews I'd been on tolerated each other long enough to get the job done. Some of the crews were tight, but never like this. Even though we'd only met a short month ago, I couldn't imagine my life before this job. It made me wonder where we'd all end up, because I couldn't imagine my life without them in it.

Suddenly the group broke into applause again, looking toward the entrance to the common room. I followed their eyes and saw Angel.

She smiled at us—one of her gorgeous, genuine smiles—and I felt my heartbeat quicken.

"Excellent work, all of you," she said to us. "What we just accomplished, others might have found impossible. You should all be proud." She swept her gaze across the assembled group. "We just have one last hurdle to clear, if you'll all come with me."

We followed Angel to her room. The room was cleared of furniture and the walls were hung with black curtains blotting out the light. A solitary screen was set up on the far wall, fuzzy with static. We gathered around the edges of the makeshift stage, out of frame. Angel stood in the middle.

She shrugged into a black hoodie, and I realized then that she was dressed in Malia's hacker gear—the hoodie and dark pants, her mirrored mask under her arm.

It seemed fitting that the Obake would be the face of our operation.

"I've masked the outgoing signal," Malia said. "You're good to go."

Angel fitted the mask over her face and drew up her hood. "Do it."

We all went silent as the line connected. It felt like an eternity, staring into the static on the screen. Until finally, the screen flared to life and Atlas appeared.

He looked fucking livid.

"Joyce Atlas," Angel said, her voice disguised behind the Obake's low timbre. "I presume you know who I am."

"Obake," Atlas said. "I didn't think you were one to gloat."

"I'm not here to gloat," Angel replied. "I'm here to offer you a deal."

"For what?" he snapped. "You've already taken everything."

"And I'm willing to return it—everything. If only you'll make it worth my while."

"A ransom," he said through gritted teeth.

"Precisely."

"What's the ransom?"

"One trillion credits."

"One—" Atlas's eyes widened. "You're insane if you think I'll pay that."

"But you will," Angel said, all cool confidence. She withdrew a little black box from her pocket. She opened it to show the camera—AXON was nestled within. "This tech cost you billions of credits, and will cost you billions more if you lose it. And if you've seen the state of your vault, you know that's not the only tech I've stolen." She snapped the box closed. "I'm sure your competitors would be very interested in seeing it firsthand."

"You're bluffing," Atlas growled.

"Why would I? It seems clear that I have the upper hand." I could hear the smile in Angel's voice. "It's all gone, Atlas. Now it's a matter of cutting your losses."

"I want my tech back first," Atlas demanded.

Angel chuckled. "Funny that you think this is a negotiation."

"Then what is this?"

Angel touched her comm. "I've forwarded you the digital copies of your tech, minus AXON. The rest is in a secure location. I will give you the location after I've received the money."

Atlas was silent for a long moment. He was in an impossible situation. And he deserved it.

"Where do I send your payment?" Atlas said, his voice low.

"I'm glad you've seen reason," Angel said pleasantly. She touched her comm again. "I'm sending you the routing information now."

Atlas tapped at the haptic screen of his comm, then looked up at the camera expectantly. A few moments later, Angel's comm chimed in answer.

"Do we have a deal?" Atlas asked.

Angel didn't immediately answer. I couldn't see her face through the mirrored mask, but I could tell that something was off. I could tell Angel was thinking, processing, weighing her options. The silence seemed to stretch on forever, all of us holding our breath. Dread washed over me, sinking into the pit of my stomach. Something was wrong.

Without a word, Angel dropped the box to the ground and crushed it beneath her boot.

"*No!*" Atlas screamed. "*No!*"

Angel's mask was impassive, the light flickering off the mirrored surface. "For everyone you've harmed, Atlas."

Atlas stared at her for a long moment, eyes wide, mouth open. Then his face twisted into a vicious snarl. I remembered what he'd said, just before escorting Angel off the premises:

there was one person who knew the system better than anyone. There was only one person who could have pulled this off. "*You*. You *bitch*. You've ruined me."

Angel said nothing.

"I'm going to ruin your life!" he shouted. "I'm going to destroy everything and everyone you love! And there's nothing you can do to stop me, Angel Huang!"

"Goodbye, Atlas," Angel said.

Then she cut the line.

The room fell silent, with only the hissing of static.

I didn't know what just happened. I knew Angel well enough to know when she'd made a rash decision—she made so few of them in her life. But what did this mean for us, the crew? I couldn't find it in me to be angry—I was just stunned speechless.

Tatiana asked what we were all thinking. "What now?"

"You do what you want," Angel answered, not turning to face us. "Atlas doesn't know who else was involved. And he won't, ever. Malia and I will have laundered the money through half a dozen transactions, and there's no trace of you in the vault. He only knows I'm involved, and he doesn't have proof of that either. I baited him into changing my credentials, and I have an alibi. He has nothing on me, and he has nothing on all of you."

We all fell silent again.

"You're all safe," Angel said. She took the mask off and pushed her hood back, shaking out her hair. "It's over."

"Angel—" I began.

"It's over," she repeated. She took in a deep, shaking breath. Then she dropped her face into her hands, her shoulders slumping forward. "It's all over."

"Angel," I said softly. I crossed the room to her, laying a hand on her shoulder. I pulled her into my arms, and she buried her face into my neck. Her cheeks were wet with tears. A shuddering sob rocked her body, and she gripped my shirt as emotion overcame her.

"It's okay," I soothed. "It's okay."

I couldn't imagine how she was feeling right now. Eight years of her life spent working toward this moment, and now it was over. I remembered what she'd said to me in the catacombs: she had no friends, no family, and now, no purpose. I wondered if it was worth it, after all this time. I wondered if revenge would ever give her peace.

I held her tighter. I could only hope so.

As I held Angel, I felt another body wrap around her—Cy, pulling us both into his embrace. Sara followed, winding her arms around us. Duke and Nakano came next, squeezing us between their bodies. Malia squished in between the others, and Tatiana clung to the outside. All eight of us, holding each other tight. I knew then that there was no way we'd ever leave each other's lives. I wouldn't let them go. Not Tatiana, Malia, Duke, Nakano, Sara, or Cy.

And never Angel.

"Stay with me," I murmured into her hair. "Don't go home alone."

She nodded. "Okay."

I'd brought home girls before her—smuggled them in and out of my room before my mother came home from her overnight shifts. And it wasn't like Angel hadn't seen the inside of my room before, not even that she hadn't slept in my bed before. But tonight was different. We were on the other side of eight years apart, the other side of a broken and mended friendship. And as I pulled her shirt above her head and slid her jeans down her legs, I knew that we would never be the same.

It was still sex, it was still Angel, but it was different this time. Maybe because *we* were different this time.

I kissed her tenderly, and she wove her fingers through my hair. She was soft and languid against me, melting into every touch. I made her laugh when I showed her the dildo Atlas Industries so graciously gifted me. I made her moan when I eased inside her. She gripped my hand as we moved together, cried out my name as she came undone. I wiped away her tears when it was over, both of us totally spent.

She fell asleep before me, nestled into the crook of my arm. I watched her as she slept.

We needed to talk. We needed to figure out where we both stood. We were so close for so long, until we shattered. I hated her for so many years afterward, cut by all the broken pieces. Now Angel was offering me another chance, to mend what she'd destroyed. I didn't know if we could do it. I didn't know if I wanted it. But for now, I was happy to hold her close, let her rest. Because we had all the time in the world now, and I had no intention of wasting any of it.

The sun had already risen when I woke up the next morning.

I blinked into the light, sitting up on my elbows to survey my room through bleary eyes. For a moment I was disoriented—I wasn't sure where or when I was. My room was still a mess, clothes heaped on my chair and strewn across the floor, my books and technical manuals stacked around a dozen half-finished models and tech kits. It was all the same. In eight years, it hadn't changed.

What was different was the person sitting at the end of my bed: Angel Huang.

It all hit me then. It was real. Everything was real. The crew, the heist, the confession—Angel. Angel was real, and she was sitting at the foot of my bed wearing nothing but her panties and one of my shirts.

"Hey," I said, my voice rough with sleep.

She looked at me over her shoulder. She was typing on her comm, but she dismissed the screen with a blink and turned to face me. Her smile was brilliant in the light of the morning sun. "Hey."

"So," I said, sitting up in my bed. "We haven't done that before."

She gave me a sly smile. "Once before."

"That one doesn't count," I protested. "We weren't together then."

Her smile softened. "Are we together?"

"I don't know," I said, rubbing the back of my neck. "Are we?"

"I think it depends on you. You know how I feel, now."

"I know how you used to feel," I corrected. "How do you feel now?"

Angel turned her eyes downward, plucking at the cuffs of my shirt. "I meant what I said. I loved you. For twenty years, I loved you. For the eight after that, I pretended I didn't. I smothered those feelings—it was the only way I could do what I needed to, keep my eyes on what I thought I really wanted. But seeing you again . . . it brought it all back." She met my eyes. "I grew up a liar, E. But I couldn't fool myself."

I sat with that, processing. After a while I said, "I cared about you too. Maybe I didn't realize it at the time, but . . ." I paused. "The weird thing is, even through all the pain and anger after what happened, I still cared about you. I still wanted you in my life, even if it was to make me miserable."

"I'm sorry I made you miserable."

I smiled. "It's still weird hearing you say that."

"Say what?"

"I'm sorry."

A faint smile crossed her face. She tucked a strand of blond hair behind her ear. "You said you used to care about me. How do you feel now?"

"Now?" I sighed. "To be honest, I don't know how I feel. We've been through a lot, Angel. I know that I care about you, I know that I want you. But I don't know where that leaves us."

She looked off over my shoulder, thinking. "The way I see it, there are two options," she began. I smiled to myself. Logical and systematic as ever. "The first is that we acknowledge that what I did can't be undone. I hurt you, E. And I don't think that wound will ever truly heal. We acknowledge that what I did was unforgivable, and we cut our losses and go our separate ways."

"Don't like the sound of that one. What's the other option?"

"The other option is that we try. Maybe we can't change the past, can't go back to the way things were, but we can try again. Try something new." She focused her dark eyes on me again. "Those are my options."

I considered it. Angel was right that what she did could never be undone. That our relationship would never be the same after that. I wasn't sure I would call it unforgivable—it would have to be, to keep her in my life. And I wanted to keep her in my life. I really did.

"I want to try," I said. "Whatever happens, I want to know at least we tried."

Angel's face lit up at that. Sitting in my hammajang room, wearing my wrinkled shirt, in the light filtering through my window—she was the most beautiful I'd ever seen her.

She moved across my bed on hands and knees, drawing close to me. She kissed me softly. I was still getting used to that softness—for so long she had been cold, hard, and unyielding. But as she kissed me in the sunlight of my old room, it was like she'd never changed. It was like I had her back.

And I'd almost blown it, if I'd called Agent McKay.

"There's something I need to tell you," I said, breaking the kiss.

Angel drew away from me, curious. "What is it?"

"The SSA contacted me. They were building a case against you and Atlas, and wanted me to be an informant."

"What did you say?"

"I almost said yes," I admitted. "When I was trapped in that tunnel and thought it was all over, I almost called them. You stopped me." I looked down at my open palms in my lap. "I just needed to tell you."

"I knew," Angel replied.

I looked up, surprised. "You knew?"

"I thought they might contact you," she said. "But there wasn't much I could do if you decided to turn on me. I could only put my trust in your word—that you wouldn't betray me the way I betrayed you."

"And you believed me."

She smiled. "You're easy to read."

"Thanks," I said flatly. I paused. "You know that means she'll still come after you, right?"

"I know. I know that she and Atlas will come for me, and keep coming for me. But I'm prepared for that." She laid a slender hand on mine. "I know what I need to do."

"What do we do now?" I asked quietly.

"We enjoy this moment," Angel answered. "Enjoy all the time we have left."

I smiled at her, laying my hand on the back of her head and pulling her in for another kiss. "I've got plenty of time."

I kissed her again, with emotion: relief, passion, and joy. Angel hummed as the kiss deepened, twining her arms around my shoulders and spreading her fingers through my hair. I turned us both over so she was lying on her back, pressing our weight into the bed. I felt my body stirring as we kissed, as Angel moved underneath me.

The opening and closing of the front door made my blood run cold.

"Edie?" Andie called. "Edie, are you home?"

"Fuck," I cursed under my breath. "Andie's here."

"Is that a bad thing?" Angel asked, keeping her voice down.

"She doesn't know about us," I explained.

"So?"

"*So*, I'd prefer it if my sister didn't find out by walking in on us."

Angel looked amused. "Hasn't she walked in on you before?"

"And it was mortifying!"

She stifled a laugh.

"It's not funny!" I hissed.

"Okay, okay. What do we do?"

"Get dressed," I said, rolling off her and out of bed. "We'll sneak you out, then you can pretend you're coming over for breakfast."

She smiled. "If you say so."

We dressed hurriedly, Angel combing her hair with her fingers and fixing her makeup as best she could. I creaked open the door, swiveling my head back and forth in search of Andie. Not seeing her, I waved Angel through the door. She followed me, heels in hand, as we crept across the living room toward the door.

But apparently Andie's mom senses had been honed by having a third child, because she called, "Edie? Is that you?" and stepped out of the galley kitchen. "Oh!" she exclaimed. "Angel, you're here."

My neck flushed beneath my collar, but Angel reacted with her usual cool confidence. "It's good to see you, Andie. Edie invited me over for breakfast, I hope that's okay."

"Yeah, of course," Andie answered, still surprised.

"What can I help with?" Angel asked.

". . . You could make the coffee?"

Angel smiled at her. "Of course." She moved away from my side, crossing the living room and entering the kitchen. Andie watched her go by, then shifted her gaze back to me. She frowned. I shrugged sheepishly. Then she shook her head, the signal that we'd talk about this later.

Andie turned and went back to the kitchen. I sighed in defeat and followed.

After the coffee and tea were made, the three of us settled around the kitchen table. "I feel like you two aren't telling me something," Andie said.

Angel answered for me. "Edie's been helping me with a project."

Andie raised a brow. "Is that what you call it?"

I had no idea which "project" she was referring to.

"I promise I'll tell you," I said to her. "It's just a little while longer."

Andie opened her mouth to reply but was interrupted by a knock at the door.

Andie rose from the table. "I'll get it, it's probably Tyler with the kids."

As she left, Angel reached across the table to take my hand. "Everything's going to be okay, E."

I raised my brows at her, surprised. "Yeah, I know."

Andie opened the door, then let out a startled gasp. "Officers—"

"Ms. Morikawa?" a woman's voice said. "My name is Special Agent Leah McKay, and I have a warrant for the arrest of Angel Huang."

I stood so fast my chair fell over. I turned toward the door, my eyes wide and my heart pounding. Agent McKay stood in the doorway, half a dozen station security officers crowded around her. She pointed at Angel, still sitting placidly at the table with her tea, and the officers advanced. "Angel Huang, you're under arrest for fraud, corruption, and obstruction of justice." An officer hauled her out of her chair by the arm and cuffed her. "Come with us, please."

"I never—I didn't—" I stammered. "How did you—"

"I messaged them," Angel answered patiently. "I gave them the files, in exchange for immunity for you, and the rest."

I stared at her. "What the fuck, Angel! We could have figured something out—"

"Don't you see?" she said. "It's the only way to keep Atlas away from you, for good." She smiled. "I couldn't let you take the fall, not again."

The officer pulled Angel along, across the apartment and out the door. I followed, pounding down the stairs and dashing to the government flyer parked at the curb. "Mx. Morikawa—" Agent McKay said sharply.

"Just one minute!" I called. "Please!"

"I'm going to prison, E," Angel said with a laugh. "And you're making me late."

"I can't let you go," I pleaded. "Not after last night. Not after this morning."

"Like you said, E. We have all the time in the world. I won't be gone long."

"How long?" I asked, my voice thick.

"Thirty-six months?"

I swallowed hard. That felt so long to wait.

She smiled. "It's nothing compared to eight years."

"Angel—"

"I have to go," she said gently.

I pushed past the officers and put my hands on either side of Angel's face. I kissed her, deeply. I kissed her until one of the officers put her hand on my shoulder and pulled me away. I stumbled backward, unwilling to let her go.

"Bye," Angel said, still smiling.

"Bye," I said, hoarsely.

Angel ducked into the flyer. An officer shut the door behind her.

Agent McKay gave me a cool look. "Whatever you did, you

better hope to God it was worth it." Then she climbed into the front seat of the flyer, and they flew away.

I stepped back onto the sidewalk, reeling. She was gone. She was really gone. After twelve hours together, *really* together, she was gone. I swiped at my stinging eyes. I couldn't help but feel like this was so unfair, so unlucky. To feel happiness like that, only to have it taken away in an instant.

Andie put a hand on my shoulder. "Edie," she said. "Please tell me what's going on."

I didn't know how to explain. How could I explain? I hardly knew where to begin.

Just then, my comm chimed. I glanced at the message, then did a double take.

It was a notification: One billion credits had just been deposited into my account. And I knew there was more. There was way more, hidden away in outer-world accounts, buried in investments and trades. More than I could ever want. More than I could ever need.

I looked up from my comm. Andie was still looking at me expectantly.

I took a deep breath. "About that project—"

Chapter 22

THIRTY-SIX MONTHS LATER

IT WAS WEIRD BEING BACK AT THE PRISON. GRANTED, I WASN'T THE ONE behind bars, but it still felt strange. The planet's gravity was stronger than Kepler's artificial g. The air was cold, and despite the smell from the strip mines nearby, it was crisp in a way that Kepler's never was. It all brought back eight years of memories: hustling cards in the prison yard, eating rehydrated rations alone in the cafeteria, sitting still as another inmate tattooed proof of the years onto my skin, standing in the warden's office when he told me that I would never see the light of day, ever again.

But here I was.

A voice drew me out of my thoughts. "Are you nervous?"

I turned toward the voice. Andie was looking at me expectantly, a sympathetic smile on her face.

"No," I answered. "I'm not nervous."

Andie bumped my shoulder with hers. "I can tell you're lying. I can always tell when you're lying."

I laughed. "You and her were the only people who could ever read me."

"Why are you nervous?" Casey asked, standing at my side. He also looked sympathetic. "You've seen her before."

"Not in person," Paige said, at Andie's side. "It's different in person."

It *was* different in person. We talked a lot over the past thirty-six months. We had a lot to talk about—our choices in the past, our decisions in the present . . . what we wanted for the future. It was all via video call, but it wasn't the same. There's so much more to communication than words. Thirty-six months had gone by without being in her space, without feeling her touch. I knew that seeing her in person would be different—but would *we* be different? Would *I* be different?

I glanced down at myself. I was still getting used to the way my clothes fit, nine months into HRT and a year post–top surgery. I wore a dark suit under a wool coat, dressed classier than anything I'd worn before. I could afford it now. But even in the years that followed, I never forgot the way Kepler almost killed me for my pride. For thinking I was better than it, better than everyone. For losing sight of who I was, what mattered to me. Still, I couldn't stop the worry that I might have changed. That I'd drifted, slowly, from the person she once knew.

"Mommy, I'm cold," Maddie whined.

"I know, honey," Andie said gently. She picked up the little girl and held her close. "It's only for a little while longer."

"Thank you for coming, Maddie," I said to her. "You're helping a lot."

Andie gave Maddie a bounce. "Say you're welcome," she encouraged.

"You're welcome, Aunty," Maddie replied.

Thirty-six months was a long time. I saw it in Maddie, Casey, and Paige. Maddie was about to start school. Casey was almost in the double digits. Paige was taller than her mom now, tall like me and Dad. I thought the gene therapy might have flipped a switch, but every doctor flatly told me that wasn't how it worked.

Thirty-six months was a long time. I had changed—had she changed too?

"There she is!" Andie exclaimed.

I lifted my head, and then I saw her.

She wore the same clothes I'd last seen her in: dark jeans and a white blouse, high heels and silver jewelry. She had grown out her hair: no longer short and blond, but long and dark. Like I remembered it, over a decade ago.

Across the landing pad, I saw her smile at me. A smile that could make anyone fall in love with her. Die for her. Live for her. Do anything at all for her.

"Edie," she said. "It's been a long time."

"Too long," I replied, starting toward her. "Way too fucking long."

I crossed the landing pad, first at a walk, then a jog, then a run. I opened my arms for her, and she stepped into my embrace. I held her close, tight like I couldn't let her go. Like I couldn't lose her again.

"I missed you, Angel," I said into her hair, my voice thick with emotion. "I missed you so much."

"I missed you too," she said, barely above a whisper.

I gave her a squeeze, then lifted her off the ground. She let out a startled gasp, then broke into laughter as I spun her around. It was such a good sound. One of my favorite sounds, I decided then.

I set her down, and she stepped back to take me in fully. She reached out to straighten my tie. "You look good," she said.

I grinned. "I'm respectable now. New money and all."

Angel laughed. "Good. Because I'm definitely not anymore."

"Once a thief, always a thief."

She smiled at me. "It doesn't matter. All I want is to go home."

"Home will be happy to have you. It hasn't been the same without you."

"That's all I want," she said, taking my hand. "All I want is to go home, spend time with family, and be with you."

"I can do that," I said, laying my hands on her waist.

I pulled her close—and kissed her.

I kissed her like it was our first. Our first *real* kiss, anyway. I kissed her like we had thirty years of history behind us—thirty years of joy, and hurt, and passion. I kissed her like she was my first, my last, my only. Because in a way, she was. There was never anyone else but her.

Whoops and cheers from Andie and the kids completely destroyed the moment, but I couldn't help the way I smiled against Angel's lips.

"Let's go home," I said softly.

We flew to Kepler crowded in the back of the flyer, the cabin filled with overlapping chatter. Maddie, Casey, and Paige spent the ride reacquainting themselves with Angel, and Andie gently redirected their questions away from prison or the heist. Paige was getting older, and maybe one day we'd tell her the whole story, but for now it was between me, Angel, and Andie.

Andie was used to the money by now. She was pissed at first, of course. I thought she'd make me get rid of it, or refuse my help. But her anger faded when the days after the heist turned to weeks, then to months, and SSA never came knocking on our door.

We chipped away at our debt rather than paying it off all at once. Despite my wild fantasies, we didn't leave the Ward or move into a fancy condo. I convinced Andie to update the furniture, though.

"Leilani's flower shop is still here," Angel said, pointing out the window as we flew through the Ward, back to my apartment.

I leaned in beside her, surveying the street. "Yeah. New hydroponic systems too. She's got choke kine flowers now."

"I thought she was filing for bankruptcy."

I coughed. "Well, someone helped her out."

Angel turned from the window to look me up and down. I grinned sheepishly. "What was I gonna use it all for? I felt like giving back." She looked disapproving. "What? I tried not to spread it around too much, but you know how aunties and uncles talk."

And did they talk. I couldn't tell you how many fucking businesses I'd invested in or buildings I'd bought over the past thirty-six months. Even with Atlas Industries in crisis—with the SSA investigation, the shareholders' lawsuit, and their founder and face in prison—there was always more to do.

We pulled up to our apartment tower and climbed out of the flyer. I held out my hand to Andie and Angel, helping them step onto the sidewalk. Andie and the kids walked into the tower and started toward the apartment, but Angel paused outside the storefront.

"Did your dad ever tell you how he met my dad?" Angel asked, eyes on the sign.

"Yeah," I answered, moving to stand beside her. "Your dad was selling cigarettes on the corner, and my mom told my dad to tell him to fuck off."

"But they talked instead," Angel continued. "Uncle Rich gave my dad his number, told him to call if he ever needed anything." She paused. "Dad told me that story every time I came home from your house." Another pause. "I wonder what he'd think of us now."

"I think he'd be happy." I grinned. "I'm a catch, after all."

Angel gave me a look, but her dark eyes were amused. "You

know he kept asking when we'd get married. He asked a lot, near the end."

"Really?" My eyes widened with shock. "I thought the old fut hated me."

"Not at all. He thought you were a good influence on me."

"Damn. Your dad really couldn't read people, could he?"

"It's why he got into so much trouble." Angel's voice took on a wistful tone. "Didn't matter how many times he got burned, he still thought things would work out. I don't think it was naivete, really, more that he couldn't give up hope that things would be better."

I touched her hand. "Things are better."

She smiled at me. "They are."

I took her hand and led her toward the apartment. "C'mon, let's go meet the others."

Together we walked up the stairs to my apartment. I touched my keycard to the sensor and the door opened with a *clunk*. Angel pushed open the door, and I steadied her when she nearly fell down the stairs at the scream of "*Surprise!*"

"What—what—" she stammered, looking around the crowded apartment.

We were all there. Andie, Maddie, Casey, Paige, and just beyond them, the entire crew: Malia, Tatiana, Sara, Cy, Duke, and Nakano. And then there was me, holding open the door and grinning widely. "Welcome home, A."

Angel took a tentative step into the apartment, taking it all in. Then her lip began to tremble, and her eyes filled with tears, and she dropped her face into her hands. We all surged forward, pulling her into a tight embrace, overlapping in our soothing.

"I just missed you," Angel whispered. "I missed all of you."

When Angel composed herself, she made the rounds hugging and kissing my family. *Our* family. We all settled in for the night, laughing and reminiscing and catching up. I drifted between conversations, taking it all in.

Cy was scheduled for his last upgrade, or so he claimed—a biofeedback LED over his heart, just for fun. He carried Maddie around, balancing her tiny feet on his palms as she squealed in delight. Tatiana played three-card monte with Casey at the kitchen table, but I didn't have the heart to tell him she was cheating. Sara, who was busy with her gym and managing her scholarship athletes, stood with Duke and Nakano in the kitchen. The two of them were still at it, funding freedom fighters across the colonies. Malia sat with Paige on the couch, conferring in low tones about the newest season of some sword-and-sorcery show. Malia was bankrolling production and taking ideas.

Throughout the night, my eyes kept wandering to Angel. She was always smiling, always laughing. It was still an adjustment, seeing her like this. But it made me happy—happier than I'd been in a long, long time.

I had all the money I could ever need, anything I could ever want. But in these past thirty-six months, I never felt totally fulfilled.

At first, I thought it was my need for more, my need to fill the negative spaces in my life. But, not long after, I realized that the negative space wasn't a fancy home, or an expensive flyer, or fashionable clothes.

It was Angel.

As I took it all in, watching my family—blood and otherwise—I realized that this was what I had been working for all my life. Not money, not notoriety, not status.

All I wanted was for us to be happy, to be together.

All I needed was my family, my home.

My Angel.

Finally, it was enough.

Acknowledgments

They say that writing is a solitary activity. But I don't think I would have been able to accomplish what I have without the people around me. This book is a true community effort, and I want to share my appreciation for everyone who has touched this book in one way or another.

First and foremost I want to thank my incredible wife. This book wouldn't exist without you. Thank you for your witty Google Docs comments, the rambling brainstorming sessions in the car, and for holding my hand through all the tears—despairing and triumphant. Thank you for being my light in the darkest times of my life. Thank you for being my rock when it felt like the world was crumbling around me. There are not enough words in the English language to describe how much you mean to me. Aloha aku no, aloha mai no.

Thank you to my 'ohana, who have been with me through the entirety of this long journey. Thank you for the joyful Zoom/Skype chats, the anxiety-soothing phone calls, and for proofreading my Pidgin. Thank you for hyping me up to everyone you know—including myself. Thank you for your unconditional love, your boundless enthusiasm, and your endless encouragement. Between funerals and weddings and book deals, these past few years have been the most challenging and rewarding of my life. You've been with me through all the highs and lows, the wins and losses, the joys and sorrows. You are the reason I'm still here. Aloha wau ia ʻoe.

Thank you to my agent, Keir Alekseii, whose unflagging support and fierce advocacy brought me here today. Thank you for the excited gifs in my DMs, the voice-note screaming, and the late-night pep talks. Thank you for always being in my corner, and for pushing me to never settle for less than what I deserve.

Thank you to my wonderful UK editors, Bethan Morgan and Claire Ormsby-Potter, whose enthusiasm and love for this book is so inspiring. Thank you for the jubilant memes, the email blasts, and the nefarious plans to take over the world. Thank you for giving me the opportunity to share my story.

Thank you to my awesome North American editor, David Pomerico, whose passion for this book is truly infectious. Thank you for the hype-up posts, the day-brightening emails, and always making sure my voice is heard. Thank you for showing me this story is worth fighting for.

Thank you to my sensitivity reader and copyeditor Raven Kame enui-Becker, whose knowledge and keen eye made this story the best it could be. Thank you for flagging all my funky commas, catching my goofy spelling errors, and for preventing me from embarrassing myself when I misread big liah as blalal. Thank you for pushing me to do right by my lāhui.

Thank you to my alpha readers, the Islander Crew, for your encouragement and insight as I struggled through the first draft of *Hammajang Luck*, née *Heist Lesbians*. Thank you for the venting sessions on Discord, bullying me for more interiority, and for challenging me to think about what I wanted this story to be.

Thank you to my beta readers and the Consolidated Critique Group for helping me shape my first drafts into a story I was proud to tell. Thank you for the all-caps comments, the hours-long voice calls, and the good-morning gifs. Thank you for believing in this book, even when I didn't.

Thank you to my incredible international and multitalented team for bringing this book to life. Thank you to APIpit for bringing Keir and me together. Thank you to all the writer Twitter chats for introducing me to my wonderful friends. Thank you to everyone who has ever left an excited comment or given me a kind word. If you aren't sure if that includes you, trust me, it does!

Thank you to everyone who has made this book possible. And thank *you*, dear reader, for opening your heart to this story.

Mahalo nui loa,
MAKANA

Makana Yamamoto was born on the island of Maui. Splitting their time between the Mainland and Hawai'i, Makana grew up on beaches and in snowbanks. Always a scientist at heart, Makana fell in love with sci-fi as a teen—they even led the science fiction and fantasy interest house at their college. A writer from childhood, fiction became the perfect medium for them to explore their interests as well as reconnect with their culture, coalescing into a passion for diverse sci-fi. They love writing multicultural settings and queer characters, as well as imagining what the future might look like for historically marginalized communities. In their free time, Makana likes to hoard dice for their Dungeons & Dragons games, defeat bosses with their guildmates, and get way too invested in reality competition shows. They currently live in New England with their wife and two cats.